...BEFORE YOU LEAP

LES LYNAM

This book is a work of fiction. The characters, incidents, and dialogs are products of the author's imagination and are not to be construed as real. Any resemblance to actual events or persons, living or dead, is entirely coincidental.

All rights reserved. With the exception of excerpts for review purposes, no part of this book may be reproduced or transmitted in any form or by any means, electronic or mechanical, including photocopying, recording, or by any information storage and retrieval system.

ISBN-13: 978-1503205222
ISBN-10: 1503205223

Text Copyright © 2014 by Les Lynam
Bōn-'Mō(z) Publishing
First Edition
Printed by CreateSpace

All Rights Reserved

Dedication:

To Elizabeth "Libby" Nelson
Who after Chapter 5 declared it: 'weird'.
Sorry I didn't write faster.

Acknowledgments:

Special thanks to my Alpha Team:
my wife, Susan; my sister, Ramona; my niece, Kari.
Thanks to my Beta-readers for their comments:
Candi T., Mollie D., Preston F., Sarah T.
Above & Beyond award: H.S. Buddy, Bryan J.
For all the technical edit assists.
Thanks to a Stranger Award: Jerry D.
Whose unbiased comments were a great help.

Table of Contents

Prologue 1

Chapter One 10

Chapter Two 37

Chapter Three 60

Chapter Four 103

Chapter Five 139

Chapter Six 163

Chapter Seven 168

Chapter Eight 182

Chapter Nine 216

Chapter Ten 243

Chapter Eleven 266

Chapter Twelve 288

Epilogue 303

Prologue
Anemone Grotto – May 11, 2216

FATHER insists the entire household gather communally for morning nutrition on the first day of each month and again on a second negotiated day near the middle of the month. Today was negotiated if you consider Father's unilateral declaration a fair substitute for negotiation.

I considered a pointless protest. Pointless, because Father's companion and the two live-in interns under his tutelage had already agreed. I know Father selected this day because of me, and for that very same reason, I would prefer a morning of solitude.

I walk into the common room and, as expected; I am the last to arrive. What I did not expect was to find Mother standing there. The instant of shock dissipates as I detect the faint halo around her and notice that she is motionless.

"LX," Father greets me, "Good morning."

"Good morning, Father," I reply, and then nod to each of the others as I greet them, "M8, KC, MLE."

"Is your anxiety level elevated?" M8 asks.

"I believe it is near equilibrium," I tell her and hope she does not detect prevarication. I cannot fully control the anticipation of the day's activities.

"Please sit," Father suggests. "Do you have a preferred order regarding your mother's holo or morning sustenance?"

"Inconsequential," I reply, though I would prefer neither. "Does Mother expect a return holo?"

"I received no relevant data during our last brief communication," Father says, "Though, I would hypothesize that the probability is high. Perhaps there will be conclusive data within the holo?"

"You have not previewed the holo?" I ask.

"I have not," Father confirms, "I expect the content to be supportive of your proposal."

"KC and I have reviewed your proposal, LX," MLE says, "We believe it is sound and compelling."

"I predict the selection board will find it meritorious of further investigation," KC adds.

"I also found it sound," M8 offers, "and logically organized."

Father nods but does not speak. I detect a minuscule twitch of his lips and wonder if it was an involuntary response spurred from emotion. I immediately chastise myself for fantasizing.

"Choose, please," Father says, "Holo or sustenance first?"

I sit. "Sustenance," I declare, "There is no need to delay any of you from more pressing matters. The holo is likely inconsequential to your lives."

"We do not consider the potential ramifications of your proposal inconsequential, LX," M8 states, and then nods to Father and each of the interns. "Please confirm that I have not erroneously enlisted any of you in my statement."

"Verified," MLE and KC say in unison. Father nods.

I feel a spike of adrenaline and push it back down. "It is gratifying," I say, "that you are supportive of my endeavors."

M8 nods.

"Do you have a preferred viscosity today, LX?" asks Father. "We all have already stated our preferences."

He refers to the meal. Nothing seems appealing today, but I know Father would not allow me to decline nourishment, especially at a communal.

"Thirty-Five percent at seventy percent viscosity," I decide, "The remainder in liquid suspension."

Father's eyes show disapproval, but he does not countermand. "Kitch," he addresses the interface for the nutrient computer, "prepare all meals requested." He moves his attention to the interns. "Reports?" he asks.

KC and MLE briefly glance at each other. KC speaks. "Kelp platform forty-two has shown a four percent measurable growth compared to the control platforms. Recommend additional platforms be added to the study."

Father nods approval. "Agreed. Add three neighboring platforms to the experiment."

KC nods.

MLE is about to report when Kitch enters and begins distribution of our nutrients. I believe she welcomes the interruption.

I dip a spoon into my Formula Ten and lift it to my mouth. I have no interest in nourishment, but force myself.

KC seems to enjoy experimenting with his provisions. Today, it appears he has requested fifty percent of his allotment dehydrated. He has a beverage vessel that is steaming, and three other containers of multiple viscosities. He crumbles some of the dehydrate onto a bowl of seventy percent viscosity, then pours a forty percent viscosity over both. He samples a bite before addressing this third container. With a knife, he dips into the ninety percent and spreads it on a sheet of dehydrate. I can only assume that his body's greater requirement for calories spurs his interest in textural experimentation.

"I have inconclusive data to report," MLE says. "The UV enhancing filters over the phytoplankton showed no measurable growth. Conversely, the zooplankton consumed twelve percent more experimental phytoplankton than the control group. We do not yet have data regarding Krill consumption of zooplankton." Her eyes studied her bowl during her report.

"Interesting," Father says. "Do the zooplankton show increased nutrient value?"

MLE continues to stare at her bowl. "A longer study seems pertinent," she offers.

Father glances at KC, who spreads paste on a second dehydrate, his first slice devoured. He returns his attention to MLE. "Data regarding increased consumption of phytoplankton?"

MLE glances at Father. "Conjecture?"

Father nods. "Proceed."

"New or increased production of enzymes that stimulate zooplankton feeding?"

"Logical," Father says, "and potentially exploitable." MLE makes eye contact with Father, and he adds, "Verification?"

Her eyes return to her bowl. "Increased resources?" she asks quietly.

"Is that a request?" Father asks.

MLE bolsters her courage and again makes eye contact with Father. "May I have increased resources to launch a study to identify the cause of the increased feeding levels of the zooplankton?"

"Granted," Father agrees with a nod, "Three weeks. I will then require your results."

MLE nods, then quickly sticks a spoonful of nutrient in her mouth. I believe the maneuver was to cover a smile. I have also used it, when necessary.

Father looks wordlessly at M8. She returns a nearly imperceptible head shake, and I am relieved. M8's field of expertise is human sexuality. The candor of some of her past reports has caused me to feel uneasy.

Father turns to me. I believe I detect another tiny twitch of his lips. Could Father be proud of my accomplishments? I allow the fantasy to run a few seconds longer before clearing my throat.

"As you are aware," I say, "today is the announcement of the four proposals that Chronos University will sponsor this year. Ten proposals remain at this selection strata."

"Initial pool?" Father prompts although he knows the answer.

"There were one hundred twenty-seven proposals submitted this year," I reply.

"And at age fifteen?" Father again prompts—and I am certain the corners of his lips curled for a nanosecond.

"I am the youngest to have an active proposal remaining," I answer, then bite my lip to curtail my own urge to smile.

"An admirable accomplishment," Father proclaims.

"Agreed," M8 and MLE say in unison.

KC quickly clears his mouth with his hot beverage. "Agreed," he adds belatedly.

"Do you wish to view your holo now?" Father asks.

I nod and the holo of Mother springs to life. She spreads her arms toward me and is openly smiling. "LX," Mother greets me, "I am so proud of you!" I flinch from her open display of emotions, but also, strangely, feel encouraged. I quickly glance around the room. MLE and KC have shifted their attention to their food. M8's eyes shift between the holo and Father. Father has no visible reaction.

"I wish I could be with you in person," Mother continues, "and hope we can schedule a live holo when we are nearer opposition. I knew you could excel in any field of study..." Her smile fades a degree. "...even History. You have impeccable genetics!" Mother turns toward M8, and I cannot see the expression on her face, but M8 reacts by glaring at me. I recognize a fleeting moment of anger before she recomposes herself. I wonder if Mother anticipated M8's location and purposefully turned? She turns back to face me and brightens her smile. "Anyway, I am certain you must be terribly nervous, but I am confident in your selection. I look forward to a return holo with your good news. Ciao, my love!" She puts a hand to her lips, then holds it toward me and blows.

As the holo fades, I wish I could fade along with it. Mother has no qualms about stirring emotions. I busy myself with my Formula Ten.

"9A seems to have embraced a full immersion into Martian social mores," M8 comments, "though I struggle to comprehend her choosing to display them before a minor offspring."

Though I do not disagree with them, M8's words only contribute to the stir of emotions that Mother began. Had I chosen to live on Mars with Mother, would I now also display emotions openly? I shudder at the thought.

"LX," Father addresses me, "Unorthodox as she may be, your mother encourages you in your academic pursuits." He pauses before adding, "As do we all."

"I arrived at the same interpretation, Father," I say, then wish I had not spoken. My intonation was far from modulated. Surely Father detected it. I look at him, expecting a rebuke. His face shows nothing. I do so admire his control.

KC abruptly stands. "I volunteer to assist MLE in constructing her research model for the zooplankton study," he says.

MLE also rises, and they both look to Father. "We currently have eighty-six minutes before our regularly assigned duties commence," she offers.

I notice they both managed to consume the remainder of their nutrients during Mother's holo. I glance down at my own bowl and wish that it was empty.

KC holds a steady gaze with Father. His courage astounds me. I spoon in a mouthful of Formula Ten as we all await Father's response.

"Acceptable," Father says, "KC, you may assist until your regular shift. MLE, I will contact your immediate supervisor and report your delay. Will an additional two hours be adequate to complete your module?"

"It will," she confirms.

I shovel in another large spoonful, swallow and reload a second. By the time KC and MLE have left the common room, I have completed my solid nourishment. I decide against rushing to empty my suspension container.

"Father, I wish to have solitude before I attend class." I attempt to maintain eye contact as KC did, but fail. After a few seconds of silence, I glance back up to see that Father stares at my beverage container. "If I could take it with me, I guarantee I will ingest it all before class."

"LX, do you require a stabilizer?" Father asks.

I battle the emotion the question has stimulated. "No, sir," I reply evenly, "I believe solitude and contemplation will rectify any slight deviation I have experienced." This time I do manage to hold my gaze on him.

"Very well," he says, after a nearly intolerable silence.

I grasp my container and head for the door.

"LX," Father says, "Acknowledgment to your mother?" He phrases it as a question, but it is not. With a slight jerk of my head, I connect to the house computer. I assemble a short text burst and move it to dispatch.

"Complete," I tell him as I continue toward the door.

"LX," Father says, just as the door opens, "I will be interested in your report. I will make myself available immediately after your class."

I turn to respond and see that M8 has stood and moved around behind Father's chair. Her hands are on his shoulders.

"I will inform you of the results immediately after class," I say, then exit. As the door closes behind me, I shudder. I wonder if M8 experiments on Father?

* * *

Two and a half hours of solitude in my quarters did not center me. I opened my portal and stared out at the kelp fields. I had hoped that their gentle undulation and shifting light reflected from the surface would soothe my mind into a low activity state, but it did not. I did observe three platforms rise to the level of KC's experimental platform.

KC is always proposing new ideas, and more than eighty percent of his ideas lead to production increases. Perhaps MLE's and KC's presence serve as surrogate children for Father since I rejected the study of Marine Agriculture? Both Mother and Father's families have long been focused on Marine research. I am an anomaly. I have both aptitude and interest in Chrono History.

When I found that the kelp fields only led my mind to wander in areas that were non-productive, I refocused my attention with yet another review of the abstracts of the nine other remaining applicants. They are all so strong. I do not believe I will be selected.

The time nears for class to begin. I settle into my seat and run diagnostics on the VR equipment. I open the channel to the upper platform, fifteen meters above me. The laser tower reaches another twenty meters above sea level where it is stabilized against the rocking waves to ensure a perfect connection to shore. The bandwidth automatically clears for me at this time of day.

I ping the class server because I dislike being first or last to class. Though the sole purpose of this final class period is to select the four to receive full sponsorship, it is still a requirement to attend. Nearly sixty students remain from the original proposals submitted. Many still hope they can modify their proposals for selection next year.

The ping shows only three have connected. I wait thirty seconds and send a second ping. Fourteen. I send a third ping after another ten seconds. Twenty-eight. I signal a full connect and find myself sitting in a virtual auditorium with at least thirty other students. In my peripheral vision, I see others materialize. Two rows in front of me there are three unstable low-rez students connecting from Luna. I wish they would log in at the back. Their flickering is very distracting.

I glance to the left and right and see that all of the seats have filled. I am about to turn around to check behind me when the professor pops in at the podium. Anyone who pops in now will buzz and sit in a red bubble until the professor releases them. Their tardiness records automatically, so the visible marking is a punitive measure. No one is late today.

I find it difficult to stabilize my breathing and realize I am experiencing an uncontrollable adrenaline spike. With a slight twitch, I connect to the house computer and signal for nanite intervention. The computer directs some of my nanites to absorb adrenaline and others to stimulate the release of extra dopamine in my neural pathways. Within two deep breaths, I am feeling more centered, and I signal the house computer to intervene as needed.

During my crisis, the professor has introduced members of the selection committee, and they have popped in behind him. The introductions and formalities are complete.

"As you all know," the professor begins, "each year, the caliber of proposals seems to increase exponentially. We have already discarded proposals that are of a higher quality than those selected for sponsorship as little as five years ago."

He speaks in an even tone that would be too soft to hear if we sat in a physical auditorium, but we each hear him as if we were at a private consultation at his desk. It may seem different for the students on Luna; I do not know.

"We are gratified by the academic excellence you all show," he continues, "It bodes well for the future of Chrono History."

He pauses, and I notice flashes from several desks around me. I quickly blink my applause function on, as does everyone else. The room briefly sparkles. The professor nods the flashes off.

"We wish to begin by acknowledging the top fifty proposals," the professor says as he raises a hand ceremonially. There are fifty desks, including mine, that glow red. The few remaining desks flicker applause.

"The top thirty proposals." My desk and twenty-nine others shift to orange. The twenty desks that remain red join the flicker of applause. The process continues.

"The top fifteen proposals." My desk and fourteen others shift to yellow. Fifteen orange desks begin to flash. "And the top ten proposals currently active." My desk is now green. I can see six other greens either in front of me or within my peripheral field of view. I do not turn to look for the other three that must be behind me.

The professor and the selection committee flash as they join the applause for a few seconds before the professor nods the applause off. All of the seats have lost their color glow except for those in green.

The words 'Deep Breaths' float between me and the professor. It is a message from the house computer, and I realize my breathing is indeed shallow and quick. I close my eyes and take deep breaths, and after four, the message vanishes.

"It has long been the tradition of Chronos University," the professor says, "to treat the top four selected proposals as equal." He pauses to look around at virtual faces and is distracted when the students on Luna vanish. They return almost immediately. Obviously a communication disruption. He continues, "But we do select numeric order of the remaining top ten solely to allow the participants to gauge if they wish to revise and resubmit their proposals." He again pauses as he looks individually at those of us sitting in green desks. I hold my breath when he looks at me.

"Number ten," he says. One of the desks in front of me dims and the professor nods to them.

"Nine." Green in my right periphery fades away, the professor nods toward them.

"Eight." I see no changes. It must have been one of the ones behind me.

"Seven." One of the desks in front of me dims. Letters flash in front of me: 'BREATHE.' I take a deep breath and signal the house computer for additional help. An inhaler pops onto my desk. I consider using it, but remember the few times I have used a stabilizer in an inhalant. It made my brain feel dull and disconnected.

"Six." I see no changes. Another one behind me? The sight of the stabilizer popping onto my desk was enough. My determination to not use it and my continued deep breaths have at least reduced my anxiety level. The lunar students disappear again. I count the green desks. Two in front of me, I turn my head slightly to the left to bring the third green desk out of my periphery. I still do not know where the fourth desk behind me is. At least I can watch three.

"And number five." The room is now dazzling with applause flashes from everywhere. It takes me a second to refocus on the three desks. They are all still green. I was not selected. I am number five. My stomach hurts. Father will be so disappointed in me.

The girl to my immediate left leans toward me. "Congratulations, LX," she says. I know her name, but can't think of it. GG? JJ? CC?

"Thank you," I say, still trying to think of her name. Five. So close. The professor nods the applause lights off, and I notice a faint green glow. It is my desk! My desk is still green! Number five must have been behind me! I am selected!

Somehow I have the cognizance to disconnect from class before I leap out of my chair. I jump around in my quarters. "I am selected!" I shout. For a fleeting second, I imagine Mother hugging me. Then I think of Father. I must control myself. KC or MLE would not behave in this manner. I concentrate on Father, picture him as if he were standing with me. Another deep breath. I stretch my mouth open wide then close it; the smile erased.

I sit back down at my desk, quickly take two more deep breaths, and then reconnect to class. I turn to CC. "Sorry," I say, "Communication glitch. Perhaps a dolphin was experimenting with cables again." She nods at me, but her eyes say she doesn't believe me.

"Thank you all for attending today," the professor says, "the four of you selected will receive information about a group contact meeting in two hours, and then we will meet with each of you individually to map out your training. Good day."

He disappears. The selection committee also vanishes. I continue to stare at the podium and am aware that students are also rapidly vanishing. Soon, I see no one else. I turn around and see there is no one behind me either. I turn back to stare at the podium only to see the auditorium dissolve away, and I am looking at my bed. I glance to my left, and then stand and walk the few steps to my portal. The kelp undulates seductively. I smile as I imagine my Mother saying, "Dances, LX. The kelp dances." I do not even try to remove the smile.

In little more than a year of intense training, I will be ready. I will take my first real step as a Chrono Historian. I will walk amongst people who are now only dust, and I will breathe the air of the Twentieth Century.

Chapter One

"Her voice was soft and cool / Her eyes were clear and bright"

Grover's Corners, Missouri, August 1995

SEAN wiped the sweat from his face, then dropped his t-shirt at the end of the driveway. August could be brutally hot in Missouri, even with the sun about to set. Some claim it's the humidity, not the heat, but to Sean, 87 degrees at sunset was just plain hot.

He picked up his basketball and started slowly dribbling toward the goal, changing hands and crouching lower to the ground as he began his drive. He feinted to an imaginary player on his left, spun away and drove down the baseline to his right and finished with a reverse layup. The ball rolled on the edge of the rim then fell back away from it. He looked skyward as he slowly shook his head.

Sean had no delusions of a career with the NBA. He might not even be good enough to play college ball, but the sixteen-year-old did imagine that the summer growth spurt that propelled him to six feet tall would get him plenty of playing time on the varsity squad during his junior year.

The high school at Grover's Corners was just large enough to compete at the 4A level. The previous year's team had lost in the finals at district; they also lost three starters as graduating seniors. With his height and a little more practice, Sean hoped to get enough starts to earn a letter. Of course, making it to state in March 1996 would be an excellent bonus.

Some of the guys in his grade had already won their letters. Mostly small, speedy guys who managed to win several medals in track. He was a little jealous, mostly of their lettermen jackets. He looked forward to having his Mom sew the 97 shoulder patch and 'GC' on his own jacket. One that he'd already planned to ask for as a Christmas present.

He fired off a jump shot. The orange orb arched toward the backboard, made contact, fell with a satisfying swish through the netting. Sean scooped up the ball and dribbled slowly toward the street, then suddenly snapped around and launched another jump shot. It careened off the rim. He moved to his left to retrieve the ball, catching it on the first bounce. He bounced the ball slow and waist high as he returned to the end of the driveway to pick up his shirt and blot his face again.

The sun had set, and soon it would be too dark to accurately gauge a jump shot. He mopped his neck and chest absently as he looked up the street. She wasn't there. Just as she hadn't been there night after night for the past two weeks. There was no logical reason to expect a repeat of that one-time occurrence, but he continued to hope that the gorgeous blonde in hot pink would come jogging down his street again, preferably in the next fleeting minutes.

Yes, he needed the practice, but *she* was the main reason he was out there at the same time each night, still hoping *she* might come back. He knew it was a long shot. It had been a random event. She had gotten lost and asked him how to get back to the campus. He had no reason to believe that she would ever come down his street again. No reason... but hope never depended on logic or reason.

Each night that she hadn't returned, his memory of the event had added embellishment. With each new day's reminiscence, her hot pink sports bra stretched a little fuller, and her matching pink jogging shorts became even shorter. She was beautiful that night he first saw her, but as he wished for her return night after night, she had transformed into a goddess.

Sean had burned the Greek letters on the back of her shorts into his memory, unable to stop himself from staring at them over his shoulder as he walked to the house to get her the water she'd requested. He still wondered if she had purposefully turned her back to him so that he could get a look.

The next day when he'd checked with the University to see if he could find her sorority house, he discovered that there was *not* a chapter with those letters on the local campus. She may have been a transfer from another college, or maybe it was simply a joke, and she wasn't even Greek. As a high school 'townie' he wasn't all that welcome on campus, even though his parents both worked at the University.

Though he'd certainly hoped to see her again, there was a third reason he'd been out shooting hoops those last several nights. He was desperately clinging to the final hours of summer that were rapidly slipping away.

School started the next morning.

Maybe then he could put an end to his fantasy. Maybe once he was in daily contact with his friends and girls his own age, this vision of a blonde goddess would finally fade away. It was senseless. Sean knew that even if she had wandered back down his street, nothing would have changed. Even though she wasn't *that* much older, there was an invisible barrier between high school and college that artificially dubbed her a woman, while he was merely a boy.

He wondered what it would feel like when he finally crossed that mythical chasm into college. Would he *feel* more like an adult? It wasn't that he didn't already feel like an adult, but when he stepped onto University property, something changed. Somehow *they* could tell he was still in high school. He was as tall as most students there, taller than many, so he wondered what the giveaway was. Would two more years of high school somehow change him from whatever it was that labeled him 'just a boy'? He wished he could grow a decent beard.

"Sean!" his Mom yelled from the front doorway, "you'd better start winding down or you won't get to sleep tonight. You *know* you can't sleep in tomorrow." A furry red blur streaked through the open door. "Maggie! Come back here!" she shouted at the family pet.

The Irish Setter bounded out into the yard and streaked to the driveway making a beeline toward Sean. Sean set the ball down and cradled her head in his arms as he knelt beside her.

"Hey, Mags! Good dog! Who's a good girl? Huh? Who's the best dog in the world?" Maggie wagged violently and licked his face.

Sean grabbed the ball as he stood and fired off one last shot. *Sssctch.* At least the summer had ended with "nothin' but net". He retrieved both his t-shirt and the ball, walked up the driveway, and then up the steps to the front door. Maggie trotted happily at his heels until they reached the door. She suddenly jerked around and started barking skyward.

"What is it, girl?" Sean asked the agitated setter. "Did you see an owl?"

She continued her high-pitched staccato bark counterpointed with low, throaty growls. Sean scanned the tops of the trees across the street. "I don't see anything, Mags." He grabbed her by the collar. "Come on, let's go inside," he said as he forcefully pulled her through the door.

He sighed, looking back at the street again. Another day with no goddess in pink and the last day of summer freedom. He closed the door.

Even if Sean had managed to look at the exact spot that Maggie saw, he wouldn't have detected the nearly invisible boxy shaped object that silently drifted away above the treetops. There was only the tiniest rippling in the stars.

* * * * *

Cars clogged the entry to the high school parking lot. Sean grumbled to himself that he should have known it would happen. No one in high school wanted to ride the bus. Even kids too young to have their driver's license begged to be dropped off by a parent rather than ride in one of the school's yellow monstrosities.

He popped the last bite of his second granola bar into his mouth and casually tossed the wrapper over his shoulder onto the backseat. He would have preferred Pop-Tarts, but he hadn't budgeted time to heat them. His Mom had yelled at him repeatedly about not getting up in time, so asking her to put his favored breakfast into the toaster while he finished getting dressed would not have been wise.

As he counted the number of cars that were slowly funneling into the parking lot ahead of him, he had to admit that she may have been right. She was *usually* right, much to his annoyance. If he'd gotten up fifteen minutes earlier, he wouldn't have been even considering sprinting to his first class. Of course, if all of these *other* clowns had gotten up fifteen minutes earlier, he rationalized, they would have been out of his way.

He finally crept to a point where he could break away. He drove only *slightly* onto the sidewalk as he scooted around and away from all the sheep heading down the first or second rows. There was no way any of the nearer spots remained unclaimed. It seemed pointless to follow the crowd.

Someone honked at him and jammed their brakes as he zipped past the fifth row. He spied an open slot in row 7 and locked into his targeted path. He parked the Taurus, grabbed his notebooks and pen and started toward the building. The clock in his dash showed that he still had 6 minutes, so he decided on a brisk walking pace. Running might not look cool, he decided, and the appearance of being laid-back about school was definitely the desired first-day look.

Someone in a shiny blue Mustang blasted his horn as Sean scooted between the rows and angled toward the sidewalk. It was Cliff Sickler. Cliff's dad owned the Ford dealership in town, so he was driving a brand new car, of course. Sean didn't particularly like Cliff, regardless of what he drove, but the fact that *he* had a cool car while Sean drove a six-year-old family car made Cliff seem all the more unlikable. He considered flipping him off, but instead rapped on the Mustang's fender and beamed him an insincere smile.

Sean didn't follow the sidewalk far. Once past the parking lot, he cut across the grass to around behind the main building. Laid out behind the three-stories of the high school were the 'expansion' classrooms.

It was only the fifth anniversary of the main structure of the high school, completed the summer of 1990, and already it was too crowded to accommodate the nearly twelve hundred students. His parents claimed that during the 1980s, voters had repeatedly been unwilling to fund a school levy in the amount needed to build a larger high school, finally passing a reduced request in 1988. The school district had accepted the compromise to be able to build what they could. The building had been almost large enough to handle enrollment the first year that it opened, but the district had been growing steadily over the past twenty years. Everyone knew it hadn't been enough, but still they regarded it as better than nothing.

To deal with ever increasing enrollment, they erected a small trailer park of classrooms behind the relatively new main building. It made no sense to Sean that somehow they found money for tacky little stop-gap solutions. The prefabricated buildings weren't *exactly* double-wide trailers, but the area still had the look of a trailer park, and had been dubbed "Schoolyard Wasteland."

Sean only had two classes in the Wasteland during fall semester, but one of them—Spanish III—was during first hour. He wasn't particularly interested in learning Spanish, but his Mom had argued that taking it as dual credit with the University would give him the option of then getting a BA instead of a BS. He had wryly commented that he thought it was all BS. Her stern rebuttal had been the standard "you'll thank me later."

He'd had an excellent Spanish teacher his freshman year, which had made it tolerable, almost pleasant. She was a native speaker, but, thankfully, equally fluent in English. Somehow the language just sounded better rolling off her tongue than it did when he attempted to speak it.

During his second year, he was disappointed to find that Ms. Gonzales had left the school. She had taught only one year while her husband was a visiting professor at the University. The airhead who replaced her was fresh out of college, taking her very first job at GC High. She had been hired primarily as a drama teacher, but on paper, she was also qualified to teach Spanish. Sean made a point of accenting the 'on paper' whenever he thought of her. He'd secretly hoped that she'd run off to join a traveling theater company or circus or something during summer break.

Sean reached the stairs down to the Wasteland classrooms at the same time as Eric Hennison. Eric, a senior, was a point guard on the basketball team. They exchanged small talk as they descended the stairs together. At the bottom, Eric turned to the left. Sean's building was on the right. He was making parting comments to Eric as he blindly turned to his right and slammed into someone.

Her books went flying as they both nearly tumbled to the ground. Sean knelt down to help her retrieve all her dropped books and papers. Once gathered, they stood facing each other.

"Thank you. That was my fault," she gushed, "I was attempting to determine which building contained my classroom. It was poor planning to look at my schedule near the bottom of the stairs."

"No, no, it was my fault," Sean insisted. "I was trying to not be late, and probably came down the stairs too fast." He shrugged sheepishly. "And I was talking to someone instead of watching where I was going."

"Perhaps we should agree we were each distracted?" she offered.

"Well, anyway," he said, "I'm glad you're not hurt." He studied her face. She had beautiful blue eyes. "I don't think I know you. My name is Sean Kelly."

She reached out to grab his hand and pumped it. "*Hola. Me llaman Alexis Townsend. Me plazco conocerle*"

"Ummm... OK. Hi, Alexis... I'll take a wild guess that you're headed to Spanish class. It's the last one here on the right," he said as he pointed the way. "By the way, class hasn't started yet."

"Oh. Sorry, I thought perhaps they expected a language immersion here. It is difficult to know relevant customs when you are new to the area."

"So that's why I've never had a class with you before, you're new to the area? Where you from?"

"New York. Upstate, not the city. I recently moved here with my Aunt Katherine."

"Oh. She start a new job with the University?"

"No. Why would you make such an assumption?"

"Good odds on that guess," Sean shrugged. "It's the reason a lot of people move to this town. The University's a major employer."

"No. She recently became widowed and wanted to distance herself from everything in New York. She randomly placed her finger on a map and selected this location."

They started walking slowly toward their classroom.

"So what does she do?" asked Sean.

"Do?"

"You know, work. What kind of work does she do?"

"Oh. She is an artist."

"You mean like painting and stuff?"

"Yes. And sculptures, and photography, all types of art."

"And she can make money?"

"No, she is not a counterfeiter!"

Sean chuckled. "Good one. But seriously she can make a living from her art?"

"Oh! Vocational compensation! Yes. No. I mean..." Her head twitched slightly. "Her husband was a very successful businessman and left her a considerable sum of money." Sean lifted an eyebrow. It seemed that she rattled off the last sentence as if memorized from a script, but he decided to let her odd delivery slide.

"Well, I hope you like it here," he said. "Hey, we'd better get inside before we're late."

"May I sit beside you?"

"Um... I guess." Her directness had taken him by surprise. "If there are two open seats together."

Standing in the doorway, they found there were only single open seats spread throughout the compact room. Sean shrugged an "oh well" smile to Alexis and sat down in one.

Alexis bent near the girl sitting to Sean's right.

"*Hola*, my name is Alexis and I am new to this school. Would it be possible for you to relinquish your seat?"

"Excuse me?" the girl said sourly.

"You are excused," Alexis replied courteously. "May I sit here?"

"No," the girl snarled, crinkling her nose as if Alexis had set a skunk on her desk. "Sit over there!"

"I would not inconvenience you with this request except Sean is my only friend, and I would feel more comfortable sitting next to him."

"Really?" The girl smiled sweetly as she turned to Sean. There was something feline about the smile. "So, Sean, you are her 'only *friend.*' I certainly wouldn't want to come between you two love birds."

"No, Megan, I just met her," Sean stammered.

Megan swept up her notebook as she stood, then moved over two seats with a surly, "Whatever." She looked back with a brief wisp of a smile, then immediately put her head next to the girl to the left of her new seat. She whispered something in the girl's ear, and they both giggled as they looked in Sean and Alexis' direction. Sean's cheeks flamed. He turned to Alexis.

"Why did you *do* that?" he hissed.

"Do what?"

"Make Megan think we were going out!"

"That statement does not make sense. Why would she believe we were going out when we only now came in?"

"Not going out! *Going out!* Boyfriend/Girlfriend! Dating! What did you call that back in New York?"

"Really?" Alexis suddenly beamed, "Simply from my request to sit here, that girl now believes that we have a romantic link?"

"Are you kidding me? Do you…"

"Sorry I was late, class," Ms. McGuire announced as she quickly clacked into the room in very high heels. "The Principal's little First Day Pep-Talk didn't allow those of us who actually have to teach out here enough time to get here. We can skip roll call today, it looks like most of the seats are filled, and I recognize most of you from last year. Did you all make it in last week to pick up textbooks?" She fabricated a smile as she took a breath.

The mumbled response from the group wasn't coherent. Ms. McGuire's propped up smile collapsed.

"All right. Let's try it this way. If you have a textbook with you, please raise it up above your head."

After some muttering and shuffling in book bags, five or six textbooks were lifted into the air. Sean noticed that Alexis held hers aloft.

Ms. McGuire continued, "You should remember from last year that we used these books almost every class period. I expect you to bring them with you. Make sure you have them tomorrow. Now then, as I said, I think I recognize almost all of you from last year," she paused as her eyes rested on Alexis. "But not you, *chica*." She approached Alexis' desk.

"*Saludos. Me llaman Ms McGuire. ¿Qué le llaman?*" She offered a limp hand to Alexis.

"*¡Hola! Me llaman Alexis. Estoy muy contento ser su estudiante,*" Alexis replied while giving Ms. McGuire's hand two swift pumps.

"*¡Muy bueno! Usted habla muy bien,*" Ms. McGuire said with a genuine smile.

"*Gracias. Usted me adula,*" Alexis replied shyly.

Ms. McGuire noisily clacked back to the front of the room. "Well, class," she said as she turned to face them. "Alexis just might set the bar a little high for some of you this year," She paused, reconstructing a bright smile as her gaze passed around the room. "Now then, let's review a little of what we learned last year." She went to the whiteboard and started writing in large flowing letters.

Sean glanced cautiously to his right and found that Alexis seemed to be watching him. His glance shifted past her, and he also noticed that Megan and Ashly were looking his way and smirking. When she'd seen she'd caught his eye, Megan pursed her lips into little air kisses. Sean turned back to face the whiteboard, and then slowly dropped his head back until he was staring at the ceiling. The first day of his Junior year certainly had *not* started the way he had imagined it would.

Spanish class didn't last all day, but to Sean, it seemed like it had. The following speech class and algebra were both incredibly boring, but at least they didn't have Alexis' watchful eyes in the room, nor was she in the study hall that fell between them. He'd begun to forget about the strange new girl as the day passed, and was glad finally to hit the lunchroom and have some time to catch up with friends he hadn't seen in awhile.

He scanned the room as he stood in line to buy a couple slices of pizza and a Coke. He spotted Raj and Kevin and waved. Kevin mimed back that they would save him a seat. Sean paid for his food, then crossed the room to sit across the table from Raj.

"Dude, what's up?" Raj offered as a greeting. Kevin mumbled a "hey" as he bit into his burger.

Sean nodded a "hey" back to Kevin and addressed Raj, "Not much. What's going on with you?"

"Nada. Just back in the grind," Raj said as he crunched a chip.

"Didn't see you any this summer," Sean offered with an unspoken, "Where were you?"

"Yeah," Raj returned flatly, "we were gone for the summer." His eyes sparkled as his face cracked a grin.

"And...?" Sean could tell Raj intended a dramatic tale, so he obligingly prompted him.

"You know my dad's in the Biology department at the University." Raj paused again for effect.

"And...?" Sean prompted again, this time with raised eyebrows.

"He got a summer research project and took the whole family." Another pause.

"And here comes the big finish," Sean said toward Kevin in mock stage whisper.

"To Florida! To study manatees!" Raj finally exploded.

"You *Dog*!" Sean yelped as he threw a parmesan packet at Raj.

"I know!" Raj crowed, "And we were less than a half mile from a huge public beach! I was in the ocean every day!"

"Is that's why you're so brown?" Kevin asked with an innocent smile.

"Kevin!" Sean said, once again using a stage whisper, "Raj's parents are from India."

"India?" Kevin bellowed with feigned surprise, "I thought they were from *Indiana!*"

"Ha ha," Raj retorted, "you guys are a riot." He tossed a chip at Sean bouncing it off his forehead. "With your Irish ancestry, you're lucky to even get freckles." They all laughed.

"Does that mean," Kevin continued as if shocked by the discovery, "that Raj isn't just short for Roger?" Raj flung a chip at Kevin who easily ducked the projectile. Kevin popped back up with a triumphant grin. "So," he asked Raj, "tell us about the wahines in the bikinis!"

"That's Hawaii; you dork," Sean chided.

"They have bikinis in Florida," Kevin returned with know-it-all bravado.

Sean rolled his eyes while shaking his head.

"Guys," Raj said in a suddenly hushed conspiratorial tone, looking both right and left before continuing, "that's the part I haven't gotten to. *Half* of the beach was topless."

"Are you *serious?*" Kevin gushed, with open-mouth and wide-eyes.

"Serious," Raj said soberly while drawing an X over his heart.

"Whoa..." Kevin grinned. His eyes glazed over as he imagined the beach.

"Well, maybe not *exactly* half," Raj considered, index finger on his chin, "there were usually more girls than guys out there."

Kevin punched Raj in the shoulder. "You *Punk!* Topless *guys* don't count!"

They all laughed again.

"But seriously... for real seriously... Lots of cute girls?" Sean asked.

"Oh yeah," Raj nodded enthusiastically, "all shapes, sizes, and colors."

"First base with any?" Kevin asked, waggling his eyebrows.

"Don't be so crass!" Raj snapped.

"I thought so." Kevin nodded, "all look, no touch. Did you even *talk* to any of them?"

"Hey! It's still better than either of *you* did this summer!" Raj huffed.

"Actually," Sean offered slowly, "I had an interesting encounter with a hot college girl a couple of weeks ago, and I *did* talk to her!"

They both turned all attention to him as Kevin requested details.

"Welllll," Sean drawled, "I was out in the driveway shooting some hoops when this hot college chick in a pink sports bra and tight pink shorts came jogging down the street and stopped to talk to me."

"Innie or outie?" Kevin interrupted.

"What?"

"Her belly button. Innie or outie? I'm just trying to get the whole picture."

"Are you kidding me?"

"No! I think outies are kinda hot! You know, especially if they have a piercing."

Sean looked perplexed. He stared at Kevin for a beat before repeating slowly, "Hot. Pink. Sports. Bra. Matching tight hot pink shorts... there was a lot to notice besides a belly button."

"How about tattoos?" Kevin interrupted again.

Sean stopped to think. "No, I don't think so. I don't know! So when I say hot girl you think pierced belly button and tattoos?"

Kevin scrunched his lips to one side, considering. "Yeah, that works for me."

Sean put his hand over his eyes and pulled it down the length of his face. "OK," he continued, "the hot chick *may* or *may not* have had piercings and/or tattoos, I didn't specifically notice. Sorry."

"So anyway," Raj inserted, "this hot college girl comes jogging up to you and says, 'hey, studly high school boy, how about it? You and me?'"

"Now who's being crass?" Sean snarled, "It wasn't like that."

"Sadly, it never is," Kevin sighed.

"OK, so she was lost and asked me how to get back to the campus. But she was still totally beautiful."

"I saw a cute blonde just today," Kevin said, "New girl, I think."

"What'd she look like?" asked Sean.

"Medium height. Trim. Kinda cute."

"I'll bet that's Alexis. I had Spanish with a new girl. Blonde. She seems kinda different. She said she's from New York. Describe her some more."

"Umm," Kevin began, looking over Sean's shoulder, "OK, I'd say about 5'5", shoulder length wavy sandy-blonde hair, blue eyes, cute little upturned nose, white sleeveless top with little red stripes, matching red skirt..."

"Whoa," Sean interrupted, "when did you get a photographic memory?"

"No, dude," Raj said, also looking over Sean's shoulder, "he's just describing her."

Sean's eyes widened as he heard a soft feminine voice behind him. "Hello again, Sean."

He spun around, "Um, hi, Alexis. Umm, hey, Kevin was just talking about you."

"How nice. Who is Kevin?"

Kevin raised his hand. "That'd be me. The tan dude on my left is Raj." Raj elbowed him in the ribs. "Ow! I thought you guys were supposed to be pacifists."

"Don't stereotype," Raj growled, "Gandhi was one guy. Does everyone assume *your* guys still plunder villages?"

Kevin looked at him blankly.

"I think he's referring to the Vikings, Mr. Olsen," Sean explained to his confused friend.

"Oh yeah?" Kevin objected, "Well my *Mom's* side of the family is *Italian!*

So, Ha!"

Raj turned to Sean and lifted a questioning eyebrow. Sean shrugged.

"You have very interesting friends, Sean," Alexis said politely.

Sean turned back to her. "Yeah, they're a laugh a minute," he muttered, then turned back to his friends. They each looked at him, then looked over his shoulder, looked at each other, then back to Sean. Raj did a quick glance up, then back to Sean with a serious stare. Sean silently mouthed a "what?". Raj repeated the glance, looked back at Sean then did a subtle head twitch in the same direction. Sean frowned as he squeezed his eyes shut, then blew out a breath, opened his eyes and managed an expansive plastic smile as he turned back to Alexis. "Nice talking to you again, Alexis." He turned back to Raj.

"I thought perhaps we could sit together during lunch period," she said to his back.

Raj stifled a snicker. Sean put the big smile back on and turned. "I was just catching up with the guys," he explained tersely, "Haven't seen them in awhile."

"That's OK," Raj said, not even trying to hide a huge grin, "We were just finished."

"I'm not finished," Kevin complained, somewhat confused again.

"Sure you are, buddy. Grab the rest of your fries, and I'll go help you with that problem you were having with your locker."

Kevin's face reflected how completely lost he was. "What problem?"

"You know," Raj coaxed, jerking his head subtly toward Alexis, "you can't get everything in it, because it's *too crowded*." He continued the subtle head nods toward Alexis.

Still confused, Kevin looked at Raj, then Alexis. Finally, his eyes opened wide. "Ohhhhh!" Kevin grinned, "Right! Too *crowded*... gotcha. I mean, yes, my *locker* is *much* too crowded. We should go have a look at that."

Sean stared daggers at both of them as they stood. Kevin crammed a fistful of french fries into his mouth then picked up his tray. "Nigh hoo mee ew, Awexis."

Raj looked back over his shoulder toward Sean as they left, still grinning. As they walked away, Sean heard him tell Kevin, "I can actually picture you sacking a village."

Alexis placed a small brown bag on the table as she claimed the seat Raj had vacated. She smiled warmly at Sean. He smiled back weakly, then took a bite of his pizza. She reached into the bag and brought out a clear container and spoon, set them on the table, then folded the bag and put it to one side.

"Have you known your friends long?" she asked.

Sean set his slice down, finished chewing, and then swallowed. "Yes. Seems like my whole life. I guess Raj goes back to 2nd grade, and I think it was about 5th grade when Kevin moved here."

Alexis opened her container and dipped her spoon into it. She put a small bite into her mouth.

"What's that?" Sean asked.

Alexis swallowed, paused, looked into the container, then back to Sean. "Simply by appearance," she asked enigmatically, "what would you assume?"

"I don't know," said Sean, flustered that she answered a simple question with another question. "It kind of looks like yogurt, I guess." Sean noticed that she glanced away with a brief twitch before answering.

"Yes. That is exactly right. Yogurt," she said, then added, "My Aunt Katherine prepares it."

"Looks...uhhh... yummy," Sean lied. He took another bite of pizza and flogged his brain for a way to tactfully draw the conversation to a close. "Is that all you're going to eat for lunch?"

"Yes."

Her terse reply irked Sean since he felt compelled to continue politely, and it agitated him that she seemed to be studying him again. "I don't know how some of you girls get by eating so little," he fumbled.

She just smiled at him.

Why did she come to sit with me if not to talk? He wondered. *And why is she staring at me?* "I guess that's how you keep your cute girlish figures." He knew he was babbling, but her silent smile was making him crazy. "So, how do you like it here?"

"It is rather loud," she replied.

Initially confused by her answer, he then realized she was referring to the din of the lunchroom. "No, I don't mean *here* here," he said, tapping the table. "I mean here like the school, the town... you know, is it very different from where you came from." Sean thought he saw her suppress a laugh.

"Yes," she smiled, "it *is* different... but also intriguing."

"I suppose some people back east think we're all a bunch of hicks."

She glanced away again in that same strange way as when he asked about the yogurt. "Hicks." She pronounced distinctly, as if she were in a spelling bee. "Hayseeds, yokels, bumpkins, hillbillies." She paused. "That appears to be rather derogatory terminology for a rural populous in general."

"Wow," Sean agreed, "especially when you string it all together like that. So is that how *you* see us?"

Alexis smiled warmly, "I attempt to not be judgmental of the differences in others." Her face shifted to become more serious. "What are your initial impressions of me?"

Sean felt the heat rise in his cheeks. He wished he didn't blush so easily, but the bluntness of her question overwhelmed him. He rejected his initial thoughts, since, naturally, he couldn't tell her that she creeped him out a little. "Oh, I agree totally," he stammered, "It's best to not be judgmental." He shoved another bite of pizza into his mouth and assessed the distance to the closest exit.

"You appear somewhat," Alexis began, then paused before finishing, "ill at ease. Have I said or done something inappropriate?"

"No, of course not," Sean protested chivalrously, "I'm just not too good at one-on-one with new people. I've known most of the people in this room for years. I guess my conversation skills with strangers might be a little rusty."

"How might I decrease my strangeness?" she asked.

Girl, Sean thought, *I don't see how you possibly could GET stranger.* But he said, "I guess it just takes time."

"Time," she mused, "What an appropriate assessment."

"Good," Sean agreed, "I'll bet by the end of the school year you'll fit right in and have tons of friends. You'll probably have so many friends you won't even remember that you ever talked with me."

Alexis sampled another bite from her container. "Or I might recall your every word verbatim."

"Or that," Sean squeaked nervously. He stuffed the rest of his pizza into his mouth and started chewing rapidly. Alexis leisurely took another bite, happily watching him. Sean swallowed. "Well, better go. I need to go to my car before afternoon classes," he announced as he stood.

"Sean," she said, "there is one more thing." She sat her spoon down.

"What's that?" he asked before downing the last of his Coke.

"Could I go home with you after school?"

Sean gasped, sucking the last drops of his Coke into his trachea. He started coughing violently.

Alexis stood. "Do you require the Heimlich maneuver?" she asked.

Sean wheezed. He had one hand on his chest, and the other held out to Alexis signaling her to sit back down. "No," he croaked, "I'm fine." He sat down and coughed a few more times. He wheezed in a couple of deep breaths then croaked, "What did you say?"

"Do you require the Heimlich maneuver?"

"Before that."

"Could I go home with you after school?"

Sean coughed again as he pointed to her. "That would be the one."

"I hope it will not inconvenience you. My aunt resides a short distance down the street from your house. It would be a minimal diversion from your usual route."

"*Oh!*" Sean said, his voice nearing normal, "you want a ride. To *your* house."

"Yes, if that would be possible."

"Um, sure. Fine. Meet me in the parking lot after last class."

"Biology!"

"Um, yeah, that's *my* last class."

"Mine, also," she smiled as she scooped another bite from her container.

"Of course it is," he mumbled as he stood, "see you in Biology."

Sean walked away, wondering if the day could get any weirder. He stopped in mid-stride. How did she know where he lived? He turned, took one step back to ask her that question, and then froze. She was watching him, her spoon between container and mouth. She smiled. He decided not to go back.

Sean dozed off a few times in study hall, then had trouble paying attention in History class. He wasn't that fond of history or that particular teacher, but his mind was focused on trying to figure out what it was that bothered him so much about Alexis.

He had first gone out with a girl in 7th grade. Three or four others after her. Nothing too serious or even anything that lasted very long. His Dad had said "have fun, but stay out of trouble. Remember, it's a lot easier to finish college first before settling down." Settling down? Like he'd even think about that in the 7th grade. He had plans to travel around and see the world, maybe even land a job that allowed him to travel a lot.

His thoughts continued to wander. It was easy for his mind to wander while the teacher droned on and on about what all they would cover during the semester and how exciting it was to learn about the past. He was still puzzling about what it was about Alexis that made him feel so off balance, and then his thoughts drifted to Tiffany.

Those rough few months of his freshman year came rushing back to him. At first, it seemed flattering for a senior girl to show interest in him. She wasn't the type to enter a beauty contest, but she certainly wasn't ugly. Cute wasn't a word he'd use to describe her. Perhaps the best and simplest term was sexy.

She was overtly seductive, he recalled, and when she first started talking to him, she somehow managed innuendo that led his thoughts toward something titillating.

In hindsight, Tiffany embodied everything Mrs. Walters had warned him about. Mrs. Walters had been one of his eighth-grade teachers who'd made a point of telling him that he'd need to watch out in high school. She warned him that a good looking boy like he would be a target for an upper-class girl to "spoil." This advice came at the Spring Science Fair where she then proceeded to explain graphically to his Mom what she meant by spoil.

Somehow, summer vacation had been long enough to purge that moment from his brain, and at the beginning of his freshman year, he was swept up by Tiffany Maxwell.

In hindsight, it was obvious that he had been just a plaything to Tiffany. Initially, she was quite the charmer. She flattered him; told him how he seemed to be so much more mature than most of the other boys in the entire high school.

Next she started buying him little things, driving him home after school every day, going out of her way to always find him between classes. He had to admit that he liked the way she treated him. It made him feel special. His parents even seemed to find her charming. She had a special level of "nice" that she portrayed to his parents. Everything seemed perfect... and then things started to change.

At first she had always asked him what he wanted to do when they went out. Before long she was suggesting what they do, and finally, by the last week they were together she was in complete control. *She* told him what time she would pick him up, what he should wear, and where they were going.

She started telling him how stupid and immature his friends were and that he should drop them. Eventually, she only took him to secluded spots out on country roads where she would pull into a field and park.

She had been an amazing kisser, he still granted her that. She pretty much taught him everything he knew about kissing.

While the history teacher droned on, Sean thought of that final Friday night with Tiffany. It had started out like every other recent date; out on a country road, park, make out. At first, it seemed great, but eventually he began to feel like he'd become an object... something that she enjoyed, but was eventually going to use up. He decided he needed to change the status quo, still wanting to believe there might be a glimmer of hope for what he felt was becoming a joke of a relationship.

He pulled back from a long kiss. She leaned toward him as he pulled away, and he put two fingers to her lips. "Tiffany," he began shyly, "I was thinking maybe we could go catch a movie. *Rudy* opens tonight."

"A movie?" Her voice had a mocking tone. "Why would we want to do that?"

"It just seems like, lately, all we do is park and make out."

She leaned into him again, nuzzling his neck, running her tongue up it until she reached his earlobe, giving it a little nip. "I thought you liked this," she purred.

"I do, but..." her mouth covered his, stopping him mid-sentence. He gave in to her advances and kissed back, but then pulled away again. "It seems like this is *all* we do anymore."

"I see," she smiled knowingly, "Getting a little bored with it?" Her right hand was behind his neck, her left hand on his chest. She had popped open two buttons on his shirt before he barely knew her hand was there. "I can understand that. Ready for something a little more exciting?" Her fingers were quick! She'd slipped the button of his jeans open and was moving his zipper down. "Is my little Sean ready to become a man?"

At that moment, he was torn, but in retrospect, it was her tone that had tipped the balance. She seemed so... condescending. If she hadn't said it in exactly that way, the night might have gone differently.

He gripped her left wrist and pushed her arm back onto her lap as he looked her in the eyes. "Tiffany... what kind of feelings do you have for me?" Her initial reaction seemed to be surprised. "Do you care for me as a person at all?" Her mouth twisted into a smile, but not a friendly one.

"What does that have to do with this?"

"Well," Sean offered slowly, "I guess I'd always imagined that the first time would be really special..."

"Oh, you don't have enough imagination to know how special I can be," she interrupted. She pulled the bottom of her shirt free from her jeans and pulled it off over her head. Sean gasped. "Now come here, baby," she purred, "I'll show you special."

At first, he couldn't take his eyes off her. He'd seen lingerie models in catalogs, seen plenty of girls in bikinis... but the sight of her frilly tangerine bra was somehow entirely different... everything was all right there... living and breathing... inches away.

Then she shattered the fantasy when she spoke, "Come on, don't be shy. I'll teach you everything you need to know. You can go to school Monday and tell all your little friends how you became a man."

Sean turned away to look out the side window. His desires and his morals engaged in a brief warfare. He was presented a golden opportunity, but something just didn't feel right. He buttoned his shirt as he stared into the darkness.

"Come on, baby," she coaxed, "I'm going to get cold. Come warm me up."

He continued to stare out the window. His hormones screamed for him to give into her, but something else held him back. Pride? A sense of right and wrong? He pulled his zipper up and buttoned his fly. "No," he said softly.

"No?" she snapped, "What do you mean, 'no'?"

He maintained his vigil of the darkness; his window fogged. He shrugged. "It just doesn't seem right. Not like this, not tonight. Let's just take things easy."

"Take things easy?" she mocked, her voice dripping with venom. *"You* don't get to decide. I'm telling you it's now or never, boy. *Look at me!"*

Sean held his gaze of the nothingness beyond his fogged window.

"Look at me!" she shrieked.

Sean swallowed hard. "Put your shirt back on, Tiffany," he sighed.

"You. Little. Punk!" she screamed. *"You* don't get to tell *me* what to do. And *you* certainly don't get to decide *when* we do it." He could hear her pull her shirt back on. He turned back to face her and was shocked when she

grabbed him by the jaw, digging her fingernails into his cheek. "*You. Are. Nothing!*" she growled shrilly, "No one *ever* turns me down!" Her eyes glistened as a single tear ran down a cheek. She turned her head away and quickly ran a hand over it.

Sean was confused... embarrassed... even a little scared. "I'm sorry, Tiffany," he offered gently. She pushed his face away so roughly that his head hit the window.

"No," she snarled, "not *yet* you aren't. But you *will* be."

Sean hadn't thought about that night since one day in the prior Spring semester during English Lit when he came across the phrase, "Heaven has no rage like love to hatred turned / Nor hell a fury like a woman scorned." The teacher indignantly explained that it was usually misquoted as "hell hath no fury like a woman scorned." Either way, Sean could attest to its validity... at least in Tiffany's case. During the rest of his entire freshman year, he often heard girls whispering in the hallway that he was gay.

He shook free from his thoughts about Tiffany, but began to wonder what about Alexis had triggered them? They didn't even remotely look alike; Alexis was (he had to admit) much cuter. Nothing about their voices seemed similar. He was sure that there had to be something about her that triggered the comparison, but he couldn't put it together.

His musings were interrupted by the bell. Only one last class, but it was Biology... and he already knew that Alexis would be there. Fortunately, so would Raj. With a University Biology Prof as a father, Raj would be a real asset in that class.

As Sean stood to leave, he was stopped by an authoritative voice from the front of the class. "Mr. Kelly. A word, please?" It was Mr. Douglas, the history teacher. "Mr. Kelly," he continued as Sean walked toward the front of the room. Sean hated when teachers called him Mr. Kelly... it always spelled trouble. "You seemed distracted today."

"Sorry, Mr. Douglas, I've got a lot on my mind," Sean said, hoping he had sounded genuinely contrite.

"Mr. Kelly, it's the first day of class, I would think your mind would be empty after a summer of goofing off. Empty and eager to soak up knowledge."

"Yes, sir... sorry." Sean dipped his head to sell his plea. "I promise I'll be paying more attention tomorrow."

"Well, Sean, I have to wonder if a two-page paper for tomorrow might help you focus."

"I don't think that's really necessary, sir. You've gotten my attention; I promise."

"Wellll," he drew out the syllable as he assessed Sean's sincerity, "I suppose I can forgive you on the first day," he said with a smile, then immediately added sternly, "But don't let it happen again tomorrow!"

"Yes, sir... I mean no, sir!" Sean promised, while thinking, *just let me go, you dick-weed.*

"OK, Mr. Kelly. I'll see you tomorrow."

Sean bolted out the door.

Great, he thought glumly, *My only afternoon class outside of the main building, and I had to be held after.* He was sure he would be the last one to Biology, which was all the way on the far side of the main building on the third floor.

"Please, Raj, save me a seat... please, Raj, save me a seat," he chanted as he flew up the stairs. He just made it through the door as the second bell rang and quickly surveyed the room. One empty seat, but at least it was next to Raj. As Sean headed toward it, Raj shifted into the empty seat. Glancing to the right of the vacated seat, Sean closed his eyes and glumly sat, with Raj now on his left. He glared at his friend, then turned to his right, valiantly presenting a plastic smile.

"Hello again, Sean," Alexis said warmly.

"Hi, Alexis." His voice dripped with sarcasm. "How have you been?" He turned back to Raj, his smile gone, and his eyes fiery as he growled one word, "*Why?*"

Raj leaned close to his ear and whispered, "Come on, man; she's cute... and I think she likes you. Why not give her a chance?"

"All right, settle down," came a voice from the front of the room, "I know this is your last class on the first day, but I'm sure you can all concentrate for another 50 minutes."

It was a grueling 50 minutes for Sean. Anytime he even glanced to his right; Alexis met his eyes with her warm smile. Raj was smiling, too, or maybe grinning, whenever Sean glanced his way.

Sean had never spent so much classroom time focused on the whiteboard, but he didn't know if he was relieved or even more stressed when the last bell of the day rang. Raj was up like a shot. Sean barely hooked his elbow before he got away.

"We need to talk, old buddy," Sean said menacingly through clenched teeth.

"Can't. Gotta go. Sorry. Maybe catch you on IRC tonight?" Raj said as he pulled away and rushed out the door.

"IRC?" inquired Alexis from Sean's left shoulder. He turned to her; resigned to the fact that he'd already agreed to give her a ride to her aunt's house.

"It stands for Internet Relay Chat. It's probably a little too technical for you to understand, but it's kind of like email, but in real-time. Some of us guys like..."

"Really?" she interrupted. "The text-based protocol that evolved from Bitnet relay?" Alexis' eyes flashed. "Still using TCP but predating MSN.NET. It would be fascinating to observe it in use." When she saw the astonishment in Sean's face, she added more subtly, "I mean, it would be interesting to see how that works."

Sean's eyes narrowed. "OK," he started slowly, "I know TCP. That's Transmission Control Protocol—the thing that makes it work in real-time. And I've *heard* some older guys talking about BITNET. What's that other thing you said? Something dot NET? MSN? What's that?"

Alexis looked away, tilting her head slightly to her right. "Not MSN, *N*SN. Network Switching Node."

"And the dot net part?" Sean asked.

"Perhaps you misheard? I said, '*Doc* Net.' Sending documents over the network. It is an experimental protocol."

"Never heard of it. Then what did you mean by 'predating'?" Sean continued suspiciously.

"Predating? When did I say predating?" Alexis asked nervously.

"Just before the NSN doc net thingy."

She twitched her head slightly to the right. "Oh... *relaying*. It relays through a network switching node over the doc net. It must be the difference in our accents. I must confess I sometimes have trouble understanding things that you say with your Midwestern accent."

"What are you talking about? *I* don't have an accent. *You* have the accent," Sean protested. "Never mind that... why do you know all about computer stuff?"

She again tilted her head slightly to the right before answering. "My Father was a computer technician in the military." She paused before adding, "He was killed during the first Desert Storm."

Sean dropped his gaze to his feet, his voice suddenly quieter, "I'm sorry to hear that. That must be tough to lose your dad."

"Yes. It is very sad," Alexis said flatly.

When Sean looked up, he noticed that nearly everyone had cleared the hall. "Hey, we should probably go ahead and get to the car."

They walked in silence down the hall to the stairs. Sean still felt there was something strange about Alexis, but considered it was just that she grew up in a different part of the country. He had to admit that it must have been traumatic to lose her father in the war.

Wait, he thought, *First?*

As they started down the steps, Sean vacillated on whether to re-introduce the topic, but curiosity won out. "Did you say, *'first* Desert Storm'?"

Alexis froze momentarily on the step she was on. Her head twitched. She turned back with a confident smile. "The first *part* of the war. The Desert Storm conflict spanned 1990 and 1991. He was killed during the first part of the conflict." She continued down the steps.

Sean was getting that weird feeling again. He wished he could pinpoint whatever it was that seemed off, but it definitely gave him chills when she came up with some of her replies. It wasn't the answers as much as the way she delivered them. She rattled data off like she was reading from a script.

Sean attempted to make small talk as they walked to the car. He hated small talk. He was terrible at it, but Alexis was even worse. She didn't make any return comment when he'd mentioned the nice weather. While he didn't really expect her to have watched *Babylon 5* or *X-Files,* he thought she might at least have some opinion about *Seinfeld* or *Friends.* He was sure every girl in the school watched *Friends.* He began to wonder if she watched TV at all. When he asked her if she liked to go to movies, Alexis turned it back on him and asked what movie he liked from summer.

"I kind of liked *Waterworld.* I thought the critics were pretty rough on it, but I guess I like Sci-Fi enough to say that it was good. Did you see it?"

He had noticed the head-twitch again before she answered, "Yes,

Waterworld. The polar ice caps have melted, and the Earth is covered with water. The remaining people travel the seas, in search of survival. Several different societies exist. The Mariner falls from his customary and solitary existence into having to care for a woman and a young girl while being pursued by the evil forces of the Deacon."

"What was that? Did you memorize someone's review?"

"What do you mean?" she asked.

"Forget it," Sean said, exasperation creeping into his voice, "did you *like* the movie?"

"Yes. It was very entertaining."

"So do you think that's maybe what the future's like? That the ice caps might actually melt and leave just one massive ocean?"

"No," she smiled. It was almost a laugh.

Why was that funny? he wondered. "OK, what do *you* think the future will be like?" Sean asked.

The smile left her face. "I could not say," she replied.

Was there just a bit of panic in her voice? "Well, you seem to dismiss the *Waterworld* theory almost as if it were a joke. I thought maybe you already had something that you imagined it would be like."

She seemed relieved. "Oh, no, I do not have much imagination. The future will probably be a pleasant place to live."

As they neared his car, Sean was torn between opening his own door and going to the passenger side first. He didn't want to give Alexis any wrong ideas, but his parents had rather firmly instilled into him some old fashioned manners. The training won out, and he unlocked and opened the door for Alexis. She slid out of her backpack and handed it to Sean before getting in. He was caught off-guard by the weight, but was even more surprised by how she easily handed it to him. He swung it into the back seat behind her. "Gosh, Alexis, did you bring home every textbook you have?"

"Yes," she replied, "I will need them to prepare for classes."

"Really? That looks like a lot. I didn't have anything assigned that's due tomorrow."

"I prefer to keep ahead."

Sean closed her door and walked around to his side. He only carried the notebooks and pen that he had when he arrived that morning. All of his textbooks were safely locked away in his school locker. He got in, started the car, put it in drive and moved through the mostly empty lot, swinging around toward the exit. He could feel Alexis' eyes on him again. When he took a confirming glance, she smiled. He looked back at the road as he prepared to round the curve that led to the main streets.

"Sean," Alexis inquired, "Do you find yourself attracted to me?"

He jerked so sharply in her direction that it pulled the wheel and the car ran up onto the curb. He jammed the brakes and turned back onto the road. "What?" he asked incredulously.

"Do you find yourself attracted to me?" she repeated.

He stopped the car and faced her.

"Attracted to you?" he echoed.

"Yes," she continued, "someone you find you would select for a w...." she stumbled, "...girlfriend."

"We only met for the first time today," Sean said, unable to keep the irritation from his voice.

"Yes, that is true," she said evenly.

Sean held his head slightly askew, holding his hands palm up at shoulder level. He refrained from saying the "duh" that typically accompanied that gesture, thinking it unnecessarily rude. Her face was blank, and he regretted omitting the "duh."

"We don't know anything about each other," he finally said in exasperation. There again, he saw that smile that was almost a laugh. That reaction was beginning to get on his nerves.

"What would you like to know about me?" she said, followed with her sweetest smile.

"Nothing!" Sean grumbled. "Absolutely nothing!" He turned back and jammed the gas pedal, chirping the tires. They rode several blocks in silence.

Alexis finally asked softly, "What has made you so angry?"

Sean was silent until he pulled up to a four-way stop sign. He turned to her again. "*You! You* make me angry!" he spat. Alexis cowered, shocked by his harshness. Sean continued with less heat as he counted on his fingers, "You make Megan move during Spanish so you can sit by me. You hijacked my lunch with the guys. Then you somehow manipulated Raj into sitting me beside you again in Biology."

At last it clicked. That was why he had thought of Tiffany, he felt like he was being manipulated... controlled. Just like with Tiffany. Alexis seemed to be trying to *force* a relationship with him.

A horn blared from behind them. He'd apparently missed his turn to go through the four-way stop. He glanced at the cars to his right and left and saw the drivers were watching him to see if he was finally going to cross the intersection. The horn behind blasted again. Sean pushed the gas.

They rode in silence for several more minutes. Sean turned into his neighborhood, then finally broke the silence, "So where do you live?"

"It is less than a kilometer east of your house, on the same street," she said in a soft flat voice.

Kilometer? Who says kilometer? "So why do you know that? Why do you know where I live?" Heat returned to Sean's voice as he added, "Are you *stalking* me? Is that it? You ambush me before Spanish class like you were waiting there to crash into me on purpose. You know where I live. You are *always* staring at me."

Alexis was silent. She faced straight ahead. Sean thought she nearly looked frightened. He turned onto his street and continued east past his house. Alexis continued to look silently forward.

Sean went through two intersections. "Well, I *still* don't know where *you* live... you're going to have to tell me." They continued another half block in silence.

"Reduce speed," Alexis finally said softly, "It is three more houses on your left. The light blue one."

Sean slowed, then turned into the driveway. The garage door was open, and bright sparks were flying. He stopped and put the car in park.

"That is my aunt Katherine," Alexis said, her voice soft, sullen. "She is working on a sculpture."

"With a welding torch?" Sean asked, just as the sparks stopped. He could then clearly see there was someone in a welder's helmet standing over some twisted pieces of glowing metal. She tilted the mask up as she examined her work. She looked their way, smiled and waved, then returned the visor to the down position and applied the torch again. More sparks flew. Sean could see in the quick glimpse he had of Aunt Katherine that there was a strong family resemblance. "That's pretty cool," he added.

"Approximately 3500 degrees centigrade," Alexis said absently, still staring forward.

"No, not the torch, I meant..." Sean decided it was pointless to correct her strange statements. He stopped when he saw the sadness in her eyes. "Look, Alexis, I'm sorry I went off on you. I just... I don't know... I just don't like the way you seem to be after me. It feels a lot like a bad relationship I had with a girl once. I didn't mean to hurt your feelings."

She finally shyly looked his way. "No, it was my fault. I made some incorrect assumptions about how to approach you. I am sorry for causing you discomfort."

"See, I don't get that either. *Why* are you approaching me? Why *me*? You seem to have picked me out... but *why?*"

Alexis opened her door and stepped out. She turned back to him. "I regret that I cannot tell you." She leaned back in a bit. "It was wonderful to meet you, Sean Kelly. You have shown me kindness, even though I have irritated you." She turned back away and closed the door. Sean popped his door open and stood up.

"Alexis!" She turned back toward him, her eyes downcast. Sean opened the back door and pulled out her backpack. "Your books?" He walked them around to her. His stomach felt queasy as he handed the bag to her. She looked so terribly sad. He hadn't meant to hurt her feelings.

He held onto her backpack as she started to take if from him. She looked up, questioningly. "Look, I'm sorry I hurt your feelings. I'm sure you're very nice." *Should I say it? Please don't take this as encouragement.* "And Raj and Kevin are right, you are kinda cute." *Please don't take it as encouragement.* She smiled weakly. "Just dial it back a little, huh? Maybe more than a little." He released her books, and she turned to head into the garage. Sean opened his door. "Alexis!" She turned to look at him. "*Hasta mañana.*"

"*Si, tal vez,*" she mumbled.

Sean backed out onto the street. *Tal vez... 'such time'... no, wait, as a phrase... 'perhaps.' What did she mean by that?*

As he rolled down the street back to his house, he decided it had to have been the weirdest first day of school ever.

Chapter Two

"Birds singing in the sycamore tree..."

SHE was less than thirty yards ahead of him, and he was rapidly closing the distance with his long strides. It had to be her. He was sure he recognized the three white Greek letters on her pink running shorts. He pushed himself harder; had almost caught up to her. His shoes hammered the street with each stride. Couldn't she hear his footfalls by now? She hadn't even looked over her shoulder.

Nearly caught her, her blonde ponytail a metronome for his pace... just a few more strides. She stopped without warning and Sean crashed into her. They both tumbled to the ground, but somehow it wasn't the street where they'd been running. It was a grassy meadow.

"I'm so sorry," Sean panted, out of breath, "I was just trying to catch up to you."

"I know, my darling Sean," she replied huskily. She turned beneath him to face him... but it *wasn't* the goddess in pink, it was Alexis! "I knew you'd come for me, my love. Hold me close, Sean. Never *ever* let me go!"

With a quick twist, she shifted his back to the ground, and she was above him. She kissed him hard on the mouth, and he felt her shudder from the passion. He closed his eyes, relaxing on the soft grass and enjoying the heat of the kiss.

Something seemed so very familiar. His eyes were still closed when she lifted her lips from his. "Is my little Sean ready to become a man now?" His eyes flew open. *Tiffany!*

He gasped, struggled, and suddenly found his arms ensnared in bedsheets. He fought his way loose then propped himself up on his elbows and assured himself that he was in his own bed. He turned his head toward the nightstand to see the red digits glowing 6:49. The alarm would buzz in six minutes.

He let his head flop back onto his pillow, staring at the shadowy ceiling and still breathing hard. His normal routine would be to hit the snooze button, sometimes twice. His heart thudded as if he actually had been running, and he knew he wouldn't be following routine. He didn't want to go back to sleep, in case the nightmare could still be lurking. He wondered what his mother, the psychologist, would make of those jumbled images, and then shuddered at the thought of her psycho-babble.

-Wide-eyed, staring at the ceiling he reviewed his dream. He was chasing the gorgeous college jogger, but when he caught her, it was Alexis... until she kissed him, and then it was Tiffany. He felt goosebumps rise on his arms. The part of him that wanted to understand what it all meant warred with the part of him that never wanted to think of it again.

The alarm buzzed, and he reached over and almost methodically hit the snooze bar, but slid the off switch instead. It might even be nice, he realized, to not have to rush so much. He threw back the tangled sheet, rolled out of bed, and headed out the door, making the bathroom his first stop.

He smelled the coffee even before he reached the kitchen and wondered how something with such a pleasant aroma could taste so nasty. Would he ever want a caffeine charge so much that he'd learn to like the stuff?

His Dad sat at the kitchen table, sipping from his over-sized mug, reading the newspaper, already dressed and ready to head to work after eating breakfast.

His Mom was at the stove, cooking the usual bacon and eggs, clad in her robe that she'd had for as long as he could remember. She stopped when she saw him and turned his way, eyes wide, hands dramatically on hips. "Who are you, and what have you done with my son?"

"Ha ha, Mom," Sean sneered, "you're so funny in the morning."

She stretched onto tiptoes to kiss him on the forehead as he passed on the way to the refrigerator. He bent down a little to ensure that it was his forehead she hit. When he looked up from pouring a glass of orange juice, he noticed her watching him. "What?"

"Are you all right, dear?" she asked with that motherly concern in her voice. "I normally wouldn't expect you for another 15 or 20 minutes."

"Something special going on at school this morning?" his Dad asked from behind the paper.

"No," Sean replied with a dismissive shrug.

"Bad dream?" his Mom suggested.

"No!" Sean snapped, "geez, can't a guy get up early once in awhile?" He sipped juice as he sat down at the kitchen table across from his Dad. His Mom scrutinized him with what Sean thought of as 'the patented Mom-Stare' as she decided whether to continue to pry. Sean tried his best to be invisible. She turned back to the stove and slid a spatula under the bacon smoothly sliding it to a plate padded with paper towels.

"OK," she said without turning from the stove, "since you're up early, would you like some eggs and bacon?"

Sean considered the offer, nearly tempted by the smell, but then realized that extra time to cook more breakfast would also mean more time for her to ply him for details about his life. "No thanks, I'll just have pop-tarts."

"Have you read the label on those things? It's all sugar!" she complained, "You're kidding yourself if you think you are eating fruit."

"Don't care."

"There are several other choices that are just as quick and better for you."

"Don't care."

"And with your youthful metabolism, you don't have to worry about cholesterol in the eggs... like your father should."

"Don't care."

"Sean, you know I only..."

"*Mom!*" he snapped, "Which word are you having trouble with? Don't, or care?"

Silence, except for the sizzling of the skillet.

His Dad lowered the paper and glared at him with the 'patented Stern Dad look.' Sean assessed his Mom's face to measure if he had to deal with 'Hurt Mom' or 'Mad Mom.' To his relief, it was 'Hurt Mom' and the repercussions would end much sooner. He hoped when she looked at him that she would see the 'Contrite Sean' face that he sometimes practiced in the mirror.

"Sean, everything I say is in your own best interest."

"I know," he answered in what he hoped was a vocal match to his posed remorseful face.

"Your father and I know that teenage years can be fraught with emotional turmoil."

Sean suppressed a smile. *Fraught? Emotional turmoil?* He bit the inside of his cheek to maintain his 'Contrite Sean' face.

"I try not to pry," she continued, "but I did notice last night at dinner that you didn't seem to be yourself. Something happen at school, sweetie?"

Sean winced. He hated when she called him sweetie. He pressed his still-groggy morning brain for something to deflect her, but found it was too early in the day to think strategically. His only option was to stall. "Aw, something always happens at school. It's no big deal."

"You know you can always tell us anything," she prompted.

OK, gotta give her something. Think. Think. Not about Alexis. Cliff honking at me in the parking lot? Nope, too minor. What else WAS there? Think! Aha! Douglas! "Coach Douglas kept me after class in History, and I was almost late for Biology," he said with a touch of whining to really sell it.

Sean's Dad lowered his paper again.

"And why," asked his Mom, "did he keep you after class?"

"I dunno," Sean started, trying to think of a quick endgame, "He said I wasn't paying attention."

"Were you?" she asked.

"Yeah." He paused. "Well, maybe not the *whole* time."

"Is this still because you quit the golf team last Spring?" his Dad asked.

Good One, Dad! Wish I'D thought of that! "Maybe. Who knows?"

His Mom turned back to the eggs, sliding two sunny-side-up onto a platter, and placing three slices of bacon beside them just as the toaster popped. She plucked one slice of toast and sat it on another plate, slid her over-easy egg on top of it, and garnished with a single strip of bacon.

The second slice of toast was quickly buttered, cut on the diagonal, and placed on the first plate, which she smoothly set in front of her husband. She set her own breakfast at the table and went to the refrigerator for orange juice.

"Well, keep us informed if you think he is harassing you," she said as she poured her juice and sat down.

Sean was quite pleased by the quick turn-around from his blundering outburst. He mentally pictured a sheet of basketball stats and put a stroke in the assist column next to his Dad's name.

He stood, went to the cabinet to retrieve pop tarts, and put them in the vacant toaster. He glanced back at the table while he waited for his breakfast to heat. His Dad had put the paper away and was dabbing toast points into his egg yolk with his right hand as he munched a slice of bacon in his left. *As they say, thought Sean, "you can take the boy outta the farm...".*

In contrast, his Mom was daintily eating bites of egg on toast from her fork, which she had been sliced off in petite portions with her knife.

He smiled. *What a pair.*

The toaster popped, and he tipped it to dump the hot pastries onto the counter. He watched his parents as he waited for the pop tarts to cool a bit. They were annoying, but he knew of other kids whose home life wasn't nearly as good as his. *Not that everything's perfect here.*

He grabbed his breakfast and headed out of the kitchen.

"Napkin!" his Mom yelled, holding one aloft until he returned to take it from her.

By the time Sean had showered and dressed, his Dad had already left for work. His Mom sat at the dining room table with briefcase open and papers spread out. She was extremely organized. Sometimes Sean thought she was *too* organized and wondered if she ever turned her psychology degree on herself. *What's that term? Anal retentive? How'd they come up with their wacky terminology?*

It was Friday, so her first class on the MWF rotation was at ten, which explained why she was still in her robe. He headed for the door. "Bye, Mom, see you tonight."

"Too grown up to give your Mom a goodbye kiss?"

"Yup."

"When you were in grade school, you never left..."

He'd shut the door cutting off the end of her sentence... but then finished it himself as he walked to his car. "...for school without kissing me goodbye." He got in the car. "Yes, Mom, but kissing is completely different now."

He started the engine and noticed from the dash clock that even though he'd taken his time in the shower, he was still early. He considered a slow drive past Alexis' house. His car was parked at the curb in front of their house, since both his parents' cars took up the double garage, and it was currently pointed toward school. Alexis' house was the other way. He sat for a moment, picturing turning the car around. "No, it's dumb to drive by her house," he told himself.

He pulled the lever into drive and started forward. "Oh, what the heck." he pulled a U-turn in the street, needing a few feet of the Wilson's driveway to complete the maneuver. "Why am I doing this? What if she's outside just as I go by? Then she could accuse *me* of stalking *her*."

The car continued down the street. There was one more intersection that he could turn onto to avoid going past her house.

He went through it.

As he approached the house, he craned his neck to see if anyone was out, but didn't see anyone. He slowed as he got closer. Every blind in the house was pulled closed. He decided she was probably already at school, no doubt waiting somewhere different to ambush him again. He turned left at the next corner, then again onto the next street over and headed toward school.

He parked closer than he ever had before, and decided that maybe there *was* some merit in getting to school ahead of the main crowd. He grabbed his notebooks and headed toward class. As he started behind the main building, he looked warily in every direction. She could be anywhere. He paused at the top of the stairs. Everyone already heading in this direction was either a brainiac or a suck-up. He was definitely too early.

He sat on the steps and pretended to tie his shoe. Then the other shoe. Then he flipped through his notebook like he was looking for something important. He went through several iterations of that same routine as he watched for the kids filing by to become 'normal.' He soon decided he had waited too long.

"Good morning, Sean," came Megan's overly cheery and melodic voice from behind him, "Waiting for your girlfriend?"

Sean stood quickly, mentally cursing the heat he felt rising in his cheeks. He wished there were some kind of pills he could take that could keep him from blushing. "Look, Megan, she's *not* my girlfriend! I told you yesterday that I'd just met her."

"So you said," she smirked.

Sean stepped into pace beside her. "Seriously, Megan, I just bumped into her before class started and helped her pick up her books. I don't know *why* she wanted to sit by me."

"I believe you, Sean," she purred, "What *ever* you say..."

"Cut the sarcasm, Megan, it's the truth!"

"Of course it is, Sean! And I'm sure Rachel was mistaken about seeing you eating lunch with Alexis. And *everyone* knows Amber is such a liar! She was trying to get me to believe that you sat with Alexis again in Biology." Megan paused in pretense of thinking. "What really bothers me, though, is Jackie saying she saw you walk Alexis out of the building and right into your car. Jackie has *never* lied to me before. I'm *so* disappointed in her. Why do you think she lied to me, Sean?"

"What the hell, Megan!" Sean exploded, "Is every girl in school spying on me?"

"Don't flatter yourself, Kelly," she laughed, "We all *know* you. No one's watching *you*. Now, when a new girl comes around, especially one as cute as Alexis, we have to keep an eye on *her*. Just in case she's a threat to steal someone's boyfriend? Imagine how relieved we all were to find out you two were already hooked up."

Sean was so incensed with Megan that he hadn't noticed that they were walking through the classroom door. "Dammit, Megan, I'm telling you that we have *not* hooked up!"

Every head in the room turned toward the door. Sean felt his cheeks flame again. Megan did her best to contain a giggle as she sat down. Sean looked to the front of the class as he sat, and found that not only was Ms. McGuire already there, but also that she was glaring at him.

"Something you'd care to share with all of us, Mr. Kelly?"

"No, Ms. McGuire." The bell rang as he sat. He glanced to his right. Alexis wasn't in her seat.

"*En español, por favor, Sr. Kelly.*"

"Ummm," Sean stalled, then haltingly pieced together, "*no Señorita McGuire... lo siento... por... la perturbación.*" As he finished, Alexis sat in her seat.

"*Señorita Townsend, ¿tiene usted una razón para llegar tarde?*" Ms. McGuire posed to Alexis.

Without the slightest pause, Alexis answered fluently, "*No, señora, no tengo ninguna excusa. Lo siento mucho llegar tarde a su clase.*"

Ms. McGuire blinked a few times. "Miss Townsend, were you born in a Spanish speaking country?"

"No, Ms. McGuire."

"Are your parents native Spanish speakers?"

"*No, señora.*"

Ms. McGuire was puzzled as she stared at Alexis. "I'm certainly not an expert, as I'm not a native Spanish speaker, but as best as I can tell, you speak with *no* English accent at all."

"*Gracias, Señora. Me siento halagado. Trato de hacerlo lo mejor posible.*"

Ms. McGuire shook her head as if trying to clear cobwebs. Determined to go on, she constructed her classroom smile. "All right, class. As most of you know, I've always used Friday as "feature Friday". We will watch an episode of a Mexican Telenovela and on Monday you will each turn in a double-spaced single page summarizing what you saw."

She went to the TV in the corner and pushed a tape into the VCR. As the program started, she moved to the back of the room to turn off the lights. The classroom became dimmer, but the windows on each side of the room, though shaded, made it far from dark.

Ms. McGuire had returned to the front and was sitting at her desk once the episode started.

Sean glanced to his right, half expecting Alexis to be looking at him as she had previously. She was watching the video. He tried to turn his attention back to the monitor, but found it difficult to concentrate. The conversations on screen flowed over him as little more than gibberish. He looked again to Alexis only to find that she was still intently watching the show.

"Alexis," he whispered. She didn't take her eyes from the TV. "Alexis," he repeated, slightly louder. Her eyes flicked toward him, then back to the screen. "Alexis, is everything OK?"

"Everything is fine," she whispered with only a brief glance his way.

"You seemed so upset last night, and then you were late to class. I was just wondering if everything was OK."

"I am fine. Will you please be quiet and watch this video?"

"Yeah, yeah, great stuff. An impossibly beautiful couple at a restaurant. Gripping drama!"

The dialog suddenly stopped.

Sean looked up to see that the man's mouth was frozen open. A sharp shard of ice seemed to gouge his stomach. He looked toward Ms. McGuire's desk and in the dim light could see her standing with the remote in her hand, frowning.

"Problems, Mr. Kelly?"

"No, Ms. McGuire." He attempted to use his contrite voice and face again.

"Following the story so far?"

"*Sí, Señorita McGuire, es muy excelente!*"

"I'm so glad you are enjoying it. How would you summarize this current scene?"

"Ummm... the young couple are enjoying a meal in a restaurant."

"That's a bit obvious, don't you think? What had the young lady just said?"

Sean hadn't a clue. He glanced at Alexis, wondering if she might help him out. Her eyes were focused on her desk. He tried to force a memory of what had just been on. He couldn't remember any of the dialog, but he did seem to recall that the woman was distraught about what she was saying. His mind raced. His past experience reminded him that the plot was always unbelievably over dramatic. He picked through ridiculous story lines and took a shot in the dark. "She was explaining that her father was very sick and asked the rich young man for help."

"Miss Townsend, is that what you saw?"

"No, Ms. McGuire."

"What do you think was transpiring?"

Alexis looked down at her desk as she spoke, "the young lady was professing her undying love for the young man who was ordered by his father to reject her."

"*Perfecto, Señorita Townsend!*" She turned back to Sean, "Mr. Kelly, perhaps you can convince Miss Townsend to be your study buddy, and you could improve your grades this year." Sean glanced at Alexis; her eyes were still fixed on her desk.

Peripherally, he noticed motion behind her and shifted his focus to Megan. Her lips pulled into little kisses that she then blew across her palm.

"And Mr. Kelly," Ms. McGuire glared, "I don't want to hear another word from you before this video is over... in English *or* Spanish." She clicked play on her remote. Sean again examined the ceiling, the second day in a row.

At the end of class, Sean was one of the first out the door. He went as far as the stairs to the main sidewalk and waited at the bottom, exchanging "hey" with a few people as they passed him, then his eyes met Megan's. She was chatting with Ashly as they approached. When she saw Sean, she started to purse her lips.

"I swear, Megan," Sean growled, "if you do any more air kisses I will smack you!"

Megan unfurled a catlike smile. "Really, Sean? Principal's Office on the second day for hitting a girl?" They walked past him, laughing as they went up a couple of steps. "Maybe you can get some real kisses from Alexis," Megan said over her shoulder. Ashly giggled. Sean closed his eyes and imagined Megan's head exploding.

He waited and watched as nearly everyone from the outside classrooms went up the steps. The over-achievers were already heading the other way, early for their second class of the day. At last Alexis appeared. In the sunlight, Sean could see that she was wearing blue jeans and a simple blue shirt with three-quarter sleeves. He wondered if the color reflected her mood. She stepped past him and started up the steps.

"Really, Alexis?" Sean said as he quickly gained the same step that she was on, "today I don't even exist?"

"Of course you exist," Alexis stated flatly, still looking straight ahead.

"So yesterday you were stalking me, and today you give me the cold shoulder?"

"My shoulder is the same temperature as..." She stopped abruptly, then continued, "I am making no attempt to ignore you."

"What do you call it, then?"

"I believe you said, 'Just dial it back a little, huh? Maybe more than a little.'"

It took him by surprise. She had perfectly mimicked his cadence and inflections, almost as if she had recorded him and played it back in her own voice.

"Will you stop a minute?" he demanded.

"I will be late for my next class, as will you," she said as she maintained her pace.

"Thirty seconds then." He grabbed her shoulders and spun her to face him. "I just don't want to feel like I've ruined your life because I don't have feelings for you the way that you want."

"Then you should not," she stated flatly. Her face showed no emotions.

"Not what?"

"Not feel like you have ruined my life. You can select an alternate emotional state."

"Look, I just want us to be OK," he insisted, "Can't we start over and just be friends?"

"Yes, we can be friends, and I have already determined that I must 'start over.'"

"You have? Good." Sean paused as he examined Alexis' eyes for any telling signs. She was silent, and too much silence always made him uncomfortable. "So... you never know... maybe with a little time... and not rushing anything... you never know," he babbled as he tried to assemble a coherent sentence.

She smiled. Nearly a believable smile, but it didn't reach her eyes. Sean dropped his hands from her shoulders.

"No, I believe I do I know," she said. "I have committed numerous mistakes. Alexis Townsend is not the girl for you, Sean Kelly." She turned and started walking to the main building. Sean fell back into step with her.

"Ummm... OK. So... all right... friends... and yeah, OK... good talk." They entered the building, and Sean started up the steps to his next class. Alexis remained on the ground floor and started down the hall. He stopped four steps up and called over the rail. "Hey, Alexis... um... you know, Raj really does think you're cute and all... so... you know...."

Alexis looked up to see him shrugging. "You truly are a fascinating person, Sean Kelly."

She smiled. It was a genuine smile this time.

Sean continued up the steps, but called down, "Right... umm... yeah... OK... good talk!"

As he sat in Speech class, Sean began to feel lighter with each passing minute. His psychologist Mom would have been proud of him. He'd talked things out with Alexis, and they were going to be just friends. He'd been afraid that she might be all crushed and gloomy about it.

He joined in with the rest of the class groaning about the next assignment—talk for ten minutes about something that made an impact on them during the summer. At least it was a no-brainer assignment. He knew he could pull off ten minutes without any prep. It seemed like something from grade school, though, "what I did this summer." He wondered if he should bring something in for Show and Tell.

Algebra class was still boring review stuff. Sean had always been good at math, it just seemed to come naturally. He particularly enjoyed the logic, which sometimes made him think of *Star Trek* episodes that featured Spock or Data bailing everyone out of a jam with logic. *Deep Space 9* really needed a Vulcan. Odo, the shape-shifter kind of filled that role, but it wasn't really the same. Vulcans were the best at logic, and previews showed that the new series, *Voyager*, seemed to have a Vulcan.

Sean felt a little apprehensive as he headed to lunch. Thoughts of his last cafeteria experience had him wondering if Alexis would want to sit with him again. That might even be a logical move to begin to establish their 'just friends' relationship.

He ran into Kevin in the hall, and Raj joined up with them inside the cafeteria. Sean noticed that his friends repeated their lunch choices. Kevin stuck with his burger and fries and Raj repeated his chicken-salad sandwich and chips. Unlike his friends, he preferred variety, so he passed by the pizza. It was Friday, so there was a fish option.

The cooks had a recurring theme of featured items each week. Tacos made an appearance every Tuesday, and normally Sloppy Joes on Wednesdays. He avoided the Monday special—Meatloaf Monday. When he'd reached the head of the line, he requested the Fish & Chips, even though he knew it was simply fish sticks piled with fries.

They sat at their same table, but Sean switched places with Raj to get a better view of the lunchroom. He didn't think Alexis would swoop up behind him, but it never hurt to be prepared.

"Hey, ya gotta love these two-day school weeks," Kevin announced just before chomping down on a full third of his burger.

"Yeah, weird, huh?" Sean replied, "Five days next week, and then labor day weekend, so only four days the following week." He dipped a fish stick into the tartar sauce and bit the end off. For just a moment, he drifted back to his younger days when he actually loved fish-sticks.

"They keep adding more in-service days for the teachers," Raj explained. "My mom is a sub, so she goes to the in-service stuff. This year they added a morning session on building student self-esteem, and an afternoon session about bullying and gangs and stuff."

"Gangs!" Kevin scoffed. "There's a major problem in little ol' Grover's Corners. I can't decide if I want to be a Crip or a Blood." He held four fries in his right hand and dumped a packet of ketchup over them before shoving them into his mouth.

"Just because we're a small town," Raj countered, "doesn't mean something couldn't happen here. You can show statistically that violence in schools is on the rise."

Sean scanned the room. He didn't see Alexis anywhere. He pushed the remainder of his first fish-stick into his mouth and took a sip of Coke.

"Statistics? Ha!" Kevin countered, "'Lies, damned lies, and statistics.'" He wolfed another third of his burger.

"Do you even know who said that?" Raj asked.

Kevin chewed a couple of times, slurped some of his Coke and swallowed. "Yeah! My dad!"

Sean craned his neck a little to the left to get a better look at the blonde most of the way across the room. He decided it was Rachel Harper, not Alexis.

"Try Benjamin Disraeli," Raj laughed, "although many Americans think it was Mark Twain."

Kevin and Raj continued their heated discussion, but Sean had started to tune them out. Alexis was wearing blue. He considered watching for blue instead of a blonde. Actually, he decided, he should be looking for blondes wearing blue. Surely she had to eat. Although he knew that some girls got by all day with only several cans of Diet Pepsi. Maybe Alexis was skipping lunch? He saw someone in blue coming in, but abruptly returned his focus back to the table where Raj was snapping his fingers in front of his face.

"Kevin and I have a question for you," Raj said.

"What's that?" Sean asked.

"What color is the sky on the planet you're currently on?"

"Yeah," Kevin chided, "Earth to Sean, come in Sean!"

They were right. He was in his own little world. The previous lunch he hadn't spent much time with his friends because of Alexis, now he was missing out with them because he was looking for Alexis. He reset his priorities.

"So, Raj," Sean asked, turning his attention back to his friends, "do you really think something bad could happen here?"

Later, during History, Sean was determined to not give Mr. Douglas any reason to think he wasn't paying attention. He *would* listen closely to every boring thing that came from the teacher's rambling mouth. He checked the clock, certain it was almost time for the bell, only to discover that a mere twenty minutes of class had passed. Even rehashing nightmares about Tiffany was better than listening to the drivel Mr. Douglas was dishing out. Sean clenched his teeth and wrinkled his brow, determined to show the History teacher that he was focused.

Mercifully, Mr. Douglas let them go five minutes early and wished them a happy weekend. Sean could actually take his time going all the way to the third floor of the main building for Biology.

He was halfway up the last flight of stairs when he heard Raj call his name. He slowed as his friend caught up to him, and they reached the third floor together.

"You're early today," said Raj.

"Douglas ran out of hot air, I guess. He let us out five minutes early. Where was your last class?"

"I was just on second floor in Trig."

"So you got to Biology early yesterday?"

"A little, I guess."

Sean paused, trying to decide how to word the next question. "Was Alexis already in the room?"

"No, she came in just after I sat down. She came right over to me and asked if I thought that you'd be sitting next to me. I said 'probably', and then she sat with one seat between us... where she was when you came in."

"Did you guys talk?"

"Some."

"About me?"

"What? No! Wow, what an ego!" Raj grinned as he gave Sean's shoulder a punch. "I asked her if she was adjusting OK to the new school. She said lots of things were different from what she expected. Then she asked me if I was born in southern Asia, and I told her no, that my parents came to the United States to go to grad school, and that I was born here, but have dual citizenship here and in India."

They entered the classroom and sat. A few others were already there. Sean wondered why some people just loved to get to class early. He looked grimly at Raj. "So whose idea was it about the seating arrangement?"

"It just kind of happened. I left my books where I was sitting but shifted over one seat to talk to Alexis. All the seats were filling up, and Dude, you were like the last one in the door."

"*You* could have sat by Alexis and let *me* sit where your books were."

"Yeah...."

Sean waited for Raj to continue. He didn't. "Yeah," Sean prompted, "but?"

Raj pouted for a moment before he blurted, "I thought you guys were like hooking up. It seemed pretty obvious that she's interested in you. Come on, Dude, she's cute! *I'd* go out with her if she were interested in me."

Most of the seats were filled by the time Mrs. Roberts came in. She was writing on the whiteboard when the bell rang. Sean glanced at the empty seat to his right. It felt odd that Alexis was going to be late again.

Mrs. Roberts continued to write on the board for a few more minutes then turned and addressed the class. "I hope all of you read the first chapter last night. As you can see, I've written some terms on the board. I'll give you a couple of minutes to look them over and then I'll start asking for some definitions."

Sean scanned the board. He knew some of the terms, even though he hadn't read the first chapter. Amoeba... he knew what an amoeba was. And paramecium, he was pretty sure that was another microbial critter. Flagellum? What the hell was flagellum?

He looked back at the empty seat beside him. Five minutes had passed since the bell rang. Sean wouldn't have picked Alexis as someone who would cut class... especially on just the second day.

"OK, who wants to go first?" Raj's hand flew up. "Raj? Which term do you wish to define?"

"Flagellum," Raj crisply pronounced, "From the Latin word for whip. Some bacteria use a flagellum as a method to propel themselves around their environment."

"Very good, Raj."

Sean was glad his friend couldn't read minds. *Raj,* he thought, *you can be such a suck-up sometimes.*

"We'll just work our way around the room from there," declared the teacher. "Sean?"

"Um, OK...," Sean stalled as he looked at the list again. "I'll take pseudopod. It means fake foot. It's how amoebas get around." He relaxed a little having answered before all the easy ones were taken.

He coasted through the rest of the class, taking a few notes here and there, but mostly doodling in the margins of his notebook. When he glanced at Raj's notebook, he saw that his friend had almost filled two pages. With a last look at the empty seat to his right, he decided to not think about Alexis anymore.

The weekend felt like summer again, particularly with the hottest daytime temperatures in the high 90s. He played some tennis with Raj, had some pickup games of basketball, and hung out Saturday night at the food court of the little mall on the north end of town.

On the down side, he had to mow the lawn Saturday morning, and then Sunday afternoon the whole family went to North Kansas City to visit his Grandma. He ended up mowing her lawn, too, which was better than just sitting around the living room and talking.

His Dad grew up on a farm in southwest Iowa, and when Sean was younger, he referred to Grandma Kelly as "Gramma On-the-farm." Though both grandmothers were widows, Grandfather Kelly had died before Sean was even born. It was rare to make the four-hour trek to the Iowa farm, usually a weekend near Christmas and then sometime around the Fourth of July. He'd enjoyed trips to the farm when he was younger. His grandma kept some chickens and even a few pigs. She had a large vegetable garden and a little apple orchard. The most fun was playing with the collie-shepherd-mix dog, or exploring the barn and trying to catch the semi-wild barn kittens. When he got older, he began to think of the farm as boring, but at least he didn't usually have to mow that Grandma's lawn.

On Sunday night, he went to his inner sanctum in the basement. It was just a corner of the family room, but that was where the computer was, as well as the stereo that no one seemed to use anymore except him. He cranked up some tunes and turned the computer on to do the assignment for Spanish, hoping he could bluff enough to at least get a "C" on the paper.

After staring at a blank screen for several minutes, he decided to log into IRC. He wasn't surprised to find several of his friends online and probably would have forgotten about working on the Spanish paper if Raj hadn't made such a big deal about needing to log off and do school work. He logged off and stared at the blank screen again. He couldn't remember hardly anything about the video.

Ready to give up and accept an 'F,' he decided to check his email. He couldn't believe his eyes. Alexis had emailed him a text file which seemed to be nearly a word-for-word transcript of the telenovela. With a little cut and paste from Alexis' file, he quickly knocked out what he thought was an acceptable paper. He emailed a short 'thank you' back to Alexis. He hoped Alexis could accept being just friends. He imagined a rather successful semester and improved grades if he had stellar help in both Spanish and Biology.

When Sean's alarm went off on Monday morning, he wondered why Saturday and Sunday during the school year were always shorter than the other five days. Hitting the snooze bar a couple of times forced him into what had become a familiar mad dash to get to class on time.

He finished his pop-tart breakfast as he waited for the line of cars to funnel slowly toward the parking lot. He made a break from the crowd at his usual spot, once again eliciting squealing breaks and horn blasts. With some quick maneuvering, he slid into the last open space in the 6th row, cutting off a bright blue Mustang. He glanced in his rear-view mirror just in time to see the driver was flipping him off. Sean returned the friendly hand sign to Cliff and felt that the second week of classes was getting off to a good start.

Somehow, he managed to make it to Spanish a couple of minutes early; no sign of Alexis. He wanted to thank her in person for the homework help. Several minutes into class he decided she wasn't going to show up.

He wondered about her again, briefly, during lunch, but was mostly caught up with Kevin and Raj's heated discussion of President Clinton. Kevin's family was strongly conservative, and he gleefully pointed out that Bob Dole currently had higher popularity percentage points than the President. Raj tended to be liberal in most issues and skillfully argued that Clinton would not only win a second term, but would usher in Al Gore as the first President of the 21st century. Sean wondered how people could get so emotionally wrapped up in political parties. His view was that politicians were all self-seeking scumbags.

The day continued to drag on; Mr. Douglas didn't seem to catch him daydreaming and he'd done some fairly impressive doodles in the margins of his notebook during History. When Alexis didn't show up for Biology, Sean began to wonder if she might be sick. Maybe the hot, humid August weather of Missouri had proven to be too much for a transplant from upstate New York?

Tuesday, everything was beginning to fall into place. The whole rhythm of the new school year was starting to feel comfortable. He survived the morning classes and was happy to join his friends at their usual table for lunch. The topic of the day was sports. Both Sean and Kevin were big fans of the Kansas City Chiefs, and though not as interested, Raj tried to keep up with the conversation. Kevin lamented the loss of Joe Montana at quarterback, but Sean was hopeful that Steve Bono would do fine, especially with Marcus Allen to dig out yards on the ground. They both agreed that the defensive combo of Neil Smith and Derrick Thomas were unstoppable, and couldn't wait for Sunday's opener with Seattle.

By the end of the day, Sean hadn't thought much about Alexis except when acknowledging that she was absent again. That evening, he sent her a short email to ask if she was OK as well as giving her a brief overview of Spanish and Biology.

On Wednesday, when Alexis was again absent from Spanish, Sean began to wonder if something serious had happened. He went out of his way during lunch to find and talk to Megan. She was the center of attention at a table with five of her friends. He decided his best approach was to start with something snarky. Megan was always up for a good slandering.

"Hey, Megan," Sean began, "what'd you think of that outfit Ms. McGuire was wearing in Spanish today?"

"For reals," Megan responded, dramatically rolling her eyes, "Where in the *world* did she find an eyeshadow in that shade?" She crinkled her nose. "It matched her blouse! Eeeewwww!"

"Must be her theater background. You know... overly dramatic makeup." Sean paused to see if Megan had anything else catty to add. When she didn't, he decided to press on. "Hey, you haven't heard anything about Alexis, have you?"

Megan's feline smile slowly appeared. "I was wondering why you came over to talk to me." She made a quick check of her entourage. "Missing your girlfriend, Sean?"

"Do we have to go through this again?"

"As a matter of fact we do, Sean, until you admit you two are a couple."

"But we *aren't*!" He clenched his teeth. He could feel all of the girls at the table lean toward him. An image of an antelope hopelessly running from a pack of lions flitted through his mind.

"Then why are you asking me about her?" Her voice was overly sweet and calm, and her eyes locked on his, her body nearly motionless. Sean recalled a documentary he'd once seen about cobras. He tried to rally his confidence. He knew showing fear was the worst thing he could do.

"I just care about her as a friend... that's it," he said calmly, bravely. "She moved to a new town, started a new school and now she's going to get behind in classes." He swallowed. His mouth felt dry. Megan's eyes were unblinking. He forced himself to continue, "I thought maybe she was sick, and I wondered if *you* knew anything. You know, girl network..."

Megan held her steely gaze on him a few seconds more, then shrugged benignly. "Nope, sorry. She seems to have dropped off everyone's radar sometime Friday morning." She did a quick survey of all the faces at her table, gathering nearly imperceptible nods. "It's almost like she just vanished. No one even saw her leave. She was just gone."

"Well... if you hear anything?"

"Oh, of course, Sean," Megan gushed dramatically, "If I hear *anything* I will drop whatever I'm doing and rush to find you to tell you the scoop." She framed a smile so big that her cheeks dimpled, then batted her eyes flirtatiously before laughing. The girls sitting at the table joined in. Sean walked away, regretting that he'd been so stupid as to ask Megan for anything.

By the end of the day, he had decided to stop by Alexis' house to check on her. As he drove from school, he rehearsed what he would say when he got there. He simply wanted to warn her that Friday there would be a quiz over all the stuff about protozoa that they've been studying. Just a twenty point quiz, so not a huge deal, but he thought she should be prepared.

He pulled into her driveway, mentally running the story one last time before he got out, then walked to the door and rang the bell. He continued to mull over what he was going to say, and how best to phrase it so it sounded friendly, but not *too* friendly. It was only moments before the door opened.

"Oh, hi, Mrs...," Sean started, then realized he didn't actually know her last name. He stood there stammering.

"Tuttle," Aunt Katherine offered warmly.

"Mrs. Tuttle, er... sorry, I guess Alexis just called you Aunt Katherine, and I never asked your whole name. Sorry."

"And you are?" she prompted.

"Oh, um, Sean... Sean Kelly. I have classes with Alexis. In school. At the high school. I live down the street, and we have Spanish and Biology together... at school... not down the street."

Katherine smiled. "I know what you mean, dear. And yes, I believe Alexis has mentioned your name. You provided the conveyance home the first day of school, did you not?"

"Yes, ma'am... umm... can I talk to her? Is she like, sick or something?"

Katherine opened the door wider and stepped back. "You should enter for a brief time, Sean, and I will relate what has transpired."

"OK..." Sean stepped into the house and followed Aunt Katherine to the living room.

"Please be seated. May I offer you a chilled beverage?"

"Oh, no thank you. I just came over to tell Alexis about a quiz in Biology on Friday. I thought since she's missed a few days; she'd want to know about it."

"That is extremely considerate of you, dear, but Alexis will not attend class on Friday."

"Oh... gosh, is she really sick?"

"No, she traveled back to New York."

Sean was startled by the unexpected news. "So..." he began uncomfortably, "I guess she really didn't like it here, huh? Did she say why she wanted to go back home?"

"No, Sean," Katherine explained, "you have drawn incorrect conclusions. She took transport to New York to deal with some family issues. She intends to return once all is resolved with her mother and her sister."

Sean was surprised a second time. "Sister? I had no idea she had a sister. Is she younger or older?"

"No," Katherine answered enigmatically, pausing and smiling as she took in Sean's look of puzzlement before continuing, "They are twins."

He tried to imagine a carbon copy of Alexis and the impact it would have made on his life dealing with two of her. He shuddered. "Twins? Wow!"

Katherine laughed gently. "I believe you must be imagining two of Alexis. Nicole and Alexis are fraternal twins. Are you familiar with that term?"

"Sure. Not identical."

"Correct," Katherine nodded. "Although you can readily observe that they are sisters, they are not identical." She paused then smiled as she added, "And they also exhibit somewhat different personalities."

Sean examined Aunt Katherine's face, mentally comparing her features to Alexis as he wondered how Nicole might look. His gaze drifted to her dangling earrings, and he noticed they seemed to subtly change colors when she moved.

"I fashioned them myself," she said with just a bit of pride in her voice as she put a hand to her ear. "Jewelry is one of my art projects that happens to be lucrative."

"I can see why," Sean said, "They're awesome. It's like they shift colors."

"Well observed! It was a rather complicated process to achieve that effect."

With the topic shifting to art, Sean began to feel more comfortable talking with Alexis' aunt. "I saw you working on something big last week... out in the garage, with a welding torch. That's pretty awesome!"

Katherine laughed her soft melodic laugh. "I find working on those large pieces very cathartic, though compensation for a completed project is rarely cost effective. I am glad you think it is 'awesome.'" She laughed gently again.

Her cheery mood made Sean feel more at ease with their conversation. "What does Alexis need to work out with her family?"

Katherine's face lost its warmth for a second. When she smiled again, it seemed to be a practiced smile. "I believe," she said softly, "that is something you will need to inquire of Alexis upon her return. It is her prerogative what she might reveal about my sister-in-law."

Sean felt embarrassed. "I'm sorry," he stammered, "I didn't mean to pry."

"Not to worry, dear. You are merely curious."

Sean considered the implications of Katherine being Alexis' mom's sister-in-law. He had spoken before he realized that he was prying again. "So Alexis' dad was your brother?"

"Yes." She looked away, her face somber. Sean mentally kicked himself for asking the tactless question. As he thought of her losing both a brother and spouse so closely together, he searched the floor for an appropriate apology.

To his relief, Katherine suddenly turned back to him, her face had brightened and her smile returned. "Since you happen to be here, would you be willing to assist me in a small matter?" she asked.

Sean felt obligated to redeem his verbal faux pas. "Sure. What's that?"

"Well," Katherine started slowly, "I have recently become affiliated with a church here, and have been invited to a ladies' Sunday afternoon gathering. It appears that a group of the women gather together to indulge in coffee and 'goodies' while their husbands watch football on the television."

Sean nodded but didn't see how he could help with that.

Katherine continued, "It is a social norm to bring a 'goody' to this gathering, and I must confess that I rarely partake of sweets; thus, I am unsure whether my contribution is appropriate."

Sean nodded again, still wondering what she wanted from him.

She hesitated before speaking again. "I have two variations of a brownie. Would you mind sampling them and judge which one you consider superior?"

"Sure!" Sean said brightly, "I wish more people would ask me for favors like that!"

Katherine stood. "Wonderful! Wait here, and I will return shortly."

She went into the kitchen, looking back briefly to see that Sean was still on the couch. She quickly went to the refrigerator and pulled out a pan of fudge brownies she had purchased from a bakery and set it on the counter. She cut two of them from the pan, placed them on a small plate, and popped them into the microwave.

"I will warm them," she called out to Sean, "to replicate the semblance of freshly baked." As she waited for the microwave, she pulled two plastic containers of frosting from a cupboard, then quietly ducked into the garage.

She pulled a small clear vial from a shelf and set it into an odd box-shaped object that glowed briefly. With the tube in hand, she slipped quietly back into the kitchen just as the microwave beeped. She opened it, set the plate on the counter, and sprinkled the contents of the vial evenly onto each brownie. It had the appearance of a light dust, not unlike powdered sugar.

"Almost ready," she called out again then opened each frosting container and spread some of the contents over the powder-dusted brownies. With a smile, she softly whispered to herself, "Thank you, Sean Kelly, you have greatly simplified this phase of the process with your presence." She picked up the plate and returned to the living room.

Sean stood politely as Katherine returned. The dark sweet smell of chocolate reached him before she did, and he was instantly hungry. "Smells great!" he said enthusiastically. They both sat on the couch, and Katherine offered the plate to Sean.

"They are the same base, but with two variant flavors of icing. One is peanut butter and the other is chocolate fudge."

Sean reached for the peanut butter one first. He took a bite and chewed. Katherine watched as he closed his eyes and rolled it around in his mouth. He smiled dreamily as he set it back on the plate then picked up the chocolate fudge brownie, putting it through the same scrutiny as the first one before setting it back on the plate.

"Which do you find more desirable?" Katherine asked.

Sean looked at the plate with narrowed eyes, then looked away and screwed up his face in deep concentration. "Well," he started as he looked back at the brownies, "you can't go wrong with peanut butter and chocolate." He picked up the first brownie and took a larger bite, eyes shut again as he chewed. An amused Katherine watched his reactions. He swallowed and looked back at the plate. "Then again," he said as he lifted the second brownie to his mouth, "some people would probably go for the double-chocolate." He took another large bite and chewed happily. Katherine waited.

He set the second brownie back on the plate. "Why not take both? Frost half with each flavor, then the ladies can decide which ones they want. Of course, if you cut smaller pieces, they might try both."

"You find the tastes to be equally pleasant?" Katherine asked.

"I'd eat them both."

She held the plate closer to him. "Please do."

He took the plate from her and said, "Mrs. Tuttle, you are pretty awesome. You handle a welding torch, make jewelry, *and* you bake. What else do you do?"

Katherine smiled enigmatically. "Oh, you might be astonished by my talents."

Sean happily smiled back as he popped one of the brownies into his mouth.

Chapter Three

"You're my fantasy, you're my reality..."

SEAN grumbled to himself as he plodded down the steps toward the Wasteland, "How can a three-day weekend fly by so fast?" He barely remembered Saturday. Sunday, the highlight was watching the Chiefs pound the Seahawks 34 – 10. He'd watched the game with several other guys at Kevin's house. Kevin's family had one of those big rear projection TV sets, which made for a *very* popular living room on game day.

Labor Day activities were only marginally better than a Monday at school. His Mom's family got together at his Grandmother's house in North Kansas City. His Mom was the middle child of three, and Sean had an assortment of five cousins that he rarely saw. There were two boys, aged 12 and 13, and three girls ranged from 15 to 18. He didn't fit in too well with either group and was happy to sit on the fringes and eat brats and potato salad.

As he slumped into his seat in Spanish, he tried to cheer himself with the thought that it was only four days until the next weekend. The seat to his right remained empty, and he found himself wondering if Alexis was doing OK.

It wasn't until he walked into the main building to go to Speech class that he first started feeling strange. He had the oddest feeling that someone was watching him. All the rest of the day, he found himself turning around, scanning the constantly moving crowd of students, unable to shake the feeling that he was being watched.

On Wednesday, besides feeling he was being watched, he began to notice an occasional tingling in the back of his head. It took him awhile, but he finally realized that the sensations were stronger when he happened to be looking at girls that he found attractive.

Thursday the paranoia of being covertly watched was so strong that he even considered talking to his psychologist Mom about what he was feeling. The tingling was also back, but it seemed different from the previous day. It was early in the afternoon when he decided it was connected to smells. When he smelled a perfume that he liked, regardless of how cute the girl was, the tingle was stronger. The tip-off came when he found he had the same reaction when he entered the cafeteria.

The culmination of weird happened Friday morning on his way to Algebra. Megan went out of her way to cross the hall and step in front of him, stopping him in his tracks. There was definitely something different about her... besides the fact that *she* approached *him*. He'd just seen her earlier in Spanish, of course, but had never noticed her in the halls before when he was heading to Algebra, and she had *never* made an effort to talk to him.

The oddest thing of all was how good she looked to him, and she smelled fantastic! The back of his head reached a new level of tingling as she stood next to him. She batted her eyes, and he suddenly had weird thoughts about asking Megan out on a date. He was only barely aware that she was talking; he was totally engulfed in how she looked, and how delicious she smelled. He took in deep breaths of her intoxicating perfume and had to fight off the urge to put his arms around her. The logical side of his brain tried valiantly to remind him that Megan was a thorn and not the rose he thought he was seeing, but that voice was drowned out by the inexplicable attraction he felt. The tingling in the back of his head had built to a crescendo, and then suddenly stopped completely. Just as suddenly, Megan said a quick goodbye and disappeared down the hall.

Sean shook his head briskly and considered a visit to the school nurse. Instead, he stopped at the closest water fountain and slapped his face with a palm full of icy water. He decided what he really needed was a good dose of logic and went on to Algebra class. The practicality of mathematics pushed his unexplained emotional torment aside.

He felt more like his old self as he headed to lunch. The feeling of being under surveillance had gone away, and there was no more tingling around attractive girls or pleasant aromas.

Lunch conversation with his friends focused on football again. They discussed in detail the strengths and weaknesses of the Giants, and determined that the crowd at Arrowhead for the home opener would give the Chiefs an added advantage. Kevin was even more concerned about his own home opener that evening. It was his first time as a starter.

When he'd finished eating, Sean noticed Megan sitting with a bevy of followers a few tables away. Curiosity got the better of him, and he decided he needed to talk to her to clarify what exactly had happened in the hall before Algebra.

He approached confidently. "Hey, Megan, what's going on?"

"Sorry, Sean, but I have no reports of Alexis sightings this week," she said, then melodramatically laying her wrist against her forehead she added, "You'll just have to continue to pine away."

Sean stepped closer, hoping to catch another waft of her delicious perfume. "No, I was just going to ask you... say, did you change your perfume?"

"Excuse me?" she said icily.

"Your perfume. You smell different than you did earlier."

"You were sniffing me in Spanish?" she said indignantly.

"No, just before last hour. In the hall, when you came over to talk to me when I was on my way to Algebra."

She dropped her jaw and crinkled her nose, giving Sean the full force of her soured face. "*What* are you talking about?" She quickly polled the other girls at her table. "What is he talking about?"

"You came up to me in the hall..." Sean insisted.

Some of the girls started giggling.

"*I* came up to *you?*" Megan asked, the tone of her voice adding an unsaid, "in your dreams."

More laughter.

Sean blinked. "Yes, just before last hour..."

Megan abruptly stood and ran a hand over the top of Sean's head. "No obvious bumps..." She held her hand over his forehead. "You don't seem to have a fever." She sniffed him, "and I don't smell any weed on you." She finished with a cartoonish shrug. "Sorry, Sean, I don't know *what's* causing your hallucinations, but I haven't talked to you all week." She picked up her things and walked away from him. The girls sitting at the table laughed raucously as they scurried to catch up with their leader. Sean felt his face flame, and quickly turned to leave the cafeteria by the door opposite from the one Megan had gone out.

Hours later, when at last the final bell of the day rang, Sean heaved a sigh of relief. He hoped Alexis would be back soon. At least he could understand her brand of weirdness.

Sean attended the home football game that night, along with more than half of the high school, and a smattering of parents and community fans. As he walked over to the bleachers, he noticed Megan. It was impossible to not notice her since she was standing in front of everyone in a brightly colored uniform, waving pom-poms, and shouting rhythmic cheers. She glanced his way, and he lifted his hand in a halfhearted wave. She rolled her eyes, but still smiled.

They had been fairly good friends in grade-school, but their paths were definitely separating as they got older. Sean knew it wasn't easy to make it as a 'popular' kid, even for a natural beauty like Megan. Still, he remembered her as being much nicer before she became so focused on being one of the social elite. She was currently focused on dancing, shaking, and jumping in sync with the other cheerleaders.

Sean started to climb the bleachers, and quickly located some of the guys that frequented Kevin's living room on Sundays during Chiefs games. He decided to sit with them. Raj was currently getting ready to go onto the field as part of the marching band. Kevin, of course, would soon be on the field as a linebacker for the team, thrilled to be a starter in his first game as a Junior.

It was an exciting game with the home team winning by two touchdowns 34 – 20. He made a mental note to congratulate Kevin for the big hit he put on Pleasanton's running back for a three-yard loss in the fourth quarter. Besides the loss in yards, the kid was on the bench for two plays, presumably waiting for the bells to stop ringing.

Saturday began with the ritualistic mowing of the lawn, but in the evening, Sean and a bunch of friends went to the movie theater and saw *Dr. Jekyll and Ms. Hyde*. Although it had some funny moments, they all thought it was mostly lame, and joked about it as they left the building.

"Wouldn't it be awesome if you could turn into a chick like that?" said Kevin.

"Why?" asked Raj.

"Because then you'd be a chick, and you could go places... you know... where dudes can't go. Like you could totally go into the girls' locker room when the girls' basketball team played, and see them change clothes and stuff."

"Ha! You'd probably just stay home and get naked in front of a mirror," Raj joked.

"I totally would, dude, if I was as hot as that chick in the movie," Kevin agreed.

"It wouldn't work," Sean declared, "you'd still be you... just in a girl's body. You'd still act like a guy, and everyone could tell there was something weird about you. Especially if you were always staring at other girls changing clothes."

"Maybe," Kevin suggested, "they would just think I was a lesbian."

"You come up with the weirdest ideas," Raj said, shaking his head.

"I don't know," Sean pondered, "I just can't see a guy pulling off acting like a girl. We're just too different. Even if you looked like a girl, anyone would be able to tell you still acted like a guy."

Sunday afternoon had them back at Kevin's house watching a nail-biter. The Chiefs had trailed the entire game, then managed two touchdowns in the fourth quarter to tie it at 17 all. Everyone jumped out of their chairs screaming when an overtime field goal kept the Chiefs' winning streak alive.

Waiting until the last minute to do homework, Sean didn't get to bed until late. By the time he drifted off to sleep, he groggily thought of the previous weekend and decided that *every* weekend should have three days instead of two.

The outside temperature dropped below 60 overnight, and it was too early in the year for the furnace to come on, so Sean clung to the warmth of his bed for a third punch of his snooze button. He stayed a few minutes longer than usual in the shower, using the hot water to get warmed up. He dressed quickly but still was late as he dashed for the front door.

"Sean," his Mom yelled, "what about breakfast?"

"Got emergency granola bars in the car, Mom," he said as he pulled the door open. "Gotta go!"

"If you would just get up ten minutes earlier..." The door slammed.

He had to park in the last row of the school parking lot, and ran flat-out to try to make it to class on time. As he reached the bottom of the stairs, he saw

Alexis was standing there. She fell into step with him as they race-walked to the classroom.

"I wanted to speak with you, Sean Kelly," she said, "but you are late. Can we talk after class?"

"Sure," Sean answered, "hey, glad you're back. Everything OK in New York?"

The bell rang before she could reply, and at the same moment as they stepped through the door. Sean smiled as she sat in the seat that had been empty for two weeks. His gaze shifted past Alexis, and he found that, predictably, Megan had puckered her lips into a kiss.

Ms. McGuire attempted to eye them sternly for their tardiness, but when she saw it had no impact, she changed her approach. *"Alexis, es bueno verte de nuevo, chica."*

Alexis' reply was fluid and immediate. *"Gracias, señora McGuire. Estoy muy contento de estar de vuelta. Espero que pronto pueda terminar cualquier tarea que me perdí."*

Ms. McGuire, on the other hand, did pause, apparently running through the translation in her head. She decided to shift to English. "I'm pretty sure you won't have any trouble getting caught up. Come talk to me after class."

She paused again, closed her eyes briefly to collect her thoughts, and then opened them brightly as she assembled an exaggerated smile. "OK, everyone else should have a paper to hand in, you can pass those all forward. Today we'll be working on written communication. I'll hand out a sample business letter in English, and I want you all to write a similar letter in Spanish."

She braced herself for the expected collective groan, then redoubled her efforts to smile as she passed out the letters.

When class ended, Alexis touched Sean's arm as everyone was standing to leave. "Could you delay your departure? I need to speak briefly with Ms. McGuire."

"Sure," Sean nodded. He sat back down as Alexis walked to the front of the room. He pretended to studiously examine something in his notebook until nearly everyone had gone out the door. He hoped Megan wouldn't see that he was waiting for Alexis. He stood when he saw Alexis and Ms. McGuire still talking.

He sauntered to the door, then walked slowly down the sidewalk, intending to stop to wait at the bottom of the stairs, but Alexis came up behind him before he got halfway there. "That was quick," he said to her as she caught up to him.

"She offered a solution that I found more than equitable. She said I was so obviously fluent in Spanish that it almost seemed pointless for me to attend class. Then she asked if I would be willing to take the average of the remainder of my grades for the semester, and replicate that average for the points missed during my absence."

"That does sound like a good deal for you. At least you won't have to watch last Friday's Telenovela." Sean paused as they started up the steps, then spoke again, "So, New York... everything OK?"

"Not precisely," Alexis began slowly, then shifted to a rapid-fire explanation, "my mother has battled depression ever since my father died. It has become steadily worse in the last year. That spurred my decision to move here with my aunt, to alleviate by half the stress of parenting two teen-aged daughters. Two weeks ago, her condition abruptly deteriorated. I returned to New York with the intent to provide assistance, but shortly after my arrival, her psychiatrist prescribed hospitalization for Mother. For the duration of my absence, we were assisting with arrangements for our mother's care, as well as gathering items Nicole would require for relocation to Grover's Corners."

Sean was stunned. "I... I don't know what to say. That's terrible. I'm sorry this has all happened to you."

"You need not be overly concerned," Alexis said, almost a little too cheerfully, "everything will work out eventually. Solutions sometimes present themselves after a reset."

"I admire your courage," Sean said. "If you need anything, if there is anything I can do to help?"

"Thank you, but I believe everything will soon stabilize. Aunt Katherine is extremely competent and capable. She will assist as we adapt."

"She *does* seem quite amazing. I met her last week." Sean said as they entered the main building. "She makes a really good brownie, too."

"I am pleased you like her. I hope you will like Nicole as well," Alexis said as they reached the stairs, and Sean started up. "She is wearing green today... your favorite color."

As Sean climbed the stairs, he had mixed feelings about Alexis being back in his life. He still hoped they could be friends, but something about her still sent a chill down his spine.

"Why does she know that green is my favorite color?" he softly asked himself.

They were starting a new topic in Speech class since they had finally finished everyone's 'summer' speeches. The next round would be a five minute persuasive speech. Sean tried valiantly to take notes as the class period was spent discussing elements of a good persuasive speech.

Once Speech class had ended, he made a rare trip to his locker and got his history book to take to study hall. Sean decided he'd better read over the chapters that Mr. Douglas had been covering since he found him too boring to listen to for the whole class period.

He got through one chapter... but found reading it was every bit as boring as Coach Douglas' lectures. History just wasn't something that interested him. Some parts were OK, especially if it was about major battles, but too much of it was just political junk of how countries jockeyed for position in the world. As he started to daydream, he decided History could be much more interesting if it were more often like *Braveheart*.

Sean had sat down in Algebra a few minutes before the bell rang. He talked with Brian Schmitt, who sat to his left. He'd known 'Smitty' since kindergarten. Brian's family had lived in Grover's Corners for several generations and weren't part of the University workforce. He and Brian got along OK... never been the best of friends, but it was easy for them to talk about random stuff.

Mid-sentence as Sean was mentioning Kevin's great performance on the gridiron the previous Friday night, someone excused herself as she passed between them. Sean's head popped up as her trailing perfume drifted to him. He inhaled deeply. It was the same scent, or nearly the same, as the one Megan had worn during the encounter that she had later claimed never happened.

Sean watched the gently swaying green skirt as the girl continued toward the teacher's desk. His gaze continued downward as he admired her perfectly shaped legs, then down to her heels that matched the color of her skirt. When his eyes glided back upward, he noted that the pale green blouse went perfectly with the dark green skirt; above the blouse was a beautiful flowing mane of chestnut hair. He quickly quizzed himself. Was it chestnut? Or was this called Auburn? He shrugged. Regardless of the correct term, it was a rich medium brown with reddish highlights... and *gorgeous*. Her soft curls lightly bounced as she moved; it reminded him of hair in those TV commercials that promised their shampoos gave hair more body. He was mesmerized as he watched her talk with Mr. Stapleton.

"So, you were saying about Kevin," Smitty prompted.

"Hmmm," Sean said dreamily. "Oh... yeah. Laid this guy out. It was great." His eyes never drifted from the front of the room.

"That must have been cool," Smitty offered, attempting to regain Sean's attention.

"Yep," Sean said absently, "It was absolutely gorgeous!"

Following Sean's gaze, Smitty decided the discussion of football was over. "She's a hottie, isn't she?"

"Mmmmhmmm... supposed to get cooler before the weekend, though, maybe some rain," Sean replied vacantly.

Smitty smiled and shook his head, resigned that Sean had checked out of the conversation. He watched him for awhile, then looked around to see if anyone else was so completely smitten by the new girl.

"Class," Mr. Stapleton announced, "this is Nicole Townsend. She will be joining us for Algebra II. Some of you may have already met her, and others of you possibly already know her sister, Alexis. I hope you all will help her to feel welcome."

Nicole lifted her hand in a shy wave as there was a smattering of soft applause. She smiled nervously, visibly uncomfortable to be on display for a room full of strangers. Sean focused on her face, and compared the resemblance to Alexis, but immediately could tell they weren't identical. Alexis was cute, maybe even pretty... but Nicole was *gorgeous*.

He studied details as he compared her to Alexis. Her cheekbones were a little higher, unless that was just a difference in her makeup. Her eyelashes were definitely longer and darker. They made her eyes the focal point of her face. She wore a sparkly green eye shadow that also made her eyes pop. It was hard to tell from across the room, but he thought her irises were green, or perhaps bluish green. The two sisters had very similar noses. Nicole's lips seemed fuller, but he again wondered if that was simply her makeup. Her lipstick was a subtle glossy red, hinting toward brick. Dangling green earrings hung down her neck, nearly brushing her shoulders. She had a beautiful long neck that was showcased by her blouse's open neckline. The neckline, and the cut of her blouse accented her curves. Sean sighed... then sheepishly looked around to see if it had been loud enough that anyone might have noticed.

"I'm afraid, Nicole," Mr. Stapleton stated as he scanned the room, "that the only empty chairs are in the first row. Unless of course someone wants to offer to let you have their seat." He chuckled at his own remark. Sean stared intently at Smitty, attempting telepathically to force him to put his hand up. "I didn't think so," Mr. Stapleton continued, "at least you'll have a better view of the whiteboard." She sat in the first row directly in front of Sean, and he could only catch fleeting glimpses of her through all the heads and bodies between them.

Mr. Stapleton had written a formula on the whiteboard: $P(E) = (m/n)$. Then he turned to address the class. "Today we are talking about probabilities. The probability of an event happening is normally expressed as a fraction. It can be zero when there is no possibility of something happening, or one when the outcome is certain. Let's consider a single die, from one to six spots on each of the six surfaces. Josh, if I were to roll this die, which would be more likely to come up, the one or the three?"

"Ummm," Josh stalled, "It would be the ummm... three!"

"Why do you say that?"

"Ummm, because it's in the middle?"

"How could you prove or disprove that using probabilities?"

"Ummm," Josh started, then smiled, "with great difficulty?" He garnered a few chuckles.

"Who can help him out?" Mr. Stapleton asked looking expectantly for hands in the air. "Yes, Crystal?"

"You can use the formula you wrote on the board," Crystal said, "The probability of one coming up is one in six, and the probability of three coming up is also one in six."

"Very good, Crystal. OK, let's suppose I rolled the die two times, and it came up five each time. I'm going to roll it again. What is the probability of it being five? Josh, you want to try again?"

"Sure. Zero!" Josh stated with certainty.

"Crystal," Mr. Stapleton asked, "what would you say?"

"Using the formula, it would still be one in six," Crystal said.

"Correct," said Mr. Stapleton.

"That's bogus!" Josh huffed, "You're not gonna roll three fives in a row."

"No, that's mathematics. The event is unrelated to what has happened before. Now if I had asked what are the odds of throwing three fives in three sequential rolls. That would be different. Who can tell me the probability of rolling a five three times in a row?"

"One in six!" Josh stated triumphantly.

"No, sorry," Mr. Stapleton smiled.

"You just said it *was!*" Josh protested.

"The first example was a single event. The second example requires the same event outcome three times. Crystal, do you know how to calculate this?" Crystal shook her head. "Anyone?" Mr. Stapleton paused as he scanned the eyes of his students. When he decided no one could answer it correctly, he went to the board and wrote as he spoke, "Suppose I told you that the probability of rolling a five twice in a row is 1 in 36?" He changed the formula on the board to now show: $P(E) = (m/n^2)$.

Sean caught on. Twice was six squared, so three times would be six cubed. He pulled out his calculator, and punched in six times six times six, then put his hand in the air.

"Yes, Sean?" Mr. Stapleton said.

"Umm one in two hundred sixteen?"

"Is that a question?"

"Umm. No, sir," Sean stated with more confidence, "it's one in two hundred sixteen."

"Correct," Mr. Stapleton confirmed as he went to the board to write some more.

Sean noticed that Nicole had leaned a little to her left, and turned her head to look his way. When she saw that Sean was looking at her, she smiled, then turned back to face the board. Sean was thrilled. He wondered if he could calculate the probability of Nicole going out with him.

He spent most of the rest of class-time mentally rehearsing how to talk to Nicole. By the time the bell rang, he'd finalized his strategy. Typically he anticipated the end of class and was ready to pop up when the bell rang. Though out of character, he needed to delay a few seconds, and stand up just as Nicole passed by his desk.

He shuffled his notebooks as several people had passed by, but none was Nicole. She was at the front, talking with Mr. Stapleton. He discarded Plan "A" and wished he'd spent more time working out a Plan "B." The classroom was already half empty. He couldn't sit there and wait for her. That would be too obvious. He needed a reasonable excuse to loiter just outside the classroom. Nothing came to mind. He stood. The room had nearly emptied. In desperation, he decided he'd have to use Plan "Z." He walked to the front of the room.

"Mr. Stapleton," he began enthusiastically, "I just wanted to tell you how much I enjoyed your examples to explain probabilities. I think I'm ready to go to Las Vegas." He laughed to signal he was joking about Vegas, but Mr. Stapleton's face was unchanged.

Lame! He cursed himself mentally, but at least it got him close enough to Nicole to inhale her perfume. He tried his best to covertly inhale deeply. He smiled involuntarily.

"That's nice, Sean," Mr. Stapleton said as he glanced briefly at Sean, then back to Nicole, "Anyway, Nicole, let me know in a couple of days if you are getting caught up, or if you'll need some extra help."

"Thank you, Mr. Stapleton," Nicole replied. As she turned to leave, she found Sean blocking her exit, standing there with a silly grin on his face. She smiled politely and stepped around him.

"Did you need something else, Sean?" Mr. Stapleton asked.

"Ummm, no. That was it. Just really *loved* the probability thing. Keep up the good work!"

He pivoted to find Nicole was now several steps away. He took four long strides and caught up to her. She glanced at him. "Hi," he said, silly grin still intact, "My name's Sean. Glad to meet you."

"Hi," Nicole said as they walked out of the classroom.

"Sean Kelly," he prompted, hoping she might recognize the name. When she didn't he continued, "I live just a few blocks down the street from you."

"Oh," she replied, "I believe Alexis may have mentioned you." She continued to walk down the hall. Sean kept pace with her.

"I met your Aunt Katherine last week, too." He paused to see if that won him any points. No reaction. "She seems pretty amazing. Her art and stuff I mean. Hey, did she make those earrings you're wearing?"

"Yes," she said warily, "she did. She presented them to me as a birthday gift."

Sean noticed he was walking a little faster. *Did Nicole just quicken the pace?* "So, I'm heading to the cafeteria right now. Is your lunch scheduled for now?"

"Yes," she replied somewhat abruptly. Sean was sure they were walking faster.

"Great," Sean stated enthusiastically, "Maybe we can have lunch together."

"Sorry," Nicole said coolly, "I am meeting someone for lunch."

"Alexis?" Sean guessed, "We can all have lunch together."

"No," she said tersely, "someone else."

"OK," said a disappointed Sean, "some other time then."

Nicole didn't reply. Sean decided Plan "Z" was a complete failure, and slowed his pace, then stopped altogether. He watched Nicole's hair bounce, and her hips sway as she continued on at her brisk pace. He took a deep breath of the perfume that lingered in her wake then sighed.

A hand slapped his back. "Dude, you're as hard to catch as those Pleasanton running backs," Kevin roared in his ear. "I've been chasing you down the hall. Ready for lunch? I'm starved. Hey, who was the babe you were walking with?"

"Hmm? Oh, yeah, lunch," Sean said absently, "I was headed to lunch."

"And the babe?" Kevin prompted.

"Oh, that was Nicole... Nicole Townsend. Alexis' twin sister."

"No way!" Kevin piped, "That's Alexis' *twin?* I mean; Alexis is cute, and all, but this one is a real *hottie!*"

Sean was slightly annoyed by Kevin's terminology, but then recognized that was as good a description as any. "They're fraternal twins," he explained as they walked into the cafeteria, "they're not identical." Raj was waiting for them just inside the door.

"Who's not identical?" he asked.

"Nicole and Alexis," Sean replied. "I was telling Kevin they're fraternal twins."

"Sororal," Raj corrected, "when you are referring to non-identical twin girls 'sororal' is more correct." He continued with an air of artificial condescension, "Of course you *could* refer to them as dizygotic twins or biovular twins if you were in Biology class."

"I just want to know which one is the *evil twin,*" Kevin said, bouncing his eyebrows up and down suggestively. "I'd have to go with Nicole at this point."

"I guess I haven't run into her yet," Raj said as they moved closer to the kitchen's service counters.

"She just came in ahead of us," Sean said. "She shouldn't be too hard to spot." He scanned the cafeteria for Auburn hair and a light green blouse. "There! Off to the right. Two tables down and over four. Brown hair, green top." He glanced across the table from her, and ice prickled his stomach. *Cliff Sickler? She was having lunch with Cliff Sickler?*

"I don't think she was in any of my morning classes," Raj said as he picked up his chicken-salad sandwich and chips. Kevin had already requested two cheeseburgers and fries. Sean scanned the choices. Nothing looked good to him. He considered taking the meatloaf since his appetite was ruined.

Sean moped through afternoon study-hall as his thoughts tortured him. *How could Nicole have lunch with Cliff Sickler? How did she even meet him? Why would she like him? He's such a loser... well, except for the Mustang. Ah, that must be it. She must have been in the parking lot when he pulled in, and she stopped to talk to him because of his car. OK, so the old Taurus doesn't measure up to a new Mustang, but surely she'll figure out that Cliff's a jerk. I mean, how can she not, if she spends any time with him. I just need to keep cool about it, and be there when Nicole's ready for a decent guy...me!*

By the end of study-hall, Sean had talked himself out of his depression. He even got a little spring back in his step as he headed out of the main building toward History, telling himself *slow and steady wins the race.* As he looked ahead on the sidewalk, he caught a flash of green... and auburn hair. *Nicole must have a class this hour in Schoolyard Wasteland!* She was at the top of the stairs, talking to someone. They pointed down to one the double-wide classrooms, and Nicole nodded. Sean doubled his pace. He knew there was a one in five chance that she would be heading to History class, and even if she wasn't he still might occasionally be able to walk with her.

He flew down the steps two at a time and quick-stepped down the sidewalk to close the gap. He was close enough to be in the wake of her tantalizing perfume before he realized he didn't really have a plan. The last time he tried to talk to her it hadn't gone too well, and the feeling of rejection still stung. He couldn't afford to make that same mistake again. He slowed to match her speed for just a few steps so he could bask in the trail of her lovely fragrance; and then he stopped to watch as she did indeed turn into the classroom for History. He waited a few seconds before entering himself.

Nicole stood at the front of the room showing a piece of paper to Mr. Douglas, who nodded, picked up his copy of the textbook, and opened it to point something out to her. She moved to his side as he flipped pages and talked. Sean sat down at his desk, the one closest to the door that he'd so proudly claimed on the first day of class.

Coach Douglas continued to talk to Nicole as the room filled. When the bell rang, he gave an introduction similar to the one Mr. Stapleton had made. Nicole again smiled, and shyly waved as she scanned the faces all looking her direction. Sean put on his brightest smile when her eyes met his. She quickly looked away, and Sean's smile collapsed.

Once again, her seating choices were limited to the front row, but unlike Algebra, not directly in front of Sean. He had a clear view of the back of her head and shoulders from an angle.

Mr. Douglas lectured for about fifteen minutes, then tried to engage the class on the covered material, coaxing their opinions. Fortunately for Sean there were plenty of people who liked the sound of their own voices enough to fill out the rest of the class period while he admired Nicole from across the room. She had beautiful hair that hung in perfect waves ending in soft curls well below her shoulders. Occasionally she would turn to hear someone behind her present an idea. Sean's heartbeat quickened each time he caught a glimpse of her angelic face. He *had* to figure out a way to get her interested in him.

At the end of class, rather than making his mad dash to be first out the door, he stood slowly and watched people file past. Nicole had gone up to talk with the teacher again. Sean slowly went out the door, looking over his shoulder one last time to see that Nicole hadn't left the front. He stopped at the bottom of the steps and leaned against the rail for a few minutes, watching the door, hoping she'd come out. Giving up, he turned back again when he had almost reached the main building. She was finally headed his way but was only at the bottom of the steps. *Another day, perhaps,* he thought. She wouldn't be talking to teachers at the end of class once she was settled in. He reminded himself that 'slow and steady wins the race' as he started up the steps to Biology.

He was on the last flight of stairs when he thought of Alexis. He could ask her for hints how he could make a good impression on Nicole. By the time he walked into the classroom he had decided that given Alexis' feelings for him, it would be pretty insensitive to ask her how to make points with her twin, but maybe he could ask general questions about their lives in New York.

He sat down by Raj, who was busy flipping pages in his textbook, and adding to his notes he had taken previously. Sean really did like Raj, but couldn't imagine spending so much effort on school. He knew that Raj had pressure at home to excel scholastically, particularly in the sciences. Sean knew his friend was destined to be a medical doctor whether he wanted to be or not. He *hoped* the Kapur family didn't also have an arranged marriage for him. Raj finally turned away from his work.

"I didn't have any classes this afternoon with your 'vision of loveliness,' did you?" he asked.

"Yeah," Sean replied, "she was in History. I didn't get to talk to her again though."

"I want to get a close-up view to see if she's really *all that*. What's Alexis think of you having the hots for her womb-mate?" Raj smiled, pleased with his little joke but Sean missed it.

"I don't know. I haven't seen Alexis since Spanish."

"I'll ask her when she gets here," Raj deadpanned.

"You'd better be joking," Sean warned, "or I might have to hurt you."

Sean didn't get a chance to find out. The bell rang; Mrs. Roberts started lecturing, and Alexis never came to class.

Tuesday morning Sean sprang from his bed when his alarm first went off. He hit the shower and got dressed, listening for his Mom to leave before he went to the kitchen. She had an 8:00 class on Tuesday and Thursday, so both parents were out the door by 7:15. As he glanced at the microwave clock, he briefly toyed with the idea of sitting down with a bowl of cereal, then quickly rejected it.

He verified the current supply of pop-tarts would last the rest of the week, and dropped two into the toaster. Compromising with his cereal idea, he decided to pour a glass of milk, and eat at the table instead of on the run. By the time he'd finished the first one, he realized he wasn't comfortable sitting still. All too often he would miscalculate time, particularly when he thought he had an excess.

He dumped the rest of his milk into one of his Dad's travel mugs and went out the front door. He took a bite of the second pop-tart as he pulled away from the curb. At the first stop sign, he took a sip of milk and fought the urge to spit it out. The milk had a slight coffee taste. He took small sips with each bite of pop-tart to mask the taste.

It was almost scary to park in the second row; he'd never gotten there so early before. He scanned all the other cars already there but didn't recognize any of his friend's cars. *What do these guys do before class?* As he got out of his car, and started walking toward the Wasteland, he contemplated the best spot to meet Alexis. She had waited for him at the bottom of the steps on Monday, so that seemed like a reasonable place to wait.

When he got to the steps, he decided to wait at the top instead, figuring he would be able to see her coming sooner than if he waited at the bottom. He watched the southwest corner of the building, expecting her to come from the parking lot the same way he did, and then realized she didn't have a car, and that she probably was dropped at the front by her aunt. He shifted his gaze back and forth to cover both possibilities, but caught movement from the south*east* side of the building. It didn't make sense. The drop off zone circled in front of the middle of the building. Why would Alexis walk all the way around the *east* side? There was no street near that side, only a bike path that went off into a recreational park area.

He watched her approach, and then saw her pause a moment when she first noticed him standing there. He walked toward her to close the gap sooner, stopping as she finished the last couple of steps between them.

"Good morning," he said cheerfully.

"Good morning, Sean," she answered, then added in a business-like tone, "You seem to be very erratic in your arrival behavior. You are typically late or precisely on time, but today you are early."

"We didn't get to talk much yesterday. I thought I would see you again, and we'd talk after Biology. Why did you skip Biology?"

"I decided to withdraw from the class. It is my most difficult subject, and I determined I would more rapidly absorb missed material in other classes if I could forgo remediation of Biology."

Sean paused to translate. He decided interpreting what Alexis said was almost like translating Spanish. "I guess that makes sense. So I'll only see you in Spanish, and maybe at lunch."

"No," she replied, "only Spanish. I needed to substitute another course, so I now attend Health during my former lunch period. I have lunch an hour earlier now, during what had been a study hour, and now I have substituted that study hour to the end of the day."

"Wow, I guess I won't see you much, then." Sean tried to reorganize his mind with this new information. He had intended to ask Alexis to sit with him at lunch, and use that time stealthily to extract information about Nicole.

Temporarily stymied, he stumbled with what to say next. "Hey, I noticed that you were coming around the building from the east side. That's kind of the longest way here."

She seemed oddly panicked. "I do not know what you mean."

"Well, assuming your aunt drops you off in the front, it would be quicker to walk through the building to get here," Sean suggested.

She breathed a sigh of relief. "Oh, yes, of course my aunt drops me at the front, but I find a walk in the morning air to be refreshing. It stimulates the blood flow to my brain."

Sean found her response overly enthusiastic. It seemed the simplest things would get the strangest reactions, but he saw an opening to bring up Nicole. "Nicole doesn't like to take early walks with you?"

"Nicole?" Her eyes flew wide with surprise. "Nicole does not join me because..." she started hastily, then twitched her head slightly to the right. Her voice calmed as she continued, "Nicole enjoys coming into the library to sit in silence and compose herself for the day."

Totally lame, thought Sean, *and she always does that little side twitch during her panic/calm swings.* He decided to keep track of whether there was an actual pattern. His thoughts were interrupted.

"You met Nicole yesterday, then?" Alexis asked. "Do you like her?"

Sean involuntarily smiled. *Like her? I think she's amazing.* "Yes," he answered with all the nonchalance he could muster, "she seems nice. Is she finding it hard to settle in here?"

"Well, it *is* different here than what we formerly experienced."

"Right," Sean said, wincing as he remembered the hick-hayseed-bumpkin remark, "besides culture shock, I thought it might be tough to catch up a couple of weeks of classes."

"No," Alexis replied assuredly, "Nicole is an excellent student. She will be caught up by next week."

Sean glanced away as he noticed several early-birds heading their way from the main building.

"Except for math!" Alexis emphasized, "She is only *average* at math."

Sean detected just a tinge of excitement in her voice and again wondered why she could be so weird over the simplest things. It suddenly struck him that Nicole might be just as weird; it was too soon to tell. He hated to think that the angelic Nicole might behave as bizarrely as her twin. Over Alexis' shoulder, Sean noticed more people were coming out of the building. He had little time before they would need to head to class themselves. He took a deep breath and decided to push. "So, did she say anything about me?"

"About you?"

"Yeah, you know. Did she mention meeting me yesterday?"

Alexis started to speak, paused, and then reluctantly said, "She has two classes with you."

"It seems like there's an 'and' or 'but' missing from that sentence," Sean prompted.

Alexis' chin dropped. "I do not wish to say..."

Sean's imagination turned cartwheels. *She told you she likes me! Woohoo! Wait... that would seem sad to you since you like me. Still, I GOTTA hear it!*

"Aw, come on," he coaxed, "you can tell me."

"Well," Alexis started slowly, "She asked me if I thought..."

...If I like her! YES! The answer is YES!

"...if I thought you might be a stalker," Alexis finished softly.

Sean's heart crashed to the bottom of his stomach like a jagged rock. "A stalker?" he gulped, "Me? A stalker?"

"She said that you waited for her after Algebra, and all but chased her to lunch. She also related that in History any time she glanced your way you were staring at her," Alexis replied apologetically.

Sean was crushed. Nicole thought he was a stalker.

"I suggested that you were merely attempting to make her feel welcome," Alexis continued, "I explained that you had been kind and attentive to me to assist in my adaptation to the new school."

Sean felt doubly crushed. Nicole thought he was a stalker, and Alexis had defended him... even though he had accused *her* of being a stalker. He was lower than pond scum. Things couldn't get any worse.

"Oh, how cute!" came a melodic voice from behind Sean. "Look, Ashly, the lovebirds are having an early morning tryst!"

Megan. He was wrong... it definitely *could* get worse. He turned to face her with clenched teeth.

"No, no, sorry," Megan continued cheerily, "don't let us interrupt. We're just on our way to class."

"Dammit, Megan," Sean growled, "I swear..."

"Yes, Sean dear, I can hear that you do," Megan interrupted, "Not very nice in front of your girlfriend."

"She is *not* my girlfriend!" Sean seethed.

"Oh," Megan said softly, her hand to her lips, "Ooohhh... I am *so* sorry!" She turned to Alexis, and continued in a soft, soothing tone, "I am *so* sorry, Alexis, I didn't realize he was breaking up with you just now."

"Megan, just *stop* it!" Sean yelled, "We are *not* breaking up!"

Megan suddenly beamed, turning again to Alexis, "There you go! It's all OK! You hang in there, girl! High School romances have a lot of ups and downs, but it sounds like you are on an up. You're *not* breaking up." She turned her smile back to Sean; it suddenly developed that feline quality.

He felt his blood pressure rising, tried to scream something at Megan, but couldn't come up with any intelligible words.

"Sean, that is an *amazing* color of red!" Megan taunted, "You know, Alexis, I think you should get a lipstick in that color. I think it would really look good on you."

Sean sputtered incoherently as Megan and Ashly started down the stairs. Megan looked back over her shoulder with a parting shot, "Don't be late for class, you two!" She finished with her signature kiss.

Sean envisioned the Enterprise firing a pinpoint phaser burst, turning Megan into a pile of smoldering ashes. Then he imagined his Mom asking him about his violent fantasies, using her soothing psychologist voice. He closed his eyes and took several deep breaths.

"We probably should go to class," Alexis suggested softly.

¡Ay caramba! Bart Simpson echoed in his head.

When Spanish had ended, Sean walked back to the main building, lost in thought, Alexis silently beside him. He was no longer in the mood to quiz her for tidbits of information that might help him make points with Nicole. It was the most stressful relationship situation he'd experienced since the big breakup with Tiffany. He liked Alexis, but just didn't feel the same attraction to her that he felt for her twin. A dark cloud of guilt hung over him as he thought of accusing her of being a stalker. He must have misinterpreted the whole thing, he knew *he* wasn't a stalker, yet Nicole thought he was. When he thought of it objectively, he could see that he acted toward Nicole similarly as Alexis had toward him. He'd told Alexis to dial it back, maybe he needed to take his own advice.

"You appear distracted," Alexis finally said.

"Hmmm... oh, sorry. I was just contemplating becoming a monk."

"But you are not a Catholic," Alexis said with a puzzled tone.

"I know, I just meant that..." Sean stopped mid-sentence, then inquired, "Why would you think that?"

"Think what?" she said. He could see that she was flustered again.

"Think that I'm not a Catholic. We've never discussed religion."

"Oh," she stumbled nervously, "Merely a guess. I do not know for certain, it was only an assumption."

"Really?" he continued to press, "With a fine Irish name like Sean Kelly, wouldn't you assume that I *was* Catholic? I think most people would."

"Of course... a complete miscalculation. The logical assumption would be that you were Catholic."

"But I'm *not*," Sean said. "My great-grandfather left the church when he married a protestant woman. Apparently that wasn't acceptable back then. It's just that the *way* you said it; you seemed to state it as a known fact."

Alexis abruptly stopped walking. "I forgot to ask Ms. McGuire information about an assignment I missed." She turned, and headed back the way they'd came.

"I thought you didn't have to make up any assignments in Spanish," Sean called to her as she retreated.

"It is a question about an upcoming assignment," she called back.

Sean stood watching her for a minute, and reconsidered his position about Alexis stalking him. He shook it off and continued walking to the main building.

He was glad he wasn't on the schedule to give a speech that day. Instead, he used the hour in an attempt to unravel the puzzle of the Townsend twins while pretending to listen to the speeches given. By the end of study-hall, he'd determined it was best to disconnect emotionally from *both* sisters.

When he later arrived at Algebra class, it was at the same moment that Nicole approached from the other direction. They both stopped, face to face, a few feet apart.

"Good morning, Sean Kelly."

"Good morning, Nicole," Sean replied as he gestured toward the door, "after you."

She stepped into the room, Sean right behind her. He inhaled her scent and wondered why it made him think of putting his arms around her, and pulling her close. He slapped his face, determined to regain his cool.

He sat at his desk, focused on Algebra the entire class period, and when class ended, he didn't even consider trying to talk to Nicole.

Sean ran into Raj on his way to lunch. They paced themselves, expecting Kevin to catch up with them before they made it to the cafeteria, and Nicole walked past them. Sean waited for her to get beyond earshot. "That's Nicole Townsend," he whispered to Raj, then inhaled deeply. "What do you think of her perfume?"

Raj sniffed, then turned his head a bit, and closed his eyes. "It seems to be lightly floral... with a fruity note... maybe peach?" He paused in concentration, then continued, "a pleasant earthy undertone... musk, or maybe sandalwood? Not sure, it's subtle."

"You really scare me sometimes," Sean commented.

"What?"

"Couldn't you just say, 'yeah, that's nice', or 'hmm, I don't really like it'."

"OK," Raj shrugged, "yeah, that's nice."

"No, really! Isn't it like the most delicious thing you've ever smelled? Doesn't it make you just want to reach out and grab her?"

"No," Raj said with furrowed brow, "but now you're scaring *me*."

"What's going on, dudes," Kevin bellowed as he corralled their heads pulling them toward each other. Raj slipped free; then Kevin released Sean.

"I just got my first close look at Nicole Townsend," Raj said while smoothing his hair, "and Sean is planning to go all boa constrictor on her."

"Cool!" Kevin nodded enthusiastically. "Hey, I'm still betting she's the *evil twin!*"

Sean tuned his friends out as they merrily tossed *evil twin* plots back and forth. He glanced ahead in line and located Nicole talking with Robbie Flanders.

At least she's not with Cliff Sickler again, he thought with some relief. *Maybe that was just a one-time thing. Maybe she's trying to see how many guys she can get twisted around her little finger. Maybe she'll eventually get to me.* He slapped himself. *Maybe I should just stop thinking about her.*

He turned his attention to the serving counter. *It's Tuesday. Taco Tuesday. Good. I'll just get my usual two tacos.* His eyes shifted between

Nicole and the counter, and his focus blurred. *Twin tacos. One with hot sauce, one with mild. Two similar but not identical tacos. One taco's definitely hotter than the other.*

He briskly shook himself to snap out of his haze. By the time he reached the counter, he had decided on pizza.

Study-hall immediately after lunch had both good and bad points. On the positive side, Sean could practically take a siesta after eating. On the negative side, he rarely got any actual studying or homework done because of his near-nap stupor. One good thing about having History out in the Wasteland was that the walk in fresh air tended to wake him up. It was difficult enough staying alert while Coach Douglas droned on, starting out sleepy would not work in his favor.

As he came down the stairs from second floor, Nicole was coming from the ground floor hallway, and they reached the back door at the same time. Sean pushed it open, politely holding it as Nicole walked through. She paused, turning her head demurely. He quickly joined her, his inner voice chanting, *Don't act like a stalker, don't act like a stalker, don't act like a stalker.*

"Thank you, Sean," she said warmly.

"Ummm, you're welcome, Nicole." They silently walked side by side. Sean's brain bounced thoughts like a pinball machine, searching for the right thing to say.

As they neared the steps down to the classrooms, it was Nicole who spoke. "I apologize if I seemed rude to you yesterday when I declined your lunch invitation."

"No! Not at all," Sean gushed. "I'm sorry that... well... that I came off like some kind of stalker."

"Stalker?"

"Yeah. Hey, it's OK. Alexis told me. And I really am sorry."

They had reached the bottom of the steps, and Nicole stepped to the side, and stopped. She pushed her hair back over her shoulder on the side that faced him.

"Alexis believes that I had misjudged you," Nicole said, shyly looking down at the sidewalk. "I made no request for her to reveal that I assessed your behavior as questionable."

"No, really, it's OK." Sean tried to sound enthusiastically believable. "I was probably overly anxious to meet you, and it just came off bad."

"Perhaps we simply should attempt to ignore earlier encounters?"

"Sounds good to me," Sean said eagerly.

Nicole thrust out her hand. "Hello, Sean Kelly, my name is Nicole Townsend. It is nice to meet you."

Sean took her hand. It felt soft and warm in his. When her perfume found his nose again, he had to fight a strange urge to pull it to his lips. She briskly pumped his arm twice, then pulled her hand away.

"Umm, yeah," he stumbled, "nice to meet you, too."

She turned, and started walking toward class. Sean fell into step. They had taken a few paces in silence before Sean spoke again, "Umm, can I ask you something?"

"What about?" she asked warily.

"It's about your perfume," Sean said timidly. *Please don't think that sounds like a stalker, please don't think that sounds like a stalker.*

"Do you find it appealing?" Her voice was soft, and a little coy.

"I *love* it!" Sean gushed. He felt the color rise in his neck.

"That is very gratifying," she said warmly with a smile.

"So... what is it?"

Nicole seemed puzzled by the question.

"I mean," Sean clarified, "what's it called?"

She looked at him blankly.

"My Mom's favorite perfume is *White Diamonds*, and yours is called?" he prompted.

"It does not have a name," she said and glanced away for a moment before continuing smoothly, "Aunt Katherine makes it."

A little tingle went down Sean's spine. *That's exactly what Alexis does! The little twitch, then the next sentence is like it was read from a script.*

"Boy," Sean said fervently, "That Aunt Katherine. She's really amazing!"

As they reached the juncture where the walkway split to the classroom, Sean decided to reassure himself. "So, we're OK, right? I mean clean slate? Just scrap yesterday?"

"Yes," Nicole confirmed, "Sometimes it is best just to start over."

Another shiver went down Sean's spine as they entered the classroom. *That sounded exactly like Alexis!*

He tried to rationalize that it was because they were twins, but there was still something disturbing about the Townsends.

Wednesday morning found Sean back in stride with his routine. He was nearly out of breath from his brisk walk to Spanish class. He breathed out a satisfied sigh as he sat down... the bell hadn't rung yet.

"You are very erratic in your arrival behavior," Alexis pointed out.

"That's what you said yesterday," Sean replied with a smile.

"It is still a true statement today."

"Maybe I just like to keep you guessing," he teased.

Ms. McGuire sprang into action the second the bell rang. She passed a book to Kristen, who was nearest her desk, then walked to the opposite corner at the back of the room, and handed another book to Jake.

"Today I want each of you to read two pages from *Don Quixote*," she announced. "Who can tell me the name of the author? Other than Kristen and Jake." She looked expectantly to Alexis, who shyly put up a hand. "Yes, Alexis."

"Miguel de Cervantes. He wrote in the early seventeenth century."

"Ms. McGuire," said Jake as he waved his hand.

"Yes, Jake?"

"You musta gave me the wrong book," he continued, "This one's title is: *El ingenioso hidalgo don Quijote de la Mancha.*"

"No, Jake, that is the correct book," explained Ms. McGuire, failing to keep the annoyance from her tone, "Cervantes was a Spanish author. That is the original title." She glared and smiled simultaneously. "And it's pronounced 'key hoe tay' not 'kwe joat'. Would you please start reading at page one?"

As class progressed, Ms. McGuire assisted anyone struggling with pronunciation and stopped each student when they had finished reading two pages.

When Alexis took her turn, she read so smoothly and quickly that she breezed through her two pages, then paused. Ms. McGuire didn't stop her, so she continued. She was near the end of the second paragraph on her fourth page when Ms. McGuire finally interrupted. "I'm sorry, Alexis, I should have stopped you sooner. I so enjoy listening to you... it's like... music. *Gracias, querida, que fue maravilloso.*"

"*De nada*" Alexis replied modestly.

Sean waited for Alexis at the doorway when class ended. "So why *are* you so good in Spanish?"

"It... comes easily to me," Alexis replied in an unsteady tone.

"And *why* do you think that it's so easy for you?" Sean prompted.

"I believe I have echoic memory, which is similar to a photographic memory, except with sound. My Spanish teacher in my former school spoke Spanish as her first language. I am able to remember her exact inflections."

"Wow. Does Nicole also have this gift?" Sean asked.

Alexis paused before answering. "Yes."

Sean continued to guide the conversation toward Nicole. "How is it working out with her moving here?"

"It has been a favorable adjustment. I believe she will enjoy this environment."

"I suppose both of you miss your old friends."

She paused again, giving Sean a sideways glance. "Yes. We both do."

"And any boyfriends left behind?"

"No... yes... I mean... none currently. Neither of us presently has a romantic link."

"Romantic link? Wow, that sounds kinda serious."

Sean watched Alexis make a small twitch before she replied, "Casual dating—movies, school dances, parties. Typical high school relationships."

He narrowed his eyes at the scripted response but pressed on, "I guess that makes it easier. I understand long distance relationships can be hard." When she didn't reply, Sean continued, "How about any interesting hobbies? Either of you have an interesting hobby?"

Quick twitch, then another scripted response, "I enjoy music, dancing, photography, and collecting Beanie Babies."

"And I like to help the homeless, and someday hope to work for world peace," Sean added, mocking a pageant voice.

"I do not understand."

"Sorry. Just messing around. So, what kind of music do you like?"

She glanced away before listing, "Cranberries, Green Day, Nirvana, Oasis, Pearl Jam, REM, Smashing Pumpkins, and Weezer."

Sean tried to replay the list in his head again, and decided she really *had* listed them alphabetically. He responded neutrally, "That's cool. I like most of them." He waited a few seconds after they climbed the stairs, assuming she'd continue to talk about music. Nothing. "Did you like REM's latest album, *Monster*? I didn't get the whole *What's the Frequency, Kenneth* thing." She still didn't respond. "So what's your all-time favorite song by REM?" He specifically watched to see if she did the side twitch thing. She did.

"I would pick *It's the End of the World as We Know It*."

"I like a little more angst. I'd go with *Everybody Hurts*," Sean said. He watched again as she looked away, longer this time. When she turned back toward him, the corners of her eyes seemed to glisten a little.

"That is very sad," she said somberly.

"That I like that song?"

"No, the song itself is very sad."

"I think that's pretty much the idea," Sean said as he opened the main building's door for Alexis. "I figured you must like a little angst from the bands you listed."

"They are all popular musicians of this era," she said as they reached the stairs, and Sean headed up.

"Hey, I'll talk to you later," he said as she headed down the first-floor hall, and then quietly added to himself, "and hopefully it won't be so *weird* next time."

He silently quizzed himself, *Why did talking about ordinary stuff seem to make her all weird? Why did she call them 'popular musicians of this era'?*

While he continued up the stairs, he decided to make a list of what he had learned. One: Alexis and maybe Nicole have photographic memories, or audio-graphic? Two: Neither of them have current boyfriends back in New York. Three: Alexis' list of hobbies sounds like a prepared reply in a beauty pageant. Four: Alexis is still weird.

During Speech, Sean thought about all the strange things Alexis had said, her odd little twitches, her total fluency in Spanish, and tried to piece together something that made sense. Nothing seemed related, just strange.

By the time he changed classrooms to study-hall, he'd also changed his puzzled thoughts to daydreams of Nicole. He wondered what she'd be wearing. She always wore something eye-catching, and it always looked great on her. He wondered why Alexis chose a more subdued look than her twin, and what made Nicole more interested in a flashier appearance. She could have stepped off the page of a teen fashion magazine. Her makeup was perfect; her hair was perfect, and her perfume sent him in orbit.

The first thing Sean noticed when he walked into Algebra class was someone in faded blue jeans and a blue cambric shirt sitting in Nicole's seat. He looked again. It *was* Nicole! Her beautiful auburn hair was tied back in a simple ponytail. This look was *not* in the daydream.

When class ended, he stood and waited for her by his desk. As she got closer, he could see that her makeup was minimal, and her eyes were a little red and puffy.

"Hey, Nicole," he said simply.

"Hello, Sean." Her voice was a subdued monotone.

"So..." he started, unsure of where to go with the conversation, "how's everything going so far?"

She started to walk briskly as they reached the hallway. "Sometimes I feel like I'm on my own in this life. The days and nights are long."

Sean took longer strides to keep pace with her. "It's gotta be hard to pack up and move to a new school, especially after you've already started classes in your old one." He waited for her to say something, but she didn't. "I hope I'm not getting too personal... but have you been crying?"

"That is not a topic I care to discuss," she said hoarsely.

"I'm sorry.... look, ummm... is there anything I can do?" Sean asked meekly.

"Everybody cries! Everybody hurts... sometimes." She doubled her pace, and Sean slowed, and let her go.

"What was *that* all about," he said softly.

"What was what all about?" Raj asked as he approached Sean from behind.

"Nicole Townsend. I'm starting to wonder if she's as weird as Alexis."

"That was Nicole you were walking with?" Raj peered down the hall. "Interesting. I didn't notice her signature scent."

Sean hadn't realized before Raj had mentioned it, but it was true, her captivating scent was missing.

They joined up with Kevin in the cafeteria and had a lively discussion about the upcoming Chiefs/Raiders game. Sean felt relieved to be talking with someone rational about something as normal as hoping Neil Smith and Derrick Thomas would meet in the Raiders backfield and crush Hostetler.

With Sloppy Joes and fries in his stomach, Sean actually fell asleep in study-hall. He jerked awake as the bell rang, and began the long trek to the outdoor classrooms. He had just gotten out the door when Nicole called out to him. "Sean, may I accompany you?" He paused and allowed her to catch up to him, and then they started walking together.

The first thing he noticed was her perfume. It was back, and as tantalizing as ever. He covertly leaned closer to her to take it in. Next he saw her hair was loose and bouncy, and that she'd applied her normal makeup. Rounding out the transformation, he was happy to see a warm smile on her angelic face.

She spoke softly. "I apologize for my earlier rudeness."

"No, not a problem... but I was a little concerned about you. You just didn't seem yourself... I guess that sounds kind of dumb since I hardly know you, but well... I guess I just..." he trailed off, not knowing how to finish.

"That is very kind of you to express concern. I experienced an unpleasant morning. It has taken considerable effort to reestablish my positive energies."

"Something bad happen this morning?" Sean cautiously inquired.

"Last evening," she corrected. "I had planned a telephone conversation with my mother, but the institution related that she was unable to accept."

"I'm sorry to hear that. No wonder you're bummed."

"I was still..." she glanced at Sean, and the corners of her mouth curled up briefly, "'bummed' this morning, and did not wish to attend classes. You must find my appearance to be atrocious."

"Are you kidding? No, you look great!"

"Really? You find my appearance acceptable?"

"Sure!" Sean lied, hoping he sounded sincere. "But especially when you let your hair back down and got your smile back."

She shifted her eyes to the ground and smiled warmly. "You are a kind and caring person, Sean Kelly."

Sean felt the color rising in his face, and tried to will it away. He happily smiled back at Nicole and hoped that things were starting to change with her. They quietly walked the rest of the way to the classroom. Sean considered taking hold of her hand as they walked, but decided that move was premature. Still, he hoped that things were progressing that direction.

During class discussion time, Nicole was actively involved in a heated topic. Sean was quite happy about it, since it caused her to turn around more, and he could see more of her face from across the room. She would occasionally glance his way, and give him a brief smile before continuing to argue her point. He found History much more enjoyable when he could listen to Nicole's melodic voice instead of Mr. Douglas' droning.

Sean was first out the door when the bell rang, but waited for Nicole. She flicked him a glance as she came out then shyly looked away. They started walking back to the main building.

"You showed no interest in entering the discussion," Nicole commented.

"I was busy listening to you."

"Did you find my points compelling?"

"Umm, sure," Sean said, realizing he really hadn't listened to *what* she was talking about as much as just listening to her voice.

"I find history fascinating," she gushed.

"Really? I think it's kind of boring."

"Boring?" Her voice was indignant. "Mankind's struggle to survive, progress, and build civilization?"

"Umm, yeah," Sean returned weakly, "It's just a bunch of stuff about old dead guys."

"'Those who cannot learn from history are doomed to repeat it,'" Nicole quoted.

"Oh, don't worry about that. I know it good enough to not flunk," he assured her.

"I was quoting George Santayana. Actually just one of the popular English translations, since it was originally in Polish."

"Who's George Santa whatever?"

"'Some old dead guy' if I were to use your terminology," she said testily.

"Sorry," Sean apologized, "I didn't mean to ruffle your feathers. Hey, it's cool if you like that stuff."

"I do not understand how you can be so indifferent. When someone studies the past, they can examine the cause and effect cycles of past decisions, and assess how those decisions shaped the future. Then when one observes a similar negative cause and effect cycle begin to take place, an attempt can be made to change it before there is a repeat of the negative outcome."

"OK, I think I understand," Sean started seriously, "tomorrow, before I tell you that History is boring, I should look back at today, and learn to keep my mouth shut." He made a point of showing all his teeth as he grinned.

"Very good, Sean Kelly," she nodded with a smile, "that is a start."

"So, you seriously, really do like history?"

"Yes, I do," Nicole confirmed. "And also recognize that all of the decisions currently being made are what shape your future."

"Yeah, that's kind of scary."

As they entered the main building, and Sean started up the stairs to Biology, he mentally added a note to his list of things he learned about the Townsend twins. Five: just because she is drop-dead gorgeous doesn't mean that Nicole isn't *every bit* as smart as Alexis.

Thursday was a near repeat of Wednesday. Sean tried tactfully to gain more information about Nicole from Alexis, but ended up in a strange conversation about candy. He had casually said something about 'life is like a box of chocolates' and Alexis started listing sugar content and chemicals found in various candy bars. When she stopped long enough for him to speak, he attempted to circle back to *Forrest Gump,* which she seemed totally clueless about until she did one of her twitches.

Nicole was already in her seat when he arrived in Algebra. After class, Sean's hope of walking her to lunch was dashed when he saw she was holding her open math book and quizzing Mr. Stapleton. He walked solo to the cafeteria where he settled into his standard lunch routine with Kevin and Raj.

He was laughing at one of Kevin's jokes when he saw Nicole walk in with Cliff Sickler. It didn't hit him nearly as hard as the first time he saw them together, but his good mood quickly soured. He didn't *hate* Cliff, but he certainly didn't like him. He wondered if 'despise' wasn't as strong as 'hate'... and decided that maybe he despised him. He returned his attention to Kevin, who had moved on to a frenzied monologue about the upcoming away football game with Henryville, their first conference game.

Sean did finally get to talk with Nicole during their walks between the main building and the Wasteland. He asked her what she missed about New York, and she asked him what he liked about living in a small town in the Midwest.

On the return trip, Nicole was still excited about History class, and Sean was content to let her do most of the talking. He did his best to toss in an occasional 'uh huh' when appropriate, and tried to not let it show how boring History still was to him. The sting from Nicole's lunch with Cliff faded as Sean happily listened to her melodic voice. He propped up his bruised ego by again reminding himself that 'slow and steady wins the race.'

Friday morning, Sean hit the snooze bar only once, managed to get a fifth-row parking space, and walked at a leisurely pace around to the back of the main building. As he came around the corner, he noticed that Alexis was nearly to the stairs coming from the other direction. She waited for him at the top of the steps and greeted him as he neared.

"Good morning, Sean."

"Good morning, Alexis."

"You are very erratic in your arrival behavior," she pointed out again.

"You are very systematic about telling me that every morning," he replied cheerily.

"You have not arrived at the same time any day this week," she reported as they started down the steps.

"I suppose you *did* get here at exactly the same time every day this week?" Sean asked dryly.

"Yes," said Alexis. "Do you find that unusual?"

Sean thought for a moment. "No, not for you. So is Nicole as punctual as you are?"

"Yes," she replied then stepped off the sidewalk and stopped. Sean turned back and stepped aside with her as she continued, "You have inquired about Nicole several times this week."

Sean glanced away from her as panic seized him. He'd hoped his questions had been careful enough to not tip Alexis about his interest in her sister. "I... umm," he stammered, "... think twins are cool, and it's interesting to find out what things are the same about them and what things are different."

"Perhaps why one is more attractive than the other?" she asked calmly.

Sean squirmed. He was completely unprepared to talk about this with Alexis. Her bluntness always caught him off guard. "No... just... different. You know. Twin stuff." His brain was freezing up, but his mouth kept desperately moving. "OK, like you both are punctual, but *you* like to take morning walks and *she* likes to go to the library, and... and, OK, you both have a similar nose but you're a blonde and she has reddish brown hair."

"Do you not feel a stronger attraction to her than to me?" she asked neutrally.

Sean was thoroughly confused. Her *words* seemed to be confronting him, but her *voice* wasn't the least bit confrontational. *Should he tell her?* He wondered. *No. I still didn't want to hurt her feelings.* "I guess I haven't really thought about it."

"Your statement seems evasive, and possibly untruthful... and your face exhibits signs of fear. What do you fear?"

Sean decided if Alexis wanted to be blunt; he could dish it right back. "I didn't want to hurt your feelings! OK? I know that you like me, and I didn't want you to know that I like your sister! OK? Are you happy now?"

He braced himself; his eyes closed, and jaw tightened. He didn't know if she would explode like Tiffany, or break into tears, or punch him in the face, but when he opened his eyes, he did *not* expect what he saw.

She smiled.

Not a crazy stalker-boil-your-rabbit-then-later-try-to-kill-you smile... she actually seemed... pleased?

"You were concerned about *my* feelings? Sean Kelly you are a very good and kind person. I do not mind that you are attracted to Nicole," Alexis said warmly.

"You're not mad?" Sean was amazed. "Or sad? Or want to kill me or anything?"

"No," she laughed, "I do not wish to kill you!"

"OK, that's good." He breathed a sigh of relief. "Wait... you didn't say you weren't mad or sad."

"I am neither mad nor sad, and I do not feel the least bit homicidal," Alexis replied.

"Good morning, lovebirds!" Sean winced when he heard Megan's saccharine greeting. Before he could think of a scathing comeback, Alexis spoke.

"Good morning, Megan," she said without emotion, "Sean and I are not lovebirds. He is interested in my sister."

Megan stopped cold; her mouth dropped. Sean nearly matched her expression. Ashly hovered behind Megan.

"He what?" Megan asked sharply.

"He is attracted to my sister, Nicole."

"And you're OK with that?"

"It was not my original expectation, but it is an acceptable alternate outcome," Alexis said smoothly.

Megan's brow knit as her nose crinkled. "You," she said as she pointed to Alexis, "I don't get." Her finger shifted to Sean. "But *you* are a scumbag!" She turned with a huff and walked briskly away, leaving Ashly scampering to catch up to her.

"He is actually a very kind and caring person," Alexis called after her.

Sean pinched himself, hoping to confirm that he was only having a nightmare. Unfortunately, it hurt... the insanity was real. He ruefully wished he had hit the snooze alarm a second time, or even a third.

"We should go on to class," Alexis said gently, nudging Sean from his state of shock.

He stumbled wordlessly into the classroom, and slumped into his chair, relieved that it was Feature Friday. He stared at the screen, mostly oblivious of the Spanish soap opera that played. He knew he'd probably have to take an 'F' on the Monday report, but at least he didn't have to do anything during class.

He spent the hour reviewing the morning's events, and by the end of class had boiled it down to only four things. One: Alexis knew he liked Nicole and seemed OK with it. Two: Megan knew that he liked Nicole and thought he was a scumbag. Three: By the end of the day *everyone* would know that he liked Nicole and that Megan thought he was a scumbag. Four: Alexis was still weird... if not bordering on bizarre.

Sean bolted for the door when the bell rang, then waited for Alexis just outside the classroom. He tried to ignore Megan's sneer and eye roll as she passed him. If she had been a cat, she would have been hissing. Alexis smiled at him as she came out. He marveled at her serene face as they started the trek to the main building.

"You really don't get it, do you?" he finally said.

"Get what?"

"The Girl Network... and that Megan is a power player."

Alexis merely looked at him blankly.

"By the end of the day... if not by lunchtime," Sean explained to her (he used the same tone as if talking to the three-year-old who lived two houses down from the Kellys), "Megan will have told the entire school that I dumped you, that I like your sister and that I am a scumbag."

Alexis thoughtfully assessed his statement before responding, "She has made an incorrect assumption, is stating a discovered fact and has made an erroneous judgment of your character."

Sean wondered if he had been fluent enough to explain it to her in Spanish if she would get it, but decided she wouldn't. They had walked most of the rest of the way back in silence before Alexis spoke again.

"People who know you will not believe you are a scumbag. I will tell anyone who asks me that we were never a couple; therefore, you could not dump me."

"Yeah, look, I'm not really worried about the scumbag thing. No one is going to 'ask you' if I dumped you, and what about Nicole?"

"But that statement was the only *true* statement," she said, confused.

"What's Nicole going to think when she hears all this buzzing around?"

"Oh, now I understand that part," she said, then added simply, "I suggest *you* tell Nicole yourself."

Sean started up the steps to Speech, and called back down to Alexis, "Thanks, Alexis," he said sarcastically, "you've been a great help!"

"You are most welcome, Sean," she replied cheerfully, "Have a good day!"

Sean stopped climbing for a moment and leaned over the rail to watch her walk down the hall. "From now on," he muttered to himself, "any list I make starts with: Number One: Alexis is weird!"

Sean was pretty sure he tanked the test in Speech class, even though he'd studied for it. His state of mind wasn't conducive to test-taking. During study-hall, he ran multiple scenarios about what to say to Nicole. None of them struck him as an excellent strategy. Just the thought of Megan spreading the news throughout the entire Girl Network made his stomach hurt. He tried to imagine her being captured by killer robots, but couldn't even conjure up a satisfying image of his nemesis being thwarted.

Every time he thought about Alexis he felt more confused. She was obviously brilliant, yet sometimes seemed totally clueless. *Idiot-Savant*? Was that one of his Mom's psych phases?

The bell rang signaling time to go to Algebra. Icy needles prickled his stomach. He tried to breathe through it and nearly hyperventilated. He'd decided his course of action and hoped he could pull it off. He rushed to get to the classroom before Nicole.

When he saw her approaching, his heart-rate doubled. He felt his stomach roil, and glanced at the water fountain a few yards down the hall. *Too far.* He couldn't get there and back before Nicole reached the door. He waited. His mouth was even drier having thought about the drinking fountain. He took in a deep breath as she approached and found that she was already close enough for a trace of her scent. Unfortunately, it didn't give him a rush of good feelings or even reduce his anxiety.

"Good morning, Sean," she greeted.

"Hi, Nicole," his dry throat croaked.

A concerned look crossed her face. "Are you all right?"

"Great," he lied, "just need a little water."

She glanced at the water fountain but didn't say anything.

"Umm... Nicole," Sean stammered. She stood there smiling which only rattled him more. "I was wondering..." He paused, cleared his throat, and coughed. "I was wondering if you had any plans for lunch today." He waited an eternity for her reply.

"No, nothing specific," she answered after a moment's thought.

"Well, would you like... I mean, would it be OK if we... could I sit with you at lunch?"

The concerned look returned. "Are you certain you feel all right?"

"It's OK if you don't want to," he rushed, "you probably already have plans."

"Sean, perhaps you should splash a little water on your face." He stood there frozen, unsure of what to do next. "Yes, we can sit together at lunch, assuming you have not succumbed to some illness."

He was in shock. She said yes. He didn't have any actual data to calculate the probability, but he had already decided that his chances were approaching zero.

He hadn't realized that he'd stopped breathing until he suddenly heard himself take a big gasp.

"I hope the water helps," Nicole said as she turned to go into the classroom.

Sean stumbled zombie-like to the water fountain, amazed. He slurped up some big gulps before sticking his hand under the stream, and then rubbing his face with it. *Now how am I going to tell her about what was running through the rumor mill?*

Nothing in Algebra class made any sense, but then nothing in his entire life seemed to make sense since he'd met the Townsend twins. He waited in his seat when class ended, then noticed that Nicole had once again gone to talk with Mr. Stapleton, open book in hand.

Sean decided to *not* wait in the classroom. He inched his way slowly toward the cafeteria. Raj and Kevin came up from behind him passing him on each side. They both were pantomiming running in slow motion. After a few steps, they laughed and turned back to him.

"Did we miss the 'I can walk slower than you' race announcement?" Kevin asked.

"I'm kind of waiting for someone," Sean answered.

"And here we are!" Raj added brightly.

"Ummm, someone else..."

"Whoa," Kevin said, a big grin on his face, "Someone of the *female* persuasion?"

"Maybe..." Sean grinned back.

"Someone who might have a sister who is *not* the evil twin?" Kevin continued.

"Will you let this *evil twin* thing go?" Sean snapped. "Nicole's not evil."

"You don't actually know that for sure," Raj said.

"Shhh," Kevin hissed looking over Sean's shoulder, "evil or not, here she comes. Good luck, buddy, it was nice knowing you."

They both quickly slipped down the hall, leaving Sean standing alone as Nicole approached. He breathed in her fragrance, and this time it *did* seem to ease his anxiety.

"Was that your friends?" Nicole asked.

"Umm, yeah... Kevin and Raj."

"If you would prefer to sit with them during lunch, I will not mind."

"No!" Sean barked, then immediately wished he hadn't said it so forcefully. He calmed his voice to continue, "No, that's OK; I have lunch with them all the time."

She smiled. "Then are you ready to enter the cafeteria?"

"Sure," he replied, already running his options of opening small talk. "It was sure hot this August," he said as they reached the door.

"Meteorologists are forming theories that link an *el niño* during the winter to summer heatwaves in the Midwest," she replied.

"Uh-huh," he nodded, wondering if *either* of the Townsends ever did small talk, "I hope it starts to cool off soon."

They picked up trays, and Sean headed toward the hot-bar serving area. He looked over his shoulder and saw that Nicole was browsing the salad bar. He remembered that Alexis ate homemade yogurt, and Aunt Katherine said she never ate sweets. His dilemma was whether to go ahead and get something he *wanted* to eat or try to choke down a salad for show. He decided that a chicken-salad sandwich was a compromise... at least it wasn't fried or covered with cheese. Nicole waited for him to pick a table. As they sat down across from each other at one of the small tables, he saw that all she had on her plate was a tiny pile of plain lettuce. He popped the top on his Coke.

"Umm... just lettuce?" he ventured.

"With a protein supplement," she said as she reached into her book bag, and pulled out a clear container. She meticulously drizzled the contents over her lettuce.

"Protein supplement?" Sean asked with a wrinkled nose.

"Yes," she answered, ignoring his disapproval, "and a balance of vitamins, minerals, and just a bit of non-saturated fat. The lettuce contains carbohydrates and fiber."

"Does it *taste* good?" Sean asked, still unable to unwrinkle his nose.

She looked as though she didn't understand the question. After giving it some thought she said, "it is mostly flavor neutral."

"Yumm!" Sean said, then immediately felt guilty for being sarcastic. "Where do you get this supplement?" he quickly asked to cover his *faux pas*.

"Aunt Katherine makes it," Sean said in unison with Nicole's reply. She smiled at him.

"So..." Sean began, "and you can stop me anytime I get too personal... are you like vegan or vegetarian or something?"

Her eyes flicked away and returned before she responded, "I do not find either term to be entirely accurate, but perhaps close to what you would define as vegetarian."

"OK, so you said you're from New York... did you live in California for awhile? Or are your parents from California?" *Damn! Why did I bring up her parents? Her dad is dead, and her mom is in a looney bin... what an idiot thing to say.*

"No, to both questions about California," she replied evenly.

"OK, umm, I guess I shouldn't say anything about what you eat, and hopefully you're OK with me eating what I want."

"That seems reasonable," she said and took a bite of her salad.

"Great," Sean said, taking a bite of sandwich.

"Was there an objective for requesting to sit with me during lunch?"

He nearly choked on his bite. *OK, she's every bit as direct as Alexis.* "Umm, well... to talk... to get to know you better."

"What would you like to know?"

First, I'd like to know if your directness is going to make this easier or harder. "Ummm, let's see... are you making friends here OK?"

"Yes."

Blunt and concise. Not making it easier. "Like, guy friends, girl friends..." he trailed off, lost on a track that had no known destination.

She smiled at him. "It appears to me there is a more specific question you are *not* asking, but wish to derive through inference."

Maybe even MORE blunt than Alexis. OK, here goes! "So are you like going out with Cliff?"

She seemed almost amused. "Not if I correctly understand your use of the terminology 'going out'"

"It's just that I've seen you have lunch with him a couple of times... and he *does* have a really cool car."

"We have a theater class together," she said matter-of-factly, "and were randomly selected for a duet reading in two weeks. We discussed which scene to select."

"Theater class? With Ms. McGuire?"

"Yes. She is very enthusiastic about dramatic interpretation."

"That's cool. Kind of like you're enthusiastic about history."

"I suppose that is a fair analogy," she replied. "Since you mentioned history, did you read the section in the book we are going to cover today? I wanted to ask you if you consider the level of nationalism reflected in the devotion to the United States Olympic teams might have linking roots in patriotic rhetoric generated during the American Revolutionary War?"

Sean was lost for the rest of the lunch period, desperately trying to follow Nicole's theories about history. He finally steered back to the one other thing that he really wanted to say to her during lunch.

"Umm, Nicole, if you hear Megan Walsh or any of her friends saying stuff about you and me... it's just because she's mad at me about something, and trying to make everyone think I'm evil. You shouldn't believe anything she says."

"Nothing?" she asked enigmatically.

"Nothing," Sean replied firmly.

She smiled as they stood to leave the lunch area. "Very well, Sean... Nothing. I will see you in History class."

"Great! See you then."

As Sean walked toward study-hall, he couldn't help but notice a sea of frowns from every girl he passed in the hall. Megan was a real pro at rapidly getting information to all corners of the school. He decided to test the waters when he reached the study-hall classroom. A quick review of faces had him selecting Kristen for his test case. Kristen and Megan were from totally different cliques, and normally wouldn't speak to each other.

"Hey, Kristen," he said in what he hoped was a friendly tone, "How's it going?"

"Hello, Sean," she replied frostily, then turned away from him.

That answered that question, he thought. *I must be the lead story in today's Girl Gazette.*

He sighed as he sat down. It didn't bother him too much, since he'd faced a similar shunning when Tiffany trashed him. For the most part, he eventually bounced back from that, and he was hopeful that there would be something more scandalous by the next week to attract attention away from him.

He wondered what it meant for Alexis and Nicole, though. Was Alexis being enthroned as a martyr? Was Nicole painted as the evil 'other woman' responsible for the breakup of the happy couple? How had Megan been spinning the story? He decided to try to study Spanish, since his life was beginning to resemble one of the telenovelas that Ms. McGuire loved to show on Fridays.

* * *

Sean was genuinely surprised to find Nicole waiting for him just outside the main building. He felt wary, but at least she didn't *look* like she was mad. They started walking out to the History classroom.

"Sean, what is a scum bug?"

He gasped as his stomach flipped. *Looks like she's heard.* "Umm, I think you mean scum*bag*, not *bug*."

"Oh. I overheard some girls in the hall say that you were one. They were talking rather loudly as I passed, almost as if they intended me to overhear. In context, it seemed to be derogatory."

"Yep, I think you could say derogatory is in the right ballpark."

"This must be in reference to what you were telling me during lunch."

"Yep." Sean wondered where this was going.

"So they were calling you a scumbag because of Megan?" she asked.

"That would be my best guess."

"Then I should ignore what they said, per your instruction to believe nothing Megan said."

"That's kind of what I was hoping," Sean sighed.

"I should also ignore that they said you dumped my sister?"

"We never went out!" Sean protested. "How could I have dumped her?"

"They seemed also to insinuate that you had a romantic interest in me," she said evenly.

"What can I say?" Sean exclaimed as he gestured dramatically, "that Megan's a crazy one!"

"Therefore, that is something else I should ignore since your instructions were to believe nothing Megan said?"

Sean's brain froze. He didn't want to confirm or deny, so he simply raised his palms, and shrugged his shoulders, smiling a nervous smile. Nicole seemed puzzled by his response, and Sean desperately wanted to change the subject.

"So... are you going to bring up your theory about how the Revolutionary War causes people to like to watch the Olympics?" he suddenly blurted.

"I believe I said my theory was that Nationalism shown in devotion to a US Olympic team could have its emotional roots in the American Revolution."

"You always say it so much better than I do," Sean said, hoping that he had distracted her.

"Do you recommend that I present my hypothesis today?"

"Yes! Yes, I do! I think it's a great hypothesis!" *I think that ANYTHING that distracts you from the rumor mill is a great hypothesis.*

"Will you support my arguments?" she asked enthusiastically.

"I'll be rooting for you!"

As they walked into the classroom, Sean breathed a sigh of relief. He had only History and Biology standing in the way of his weekend.

When History class had ended, Sean felt conflicted whether to wait for Nicole or not. Fearing a return to the earlier Megan discussion, he decided to leave. He rationalized he wasn't *exactly* dodging her; he was just closest to the door.

He had nearly reached the stairs before he heard Nicole call out his name. He turned, put up a brave smile, and quietly chanted to himself, "Please don't bring up the Megan rumors, please don't bring up the Megan rumors."

"Sean, I have need of clarification," she announced as she reached the steps.

He braced himself, still unsure what to say if she asked him again if he liked her. "What's that, Nicole?" he asked, trying to keep his voice level.

"Why did Matt declare me to be a fascist communist?"

Sean's laugh exploded in a relief of tension as they started up the steps.

"I did not intend for my question to sound humorous," Nicole said sulkily.

"No, no," Sean said, breathing a sigh of relief, "I was laughing about something else."

"He seemed rather vehement in his assertion," she continued.

"Well, Matt is kind of out there on the tip of the Right Wing."

Nicole glanced away then back. "Politically Reactionary? I suppose that could explain a deep-seated opposition to both fascism and communism, but it does not explain his assigning either ideology to me."

"I think he just got mad about some of the stuff you said."

"And the two ideologies are not exactly mutually compatible," she continued.

"He's kind of a big flag-waver."

"There was nothing in the presentation of my hypothesis that even insinuated an adherence to either philosophy."

"Come on. He didn't like what you said, so he was trashing you!"

"Oh!" she said thoughtfully, "rather than refute my position, he attempted to discredit me personally? What an unusual tactic."

Sean did a mental happy dance when they had reached the main building. He had only one more class, and then he could get away for a couple of days. They climbed one flight of steps together, and Nicole started down the hall of the second floor. Sean called out to her, and she turned back.

"Hey, have a great weekend, OK?"

She smiled mischievously and nodded. "I hope your weekend is also enjoyable."

Sean climbed the last flight of stairs to Biology. *One more class.*

Chapter Four

"You can go sleep at home tonight / If you can get up and walk away"

"SEAN!"

Sean looked over his shoulder to see Nicole briskly walking his way. *Now what?* He slowed his pace to let her close the distance, but kept moving, walking backwards as she caught up to him.

"Hi, what are you doing?" she asked.

"Going home. Last bell? Friday?" Sean shrugged as he pivoted back around.

"Certainly... but my inquiry regards your short-term plans," clarified Nicole as she fell into step with Sean on her left.

What's she up to now? Is this finally about Megan's gossip? He continued to walk toward the parking lot. Nicole walked with him.

"The usual, I guess. Grab a snack, listen to some tunes, and maybe shoot some hoops... I don't know. Why?"

"Oh... I thought perhaps you studied when you got home from school."

Sean stopped in his tracks. Nicole took another step, then swung around to face him.

"Are you kidding me? Nicole, it's Friday. We're free, why would I want to study?"

Nicole's smile faded as her eyes drifted to the ground. "Oh."

She drew little circles with her shoe tip, then brought her eyes back to meet Sean's. She smiled coyly as she continued to draw with her toe, glancing back and forth from her foot to Sean's face. "I had hopes that you might assist me with math," she said shyly.

Although Sean wanted to retreat from the whole week and settle in safe at home, he couldn't deny that he found Nicole alluring. Her hair was perfect. Her clothes were top of the line. Her voice like a song... and she appeared to be warming up to him. A light breeze brought her perfume to his nose, and he smiled reflexively.

"What's *really* going on, Nicole?"

"Honestly," she said, "I am finding it difficult to comprehend this second year of Algebra. Perhaps it is because the book is a different book from the one in my former school or the difference in teachers; perhaps an expectation that everyone has learned the same information from first year Algebra, but I am not absorbing the material." She paused long enough to brighten her smile again. "I spoke with Mr. Stapleton and he asked if I had talked to anyone else from the class. And *you* seem to be doing well, so I thought if I asked you for assistance, that you could tutor me? Take pity on the new girl in town... please?"

"Seriously, Nicole... on a Friday? Haven't you got anything better to do on a Friday?"

Her eyes dropped to the ground again.

"You have decided that you do not like me," she said with just a trace of pout in her voice.

"What? Where'd *that* come from? Nicole, I barely know you... or Alexis for that matter. Maybe things were different where you came from."

"New York... upstate, not the city," she slipped in quickly.

"Maybe things were different in New York," he continued, "but in the Midwest, we let things just kind of develop over time. You both seem to try to rush stuff."

Nicole's lower lip protruded a little.

"Look," Sean explained, "it'll take awhile to adjust to a new school, a new town... a whole new life. And it'll take awhile for people to warm up to you. Give us a chance, Nicole, and give yourself a chance. I don't really know yet how I feel about you. I mean, you seem really nice... but you and Alexis just are kind of... I don't know... different. Maybe you're just used to a faster pace of things."

"I am sorry, Sean. I *do* want to fit in. I was hoping you might assist. I understand if you do not like me. I am sorry I have bothered you."

"I like you fine, Nicole... so far. Like I said, I don't really know you yet."

Nicole's brilliant green eyes sparkled as they locked with Sean's; her bright smile spread across her face again. "Then you *do* like me? Do you consider me pretty?"

"Nicole! What... what kind of question is that?"

"An honest one. I think you are wonderful. Since *I* have been honest, you can as well. I wish to know if you honestly think of me as pretty."

Sean's face flushed red as he turned his eyes to the ground. "Um... really, Nicole... we...um... we don't quite come right out and say stuff like that around here... well not this soon after meeting someone."

"Why is time a factor?" she challenged.

"What?"

"Time... how does time become a factor? Do you anticipate that my appearance will change a great deal in the next few days, or even weeks?"

"Well, no, probably not."

"Then do you have reason to believe that your perception of beauty will undergo a significant shift?"

"Well... no... probably not a lot," Sean repeated.

"Therefore; since I am unlikely to change and you are unlikely to shift values in the next few days; we can best assume that you have already established in your own mind what you find pleasing and that you have measured my appearance with regard to your vision of the mythical ideal beauty. I suspect that you have even already thought of me as a number on a scale, so why not answer me honestly... Do you think I am pretty?"

"Nine," Sean said softly.

"Nine?"

"Nine," he confirmed.

"Let me quickly verify that even though you have some German ancestry, you do not have bilingual skills in German."

"What?"

"*Nein* means 'no' in German," explained Nicole. "I wanted to clarify that you have not shifted into a secondary language to refuse to answer my question."

"Um... *nein* ... I mean, *no*," Sean stumbled as he became more flustered.

"Then I can infer that you do find me pretty, assigning me a score of a nine out of ten," she reported. She seemed quite pleased. "For the sake of comparison, how would you score Alexis?"

Sean blushed even brighter.

"Nicole... I... we... you...um, this honesty thing is kind of different... I mean, not that being honest is *bad*, it's just that... well, around here, we'd normally take a lot more time before getting to the point of saying someone was pretty... to their face, I mean." He glanced at her then looked back to the ground. "For instance, it would've been more normal if I'd, you know, just kind of casually mentioned when hanging out with the guys that I thought you were, you know... kind of cute." His eyes flicked to her face for an instant, then back down. "And then eventually the guys would be talking about it in the halls or something, and some girl would overhear and then mention in the bathroom that she heard Jake say that Sean said that he thought Nicole was cute. And then someone else would come up to you sometime and say something like, 'The other day I heard Kristen say that she heard that Jake heard Sean say that you were cute.' Then you'd find out."

"Very inefficient," declared Nicole, "That process could take weeks. What is the point of the subterfuge? I find you attractive, you said you think I am a nine, and there is nothing that time or Kristen or Jake or further extraneous rhetoric could add or detract from those concise statements."

"Does everyone in New York talk and act like you?"

"Are you attempting to distract me by pointing out that I do not have your charming Midwest twang for an accent?"

"No, well, maybe... *what twang?* I don't have an accent *you* do... and that wasn't what I meant anyway. None of the girls around here talk the way you do... you sometimes sound more like a Vulcan or something."

"Vulcan?" Nicole glanced away for a moment, and then turned back with a smile. "Oh, *Star Trek*... I have never watched that."

"I just meant that you kind of talk like a Vulcan, all logical and stuff. It's... different."

"I did not realize that it was offensive to be logical."

"No, that's OK," Sean backpedaled, "I mean, you don't *have* to be like all the girls around here. I suppose being logical and direct can be good... once I get used to it. Maybe even kind of nice."

"Good. Then may I go home with you?"

Sean blushed again but laughed. "I've already been through that one with Alexis. You want a ride home to *your* house."

"No, I am requesting to go to *your* house."

"Well, um... OK, now we're back to awkward again. Look, Nicole, just because we've rushed the part about saying that we like each other... well, let's not jump into anything too quickly that we might regret later."

"What is there to regret about Algebra?"

"Algebra? Oh... right... you want help with math," Sean laughed nervously, "I'd already forgotten you asked for help with math."

"Why, Sean... whatever else *could* you be thinking about?" Nicole's eyes twinkled. Sean looked at the ground again. His skin felt hot from all the blushing he'd been doing. "Which is your vehicle?"

They walked over to Sean's '89 Taurus. 'A practical, safe car,' was how his Dad described it. Other guys got new Berettas, Avengers, Mustangs, Cameros, but Sean's Dad had to be practical and get him a seven-year-old family car. He unlocked the passenger side and opened the door for Nicole. She slid in.

As Sean walked around to his side, he paused just a second to admire Nicole's hair through the rear window, a smile spread across his face. "OK, so she's different. She's still drop-dead beautiful," he mused.

He started the car and pulled onto the street. "Say, how do you know that I have German ancestors?"

"Why do you ask that? I know nothing about your ancestors." There was tension in Nicole's voice.

"When you were talking about '*nein*' meaning 'no' in German... you said something about me having German ancestors. Why would you know that?"

"Oh... merely a supposition. There was a great influx of German, Irish, and Scandinavian settlers in the Midwest in the 19th Century. It is likely that most people in this vicinity have at least some German heritage," she laughed nervously. "Do you?"

Sean had that same chill he felt when he confronted Alexis about knowing odd things about him.

"Well, yes... and I suppose you're right that a lot of people around here would. I hadn't really thought of that." He glanced her way. "You know, you're so incredibly intelligent, are you *sure* you need help with Algebra?"

"Unfortunately, I do. I am hopeful that you can easily enlighten me."

"You're pretty good at flattery, you know."

"I am only stating what I perceive to be fact. Would you consider it flattery if I praised your choice in automobiles?"

"No... I'd think you were pulling my leg."

A puzzled look crossed Nicole's face. "I am not even touching you, why would you infer that I was pulling on your leg?" She twitched slightly to the right before turning back with a smile. "Oh, stating something false to be true for the purpose of teasing. No. I was simply reflecting that the 1989 Ford

Taurus has a high safety rating in both head-on and side collisions. Selecting safe transportation seems very practical, therefore, I stand by my comment that you have a good car."

"Have you been talking to my Dad?" Sean laughed.

"Not yet," she replied.

Something about the way she replied gave Sean a chill. He shook it off and then he laughed again. "Nicole, I think it's going to take me awhile to get used to your sense of humor."

"Yes, perhaps. I also struggle to understand what *you* find humorous."

They arrived in front of a beige raised ranch with a two car garage. Sean pulled against the curb and shut off the engine. They got out of the car and walked up the driveway and then the sidewalk to the front door. Sean turned the handle and pushed. It was locked.

"Hmmm, that's odd. My Mom's usually home by now," he commented, "She teaches at the University and is normally finished with classes and office hours before I get home."

"Perhaps she had a departmental meeting this afternoon," Nicole offered.

Sean pulled his keys from his pocket and unlocked the door. They stepped in.

"Maybe."

Sean immediately saw the blinking light on the phone, crossed to it and pushed a button.

"You have one new message," the dispassionate not-quite-human voice reported.

After a beep, Michelle Kelly's voice came from the tiny speaker, "Sean, I hope you think to check the machine. The Dean decided he had to have a meeting with our department this afternoon from 3 until 5. Said it was the only time he could get everyone together for the next couple of weeks, and he had something *vital* he wanted to talk to everyone about. Why is everything always *vital* with Deans? I'll still get home before your father, but I think I'll just pick something up for dinner on the way home. I hope you didn't already have pizza today, because that's what I think I'll get. Don't forget to let the dog out of the basement. Let her out into the yard for awhile and then let her back in. Well, I suppose you should know how to take care of the dog by now. Anyway, see you around supper time. Bye."

"Guess you were right about the meeting. Say, are you psychic or something?"

"Psychic?" Nicole asked then glanced away momentarily. "Oh, a paranormal ability to gain knowledge by a special mental phenomenon such as telepathy or extra-sensory-perception. No, Sean, I am not 'psychic,'"

"OK, I've changed my mind about the Vulcan thing, you sound more like Data on TNG." He took Nicole's book-bag from her and dropped it in a chair. "Hey, do you like dogs? Maggie's a real sweetie. I'll try to keep her from licking you to death."

Sean stepped into the country-style kitchen and crossed to a closed door and grabbed the handle. Nicole stood in the kitchen doorway, nervously glancing from Sean to the door.

"Come on. Come here and meet Maggie."

"I am not very comfortable with household pets, Sean."

"Well, you'll change your tune when you meet Maggie. She loves everyone."

Sean opened the door, and an Irish Setter leaped out and excitedly started licking him, her tail thumped against the door.

"See, isn't she a sweetie?"

Maggie looked toward Nicole and froze. Her tail dropped, her hackles rose, and a low growl rumbled from her throat.

"Mags! What is the matter with you? Stop it! You never act like this." Maggie broke into a threatening bark. Sean grabbed her by the collar. "Stop it! Maggie, stop it!" She continued to bark and tried to lunge toward Nicole. Sean held her by her collar. "I'm sorry, Nicole, I've never seen her act this way before. I'll put her out in the back yard."

Nicole covertly stuck her hand into her book-bag a pulled out a small cylinder. She pressed one end, and a fine mist spritzed onto her right hand.

"If you could hold onto her collar while I come closer? And also hold her muzzle closed?"

Sean restrained Maggie as Nicole had asked. Nicole slipped the cylinder back into her bag then took measured steps toward them. Maggie continued to try to lunge as Sean held her.

Nicole stepped slightly to the side of them and held her right hand out. Maggie continued to growl, but sniffed at the outstretched hand. Nicole moved her right hand closer to Maggie's nose and scratched the dog's ear with her left hand. The growling stopped, and Maggie docilely sat down. Sean released her muzzle but still held her collar. Maggie licked Nicole's hand and started wagging her tail. Sean released her collar. The Irish Setter continued to sit calmly as Nicole bent close and gave her a hug.

"OK, that was weird and then weirder." Sean scratched his head. "First, she never acts that way, and then what made her suddenly calm down?"

"We could surmise that she reacted instinctively to a stranger invading her territory, but then realized that I present no threat as reinforced by your non-threatened stance toward me," Nicole theorized.

Sean stood and crossed to the back door.

"Come on, Mags, wanna go outside? Come on girl."

He opened the door, and Maggie trotted calmly over and out into the back yard. Sean looked back to Nicole. She shrugged.

"OK, besides being an expert on History, car safety, and a walking dictionary, now you're a dog trainer, too?"

Nicole shrugged again and simply smiled.

"So you're going to play the part of the mystery woman, huh?" Sean moved to the refrigerator and pulled the door open. "Want a Coke?"

"Empty calories and a caffeine-fueled adrenaline charge? No thank you. Perhaps I could prepare us both something a little healthier?"

"Healthy? I guess I should have seen that coming. What do you have in mind?"

Nicole quickly scanned the shelves of the refrigerator followed by a quick head twitch. "I see orange juice and yogurt. With an added fruit, I could prepare smoothies."

"Strawberries work? I think there are some strawberries in the freezer. They're from my grandma's farm."

"That is an excellent suggestion."

Sean piled the ingredients onto the kitchen counter and pulled a blender from a lower cabinet.

"OK, dazzle me with your chef skills now."

"Dazzle you? That is an interesting word choice," Nicole said enigmatically. She plopped some yogurt into the blender and added some of the frozen strawberries, finally topping it off with orange juice. She replaced the lid and examined the row of buttons on the base of the machine. Sean reached in and pushed a button to start it spinning.

"I always go straight for the top speed," he said as he got a couple of glasses out and set them on the counter.

Nicole stopped the motor and poured a little into one of the glasses. "Taste?"

Sean took a sip that puckered his lips. "Mmmm, yummy."

"Really? Your facial expression does not match your words. Being honest is not really something that comes naturally to you, is it?"

Sean answered sheepishly, "Well, I don't want to seem ungrateful... but it is a little sour."

"I believe 'tart' would be an appropriate term, but in your case, since you are accustomed to drinking carbonated high fructose corn syrup, perhaps you are preconditioned to skew tart to sour. I assume you have something to employ as a sweetening agent?"

"Well, yeah... there's sugar in that canister right there."

Nicole opened the canister and pinched a few grains and touched them to her tongue.

"Highly refined sucrose extracted from either cane or beets," she said clinically. "You realize this will spike your blood sugar level spurring increased insulin production to counteract it."

"Really? I thought it would just make the smoothie taste better," Sean grinned.

"I hope you do not mind that I pour mine before adding any of this." She poured part of the smoothie into one of the glasses. "How much would you like me to add?"

"I don't know? Half a cup?" Sean shrugged.

"You cannot be serious."

"OK, how about a couple tablespoons?" Sean said as he opened a drawer and fished out the measuring spoons.

Nicole carefully leveled off a tablespoon and added it to the blender. She reluctantly repeated with a second tablespoon then started the motor up. She looked up and then pointed to the back door, "I believe I heard the dog."

Sean went out the back door, and Nicole rushed to her book-bag. She selected a small vial and dumped the contents into the blender and replaced the lid. When Sean came back in with Maggie, Nicole poured the rest of the smoothie into Sean's glass and handed it to him. He took the glass and headed out of the kitchen with Maggie happily trotting behind him.

"Let's sit in the living room," he called over his shoulder.

Nicole picked up her glass and followed. Sean had already sat down on the couch. Maggie sat at his feet, looking anxiously at him, hoping for a share of whatever he had. Nicole grabbed her book-bag and sat in a stuffed chair adjacent to the couch, dropping her bag at the side. She pointed to the glass in Sean's hand.

"Your opinion?" she asked.

"Well... it's good... I guess." Sean smiled sheepishly. "Good for me anyway, huh?"

"Better for you than what I assume you normally ingest."

"Whatever you say... bottoms up," Sean toasted, just before chugging his drink and puckering his lips. He sat his glass on the end table between them. Nicole took a sip of hers and then set her glass next to Sean's. "Hey, I got a CD by this new band, "Ben Folds Five"... want to hear it?"

"Perhaps later," Nicole said as she made firm eye contact with Sean. "Sean, I have something I wish to relate to you."

Sean leaned back and raised his eyebrows. "Really? Sounds serious. Something about how hard it is to come live in the middle of nowhere?"

"Not exactly," Nicole answered as she reached into her backpack and pulled out a tiny electronic device. She pressed a button, and a miniature screen lit up. "You see, I am not actually from New York." She pressed another button and glanced at the screen. "As you hear what I say, you may have the urge to be frightened, but I assure you that no harm will befall you."

Sean leaned forward; his brow furrowed. "What are you talking about? What's that thing?" He tried to reach over to her, but fell back. "What the..."

"Do not panic, I simply needed a slight impairment of your mobility until I could complete my explanation."

"My mobility?" Sean tried to rock forward, but fell back again. "*What did you do?*"

"Sean, you are unharmed. I added nanites to your drink. They executed two separate tasks, neither of which will cause you any long term harm. As you have discovered, one of the tasks was to inhibit the motor skills needed to make your lower body move as you wish."

"What the hell?" Sean shouted. "Who *are* you? *What* are you? Some kind of space alien? Oh crap, you're going to experiment on me, aren't you? Am I being abducted? Kevin was right! You *are* the *evil twin!* You're not going to eat my brain, are you?"

"Please, calm down and listen. I am not going to harm you, and I am *not* a space alien. I was born on this planet, just as you were," she said as she moved the tiny device closer to Sean's head. "Verifying... yes, the second group of nanites reports they are in place. The next phase is best-explained visually. Look at me, please."

Nicole touched a place on her neck, and she became blurry. Sean shook his head, not believing his eyes, which rapidly widened. Alexis sat where Nicole had been.

"And again," she said as she touched the spot on her neck again. Another little blur and Aunt Kathrine was sitting where Nicole/Alexis had been. She smiled, and touched her neck and became Nicole again. "I believe you prefer to be with Nicole." She glanced again at the device in her hand. "I assure you, I was born on this planet... well, from your perspective I *will* be born on this planet. I am from the 23rd Century."

"What *are* you? Are you like a T-1000? You are, aren't you? You're a shapeshifter and hunting me down. I'm like John Connors, and you have to kill me, right?"

Nicole glanced away, then back at Sean, looked a little puzzled and glanced away again. "I apologize; I am experiencing difficulty interpreting what you just said. Are you making reference to characters in a movie... *Terminator?*"

"*T-2... Judgment Day,*" Sean corrected, "I somehow stop the robots in the future from taking over, and you've come back to destroy me, so it never happens."

"Again, I apologize, I was not prepared to know the entirety of the popular culture from this time-period. Allow me a few more seconds as I assimilate the movie you have mentioned." She looked away again for several seconds and then looked back with a curious smile. "My goodness, I had no idea meeting someone from the future would invoke such bizarre thoughts. I am not a robot or android, nor on a mission to alter the future. Quite the opposite. I take great care to make sure that I do *not* contaminate this time-period. Even your knowledge of my identity could change the future."

"So you *are* going to have to terminate me," Sean howled.

Nicole looked genuinely surprised. "No, Sean, if I terminated you I would nullify my own existence. *You* are my great-great-great-great-great-grandfather."

"But, you said I couldn't know about you, but I already do... so...wait... great-great-great-great-grandfather?"

"No, you missed one generation. Regardless, you *will not* remember any of this. That is the second nanite task. They released a chemical in your brain that will inhibit you from transferring any short term memories into long term memories. When you next sleep, you will wake up with no memory of any of this. Oh, and if you do not mind, I would prefer to drop all disguises."

Nicole tugged on her long auburn tresses and pulled her 'face' off over her head, revealing short black hair. Another push on her neck and her form changed again. This time her curves disappeared, and 'she' was sitting there in a silvery skin-tight suit that now covered a masculine body.

"You're not even a girl?" Sean gasped.

"No, sorry for that layer of subterfuge, but it seemed the best strategy to gain a close association with you in a short time-span."

"And Alexis… you're Alexis, too? And you're your own aunt?"

"Alexis was a miscalculation. My intent was to design her to be very attractive to you. I based her appearance on the woman who you will eventually marry... regressed to your current age, of course."

"*Marry?!?!* Alexis is my *wife?*"

"That is an oversimplification, and not entirely accurate. Alexis has a close approximation of the physical appearance of the woman you will eventually marry, regressed to age sixteen. My miscalculation was that at this age, you would be predisposed to an attraction to Alexis. Of course, the *physical* aspect is not all there is to forming a relationship. I believe I also made some social mistakes that further limited your attraction to Alexis. During the time you assumed Alexis was in New York, I conducted further research that would make 'Alexis 2.0' –Nicole– more appealing to you. She is a little more voluptuous, has longer darker hair and green eyes, and is an amalgamation of some of the girls you currently know and find attractive. I gathered data from your brainwaves. I should explain that today is not the first time that you ingested nanites. There were some in Aunt Katherine's brownies. I also did a study of what scents you found stimulating and developed a perfume that you would find alluring."

"And I appreciate you taking the extra effort to study me and dope me up with future-infested food and drink," Sean spat.

"That tone in your voice… that is sarcasm? It is difficult for me to understand sarcasm, but it seems to be integral to 20th Century teen-aged conversation. I find this a fascinating era."

"I'm so glad to be entertaining," Sean said dryly, "and yes, sarcasm again, Future-Boy. So tell me about these nanite thingies. Was that what caused the tingling I felt last week?" The visitor from the future nodded. "Wait... that time Megan came up to me in the hall... that was *you*?"

"Yes, that was the final test of the perfume I formulated, including pheromones to enhance physical attraction. I selected the guise of Megan for that test, since it is apparent you typically have negative feelings for her."

"No wonder she thought I was nuts," Sean sighed. "OK, if you're not a killer robot, what *are* you doing here?"

"Research. You might be surprised by the number of people from your future observing the 19th, 20th and 21st Centuries. Scholars find the acceleration of change and exponential increases in knowledge as well as social upheavals from these three centuries fascinating to study. Most observe in cities on either coast of this continent, however, as my ancestors in this time-period are primarily from the middle of the continent; my research is somewhat unique."

"So, you're telling me you've come to watch me like some lab rat? The whole Alexis throwing herself at me and Nicole needing math help… all just to get close enough to paralyze me and do some sick experiment?"

"I am not going to experiment on you, Sean. We cannot do anything to anyone in the past for fear of changing our present… your future. All research is by observation only."

"Then what's with the drugged smoothie? If you just want to observe me and this time-period, you could have just walked around shapeshifting to your heart's content, and no one would ever catch on that you were some future freakazoid on a field trip."

"Technically, the nanites are not drugs. They paralyzed you by inhibiting electrical signals from your brain to your lower nervous system. The chemical that inhibits your brain from storing your experiences into long-term memory is found within your own body… merely manipulated like your nervous system."

"Easy for you to say. *I'm* the one with little robot spiders running around inside me. I'll bet you wouldn't be so calm if you had them in *you*."

"Actually I do. By the late 22nd Century, medical nanites replaced all other forms of disease prevention and body rejuvenation that had previously been developed. Everyone from my time has nanites in their body, they augment several natural systems."

"Seriously? And they don't ever malfunction and shoot sparks or go crazy and try to take over your brain?"

"You obviously have no understanding of the technology. Nanites vary in size from one-tenth to one-fourth the size of a human red blood cell. It takes hundreds of them working together to accomplish even simple tasks. A single nanite malfunction would drop it out of its work-group... and they do not 'spark' or try to 'take over your brain.' They are too simple to have any individual higher artificial intelligence."

"Still, pretty creepy," Sean complained.

"Everyone accepts the technology available in their formative years as normal. Would you not think that if you told someone from 250 years into your past about how you use microwave radiation to heat food that they would think it was 'creepy', or perhaps even some evil magic?"

"I guess I never thought about George Washington trying to use a microwave. OK, so creepy nanites aside. What do you *want* from me? And who *are* you... besides my great-great-whatever-great-grandson? I don't think I'm going to call you 'Nicole' anymore."

"In my home time-period, I'm usually addressed as 'LX', it is a shortened version of my longer designation, 'KLE1752-NI28-949-LX'. I have traveled to 1995 to observe you and this era for my research, but I also require your assistance for my next jump back."

"'LX', huh? I guess that's how you came up with 'Alexis.' How'd you come up with 'Nicole'?"

"Ah, well, you cannot say that people from the 23rd Century are devoid of humor. That is a humorous play on a part of my name as well... NI28."

Sean raised an eyebrow. "Wow, I'd probably be rolling in the aisles if I had any idea what you were talking about."

"NI and 28? Nickel. From the Periodic Table? Element number 28 and the abbreviation Ni? So, Nickel is close to a common name from your century—Nicole. Do you not find that ironically humorous?"

"You bet, brainiac, that's a total crack-up. I'd love to see what a stand-up comedian from your time is like." Sean's voice continued to drip with sarcasm. "And your 'Aunt Katherine' disguise? Where did you come up with that?"

"Ah, that is different. Katherine is the most common female name of all of my known ancestors. It just seemed that a matriarchal identity needed a matriarchal name."

"OK... I suppose that since I don't want to just call you 'Future-Boy' and I'm *not* going to call you 'grandson', I'll need to call you something," Sean declared. "How about I use 'Alex', since that's close to your real letters...numbers...designation thingy?"

"I find that acceptable." Alex checked the tiny screen on his nanite interface. "It appears that your heart-rate is slowing, and your blood pressure is dropping back to a normal range. Perhaps you have decided that I am not going to 'eat your brain'?"

"Well, I guess if you were going to kill me, you could have easily done that by now. And other than not having control of my legs, I guess your little 'bugs' you put in me don't seem to be doing any damage. I'm still not so sure that I won't wake up from a crazy dream any minute now. Wouldn't *you* find it a little crazy if someone from your future dropped in on you?"

"I would not, since in fact, they already have. Since we are aware that time-travel is possible, we can logically expect someone from our own future to visit their past to gather historical information as we do. They do not have to keep their presence a secret, however, any information that did not already exist in my own time cannot be revealed. They excel at time-contamination procedures, as one might expect; they have had generations of experience to draw upon."

Sean's eyes lit up a little. "So, can you go visit them in *your* future? That would be so cool to see what kind of cool stuff gets invented."

"No, I cannot travel forward past my own time-period without the assistance of someone from further in the future. Beginning with your generation, I also must have the assistance of someone from my past to accurately extend further into the past. Besides, no one could observe their own future without having some effect on their present. The possibilities of creating a cataclysmic paradox would keep anyone from the future from voluntarily taking someone forward from their home time-stream."

"Cata-para what now?"

"Obtaining knowledge from the future could cause something to come into reality before it historically should. That creates a paradox, or at least it could. Suppose that you took something as simple as a 20th Century cargo aircraft to the early 19th Century and merely dropped food, water and other supplies to Napoleon's troops in their effort to invade Russia. They would not even need to know that someone from their future was assisting them. Nor would they even require weapons from the future. Something as simple as supplying provisions to the invading army could have caused the French to be successful in their campaign. A 'miracle' happens for them, from something that you consider to be a normal function in your own era. That small 'miracle' allows Napoleon's empire to expand, last longer, and from that point forward, governments would change. Some soldiers who historically died in battle would then live, and perhaps sire children that historically could not exist. Other people who lived, are instead killed, and their children who should have been born will never be. The changes that ripple forward into time could alter history so drastically that the political climate in the mid-20th Century could become even more charged. With those changes, the restraint from using nuclear weapons might not occur, and the entire Earth might then become a glowing dead ball circling the sun. You would never exist. Therefore, I would never exist. That is an example of a cataclysmic paradox."

Sean's eyes were saucers. "Wow. Extra groceries for Napoleon ends the world. Scary stuff," he ventured. "OK….I guess asking for a little trip into your time isn't going to happen then, hmmm?"

"I am sorry, Sean, no. Regardless, you will not remember meeting me or having this conversation. Simply knowing about me could alter your future, and therefore change my past."

"So, if that's the case, why are you even talking to me?"

"Primarily because I need your assistance to move back another generation in time."

"Of course you do. I'm sure my vast knowledge of 20th Century time-travel will be a great help to you. You'll probably be interested in all my theories about the Emmett BROWN flux capacitor." Sean threw his hands in the air. "What the hell are you talking about?"

"Ah, more sarcasm. I find it astounding how it seems to flow out of you as a natural form of conversation. If I were more of a linguist, I would want to do a long-term study of sarcastic communication. However, my primary focus is on how seemingly minor incidents contribute to future changes… as well as a little personal family history for my own amusement. But to answer why I need you, it is to obtain a DNA sample."

"DNA sample? Oh, I get it now; you're going to clone me and use the clone as spare parts in the future. So what you're not admitting is that the future is really radioactive, and everyone is sterile and you've got to bring DNA from the past to keep the human race from dying out."

"Sean, while I am aware from historical records that you were described as an avid fan of the Science Fiction genre, I had no idea that it influenced your ordinary thought processes. I am not taking your DNA to the future. I need it as a guidance system for my travels to the further past."

"OK... not following you at all. *My* DNA is a guidance system? You're going to have to explain that."

"I will try. First, though, let me propose an analogy. Do you believe that you could explain to *your* great-great-great-great-great-grandfather how 700,000 pounds of metal, plastics, glass, rubber, humans, and their cargo can be accelerated to 900 kilometers per hour, lifted 8 kilometers into the atmosphere, use radar and other devices such as an altimeter to ensure that it all arrives from point A to point B safely... and have him understand it?"

"Great-great-great how many? How far back is that?"

"About the time that the steamboat was being invented. I am sure you would have no trouble explaining a turbojet engine, and the whole concept of thrust and lift to someone who finds traveling in a boat powered by boiling water innovative."

"OK, I get it. I'm too stupid to understand your time-machine."

"No, Sean, not stupid. Ignorant."

"Oh, *that* makes me feel so much better," Sean sneered.

"Ignorance does not mean that you cannot learn. It simply implies that you have not yet learned. My reason for citing that example was to point out that there are so many scientific complexities that happened over time between now and my time that are needed as background knowledge to understand time-travel. You *could* learn it if you were willing to devote the next five years of your life to studying mathematics and physics beyond what is known in 1995. Of course you would also require a teacher who understood it all and was willing to teach you."

"OK, *fine!* I won't understand what you tell me about time-travel."

"You may understand basic concepts, but for the intricate detail, it might be better for you to just assume that it is magic," Alex suggested.

"Magic. Great. So hit me with the caveman magic version of how time-travel works."

"Very well. Let us begin with the jet airplane model already mentioned. Some similar elements come into play. In both models, there is a force that needs to be overcome. With the aircraft, that force is gravity. With a time-machine, the force is the flow of time. In your time, you solve the gravity issue with enough power to provide thrust for an aerodynamic design that creates lift."

"In my time?" Sean interrupted. "You don't have jets in the future? Oh. My. Gosh… anti-gravity belts! Everyone has anti-gravity belts and just fly around like birds."

"Not precisely. Let us simply say there is a more efficient way to travel."

"You have *got* to be kidding!" Sean whooped, "You've got teleporters like *Star Trek*? You just beam from one place to another? That has got to be so cool. I'd *love* to try that."

"No. No teleporters, sorry."

"Then what?"

"Twentieth Century terminology that comes closest is a dimensional shift. The molecules of a particular object are shifted out of phase with regard to this dimension, and then with a power source and guidance system, the phased object can be moved in proportionately lesser distances in the alternate dimension which equate to much larger distances when re-entering this dimension. Those distances can be in either space or time or both, dependent upon the dimension one has shifted."

Sean squeezed his eyes shut. "I'm sure that's really awesome… but maybe you're right about the magic thing. Shift dimensions?"

"How many dimensions do you understand to exist?" asked Alex.

"Three. Height, Width, and Depth. Well, I suppose some consider Time a 4th dimension."

Alex nodded thoughtfully. "So, it appears quantum physics is not taught to students your age in this era?"

"Um… not that I know of… so I guess you were lying when you said you needed help with algebra."

Alex tilted his head slightly away and then back.

"It appears that physicists of your time-period have formed theories about 6, 10, 11 and 26 dimensions, with no concrete evidence of any beyond four at this time. You need to accept that there are multiple dimensions in time similar to the way there are the three dimensions of space. We phase directly into another dimension, move slightly relative to that dimension, but emerge back to the original dimension a great distance in either time or space."

"How can moving a small amount equal moving a big amount?"

"Relativity. To begin, let us only deal with physical distance without moving in time. For example, suppose you were standing on the Earth's equator and had the ability to become dislodged from physically standing on the planet. At the equator, the spin of the Earth is approximately 1670 kilometers per hour. If you were simply able to remain dislodged for 15 minutes..."

"So you were born somewhere in Europe?" Sean interrupted.

"No," replied Alex, "and my place of birth in not relevant to this discussion."

"You keep saying kilometers... so I figured you're from Europe."

"The unit of measurement is not important for this example."

"Then do it in miles, if it's not important," Sean challenged.

Alex's head twitched slightly. "Very well. At the equator, the spin of the Earth is slightly more than 1000 miles per hour. If you were simply able to remain dislodged for 15 minutes..."

"See, miles per hour is a nice round number," Sean said smugly.

"Actually, without rounding *down*, we would be dealing with 1037.69 miles per hour," Alex returned with equal smugness. "If I may continue?"

Sean shrugged.

"If you were simply able to remain dislodged for 15 minutes, you would be 250 miles west of your point of origin, without expending any energy beyond what is initially needed to dislodge."

"I move 250 miles west by standing still?" Sean questioned.

"Yes, if you free yourself from the Earth's rotation, in 15 minutes that rotation would move the spot you *were* standing on 250 miles to your east. Thus, you would be 250 miles west. Of course, this assumes you are breaking free only from the Earth's rotation on its axis, and not also from the Earth's orbit around the sun. If you dislodged completely, you would be almost 17,000 miles away from the Earth, exploding in the vacuum of space, assuming you were devoid of a pressurized vehicle or spacesuit."

Sean's eyes glazed over.

"The speed of Earth's orbit around the sun is about 67,000 miles per hour," Alex added.

"So, if I completely come loose from the Earth, in 15 minutes I'm 250 miles west and 17,000 miles into outer space?"

"As long as you also assume that you remain in relativity to the sun. If not, we would also need to calculate the speed that Sol is rotating around the center of the galaxy."

"No, let's not calculate that!" Sean closed his eyes and waved his hands. "OK, so I just accept that you've got a way to move tiny distances in another dimension and translate that into big jumps of space or time." He curled his lip. "I think I'm feeling better about the magic explanation."

"That is probably a good compromise. It would take too long to explain even using elementary and broad terms."

"So… why don't you just show me?" Sean suggested.

"Show you? Show you what?"

"Take me on a little trip in your magic space/time-ship."

Alex frowned. "That would not explain the process."

"Sure," Sean insisted, "learning by first-hand experience."

"And if you were to allow someone from 200 years in your past to ride in your automobile, that experience would teach them about internal combustion engines?"

"No," Sean argued, "it would teach them what it was like to drive a car. Not really necessary to understand the mechanics of the engine to understand how transportation in a car works. They'd observe the steering wheel, the accelerator, and the brakes. They'd see the scenery passing by at 60 miles per hour, and after awhile they'd just get a feel for it."

"You believe you would 'get a feel' for time-travel simply by experiencing it?" Alex asked.

"Sure, I could watch what you do, and watch time go whizzing by backwards, and, you know, get a feel for the whole scene. I could probably learn how to run your ship just by watching for awhile."

Alex stared at Sean in disbelief. "Your rationalization will not work, but I am willing to take you on what you would call a 'short hop.'"

"Really? That's awesome!" Sean enthused, "So do we have to stay on Earth? Could we hop to the moon and maybe watch Apollo 11 land? That'd be way cool."

Alex's brow furrowed. "I must not correctly understand your idiom 'short hop.' You consider twenty-six years and 385,000 kilometers to be a 'short hop'?"

"Well, *I* don't, but I figured that *you* did."

"I do not," Alex corrected. "I will counter-suggest no change in space and perhaps a few weeks in time. Think back, was there any time in the past few weeks that you had an intense sensation that someone was watching you?"

"I take it you don't mean when Alexis was stalking me?"

"I did *not* stalk you," Alex snapped. "But yes, more of an eerie sensation."

Sean began slowly nodding. "Yeah, a couple of months ago, when I was shooting hoops at night, I had kind of a creepy feeling that something was watching me. Was that you?"

"The reaction was actually to your own self... but I am certainly going to have been there as well."

"Did you just say, 'going to have been there'? I'm not a language expert, but that doesn't sound grammatically correct."

"And yet it is since it is Future-Past-Tense."

"Future-Past-Tense? Not Future Tense, or Past Tense... but Future-Past-Tense?"

"That is the best way to describe an event that has already happened relative to now, but since we have yet to experience it in our linear time-stream, it is also yet to happen. Or taking it just from your current perspective in your time-stream, the event is in your past as well as your future. The past you *has* experienced it, and the future you is *going* to experience it."

Sean closed his eyes with a pained expression. "OK... ummm... let's seriously go back to the idea that it's just magic and that I'll think it's really cool."

"It is good that you have come to accept your ignorance," Alex remarked.

"I think it would be *better* if you would stop calling me ignorant."

"Would uneducated or unlearned be more acceptable?"

"No... let's leave me out of this," Sean insisted. "You do magic, and I think it's cool, OK? You don't have to refer to me as ignorant or stupid or a caveman or anything. I'm just a sci-fi fan who thinks this is cool." Sean glared at Alex for a couple of seconds. "So how far away is your time-machine?"

"Less than a kilometer from here... or 'a couple of blocks' as you might say. It is in the back yard of 'Aunt Katherine's' house."

"Yeah... that's another thing. How'd you manage that? Getting a house and all?"

"Do you really want a full explanation, or would 'magic' suffice?"

"Well, I might want the details later," Sean decided, "but for now, let's go take a wild ride into the past."

"Very good. It is only a short walk from here."

"Yeah... speaking of walking... that would be nice to be able to do that again."

"Of course. One moment."

Alex adjusted his hand-held device.

"Owww," Sean complained, "What's the deal? It feels like my legs are all prickly, like when circulation is cut off, and your leg falls asleep."

"It is merely a side effect of re-establishing the electrical impulses. It should be very short in duration."

Sean stood up and swayed slightly before he recovered his balance.

"That feels better. OK, let's do this!" He turned to the dog. "Maggie... back to the basement for you, girl."

"It would be best if I resume my appearance as Nicole," Alex commented, "in the event we meet anyone along the way."

Maggie reluctantly went through the door that Sean opened for her while Alex pulled his 'face' back over his head and pushed the hidden nub on his neck. He shimmered briefly as he changed his appearance to Nicole.

Sean and 'Nicole' went out the front door, and Sean turned to lock it. As he slid his keys into his pocket and stepped off the front step, he paused and looked back at the lock, and then to Nicole.

"So, do you lock your doors in the future?"

"In a sense," Nicole related, "Each home can detect anyone attempting to enter, and allow access to those that are in the database. If the person is unknown, the house computer requests of someone in the home to validate the person wishing to enter. If they are not validated, the house will not allow them entry. My own home is even less approachable."

"That is so freaky that you sound like Nicole again. Is that hard to do?"

"I do not have to *do* anything," Nicole replied, "The voice modulator in the suit alters the pitch of whatever I say to fit the designed voice for Nicole. I could disengage it if you preferred."

"Nah, that'd probably be freakier to have you look like Nicole and sound like Future-Boy... I guess I'll just be taking a walk with Nicole. Hey, did you know that you're a *lot* less cute now that I know who you are?"

"My appearance as Nicole has not changed. It is only your perception, which is probably driven by your heterosexual machismo that refuses to allow you to think that another male is attractive. Therefore, Nicole is less attractive, since you now know that I am male."

Sean frowned. "Do you have a phrase in the future that would translate, 'shut the hell up'?"

Nicole smiled. "Sean, I believe I could study you for years and not begin to understand you."

"Right," grunted Sean, "More walking…less talking."

"But there is so much I still want to know about you."

As they reached the first corner, Sean noticed a couple of guys down the block to their left. One was wearing a lavender T-Shirt, and the other one, in a blue shirt, seemed to be waving at them. They were too far away to tell if it was anyone he knew, and he didn't really care, he was far more interested in getting to the time-machine than talking to someone on the street.

"What do you want to know about me?" Sean asked, "Don't you have it in some computer history book about me?"

"While it is true that there is a great deal of data about your life, it is quite different for me to experience being with you."

"So, did you memorize a bunch of stuff about me and about this time-period? And how come you seem confused about stuff for a minute and then seem to know all about it? You quote stuff almost like it was an encyclopedia entry."

"I have researched this time-period and what information I can find about you, but it is difficult to limit what I know about you to only 1995," Nicole explained, "Remember, in my time, you have lived your entire life. And since there are various nuances of data, I cannot have memorized everything. I have a link to my computer for help with your odd references, such as your *Terminator* references. While I am certain that many people your age in 1995 know all about those movies, I have more references to Arnold Schwarzenegger as the Governor of California."

Sean laughed. "I think you've got your actor/politicians mixed up. Maybe you mean Ronald Reagan?"

Nicole tilted her head slightly to the side.

"My error. I am off a few years… but he *will* be the Governor of California."

"You've got to be kidding me," Sean blurted, "Are you sure it's the same guy? Bodybuilder. Action Movie Hero. Foreign accent. He becomes a Governor?"

"I find it intriguing that in the late 20th and early 21st Centuries there are many people in the entertainment industry that become elected to some level of government. That is one of the more fascinating things about this era, the majority of the populous seem to align celebrity with leadership qualities."

"OK, you said that you can look up stuff that you don't already know on your computer, but you don't have time to do that. You just seem to suddenly 'know' this stuff."

"It is a relay link, reliable up to about 10 kilometers," Nicole explained.

"You're losing me again."

"I make queries of the computer in my vehicle. There is still a considerable amount of radio bandwidth available in 1995; your fascination with cellular telephony and constant connection to others and the internet are still a few years away. My base computer is loaded with all data related to the late 20th century and early 21st century, including obscure popular culture references."

"OK, but you don't use a keyboard or a mouse," Sean argued, "or even use voice commands. So how do you look stuff up on your computer?"

"Oh… sorry, it is all such an integral part of me that I forget it is something you would not understand. I have a cyber-interface in my brain. I can link directly to the information I need by mentally forming a particular query. The computer dumps the data back to the interface, and it feeds it into my consciousness. It is nearly instantaneous. It takes a little longer to absorb audiovisual material. The most efficient way to assimilate some of the information about your *Terminator* movie was to upload parts of the movie to my brain."

Sean stopped in his tracks. Nicole stopped within a couple of steps and turned back to him.

"What is wrong?" she asked.

"You download movies into your brain?" Sean marveled.

"I could, but in this instance only scenes that were relevant to what you were talking about."

"But you could watch them in your head?"

"It is not exactly watching them; it is more of a memory of watching them. I did not have them projected onto my retinas, just into my visual memory."

Sean's jaw dropped. "You remember seeing a movie that you've never seen?"

"Although that phrasing makes it sound paradoxical, I suppose you could put it that way."

Sean stood silently for a few moments before a big grin slid across his face.

"That is *so awesome!*"

Nicole reacted with puzzlement.

"OK," Sean continued with enthusiasm, "so this summer's big *Batman* movie. You can download that into your head?"

"If I so desired. Can you clarify which of the various titles you refer?"

"*Batman Forever*.... Wait.... How many more are there?" Sean yelped, "What's the next one called?"

Nicole tilted her head away and then back.

"*Batman & Robin*. It is not as financially successful," Nicole advised. "Interesting. The name Arnold Schwarzenegger again."

"No Way!" Sean gushed, "Arnold as Batman?"

"No, he characterizes a villain. Mr. Freeze."

"OK, so you could download this movie into your head, even though it hasn't been made yet," Sean asked.

"Your perspective that it has yet to be made in this time-period is irrelevant. My computer was loaded over 200 years into your future."

Sean rolled the idea around his brain before speaking again. "So, is there any way *I* can see it?"

"See what?"

"The movie that hasn't been made yet... the one with Arnold," Sean clarified.

"Will you not simply go to your movie theater when the film is released?"

"No, I mean can I see it *now?* Can your computer play it on a monitor that I could watch?"

"Why would you wish to do that?" Nicole asked, "You will not remember seeing it."

"You are such a buzzkill," Sean growled. "It would still be cool to see."

They started walking again.

"Do you still have movies in the future?" asked Sean.

"We still have entertaining fictional stories, but the technology you speak of is no longer relevant. No one is interested in 2D passive entertainment."

"So, you have like holodecks, like in *Star Trek*?"

"Rather than attempt to explain the complexities of how it is different, I believe I will simply say 'yes.'"

Sean continued to press, "So, you've got all this cool stuff in the future, and you came back to my primitive time so you can see how boring it was?"

"Would you not find it interesting, and perhaps even somewhat entertaining to go 250 years into your own past and actually experience the life of one of your ancestors?"

Sean tried to imagine visiting the eighteenth century. "OK, I see what you mean. Yes, that would be incredibly cool," he agreed. "So, you're having *fun* doing this? I guess it's good to know that people in the future still have fun."

"Well, it *is* research," Nicole started, "but I did not claim it was boring research. Yes, Sean, it is 'fun.'"

They came to an intersection and waited until a car slowly passed by. Nicole started to cross the street but turned back when she noticed Sean wasn't moving.

"Now what is wrong?" she asked.

Sean stared off into space.

"Sean?"

His eyes slowly drifted back to meet hers.

"I just realized... I'm dead before you're even born," Sean murmured, though obviously lost deeply in his own thoughts.

"Yes," she acknowledged simply.

"And even my children are dead before you're born."

"That also is true."

"That's just kind of freaky. You're talking to someone who's been dead at least 100 years."

"No, I am talking to someone who is alive, 16 years old, and existing in the year 1995."

Sean shook his head. "But everything I've done," he argued, "everything I'll ever do is just history to you."

"You seem to find that emotionally distressing."

"My whole life... everything I've experienced so far. Is that even a paragraph to you?"

"Sean? Why are you becoming emotionally unbalanced?" There was concern in Nicole's voice.

Sean stared off into space again. He shook his head, put his hands on his hips. He looked down and then shook his head again then deeply sighed.

"I don't even know my great-great-great-grandfather's name. Let alone anything about his life. I think that everything I do is so important... but my whole life might be *nothing* to you."

"You should recognize that the ability to record events of individual lives becomes exponentially easier over time," Nicole asserted. "Your great-great-great-grandfather had little free time to record details about his life, and certainly did not have tools that made it easy even if he were so inclined."

"You don't get it," Sean complained, "I think I'm so important, and you're standing right here like some bizarre future mirror showing me that I'm nothing but dust from where your life exists. I'm totally insignificant."

Nicole paused, then took a step toward Sean. She put her arms around him and pulled herself closer.

"Grandfather Sean," she whispered almost tearfully into his ear. "You are *not* insignificant."

Another car rolled up to the intersection, and a teenage boy hung his head out of the window and yelled, "Hey! Get a room, you two! Woohooo! Hurry up and kiss her, Sean, or we'll miss it."

The car turned the corner and sped away, squealing tires as the sound of laughter moved down the street. Sean pushed Nicole away. His face flamed.

"So, I'm a big football star during my life, right?" Sean snapped fiercely. "Or win a Nobel Prize for literature? Oh, wait, I know, I become President of the United States."

"No... but that does not mean you are insignificant," Nicole said gently.

Sean took a deep breath and closed his eyes for a moment. When he opened them again, he forced both a smile and a breezy tone into his voice. "Do you even still have football in the future?"

Nicole was confused by his sudden change in demeanor. "Not in the way you know it," she said slowly, "It is a virtual game that some children play, but not a physical contest between people as it is in this time."

"Not physical, huh? How about hockey?"

Nicole started to answer and then paused to give Sean a long look. "You wish to change the subject because you are embarrassed that I hugged you. I am sorry my actions were inappropriate."

Sean stepped off the curb and moved quickly across the street. Nicole had to run a few steps to catch up. "Sean, I sincerely apologize. I allowed my emotions to overcome me for a moment. You seemed to be irrationally morbid about your significance; I felt I should do something to comfort you. We are not all without feelings and emotions in the 23rd Century, but I am sorry my reaction was not helpful."

Sean paused again. He put his hands in his pockets and shrugged his shoulders. "Ah, don't worry about it....*Grandson*... I just freaked out a little. I'm OK now." He turned to her with a stern look. "But no more hugs, OK? Let's get to your time-machine before those clowns in that car circle back around."

Sean started off again at a brisker pace. Nicole pulled up beside him and matched his speed. "Do you believe me when I say that you will not have any knowledge of me as someone from the future, or remember anything that we are doing today?"

"I guess so. Seems kinda crazy, but no more than traveling in time I suppose."

"I still do not understand why it seems important to you to do this when you know you will not be able to remember it."

"Because I want to *feel* it. I want to *have* the experience. I want to *know* right now what it's like, even if I can't remember it in the future. I still have *now*. I can live in the now. You might be able to erase what I saw, but I can still experience *now*."

They turned up the sidewalk to 'Aunt Katherine's' house. Nicole put her hand on the doorknob and paused. She turned her face to look directly into Sean's eyes. "It truly is quite an experience to get to know you as a real person, Sean Kelly."

Sean looked away sheepishly. "Don't go getting mushy on me again, Future-Boy. Let's just go see that time-machine, huh?"

Nicole opened the door and stepped in, Sean a step behind her. He was surprised when Nicole shouted, "Aunt Katherine; I am home," but shocked when he heard the reply from upstairs.

"Up here, dear, putting away the laundry," came Katherine's voice.

"We have company. I brought Sean along," Nicole shouted.

"That is nice, Nicole, go on into the kitchen and get a snack, and I will be down later."

Nicole led the bewildered Sean into the kitchen.

"I thought you said *you* were Katherine and Alexis."

"I am," Nicole smiled.

"Then who was that?"

"The house."

Sean cocked his head and squinted one eye. "The *house?*"

"Yes, it is programmed to do simple conversations as any of the people who are programmed to live here. I addressed it as Katherine, so it answered in Katherine's voice. Listen." Nicole leaned out of the kitchen doorway. "Alexis, are you home?"

"What do you want, Nikki?" The voice from upstairs was now that of Alexis.

"I thought you might want to come down and talk to Sean."

"I cannot at this time. I am not suitably dressed."

Nicole came back into the kitchen and smiled at Sean. "Using only your audio perception, you are led to believe that all three of us are currently present."

"You've got a *seriously* cool house!" Sean gushed. "Hey, can I get one of those to talk to my parents while I sneak out of the house?"

"Perhaps the nanites are already affecting your memory. Do you not recall that I told you that you cannot have anything in this time-period that was invented in your future?"

"I'm just saying it'd be cool to use that way. You obviously don't appreciate a good scam."

"Let me show you one more variation." Nicole touched her neck and changed to Aunt Katherine and then called out through the doorway, "Nicole; Sean is here. Should I send him up?"

"*No way!* I am not *dressed*. Perhaps you could bring my blue jeans to me? They were in the dryer."

"Of course, dear." Katherine went to the laundry room and took a pair of blue jeans out of the dryer then headed upstairs. In a few minutes, Nicole came bounding down the steps. "Greetings, Sean Kelly, I am pleased you could come to my house. Did you decide you were willing to assist me with my algebra?"

"Ha, ha," Sean said dryly. "OK, neat parlor tricks and maybe you *do* have a sense of humor after all. I suppose if I didn't know the trick, I'd have been fooled by that transition."

"I have not previously used it to deceive anyone in this time-period and wished to test it."

"House," Sean spoke toward the ceiling, "make me a peanut butter sandwich."

"What are you doing?" asked Nicole.

"Seeing how much stuff the house can do. Can it make me a sandwich?"

"No."

"Pthththt… some future house. Can't even make a sandwich."

"This is a 20th Century house, augmented with a 23rd Century computer. Does your house make you a sandwich?"

"No."

"Then why would this one?"

"Because it'd be cool."

"I am beginning to detect a pattern," Nicole commented, "It appears 'cool' is paramount."

"Does your house in *your* time make sandwiches?"

"It is equipped to assemble simple meals, yes."

"That is sooooo awesome," Sean bubbled with enthusiasm.

"If you are hungry, I can prepare some food."

"By hand?"

"Yes."

"Well that's boring," Sean complained. "No, I'm not hungry. Just wanted to see something cool and futuristic." He bounced his eyebrows, "So, how about that time-machine?"

"It is out the back door, follow me." Nicole led Sean through a patio door that opened onto a small deck. He followed her down the steps into the back yard, where she turned back to him with crossed arms and an enigmatic smile. Sean stood beside her and looked all around the yard.

"So, is it disguised as a tree?" Sean finally asked.

"No. It has a pass through exterior coating that gives the illusion of near invisibility by projecting on all sides what you would see if it were not sitting there," Nicole explained.

"Wow, that's way cooler than a blue police box."

"Perhaps you are aware that many scientific designs are based on things first imagined in science fiction?" She quickly surveyed the adjacent houses. "Since there is no one around, I am going to change back to myself if you do not mind." Nicole touched her neck and pulled on her hair. As the upper mask came off, her body shimmered and became the silvery clad LX.

"Knock yourself out," Sean quipped.

Alex gave Sean a puzzled look. "How would becoming unconscious be pertinent?" He put up a hand to stop Sean from replying. "Never mind, it must be an idiom."

Sean gave the yard another scanning. "So, if it's invisible, how do you *find* it?"

Alex took three steps forward and reached out a hand over what appeared to be thin air. With a slight shimmer, a nondescript boxy shaped object about the size of a golf cart appeared.

"OK, so making your ride *look* cool obviously isn't important to you."

"It would not enhance the functionality. The size and shape accommodate two people as well as the computer system and the power interface. Since it is normally all but invisible, there is little reason to employ a decorative exterior." Alex moved his hand slightly and a door slid open. He slipped inside and called back to Sean, "You still wish to experience this?"

"You bet!" Sean said enthusiastically as he stepped through the opening. He found himself sitting on a lightly padded seat, cranking his head in every direction to try to take in the interior. "Kind of cramped, don't you think?"

"It is both sufficient and efficient. We will spend very little time in here, so there is no need for a design to make it more comfortable."

"Hmmm... so, no buttons, dials, slider bars, lights, switches, joysticks... How do you fly this thing?"

"Ready travel mode," Alex declared.

Suddenly a flat panel in front of them lit up with pictures, shapes, icons, boxes, bars and other symbols foreign to Sean. Alex put both index fingers on a box and pulled them apart. The box expanded and hovered in front of them, suddenly in 3D.

"Oh wow oh wow oh wow... that is *major* cool," Sean raved.

"It may interest you to learn that much of this technology is invented during your lifetime. It is refined over the years, of course, but it becomes a standard interface that people are comfortable with and continue to use. It is not unlike the steering wheel on your vehicle, which is the same general design as deployed on the Model T, but improved and enhanced over the decades."

"Sure. Whatever," Sean said dismissively, "Skip the history lesson, let's blastoff!"

"We do not 'blastoff', it is more of a gentle nudge," Alex corrected.

"Nudge? Come on, don't you have to get up to light speed and break some kind of time-barrier?"

"Not at all. It is more of a series of complex calculations, which the computer handles, followed by a series of inputs as to which direction we are going to slide dimensionally. The first step is to nullify gravity, so there are no friction points when we slip into another dimension."

Alex slipped both hands into the 3D display in front of them. Sean watched in awe as Alex's fingers flew, somehow creating new shapes and almost as quickly pushing them off the screen. Lines of mathematical equations scrolled across the screen and then he paused.

"Which is followed by briefly expelling air to separate the craft physically from the ground."

He touched a green icon and blinked his left eye multiple times in what Sean decided was some type of code. There was a sharp brief hiss.

"That's it?" questioned Sean, "You wave your hands around like some mad conductor, then start blinking your eye like you've got sand in it, and all you get is one little pffft? I suppose we're now defying gravity?"

"I would use the term 'nullifying' rather than 'defying,'" Alex proposed, "'Defying' has an almost arrogant connotation that sounds more aggressive than what we are actually doing."

"But we're flying… or floating, whatever?"

"We are approximately 30 centimeters above the surface of the Earth neither supported by any object nor thrusting against gravity as you would in your hovercraft."

"As if I had a hovercraft," Sean corrected.

"I did not mean you personally. I meant it as an example of how this could be simulated with 20th Century technology."

"Not that it wouldn't be awesome to have a hovercraft," Sean mused.

Alex put his hands around a small green cube and compressed it to one-tenth of its former size then flicked it to one of the far corners of the screen. He pulled a smaller red cube to the size of the one he had minimized, rotated each of the six sides to the front and blinked commands before moving to the next surface.

"Normally, this would take a few more minutes of calculations, but since we are vaguely assured that this was, as you claimed, 'a couple of months ago,' we can assume whatever 'short hop' I set for that approximate time will be correct."

"And why can we *assume* that?" asked Sean.

"Because you have already related that it happened. It is logical to assume that since we are looking to randomly travel to your past that the randomly selected time will be when it has already happened."

Sean blinked several times as he screwed his face up in concentration. "OK, so because it *already* happened, what we are about to do will *cause* it to happen?"

"Exactly."

"Because we *randomly* choose a time in my recent past, it goes to a specifically *known* time where an event happened, but is also *about* to happen, and that time coordinate doesn't have to be calculated because it's random?"

"Yes!" Alex confirmed, "I believe you are beginning to understand the concept."

"Hmmm… I thought I was just talking in circles," Sean confessed.

Alex nodded thoughtfully. "There *is* a circular nature to this particular event."

"OK," Sean posed, "What if I remembered *exactly* when this happened and told you the date and the time and place and everything?"

"Then I would have done more complex calculations to make sure that we arrived at or near those coordinates."

"Which is how you would normally do this?"

"Yes."

"And we will have ended up in the same place?"

"Approximately."

"OK, so after we *randomly* travel there, we would then be able to find out *when* it was, and then put in the complex calculations to arrive five minutes earlier and let's say 50 yards away, and then we could watch ourselves materialize from the future? Or wait, that would then be the past… or the past-future? Would it be past-future or future-past? I think I'm getting confused again."

"Perhaps it is time to employ the previously agreed upon strategy?" Alex suggested.

"Which is?"

"That you simply think of what I am doing as 'magic.'"

"That might make it easier on my brain," Sean agreed.

"And I do not believe that having three iterations of yourself at a single moment in time would be prudent."

"Why? What would happen?"

"It is possible that the three iterations of Sean would merge and create a Black Hole which would pull the entire solar system into itself."

Sean's eyes opened wide. "Whoa! Seriously?"

"No," Alex smiled, "I am merely pushing your leg."

Sean exhaled a huge sigh of relief but then crossed his arms, squinting an eye at Alex.

"*You*," said Sean sternly, "have a warped 23rd Century sense of humor."

"But I have observed that sarcasm, humor and attempting to fool others into believing that lies are truths seem to be important to teenagers in this century," Alex countered.

"Maybe..." Sean punched Alex lightly on the shoulder. "But don't give up your day job. And it's *pulling* my leg, not *pushing*."

"I fail to see how any manipulation of your leg equates to the idea of lying for the purpose of humorous trickery. However, I have made a mental note that it is *pulling*."

Alex pulled open a new series of cubes and boxes and methodically touched an icon in each of them in combination to blinked commands.

"Sean, I have now completed the sequence. Are you ready for departure?"

Sean looked around and over each shoulder.

"Don't you have some kind of seat belt or anything to strap in with?"

"The internal inertia of this cabin is null," Alex explained.

"What?"

"You will not need a seat belt. Your body will not move in any direction that is in opposition to the interior of this ship, therefore, you will not require restraint."

"So, I won't even be able to tell that we are traveling through time?"

"I did not say that," Alex said with a slight shake of his head. "Since this is your first experience..." His voice trailed off as he handed Sean a small sheet of plastic.

"Open this end and place the opening around your mouth, please. It will expand as needed."

"What is it?"

"It will contain expulsions from any reverse peristalsis that you may experience."

Sean stared blankly. He opened the bag, examined it, placed it over his mouth and then pulled it away, sending Alex an accusing look.

"A *barf* bag? You're giving me a *barf* bag?" Sean protested.

"Dimensional shifting often causes an imbalance to the novice traveler's equilibrium, experienced as nausea. It could be equated to how some people in your century react to air or sea travel."

"And people of 'my century' also ride roller coasters and other crazy stuff just to get that kind of thrill, so bring it on. I don't get seasick," boasted Sean.

"Will you keep the bag in your hand simply as a precaution?" Alex asked meekly.

Sean crossed his arms and delivered a stern look to Alex. Alex looked away.

"Fine," Sean huffed. "I'll humor you. I'll hold onto the bag."

"Thank you," Alex said softly, then shifted to lecture mode, "Before I initiate this final sequence, I will broadly attempt to explain what is about to take place. The most distressing portion of the sequence is during the actual shift into another dimension. Once there, we will travel a relatively short distance; which in reality is an interval of time in that dimension." He paused to assess Sean's grasp of the concept. "If you could observe it, it would appear to be a short distance of space since space and time do not operate in the same manner as they do in our home dimension. In this particular dimension, it is normal for time to flow backward, relative to our home dimension."

Sean's eyes were becoming glassy. Alex continued, "All of this takes place in a few heartbeats. However, the time may seem distortedly long to you, or it may seem instantaneous." He shrugged. "You cannot trust that any of your senses will deliver correct information to your brain. After repeated excursions into alternate dimensions, your synapses begin to adapt to process the experience correctly, but on your initial trip, it may appear very chaotic." Alex paused to give Sean a quick reassuring smile. "You are certain that you wish to continue?"

Sean sat quietly for a moment. His face was expressionless, lost in thought. Suddenly his eyes twinkled, and a big grin spread across his face. "Punch it!" he said excitedly.

Alex nodded, placed each index finger into the holographic control panel. He tapped a small cube with his right finger and blinked out a code as it drifted toward his left.

The instant the cube touched Alex's left finger, Sean was awash in a bright flash of colors. He saw every color he could identify as well as some he couldn't... and pitch blackness... all at the same moment. He heard a roar blare in utter silence. His skin felt like it was freezing hot. His fingertips tingled numbly. His tongue felt like an explosion of salty-sweet with bitter sourness. He smelled the delicious aroma of freshly baked bread waft through the foul stench of a sewer. He was upside down while right side up, violently spinning in a serenely calm motionlessness. The eternity of the experience was over in moments.

"We have re-entered our home dimension," Alex announced, "two months into your immediate past."

Sean was pale. He groggily looked in Alex's direction, then quickly pulled the bag against his mouth as his stomach erupted. The bag expanded to contain what was left of his smoothie.

Chapter Five

"I'd save every day like a treasure, and then / Again, I would spend them with you"

"SEAN? Can you hear my voice?"
mmmm
"Can you see me?"
Mmm-hmm
"Are you ready to sit up?"
Ummm... uh-uh.
Sean was flat on his back lying on the grass. Alex had knelt beside him.
"Are your senses returning to normal?"
"Define 'normal,'" Sean mumbled.
"'Normal' is based on long-term sensory observation which sets the standard by which other atypical occurrences are compared. Do your surroundings appear to be as you would expect them to be?"

Sean propped up on his elbows and looked around.
"Where are we?" he asked.
"What do you observe?"
"The backyard of your house?"
"Good. That is correct," Alex confirmed. "What else do you sense?"
"I feel a little hot."
"Yes. Good. What else?"
"The light is dim. I can't see as well as I should."
"Also good. Anything else?"
"I hear a buzzing in my ears. Don't tell me *that's* good. I know *that's* not normal."
"In this case, that *is* also normal," Alex assured him. "The sound you hear is *Hemiptera Auchenorrhyncha* collectively vibrating their tymbals to attract mates."

Sean stared blankly at Alex.
"I believe the common name you use is cicada."
Sean's stare persisted.
"You are warm," Alex continued unfazed, "because it is the hottest part of

your summer. The light appears dimmer because it is nearing sunset."

Sean sat up straighter and leaned toward Alex to look him in the eyes.

"It really worked? We traveled backward in time?"

"That is what you wanted to do, is it not?"

"Well, yes... but... I mean... Did you *see, hear,* and *feel* all those things that *I* did?"

"No. But then technically neither did you."

"What do you mean? I went through some pretty crazy stuff!"

"The phenomena you experienced was due to your body being shifted into another dimension. The shift has a curious effect on the brain, which attempts to find a familiar perspective to explain the observed occurrence. I warned you that it could be very distressful."

"You compared it to motion sickness. That was *nothing* like motion sickness. That was..." Sean's voice trailed off as he tried to replay the experience in his head.

"Yes?"

"I don't *know* what that was."

"It is rather indescribable," Alex suggested.

"OK, I get it. You didn't describe it to me because you *can't*. And neither can I." Sean refocused on Alex. "But, you didn't experience it like I did, did you? Why not?"

"Redundancy?" Alex shrugged. "Multiple trips seem to allow the brain to begin to accept that it does not need to interpret the phenomena as a known experience. One can also minimize the effect by employing a focal point at transition. You would adapt if you also made several trips."

"And how many more trips will I be taking?" asked Sean.

"I will return you to your normal time-stream. Your second –and last– trip should be less stressful than your first."

Sean got to his feet. "OK, now that we're here, let's go see this thing that already happened."

Alex stood with him. "What do you remember about that evening?"

"Not a lot, it was pretty normal, I was just in the driveway shooting some hoops, when suddenly I had this weird feeling that someone was watching me."

"We should approach your house and determine how close we can get before you react. I am referring to the other you, although *you* will also feel that same sensation that you have already felt. The past you... the present you will experience the same feeling."

"The present me?"

"Perhaps we should assign labels," Alex decided, "The you whom I am currently addressing, we will label 'present you', and the other you that we encounter we will refer to as 'past you,'"

"I can see why you didn't want there to be three of me at once," Sean exclaimed, "This is beginning to sound like that 'who's on first' routine."

Puzzled, Alex twitched a query to his computer.

"There is too much data to sift through for 'who's on first.' Do you have additional information?"

"Oh, it's some old comedy thing from like a million years ago. Three Stooges or Laurel & Hardy or Abbott & Costello or someone," Sean shrugged. "Maybe even the Marx Brothers... I don't really remember. Something my Dad had me watch one time 'cause he thought it was funny. I guess it was. It was in black and white, so it was like ancient."

Alex tilted his head again.

"Yes, now I have something. You consider the 1940s to be ancient? It *was* Abbott & Costello. It appears to be mistaken identity of players with odd names on a baseball team."

"I don't know," Sean shrugged.

"Third base," Alex announced.

"What?"

"What is on second," Alex declared.

"Who are you talking about?"

"Who is on first."

"Why are you doing this?"

"Why comes near the end of the comic routine. Your statement is out of sequence."

"What?"

"What is on second."

"OK, just stop," Sean shouted, "I don't want to replay the thing. I don't even know it."

"When you said, 'I don't know' I assumed that you were instigating a recitation of the comic routine. You employed a key phrase."

"You can be really weird sometimes," grumbled Sean.

"Since you initiated the reference, I thought you might be revisiting the comic wordplay. I was mistaken. My apologies," Alex said with a slightly frosty edge to his voice.

"Are you mad?"

"Are you questioning my sanity, or asking if I am angry?" Alex's voice was still icy.

"You are mad! Angry. Whatever."

"I may have reacted badly to your inference that I was 'weird.' I believe I have now recovered my emotional equilibrium."

"No. That's OK," Sean chuckled. "You can be mad at me for calling you weird. I'm just surprised when you show emotions. You act all Vulcan most of the time."

"I attempt to remain dispassionate, as any good researcher should, but I must admit I am confused by my reactions to being with you. Experiencing your daily life with you is considerably different from reading about your life. You elicit emotional responses from me that I had not envisioned."

"Would I be guessing right to say that you haven't spent time like this with one of my kids or grand-kids?"

"That is correct," Alex confirmed, "1995 is the first stop on my studies."

"Why me first? Why not go all the way back to wherever you want to start and move forward?"

"I need additional information to enter earlier time-periods successfully. *Your* generation is the first to have accurately recorded the data from your genome and store it in a database. I have to stop here until I can obtain a DNA sample from your father to make the next jump back."

Sean nodded and pointed a finger at Alex. "Yeah... you were starting to tell me about that earlier."

"Correct. I believe our conversation moved onto a tangent about dimensional shifting and never returned to the guidance system. A DNA signature is a traceable format that consistently moves through the space/time continuum. Scientists in the mid-twenty-second century discovered a way to use it as a beacon when traveling in another dimension... *will discover,* from your perspective. The signature is unique, so when entered in the computer of the dimensional vehicle, a path back into this dimension is clearly marked. Without it, the re-entry to this dimension could have unexpected results."

"So, without my Dad's DNA, if you tried to go further into the past you wouldn't be able to get back to here... Earth... this dimension... or whatever you want to call it?"

"Without a beacon, re-entry could be anywhere or any when. Not unlike sailing in the middle of the ocean without any form of guidance system," Alex explained.

"Yikes! You mean you'd be lost in some limbo place?"

"No. I can always map back to any other recorded DNA streams. I also drop a strong dimensional beacon wherever I leave, so I can always return to that exact time and space. I could not accurately re-materialize anywhere earlier than 1979 with the information I currently possess."

"So when we did this little two-month hop, we zeroed in using my DNA?"

"Yes."

"So you could follow my DNA back another 16 years?"

"Correct."

"And you already had my DNA code because it was in some database? Why's that?"

"During your later lifetime, it will become a routine medical procedure to map and store individual genomes. Initially, it was to study various strands with regard to medical conditions. A comprehensive database gave scientists the opportunity to compare across the entire population."

"So who came up with the wacky idea to use it for time-travel?"

"You might be pleased to learn that it was one of your great-grandchildren who developed a theory that eventually evolved into the DNA beacon."

"Really? One of *my* descendants invents time-travel?" Sean beamed.

"That is not what I said," Alex corrected, "I said she developed a theory that was adapted to use for the DNA beacon. She was using it as a medical linkage from generation to generation. It happened to be elemental when designing the DNA beacon, but she was not involved directly with the team who developed it."

"Still... pretty cool, huh? My great-granddaughter. So that would be what? Your great-great-grandmother?"

"In this case, my great-great-great aunt. You have several great-grandchildren. Only one links to me, and she was not the one."

"Oh...I guess I never thought of it that way. I guess being an only-child affects my thinking about getting from me to you."

"It is easier to follow the branches backward," Alex offered, "and I already have the recorded genealogy."

"OK, that's enough science and history for now... or should the thing about my great-granddaughter be called 'future-y'? Anyway... let's go find me! Or 'Past Me,' whatever."

"I still believe you will find it a little unsettling, but that is the purpose of this jump, so I am prepared to move to the observation point."

Sean looked at Alex with a critical eye. "Are you going like that?"

"Like what?"

"The shiny suit. Kinda screams 'Future-Boy'... or weirdo or something."

Alex tapped a spot on the left side of his neck, shimmered and then appeared to be wearing the identical blue jeans and light blue t-shirt that Sean was wearing.

"OK," Sean complained, "now we look like sadly mismatched twins. Can you at least change the color of the shirt or something?"

Alex changed the t-shirt color to green.

"Better," Sean grunted. "OK, let's go."

Sean headed toward the deck where they came out.

"You will be unable to go that way," Alex said.

"Why not?" Sean turned and caught up to Alex, who was already at the backyard gate.

"You will soon see why I am going this way."

They walked into the front yard. There was a realty sign near the driveway with a "sold" sign on top of it.

"As you can see, I have not yet moved into this house."

"I kinda forgot we jumped back a few weeks. I mean, seems like we just came out that back door, but I guess that won't happen for several weeks from now. Kinda weird to think about," said Sean. "I hope no one sees us and thinks we're trespassing."

As they headed back toward his house, Sean took in all the little differences not seen on the walk over to Alex's house. The grass was brown in the August heat. Summer flowers that were now in full bloom had already gone dormant on their earlier walk. Cars were parked in different places or not even on the street.

When they reached the last intersection before Sean's house, Alex stopped. "You realize that we cannot simply walk up to your house. Past-You is already there."

"Right," Sean acknowledged, then pointed to his left. "We can cross the street here, then go down the alley and then we'll cut between the Young's and the Peterson's houses. That will give us cover to reach the Wilson's hedge, which should get us close enough to see my driveway."

They carefully crept along the path that Sean had laid out, and crouched behind the four foot hedge across the street from Sean's house. They found a spot where they could peek through the hedge and see the driveway, as well as hear the sound of a ball bouncing. It was Sean, dribbling the basketball, shooting and getting his own rebound or retrieving the ball when it went through the net. They watched silently for a few seconds.

"Wow," Sean whispered, "I thought I was more athletic than that. I can't believe I just missed that easy hook shot, and I don't look as tall as I think of myself." He shook his head in disbelief. "You said this might be unsettling, but it's more like demoralizing. I obviously don't have a future in the NBA."

"At some point soon, the Past-You should become uneasy," Alex explained. "He/You will sense your other existence, although the Past-You will not know that is what he is sensing. Have you... Present-You... felt anything unusual?"

Almost as if cued, the Sean across the street stopped dribbling and held the ball. He looked all around before settling his focus across the street where Alex and Sean were crouched behind the hedge. The shadows of late evening were growing longer, and Past-Sean was becoming more uneasy.

"Is someone over there?" he called out. "Hello? Come on out."

Past-Sean cautiously started across the street.

"You did not tell me that you came over to investigate," Alex said in a quiet panic.

"I guess I forgot," Sean said with a shrug.

"We must attempt a silent retreat."

"No, we don't," Sean said confidently with a sudden grin. "I just remembered why I didn't make it across the street."

"Hi... excuse me," came a soft feminine voice from a few yards up the street, "can you tell me which way campus is from here? I think I might be lost."

A pretty, well-toned girl jogged up and stopped Past-Sean in the middle of the street. She wore a hot-pink sports bra with matching running shorts. Her skin glistened in the fading sunlight, a delicate sheen of perspiration.

"It's *her!*" Present Sean gushed, immediately slapping his hand over his mouth, hoping his loud whisper hadn't carried to the street. When he removed his hand, his face framed a goofy grin. "How could I have forgotten this was the night that *she* came along?"

Sean refreshed his vision of the goddess in pink. Her long blonde hair was pulled back into a simple ponytail. Her running shoes were also a matching pink, including the little pink puff balls on the back of her shoe-height socks. She was trim and alluringly muscled with a flat belly that showed just a trace of abdominal ripple. Past-Sean's mouth dropped open as he stared at her.

"Oh, that is *disgusting*," Sean whispered to Alex, "I can't believe I... he... so blatantly checked her out. Now he's... I'm... just staring at her boobs. What a jerk! It makes me sick seeing what a dork I am from this side of me."

"Hi. My eyes are up here?" She held a hand near her face and snapped a finger. "So... do you know which way it is back to campus?"

Alex tapped Sean's shoulder lightly. "I must depart," he whispered, "remain here until I return."

Crouching low, Alex crept back along the hedgerow and disappeared between the two houses into the alley.

Past-Sean snapped out of his trance and blushed when he looked up at the girl's face. "Um, sure, it's that way," he said while pointing toward his house. "You just go back down this street the way you came and then take your first left. Keep going for about four blocks, and then kind of veer off to your left some more. You should see the edge of campus then."

"Thank you," she said, then turned on a brilliant smile. "Could I trouble you for some water, I need to re-hydrate."

"Um, yeah, sure. Let me go into the house and get some."

Past-Sean nearly tripped up the steps as he stared at her over his shoulder. "I hope tap is OK. I can put some ice cubes in it."

As Past-Sean went into the house, the girl turned her gaze to the hedge where Present-Sean crouched. She started directly over to him. Sean held his breath as she walked up to and around the hedge and stood over him. He sheepishly looked up to her, then stood, making sure his eyes stayed above her chin.

"Um... I'm not a peeping tom, if that's what you think."

"No," she replied, "I think we only have a few minutes to vacate this spot."

"Um... I can't," Sean stuttered, "I'm... uh... waiting for my friend to get back."

"You do not know who I am?" The blonde pulled on her ponytail and her "face" slid up to reveal Alex. "We *do* still need to have departed before Past-You returned with the water."

"*Nooooo!*" Sean closed his eyes and slammed his fists against his temples. "Have I met *any* girls in the past two months that are *not* you?"

They had slipped between the houses and part way down the alley before Sean spoke again. "OK, so... wait... I'm confused. You were still with me when the other you came running up as the hot chick. *Then* you left. Like maybe three minutes ago, and then the other you came over from the street and now we're following where you left just a few minutes ago." He paused as he tried to make sense of what he had said. "Are we going to catch up with you if we run?"

"No," Alex assured him.

"Also... before we get back to the sidewalk... could you switch your body back? That hot-girl body with your head on it is freaking me out. And I hope you realize you have *totally* destroyed one of my favorite fantasies."

Alex stopped a moment and adjusted the controls on his neck. He shimmered briefly then reappeared in jeans and a blue T-Shirt.

Sean pointed to his shirt. "Ummm... the twin thing?"

"What 'twin thing'?"

"Remember, you changed your shirt color so that we weren't dressed identically?"

Alex rolled his eyes as he pressed the neck control again. His shirt started randomly rotating through a rainbow of colors. "Let me know when I have achieved an acceptable color."

"That sounded kind of sarcastic... and did I see an eye-roll?" Sean slapped Alex on the back. "See, you *can* learn how to fit in."

Alex released the control and his shirt color stopped on lavender. He looked thoughtfully at Sean.

"It was unintentional to speak sarcastically, and I was not aware that I rolled my eyes." He paused, deep in thought, then continued, "It just... *happened.* I should make a note of this for my research," he said enthusiastically. "Is it possible that I am adapting your ways simply by cultural immersion?"

Sean shook his head in disbelief, then started off at a trot. "Come on," he said over a shoulder, "Let's try to catch the other you. It'll be fun!"

"But we did *not* catch the other me. I would know if we had."

"Let's try it anyway." Sean quickened his pace, and Alex lagged after him. Alex was several seconds behind when he caught back up to Sean at the gate to the back yard. Sean pointed into the back yard.

"I just saw the other you close the door... and check it out! There are *two* time-machines."

Alex was puffing as he pulled up next to Sean. "It appears... that we *did*... make it here... before I completed... the calculations to jump," he wheezed.

"Dude. You are out of shape! Not enough exercise in the future?"

"We *do* have routines to keep our physical bodies... in good working order," Alex said between deep breaths. "However, when I exert myself... while exercising I have a controlled... environment. This heat, humidity and oxygen level is more... stressful than the environment to which I am accustomed,"

"Right," Sean said as he crossed his arms, "Sounds like a lame excuse to me." He turned back to the backyard. "Whoa! Check it out! The first ship is levitating."

The shimmering shape rose about 5 feet off the ground, and for a moment, the boxy time-ship became fully visible. There was a soft *whuft* and the ship disappeared completely.

"That was pretty awesome," Sean declared, "except for the sound effects. That was kind of wimpy. Just a little poofie sound. You need some dramatic sound effects for a really cool take-off."

"There are *no* sound effects," Alex insisted. "Shifting into another dimension would be completely silent if not for the simple fact that a vacuum is created when the ship leaves this dimension. That sound you heard was the air rushing in to fill the void that was created."

"Still…. Kinda wimpy."

When Alex had no reply, Sean continued, "OK... so, how about explaining why there were *two* time-machines sitting in the yard?"

"There were *not* two," corrected Alex, "It was merely two iterations of the same object overlapped from two segments of the time-stream. It is no different than there being two Seans and two of me in existence at the same time."

"Yeah, well there was two of *me* because you used a time-machine to drag me back here, and I was already here. But there's only *one* time-machine. Why would I see two?"

Alex crossed his arms; a look of exasperation darkened his face. He spoke slowly enunciating each syllable, "Let us call the time when we initially arrived 'Event Zero.' Let us also call what you just saw –the ship vanishing– Event Zero plus 30 minutes. The vehicle that you just saw vanish had occupied that spot for the 30 minutes spanning Event Zero to Event Zero plus 30 minutes. I needed to arrive in time to distract Past-Sean from crossing the street to Present-Sean at Event Zero plus 20 minutes."

Sean scrunched his eyes tightly shut and forced a single nod at the end of each sentence.

Alex continued, "I arrived at EZ plus 10 minutes, which allowed enough time to prepare my appearance and to get into position. Since the ship was sitting there for the 30 minutes spanning EZ to EZ+30, I had to park the ship as it arrived at EZ+10 *behind* the iteration of the ship already in place, thus for 20 minutes they coexisted in the same time-stream."

Sean kept his eyes shut tightly. He moved one fist over top the other, shook his head slightly, and then interlaced his fingers. He pondered that configuration for a moment then shook his head again. He then grabbed his left wrist in his right hand and his right wrist in his left hand. He grimaced, chewing the left corner of his lower lip. He opened his right eye, and with head slightly askew, he opened his left eye to look dubiously at Alex.

"OK… got it," he finally said as he dropped his grip on his wrists, "So… now what? Shall we get back to the future? Well… *my* future, not *your* future. I don't want to be late for dinner."

"That will not be a problem," Alex replied just a bit smugly as he crossed the short distance to the remaining craft. The door slid open, and he motioned for Sean to enter. Alex slid in beside him.

"So, I guess it looks the same," Sean ventured, "I guess it's *not* a different time-machine. Still seems a little weird. And with all these little jumps you're making, are you sure the battery is charged up enough for another hop?"

"Compared to 20th Century technology, it has a nearly infinite power source. I do not know how to explain it to you with terminology that you could understand. Perhaps we can call it 'magic'?"

"Sure, whatever," Sean said, then grinned mischievously, "About how many years do you get to the gallon? How often do you have to change the tachyon particles? Do you have a regular schedule for rotating the flux capacitor?"

Alex was puzzled. "A 'flux capacitor' is a fictional designation. You cannot create, destroy, nor alter tachyon particles, and your reference to gallons is irrelevant. This vehicle does not use a liquid fuel."

Sean smiled even broader. Alex paused while he evaluated Sean's grin, then ventured, "Would this be another example of leg pulls?"

"Come on, Future-Boy," Sean replied, tapping a fist lightly against Alex's shoulder, "If you're going to treat me like a caveman, then I'm going to harass you a little. Anyway, you need to learn when people are joking around if you're going to spend any time in this century."

"I can tell jokes." He tilted his head slightly to the right, and then back. "Your mother's mass to volume ratio is such that she is the gravitational core of a small solar system."

Sean raised an eyebrow. "Was that a 'yo mama so fat' joke? Wow, those didn't survive very well."

Alex frowned, then twitched a little to his right. "Knock, knock."

"Oh, don't *even* try that. Can we just blast off?"

Alex turned to the console, pulled open the 3D controls and began to manipulate shapes and blink commands as text boxes opened to him. He paused to look back to Sean.

"I have devised a simple experiment that may decrease the level of nausea you experience during this jump." He touched a small icon, and a 3D image of a tall blue rectangular box appeared in the middle of the control field. It was spinning and had a small flashing blue light on the top surface. "If you focus on that object, it may keep your senses from going into over-stimulation. Also, here is a sound to focus on. You might find it familiar."

The cabin filled with a wheezing, trumpeting sound that ended in a 'whumph' only to repeat itself over and over.

"Now *that* is a sound you can time-travel to," Sean laughed.

Alex handed him another plastic bag. "In the event the experiment fails."

He tapped a green icon and the boxy ship rose slightly, became fully visible, and then vanished with a soft popping sound as the air molecules rushed together to fill the void created.

Sean opened his mouth and wagged his tongue from side to side. It seemed that he tasted something salty/sweet that was at the same time bitter and sour.

Alex batted a spherical shape to his left, and the rotating box vanished as the sound stopped. He blinked three more commands, and the control field shut down, and the door slid open. It was dark. He stepped out and spoke, "lights."

Sean peered out the open door. He felt a bit disoriented, but nothing like his first trip. He expected to see the same yard that they had been sitting in, but he saw an off-white concrete wall less than six feet away.

"It appears that you have made it through your second trip with considerably less distress," Alex commented.

"Yeah, well it was a quicker trip," Sean replied, "Or wait... maybe it took longer and we went slower?"

"Neither. Your concentration on the visual image and sound kept your brain from imagining most of the sensory overload that you experienced the first time."

"Still had that odd series of consecutive tastes, though... it was like a vinegar candy dusted with salty cocoa powder." Sean wrinkled his nose and shuddered. "So if I sucked on a peppermint would that go away, too?"

"Perhaps, however repeated trips tend to minimize the sensations."

Sean stepped out of the time-vehicle and looked around the room. "Where are we? This isn't your back yard. Are you sure we made it back to the right place and time?"

"Look around and tell me what you infer from what you see."

Sean scanned the four walls and noticed that directly behind them was a folding door. He looked up and saw the counterbalance springs on each side. "We're in a garage."

"Correct. I need...," Alex started, then paused, "umm... to do some maintenance on my vehicle. I assure you, this is my garage, and that we've returned to the September afternoon from which we departed."

"Maintenance? On the 'nearly infinite' powerful time-ship?"

"Errr... yes. Nothing major. Only a small adjustment," Alex said apprehensively. He cleared his throat. "We should return to your house."

They walked through the door leading to a short hall past the laundry room and into the kitchen. Sean eyed Alex suspiciously. He had never heard Alex stammer when talking. *What was that really about?* he wondered.

As they passed through the front door, Alex pulled the door shut and paused. "House: secure."

"Well, I guess that beats carrying a key," Sean said as the lock clicked.

They came down the front steps and headed toward the street. Alex turned left at the sidewalk. Sean had taken a step to the right.

"Unless you dropped us into a backwards universe by mistake, my house is *this* way," Sean said over his shoulder.

"That is true. However, if you would accompany me this direction; there is something I would like you to observe."

Alex again turned left when they reached the corner.

Sean gave Alex a sideways glance. "Can I ask you something?"

"You already have," Alex replied.

"Huh?"

"When you made the inquiry requesting to make an inquiry. That has a level of redundancy."

"No, it's just a polite way to bring up something new in a conversation... and maybe something a little... I don't know... uncomfortable."

"Why would you not simply say that you wish to broach a new topic of a questionable nature?"

"*Fine!* I want to broach a new topic of questionable nature," Sean said hotly.

"Proceed," Alex replied calmly.

They took nearly a dozen steps in silence as Sean tried to figure out how he wanted to phrase his question. "So what's it like being a girl?" he blurted out suddenly.

Alex paused before answering. "I believe I am unqualified to answer that question since I am male."

"Yeah, but... you know... Nicole... Alexis... the hot blonde jogger..."

"...Are all fictional personae... disguises, if you prefer."

"I know that *now*," Sean snarled, "But that's not what I'm talking about. I mean... it's *you*..."

Alex struggled to follow Sean's line of reasoning. "That is correct," he returned slowly, warily.

"So I don't get how you do it."

"I do not believe I can explain it, to your satisfaction, in terms that are relevant to 20th Century technology," said Alex. "The pseudo-body suit is nearly as complex as time-travel."

"No... not the hocus-pocus techie magic part," Sean said, exasperation creeping into his voice. "How do you *become* them?"

They took several paces as Alex again attempted to understand Sean's question. "It is the *technology* of the pseudo-body suit that allows me to alter my appearance."

"You're not getting this at all!" Sean growled in frustration. "OK, so try this. Kevin and Raj and I saw this movie where this guy drinks a potion and turns into a woman, and we were talking about it after the show and started goofing around about what it would be like to change into a woman. I said it just wouldn't work. Even if Kevin suddenly looked like a woman, I'd still know it was him because he'd still act the same. So how do you do it? How do you make it believable?"

It was quiet again while Alex considered Sean's question, twitching several queries to his computer as they walked. They crossed over a small culvert and Sean looked back toward Alex's house. He glanced down at the little creek that ran behind the houses and saw it was nearly dry. Even in the Spring, it could barely be called a creek. It was more of a channel for water run-off from the yards, but it stayed wet enough for the trees that grew all along it. Those trees were tall enough to shield the back yards from view, and though Sean could see the roof of the house, he couldn't see any of Alex's backyard.

They reached the end of the block and turned left again.

"I am skeptical that any answer could satisfy your question," Alex finally ventured, "as it does have several levels of complexity. Since you are not asking about the technical part of the transformation, should I assume you are asking about my simulation of alternate personalities?"

"Yes...No...*I don't know!*" Sean's temper blew. "I don't even know half the time what you're *saying!* What *I'm* saying is: you *look* like a girl, you *act* like a girl, you *sound* like a girl, you *walk* like a girl, and especially in Nicole's case, you *smell* like a girl!"

Alex recoiled slightly from Sean's outburst. "As I said," he offered cautiously, "several levels of complexity. I will do my best to simplify my response." He paused, then gingerly continued, "Since they are mostly technical issues, I will table the discussion of look and sound. We have already discussed my research to determine a scent you would find alluring. The walk is mostly a *result* of the tech, which creates an altered physiology. That leaves the most ambiguous term, act." He paused again, fearing Sean might challenge any of his assessments. Then continued, "I have accessed scholarly research, as well as samples of popular culture references and have concluded that there is enough evidence to support that gender differences—though certainly physiological—are framed by cultural influences when you speak of *acting* like a girl."

"The word 'simplify' must have a different definition in the 23rd Century," muttered Sean.

"It can be argued that gender roles will conform to the societal norm of the community or culture. Let me present two extremes that currently exist in 1995 with regard to female clothing. There are some cultures in Asia that dictate that a woman may not allow any part of her body, other than her eyes, to be seen in public. At the same time, there are tribal cultures in both Africa and South America where both men and women wear nothing more than a loin cloth. With regard to your own cultural biases, you might declare the former to be ridiculous and perhaps find the latter embarrassing."

"*My* cultural biases?" challenged Sean, eyebrows raised.

"That was not intended to be interpreted as a *personal* bias. I speak of the general norm of the culture you are part of – late 20th Century North American. That provides a segue into the topic of norms evolving within a culture, over *time*. To 'act like a girl,' would elicit a different perspective between your time-period and the late 18th Century. What could be considered modest dress by your standards would seem outrageous to those living 200 years ago. Although I suspect your ancestors would find that the liberties evolved in woman's speech would be equally shocking."

"What does this have to do with *you* acting like a girl?"

"My suggestion is that over time, gender roles fluctuate. Specifically, I propose that if someone from 1795 observed human behavior in 1995, they might feel that women tended to be more masculine and men more feminine than those from their own time."

Sean's eyes narrowed. "Great! What does *that* have to do with *you* acting like a girl?"

"I was attempting to create a background for my suggestion that gender difference in my own time is more physiological than cultural. If I replace the mythical observer from 1795 with yourself and then allow you to observe human behavior in my own time, you would reach the same conclusions about masculinity and femininity."

Sean struggled to make sense of what Alex had said. He gave up. "OK... but I swear, if you say I need to get more in touch with my feminine side, I'll punch you."

"Noted," Alex said with a gulp, then added softly, "I believe the threat in your statement supports my argument."

They walked the rest of that block in silence, Sean deep in thought. He liked Alex... mostly... at least when he wasn't being annoying, but he was growing tired of Alex's super-intellectual approach to everything. The 'mythical observer from 1795' had gotten Sean thinking about being transplanted somewhere in time. He wondered if *he* would seem alien to *his* ancestors if he could go back 200 years and meet them. He imagined the rougher life they certainly would have faced near the end of the 18th Century. If he remembered his history correctly, the street where they were walking would have been unsettled territory in 1795. Territory claimed by France but only settled mostly along the Mississippi River.

He couldn't fully imagine what life would have been like, but he was pretty sure he wouldn't know how to survive. He didn't know how to hunt, let alone skin and butcher game. Sean *had* been fishing a couple of times when he was younger, but his Dad baited his hook and took the fish off the line when he'd caught one. He had no clue how to ride a horse, or milk a cow or have any other skills that he supposed would be basic to frontier life. He felt *ignorant* compared to his distant grandson and would be *useless* to his distant grandfather.

"Are you experiencing post-travel nausea again?" asked Alex.

"What? No. Why'd you say that?"

"You have stopped speaking, and your eyes appear to be slightly unfocused."

"I was just thinking; that's all."

"I see," Alex replied then added after a pause, "A quarter for your thoughts."

"Penny," Sean said with a trace of a crooked grin. "It's a '*penny* for your thoughts' not a quarter."

"My mistake. The phrase originated in the 16th Century or earlier. I thought perhaps the monetary value of one's thoughts had inflated."

"No, just a penny. Maybe a hundred years from now it's more."

"Some things about language change slowly. Some words or phrases evolve while others remain constant, yet others fall into disuse and are eventually forgotten."

"You know *everything*, don't you?" Sean suddenly exploded.

Alex froze. Sean took another step, then pivoted to face a cringing Alex.

"I have irritated you again," he said quietly, averting his eyes. "Do my failed attempts to use idioms anger you?"

"No," Sean replied without thinking. "Well, maybe a little. But that's not it."

Alex continued to look down and to his right, waiting a few seconds before venturing a question, "Could you please explain what *did* cause you to become angry?"

Sean looked away. He clenched his jaw, shook his head, rubbed his hand across his face, looked back at Alex then looked away again. He felt guilty about scaring the guy.

"It's just..." Sean looked at his own feet then back to Alex. "It's just that you *know* everything. You're my age, but you're some kind of super-genius."

"My I.Q. measures in the upper reaches of normal, but it is certainly not at the genius level."

"*See?* You even know that you're *not* a genius. So what's that make *me?* A retard?"

Surprise crossed Alex's face. "I thought use of that term was a taboo in this time-period. My studies show that the generally accepted term used in this era is 'mentally challenged.'"

"Do you *have* to analyze *everything?*" Sean barked.

Alex paused again for several seconds, then he quietly said, "That is why I am here. To learn, to analyze, to document what I experience."

Sean's temper flared again. "And that makes *me* a lab rat. Am I chasing after the cheese correctly? Is it time for an electrical shock to see what I do? Is that why we went around the block this way? To see if the lab rat can find his way back home when you change up the maze?"

Sean stared daggers at Alex, jaw still clenched. Alex's face was passively blank. He stood submissively like a scolded puppy. He opened his mouth, but then closed it again without speaking. He blinked.

"I do not know what to say," he finally offered in a soft, trembling voice.

"*Really?*" Sean continued loudly, "I'm amazed! I thought you knew *everything*, but you don't know what to say?" He threw his hands in the air and continued to rant. "What's the matter? No data in that computer of yours that tells you what to do when a caveman goes off on you?"

Alex's posture straightened as he fixed a gaze on Sean's eyes. "You are *not* a caveman," he said forcefully, "Simply because I originate a few hundred years into your future does not mean I consider you a caveman."

Sean's rage had dissipated as quickly as it had flared. "I still *feel* like one," he complained bitterly, "You know everything about me, you know all about language and things about this time-period that *I* might not know… and I *live* here. I mean… sometimes you seem really cool, and it's just awesome to be with you, but sometimes it's just… *frustrating*… 'cause you make me feel so stupid."

"That is certainly not my intention. Nor do I wish for you to feel as if you are an experiment." Alex smiled as he continued, "It has been unexpectedly enlightening to get to know you as a real live person. I have been fascinated by your reactions to your discovery that I am from your future. You quickly overcame your initial fear, then embraced the idea even to the point of desiring to experience time-travel." His smile faded. "I do not, however, understand your current attitude. You seem determined to compare yourself to me with a goal of finding yourself inferior. I do not understand what I have done or said that would create that type of reaction. Nonetheless, I apologize for whatever it is about my presence that causes you negative emotions."

Sean took a deep breath, then released it slowly. His jaw unclenched and his face relaxed.

"OK, I get it that you aren't taunting me and trying to make me feel stupid, and maybe you don't even show off intentionally, but that doesn't change what I see and hear you say. Even if by some future measurement of I.Q. you don't register as a genius, you still are compared to me. When you talk about stuff like how hard it would be for me to explain a jet plane to one of my ancestors from 200 years in the past, it got me thinking. I couldn't fit in there. I couldn't survive in their rugged world. So that makes me a nobody. I'm dumb compared to you, and would be useless in the past."

As Alex reflected, he repeatedly twitched slightly to his right, then looked slightly up and left while he sifted through the information he had pulled from his computer. Sean watched him closely.

"You have detected that I occasionally have a facial tic," observed Alex.

"Best guess is that you're somehow connecting to your ship's computer, but I have no idea why."

"Perhaps you could think of it as 'cheating.'"

"Cheating? I don't get it."

"Using an unfair advantage... a hidden source of information," Alex replied. "I would not be able to function in this time-period without preparation. I spent months assembling data needed to prepare myself for this and earlier time-periods. Using a technique most closely equated to your 20th Century 'sleep learning,' it took several days to assimilate that data and to become fluent in English as it was spoken, *is spoken*, in this era. The 'cheat' is when I come across something that I do not readily understand; I can quickly research and generally come up with an answer at nearly the speed of thought. It gives the illusion of 'genius.' You suppose that you would fail to adapt to the past should you find yourself there, and that would most likely be true without preparation. However, if you were to spend time learning about the past and developed the necessary physical skills, you could succeed. It would be a rare individual who could move even one hundred years from their own time-period and readily be able to assimilate. That is certainly one of the more fascinating things about visiting the past, to fully experience the differences, to observe how everything works as history unfolds before your eyes." Alex sighed happily before he continued his lecture. "You have the skills that you need to survive in this present time. As you grow older, you will adapt to your environment even as it changes and evolves. That is universal for survival. You learn what you need to know to survive the environment in which you exist."

Sean considered before he spoke, "I didn't really think about it being work for you. I didn't even imagine that you spent time preparing. You make it look like it comes to you so easy, but I see now that it looks that way to me *because* of the time you spent preparing. I guess I can even see how I could learn to survive in the past if I spent time working at it. It'd probably take me years, though." He glanced away, a little embarrassed. "OK, I'm sorry that I went off on you."

"Apology accepted," declared Alex. "We need to walk briskly for the remainder of the journey to your house. I had not calculated that we would stop for this conversation."

He set off at a quicker pace, and Sean fell into step. They rounded the corner that led back to the block where Sean's house was. As they started up the street, Sean spied a couple crossing the street at the next corner. Although too far away for positive identification, Sean thought he recognized them.

"Hey!" he shouted, "that's Nicole! And she's with... me?"

He impulsively waved at them, but they continued across the street without a return acknowledgment. He stopped and grabbed Alex's shoulder and spun him around.

"What the hell?"

"And now you know why I wanted to take a longer route. Since we did not meet each other directly as we left earlier, it seemed logical to come this way."

Gears whirred in Sean's brain. "So that's why you parked in the garage? Because we came back to your house before we even left? Was that on purpose, or is it just hard to pop in at the exact time that you want."

"It was by design. I could have landed us in the back yard at one nanosecond after we initially left, but I also thought it best to eliminate all the time spent walking between the houses."

"Why? What difference does it make? This isn't because of what I said about not being late for dinner, is it?"

"Let us continue to your house," Alex said as he returned to his brisk pace. Sean took three long strides to catch up. "It is because you might notice the gap if I had not made allowance for the time that we were gone."

"Again, why does it matter?"

"Because none of this will remain in your memory, and you might be puzzled by the hour that somehow became missing from your life."

They turned right and walked in silence as they passed the two houses that lay between the corner and Sean's house. Sean pulled out his keys, unlocked the door, and they entered the house.

"So now what?" asked Sean.

"I still require a sample of your father's DNA."

"What, like a blood sample?"

"While that would indeed work, I believe we can find something less invasive. We should be able to find some epithelia or hairs on his pillow."

Sean raised an eyebrow. "What are epithelia?"

"In this particular case, skin cells that have flaked off. There should be a plentiful sample of them as well as hairs where he sleeps."

"He uses a brush to comb his hair. I'll bet there's lots of hairs in that; he's starting to bald."

"That should do nicely," Alex confirmed.

Sean went up the stairs and retrieved his Dad's hairbrush. He handed it to Alex who pulled some hairs from the bristles and put them into a small clear vial that instantly sealed itself. Alex returned the brush to Sean, who replaced it in the upstairs bathroom. When Sean came back down the stairs, he found Nicole standing where Alex had been. He stopped at the bottom of the stairs; apprehension crept across his face.

"So, this is it?" Sean asked, warily. "You're going to wipe my memory like you said?"

"If I may correct your terminology," said Nicole, "as I told you when I first revealed myself, the nanites that you ingested released a chemical that will prevent you from storing the memories of the past eighty-eight minutes. The 20th Century medical term is anterograde amnesia. Your short-term memory always resets itself when you lose consciousness, most commonly by sleeping. You have been inhibited from storing your experiences into long-term memory. Although the results are the same, I technically am not 'wiping' your memory."

"I guess that's the *up* side of this," Sean said sarcastically. "I won't remember you correcting all the things I said."

"Sean, please sit on the couch where you sat when we came in from the kitchen."

Sean reluctantly complied. He pursed his lips, and his voice was unsteady as he spoke, "You don't *have* to do this. I won't *tell* anyone. I can keep a secret."

"I understand your desire to bargain, and I accept that you truly believe you could keep this secret, but you cannot. Not for an entire lifetime. This experience would always be remembered as a tremendous event to you. It is human nature to need to share such events. Given the near impossibility that you could keep everything secret, it would still alter the way that you proceed with your life. While unlikely that any change would be *cataclysmic* to the future, I cannot be certain of that."

"OK, fine! Do your worst," challenged Sean. "Wipe out my memories. I don't think you can *do* it. I *will* remember what happened. You're right; this is the biggest thing that ever happened to me, and there is *no way* that I'll forget this. So go ahead. *Try!*"

"Sean..." There was sadness in Nicole's voice. "You are exhibiting several levels of the grieving process." She paused. "I also feel loss and must admit that it is confusing to me. I had not anticipated that I would feel such a strong bond to you in such a short time. I thought there would be no harm in spending time with you as my real self. I knew that you would be unable to remember anything about the incident, and I selfishly wanted to observe how you would react to meeting someone from your future." She briefly smiled at the memory. "And while that part was very enlightening, in the end, there is harm... to me. I will remember and feel the loss of this level of friendship and brief camaraderie that we experienced. It was... fun... or as you might say, 'it was cool.' I believe it will be more challenging for me to be able to relate to you now only as Nicole and Alexis. When I spend time with you as Nicole, I will regret that *I* have memories of this afternoon's adventures while *you* cannot remember any of it."

"So you're going to stick around?"

"For a short time. There is more data to gather here, and then I will depart to visit your father in 1969, when he is age sixteen."

Sean sprang up, grabbed Nicole's arms, and pulled her close. Their eyes were mere inches apart.

"I want to go!" Sean said forcefully.

"Go where?"

"To the past... with you. I want to go see what my Dad was like when he was my age."

"You know that I cannot allow that, and even if I did, I would still keep you from retaining any memories."

Sean released her arms and stepped back. He seemed more relaxed and smiled a little as he launched into a sales pitch. "No, wait, think of what a great *experiment* this would be. *You* can be the only person from your time who has witnessed the reaction of someone meeting *their own Father* when they were both *the same age*. I'll bet you can get some kind of paper out of this. Assuming you still write papers in the future."

Nicole was intrigued. "You are correct that no one has attempted that type of study." She mulled the idea over. "It *could,* indeed, have some very interesting observations." She was *very* intrigued. "I will require time to analyze the risks and rewards of such an experiment."

"Can't you just say, 'I'll think about it?'" Sean chuckled, "You really *are* too nerdy to fit in very well around here."

"As you wish," Nicole replied, then enunciated each word as she parroted, "I will think about it."

Sean sat back down. "That's all I'm asking," he said with a wave of his hand, "Just think about it. Think how cool it would be... oh, and don't forget that you'll probably be *famous* after you publish your findings. Who knows? Maybe that'll be a huge event in your life. When you get back to your own time, you can really wow 'em with what you saw." Sean crossed his arms. "OK, so if you think you can erase my memories, go ahead. What do you have to do? Do you need to…"

Nicole had flipped a switch on her little hand-held device and Sean was unconscious.

"Sorry Sean, determination is irrelevant. The scientific fact is that your memories of the last ninety-three minutes will not be stored." She unfolded his arms. "Now, something seems missing. Yes, the dog was in here."

Nicole went to the kitchen and opened the door to the basement. Maggie was already pressed against the door and pushed her way in. Nicole followed the dog back to the living room.

"Come, Maggie, you need to sit where you were."

She positioned the dog at Sean's feet and sat back in her own chair. She retrieved a static picture of the room that she had stored on the computer. Everything was where it was moments before she revealed her secret. Holding her tiny device above her backpack, she pressed a button then dropped it into the bag. Sean stirred. He blinked, looked a bit perplexed.

"So, Ben Folds Five? Are they talented?" Nicole asked.

"Hmmm? Yeah. What?" Sean slowly scanned the room. "Wow, I feel like I just zonked out for a second. Did you just say that you had something you wanted to tell me?"

"No. It was something unrelated. Never mind. Why not play your CD and then I need to ask you some questions about algebra."

Nicole reached for her glass and took a sip of her smoothie. She was glad Sean had already finished his, or he might have noticed it had melted. She tried to put on a convincing smile, but behind the disguise, Alex did feel a loss. He truly had *not* anticipated such an emotional upheaval.

Chapter Six

"But it would be nothing, nothing / Without a woman or a girl"

HAD anyone actually bothered to track the movements of Alexis Townsend, they might have noticed that every other day before her second class she went into the first-floor girls' restroom. Since that was a relatively conventional action, there was really no reason *to* notice. Neither was there any reason to notice that she also immediately went to the stall farthest from the door. And because no one noticed those mundane actions, there *was* no one watching to realize the very remarkable fact that Alexis Townsend *never came out* again.

Alex quietly sat in the far stall reviewing choices for 1995 clothing styles found in his database. Fortunately, his computer did most of the real work, sifting through the massive amounts of data and selecting options that were age appropriate and not overly formal for school-wear. That still left hundreds of possibilities, but Alex had further narrowed the field by uploading scanned images of girls that he had seen in the school hallways as reference points. In general, the rural Midwestern population skewed a little toward the conservative end of 1995 fashion. He purposefully had selected Nicole's wardrobe to be a little flashier than what he chose for Alexis. The goal was to be on the verge of what people of the late 20th century considered 'sexy' without being so overt as to draw censure from the school administration.

On this occasion, Alex decided Nicole should wear a charcoal skirt with a hemline 5 inches above the knee, a red/gray plaid top with three-quarter sleeves, and charcoal knee socks. Her shoes, lip gloss, and nails were matched to the red in her top, and her eye shadow was a smoky gray. He vacillated with his decision whether to add a red beret. It may have been a little beyond the norm of what girls of a small Missouri town would wear, but there was some leeway to be a little edgy since the Townsend twins background story had them hailing from New York. His main criteria for selection, however, was always based on what Sean Kelly found attractive. While that factor was no longer as critical since Alex had obtained Jonathan Kelly's DNA, he still wanted Sean to be attracted to Nicole. As a compromise, he had decided to remove the pheromones from Nicole's signature perfume.

The pheromones had probably always been unnecessary. Based on research he had done, Sean would have found Nicole attractive without them. Before talking with Sean as himself, Alex hadn't realized that his research had an unexpected physical effect on his ancestor. It appeared that Sean experienced a tingling sensation in the back of his head when the nanites had broadcast bursts of data. Alex logged the atypical reaction and made a note to add an anesthetic component to any future experiments of a similar nature. Regretfully, he had lacked any means to predict the effect of nanites on an adolescent human who had previously been nanite-free. By his century's standards, nanites were as commonly symbiotic with humans as the bacteria that live in the gastrointestinal tract. *Everyone* in the 23rd Century had nanites introduced into their systems while in utero.

He set his thoughts aside and returned to the task of transitioning from Alexis to Nicole.

Once satisfied that no one remained in the restroom from Alexis' arrival, Alex stood and pushed the door open. Nicole calmly walked out, drawing no attention from any of the girls lined up in front of the mirror checking their makeup. She paused only briefly to admire her red beret, and then exited the restroom and went up the stairs to the second floor to attend French class.

Since French was as easy as for Nicole as Spanish was for Alexis, it was tedious to endure the simplistic teaching methods used. Alex had spent several weeks in his own time becoming fluent in late 20th Century English, French, German, Russian and Spanish to the level of a native speaker. The non-English languages were easier, since there was no requirement to add idioms that were unneeded for simple classroom conversations. He had discovered too late that his fluency had caused some added attraction in Spanish class that he hadn't anticipated or wanted. Alexis smoothly spoke with a competency beyond what could be expected from even the best student. Since Nicole had started classes later than Alexis, Alex was able to adjust her French fluency level downward. Unfortunately, Alexis had already demonstrated perfect Spanish and had to maintain at that level. German and Russian had been a superfluous whim that he had added to his language learning package.

English was a frustratingly different problem since English was Alex's native tongue in the 23rd Century. It was easy to *logically* accept that the language had always been evolving, but maddeningly difficult to make the adjustment to those changes. So many words and phrases common in 20th Century English had become archaic and no longer used. Some pronunciations or meanings of words had changed, even though the word was still used. However, the most challenging element was blocking the use of common 23rd Century words and phrases that had no meaning in the 20th Century. Linguists had struggled for decades to develop a learning package that could deal with all the major changes, but more importantly teach the nuances needed to sound proficient to native speakers. The real breakthrough was when they developed a way to program automatically for different regional accents.

As with any language, the major difficulty was idioms. Although the learning module did its best to include the most frequently used slang and euphemisms of late 20th Century English, it was impossible to load them all, especially in the context of *when* to use them. That made it all the more critical to have immediate access to his computer for instantaneous look-up.

The method Alex had used to learn 'old' English was the same as each of the other languages, and with each minute he spent in a 20th Century classroom he grew more appreciative of the technique used in his own time. If he attempted to explain the method—using only 20th Century terminology—the closest he could come would be 'downloaded,' although that wasn't entirely accurate. The nanites in his brain provided a direct interface to a computerized learning module which was most efficient when the brain was at rest, particularly in the REM cycle of sleep.

REM, he thought, *odd that the word now triggers songs of the band REM.*

He forced the thoughts from his mind before they could take root. It still surprised him that the emotional impact of the music had been so strong. He twitched a quick connection to his computer and pushed all of the music files into an archive to keep them out of active access.

Now that Sean had become aware of the small physical tell when Alex accessed his computer, he needed to decide what actions should be taken. He probably should 'suggest' to Sean that he stop noticing the physical tic when Alexis or Nicole accessed the computer for data.

How would I explain that process using only current terminology? He wondered.

He connected again with his computer to query 20th Century terminology and came up with *Hypnotize.* He assimilated several contemporary news magazine articles for a greater understanding of what that meant. Other than the 'trance like state' needed, it was similar to the art of *suggestion*. The main difference was that the mental alignment of brainwaves with the subject was attained mostly through nanite tech, but it *did* also require focused thought in congress with the spoken suggestion.

It wouldn't be the first time he had used the technique in this century. He wouldn't have been able to attain the plausibility of being two people without this skill. While Nicole went to French class for second-hour, Alexis was enrolled in an American Literature class. Each teacher had received the 'suggestion' that even when Nicole or Alexis hadn't attended class, the teacher would believe that they *had* and mark them as present in their attendance books. With a tiny observer-tech on the back wall of each classroom, the base computer could track any needed assignments and even have them prepared for submission. Since Sean was in neither class, it worked well to alternate days. During the class periods with Sean, the 'other sister' always had a study-hall or lunch period. The ruse had worked flawlessly.

However, the very next day would be the first time Alex would need to use an alternative. Nicole had a test in French while Alexis needed to take an exam in American Lit. Alex didn't enjoy having to do short-hop time-travel to be physically in both places at once, it made him feel jittery. Logically, he knew that the uncomfortable feeling was due to sensing his 'other self' in the same building... but he still didn't enjoy it.

To make the most of crossing his own timeline, Alex concluded it was also an opportune time to meet with Sean as both girls simultaneously. He decided that just before Algebra class would be a good time to reinforce visually that both twins *could* be in the same place at the same time.

In some ways, Alex was pleased that his miscalculations with Alexis had forced him to create Nicole as a second personality. It added to the depth of his data to observe Sean's differences in relating with each girl. The idea to make them twins was simply to facilitate scheduling both in classes with Sean, but Alex found it amusing that Sean's friend Kevin had decided to label Nicole as the *evil twin*. The concept was even more entertaining once he had made some queries on the topic and found many stories in books and television shows that used the *evil twin* as a plot device. He even briefly considered playing out the role, but in the end rejected the idea as too frivolous. It had been fascinating to find that Sean himself had fearfully referred to Nicole as the *evil twin* when Alex had unmasked his true identity.

That, too, was an interestingly complex layer in Sean's behavior. Sean had treated Alex differently than either Nicole or Alexis, well beyond what Alex had imagined. Beyond that, the most unexpected outcome was how it had affected him personally. He had no expectation for how much he would enjoy being with Sean as himself in an almost peer relationship. Once Sean had accepted the truth of who Alex was and gotten past his initial fears, they had somewhat... bonded. Alex had even begun to appreciate Sean's many sarcastic remarks.

There was a profound disparity in the way Sean spoke to Alex compared with either of the twins. He supposed it was possibly a function of the difference in same-sex / opposite-sex relationships, as he had noticed similar patterns when observing Sean with his friends; Raj and Kevin. It was something that he knew he would never have with Sean as either Nicole or Alexis. It was something that he wanted to experience again.

He had to admit that Sean's proposal to join him to travel to the past to meet his own father at age 16 was intriguing. Everything in his training told him that it was a reckless idea, still he felt he should give it further consideration. But first, he had already decided he would spend some more time with Sean as himself, unmasked as Alex... the 'boy from the future'. It would be difficult to accomplish, but he was formulating a scenario that he thought would succeed. There would be plenty of time to think about it as he suffered through another primitive language lesson.

Nicole walked into French class and sat down just as the bell rang.

"Bonjour, class!"

"Bonjour, Mademoiselle Faye," the class responded in unison.

Chapter Seven

"Tonight's the night, I'm gonna push it to the limit"

U   **PS** *and downs*, Sean mused. The start of the '95 school year hadn't been like any other, but regardless of the crazy events of the prior week, he did finally get to spend some non-classroom time with Nicole, if only because of mathematics. He was more than happy to help her with Algebra, but she seemed to pick it up so quickly that he wasn't really sure why she was struggling in the first place.

She had listened carefully, almost studiously, when he played the Ben Folds Five CD. It was like she had never listened to music before. When it finished, he had asked her if she liked it, and her response was to point out that many of the *lyrics* were sad but that the music *wasn't* sad. Then for some reason, she had almost laughed when *Best Imitation of Myself* played. He decided it might take a long time to figure out Nicole Townsend.

One thing he thought he had certainly figured out was that her whole family was on some kind of health-food kick. He personally would have preferred more sugar in that smoothie Nicole made, but she'd seemed appalled that he wanted any sugar at all. He'd seen Alexis eat yogurt. Observed Nicole eat mostly plain lettuce drizzled with some homemade protein supplement dressing. And although Aunt Katherine had made some pretty tasty brownies, she wouldn't eat them herself. If he did ask Nicole out on a date, he knew it wasn't going to be to McDonalds.

Overall, he had to admit that he mostly enjoyed being with her, even if she was a little different. Not only did she have a slight accent, but she seemed to have a larger vocabulary than any other girl he'd ever met... not counting Alexis. At times, he also wondered if she knew more about history than Mr. Douglas. Sean had noticed several times that his History teacher seemed amazed by things that Nicole said in class.

Even with all of the areas where she seemed at genius level, there were times she seemed clueless. Watching her as she listened to the CD was like watching a child discover a butterfly, and *neither* of the twins seemed to know anything about TV shows. He wondered if they had been raised in some sheltered environment that kept music and TV away. Despite the mystery surrounding the Townsend twins, or possibly because of it, Sean found he enjoyed being with each of them. It just happened that Nicole was also drop-dead beautiful.

Other than the fleeting minutes he had spent with Nicole, the best part of the weekend, as always, had been hanging out with the guys. He had to mow the lawn on Saturday, but the rest of the weekend had been free.

Sunday's Chiefs game had been another nail biter. It was the second week in a row that the game went into overtime, but at least they beat the hated Raiders. It had been the defense that won the latest game. James Hasty picked off a Hostetler pass and ran it back for a touchdown. Sean was beginning to have doubts about the offense, especially Bono at quarterback. Two weeks in a row, regulation play had ended with a 17-17 tie, but the bottom line was still a 3-0 start to the season.

When he returned to school on Monday, Sean was determined to lay low. He assumed that the girl network was still busy spreading the tale of what a scumbag he was. To his surprise, the big story that broke over the weekend was that Ashly's boyfriend, Matt, had been seen flirting with some Henryville girls at the concession stand during the football game on Friday night. The one redeeming factor about the Girl Grapevine was that the latest gossip was the *only* gossip worth spreading. Since Ashly was in the upper level of Megan's entourage, Megan made sure that the word got out that Matt was lower than pond scum.

Sean supposed that Matt's rise to scumbag of the week was aided by the fact that he and Alexis still walked together back to the main building after Spanish. It was hard to maintain scumbag status when the woman who was supposedly wronged was openly friendly with the former scumbag. Not only had she not acted hurt, she gave the appearance to all that she encouraged Sean's interest in her sister. She told Sean that Nicole had related what a great help he had been with Algebra and that she had also enjoyed meeting his dog. Her enthusiasm led Sean to wonder what *their* relationship had become. Did Alexis no longer have a crush on him?

Higher on his list of things to wonder about was where his relationship with Nicole was going. Monday, she had walked with him to the cafeteria after Algebra, but then said she wasn't going to eat because she needed to go to the library. While disappointed, that left him free to sit with Kevin and Raj, and they had all recapped the Chiefs/Raiders game. Kevin was already looking forward to the next game at Cleveland. He was confident the Chiefs would continue their winning ways, even though the Browns were 11-5 in the '94 season and 2-1 after three games in '95. Besides the conversation, Sean also enjoyed a deep-fried chicken fritter sandwich with fries that he would have forgone in Nicole's presence.

Monday afternoon, he had walked with Nicole to and from History and felt more at ease talking with her. He no longer feared that what he said might make him seem like a stalker and for some reason he no longer felt the almost irrational urge to touch her. Her perfume seemed to be less intoxicating, although he still thought it was the most delicious scent he had ever experienced.

There were some things about the trip back to the main building that Sean was less than thrilled about. Nicole was always so excited about whatever went on in History class that she wanted to keep talking about it. Sean had tried to picture himself becoming interested in History, but struggled with the idea. He had decided that there were two things that could potentially be big issues in what he hoped was an evolving relationship: health food and Nicole's love of History.

Sean tended to daydream of Nicole during study-hall and Tuesday morning was no different. Earlier, during the walk back to the main building after Spanish, Alexis had mentioned having something important that she wanted to talk to him about, but wouldn't say what. He still liked Alexis – as a friend – but listening to her accent only made him think about being with her sister. When the bell that ended study-hall finally rang, he snapped back to reality and headed toward Algebra class. He was beginning to get his timing down to 'coincidentally' arrive at the Algebra classroom just as Nicole got there.

"Good morning, Nicole Townsend. How are you today?" he said formally.

"I am doing quite well, Sean Kelly. Thank you for inquiring."

They smiled at each other. Sean felt it was kind of flirty to call each other by their full names like that. Of course, Alexis and Nicole had initiated the formal greeting, but he kind of liked it.

"Are you ready for another exciting hour of mathematics?" Sean asked.

"I think I am," Nicole replied, "I had someone tutor me last Friday afternoon, and I feel much more confident now."

"Nikki!" A familiar voice called from behind Sean.

"Lexi, what are you doing here? I thought you had lunch this hour," Nicole called past him.

"I do," Alexis confirmed as she slid between Sean and her sister, "but when I checked my book bag, my lunch was missing."

"I believe I have some money, Lexi... if you wish to purchase something to eat."

"No, Nikki," Alexis argued, "Aunt Katherine assembled two lunches this morning. Could you check in your book bag?"

Nicole opened the side pouch of her book bag and pulled out two small brown paper sacks. One had an "N" and the other an "A." Alexis reached for the sack with the "A."

"Your book-bag was in the kitchen this morning and Aunt Katherine may have assumed it was mine and placed my lunch in it. Then when you entered, you must have added your own lunch in without seeing mine."

"Sorry, Lexi."

"It is all right, Nikki. I have it now."

"Hey," Sean interjected, "I think this is the first time I've actually seen you two together."

"Yes, it is," the twins said simultaneously.

"Jinx," Sean said with a grin. Nicole looked at him blankly, but Alexis smiled.

"It is a custom to say 'jinx' when two people say the same thing," Alexis explained to Nicole.

"You must have learned that only recently," Nicole said.

"Yes, very recently," Alexis answered.

"And now I *also* know what it means," Nicole said with a conspiratorial smile.

Sean looked quizzically from one twin to the other. He got the feeling there was some kind of an inside joke going on, but he couldn't figure out what it was. He also tried to covertly use the opportunity to compare the two girls side by side. There was a distinct familial likeness, but Nicole had higher cheekbones that seemed to make her face seem longer and slimmer. He had thought she was also a bit taller than Alexis, but then noticed that Nicole wore heels, while Alexis chose flats. Alexis had very pretty blue eyes, but Nicole's green eyes sparkled like emeralds. Nicole's auburn hair was several inches longer than Alexis' sandy-blonde, but they both styled it similarly. They each had a very cute, nearly identical, upturned nose. Nicole wore colorful dangling earrings, much more dramatic than Alexis' simple gold hoops. The most striking difference, Sean observed with a sigh, was that Nicole was a lot curvier, and dressed to show it off.

"Time for me to depart," Alexis said over a shoulder as she zipped down the hall toward the cafeteria.

"Goodbye, Lexi," Nicole called after her, "sorry about the mistake."

"So," Sean said with raised eyebrows, "Nikki and Lexi, huh?"

"It is what we have called each other since we were small children."

"Kinda cute," Sean said, still smiling, "So, should I call you Nikki?"

"No," Nicole answered flatly then turned to go into the classroom. Sean followed her in, and they both got to their seats right as the bell rang.

After class Sean waited by the door for Nicole, then started walking together toward the cafeteria. In some ways he was surprised with how at ease with her he was becoming, even though it had only been just a few days. Admittedly, the stress of defining their relationship within the bounds of Alexis' crush plus his initial bad first impression on Nicole had made it seem longer.

Not everything felt comfortable, however. Lunch was still a touchy area since he still wasn't sure how she'd react to the things he chose to eat. Tuesday meant there would be Tacos. He wondered if Nicole would consider tacos to be a relatively healthy food. After all, he rationalized, they had at least two vegetables in them. Was that enough to negate the greasy hamburger hidden underneath? Focused on his contemplation of lunch, he hadn't noticed that Kevin had slipped up behind them.

"So, Sean, are you going to blow us off today?" Kevin asked as he shoulder-bumped Sean almost into Nicole.

"Hey, Kevin," Sean mumbled, "Ummm, yeah, I guess I'm sitting with Nicole today for lunch."

"No, please sit with your friends," Nicole offered.

"That's OK; I can hang out with the guys some other time. I said I was going to sit with you."

"There is nothing that makes the seating arrangements mutually exclusive," Nicole pointed out.

"Oh... heh heh," Sean laughed nervously, "yeah... you probably don't want to sit with these guys, they can be kind of... out there."

Raj was waiting for them just inside the door. "Out where?"

"Will it embarrass you to sit with me and your friends?" Nicole asked Sean.

"Embarrass me? No! I just thought they might do something stupid to embarrass you."

"We wouldn't want to do that, would we, Kevin?" huffed Raj, "let's grab some lunch and leave these two to themselves."

Nicole looked at Sean as his friends moved away. "Though not expert at judging others' emotions, I believe you have caused Raj to feel irritated."

"Maybe," Sean shrugged, "but he'll get over it."

"I believe I will sit with *them* today," Nicole announced defiantly. "You may also sit with us if you choose."

"OK," Sean conceded, "if that's what you really want." He began to imagine all the ways things could go horribly wrong.

"I will wait for you as you select your food, I have my lunch." she said as she held up a small brown bag emblazoned with a magic marker 'N.'

Sean selected the tacos, after agonizing about the options. He decided that if his food choice was the worst thing about lunch; he would still be in pretty good shape. If it wasn't, then at least he still got to eat something he wanted. He picked up a tray and put two tacos on it, then grabbed some sauce packets. He pulled a Coke from the cooler and got in line to pay.

As he started to rejoin with Nicole, she headed to where Raj and Kevin were already sitting. Sean followed and hoped for the best. She sat down across from Kevin and Sean sat beside her, across from Raj.

"Kevin," Raj said as they sat, "you should gulp down half of your Coke and belch loudly... we wouldn't want to disappoint Sean by not embarrassing Nicole."

"OK, Raj," Sean said, "I'm sorry I said that."

Raj stroked his chin as he feigned thinking it over. "Apology accepted," he finally said, then turned to Nicole, "Hi, I'm Raj Kapur."

"I am pleased to meet you, Raj; I am Nicole Townsend."

"Yeah, we know who *you* are," Kevin said with a grin, "I'm Kevin Olsen."

"Hello, Kevin," Nicole said, smiling confidently, "but you may not know me as well as you believe, I am not the *evil twin*."

Kevin threw and accusing look at Sean, "You told her I said that?"

"No!" Sean protested, waving the idea away.

"I am afraid," Nicole said softly, "that I overheard it in the hall. Your voice projects very well. Do you participate in dramatic presentations?"

"Oh, he's all about the drama," Raj snickered.

"I didn't mean anything by it," Kevin said sheepishly while simultaneously elbowing Raj in the ribs, "I was just joking around."

"I do not mind," Nicole said warmly, "Truthfully, I find it rather amusing."

"Really? Cool!" Kevin said, then took a massive bite of his cheeseburger.

Nicole took that as a cue to open her lunch sack. She lifted a small transparent container and spoon out and sat them on the table, then neatly folded the bag and put it to one side. Sean couldn't ignore that it was almost the precise motions that he had seen Alexis make the first day they met.

"Wuhssat?" Kevin said, still chewing.

Raj punched him and hissed, "Swallow first, big guy."

Kevin took a big gulp of Coke and swallowed. "Please madam," he enunciated with his best attempt at a British accent, "if you wouldn't mind my inquiry, what, pray tell, are you about to consume?" He turned to Raj and gave him a big cheesy grin just before he re-stuffed his mouth with a handful of fries.

"Yogurt," Nicole answered.

Kevin started to speak, but put a finger in the air to hold his place. He turned to Raj and did an exaggerated chew then sipped his Coke before continuing. "Really? Doesn't look like it. My older sister eats yogurt all the time, and it doesn't look like that."

"It doesn't?" Nicole asked nervously.

"Her Aunt makes it," Sean jumped in, "it's authentic, you know, kind of like what Bedouins make."

"Oh," Kevin said, nodding as if he understood, "my sister only eats Dannon strawberry. I've never seen the Bed Owens brand."

"It's not a brand; you dolt," Raj said, "Bedouins are a nomadic people in the middle east."

"Oooooh," Kevin said with raised eyebrows, "so, some cousins of yours are in the yogurt business?"

"You are such a..." Raj started but was drowned out by Sean.

"GEEE!" Sean said loudly, "I'm sure glad we aren't going to do anything that would be embarrassing!"

Raj and Kevin both looked down, then contritely looked at each other, then at Sean. Raj finally looked toward Nicole. "Sorry," he said softly.

"Yeah, sorry," Kevin echoed.

Everyone sat silently for a moment before Raj picked up a potato chip and tried to crunch it quietly. Sean scowled at his friends, then nervously glanced toward Nicole. She calmly dipped her spoon into the container and daintily put a small bite into her mouth as if nothing had happened. Sean sighed and took a bite of his first taco.

"So," Kevin finally said to Nicole, "New York, huh?"

"Yes. Upstate, not the city."

"I lived upstate when I was a kid," Kevin continued, "What town are you from?"

Sean heard Nicole take in a sharp breath just before he saw her do her twitch. "Isn't that interesting," she said nervously, "what were you doing in New York?"

"My dad taught at SUNY Binghamton before we moved here."

Nicole did another quick twitch, then breathed out before she spoke in a calm voice, "We lived north of there, in Syracuse...near the Onondaga Lake."

Sean had decided that he'd seen the same pattern in both Townsend girls. If there was a question that seemed to make them nervous, next came a little twitch, then the calm answer. He couldn't make sense of it. The nervous twitch he could understand, especially since he knew their mother had mental problems, but what was there about it that calmed them down?

"We moved here the summer I was ten," Kevin said, "I think we probably went to Syracuse a few times. Hey, maybe we crossed paths in a mall or something."

"That is extremely unlikely. There are more than 500,000 people in the greater Syracuse area," Nicole replied.

"Yeah, but wouldn't it be cool if we did, you know, like just bump into each other when we were kids? Too bad we can't go back in time and check it out."

Nicole gasped.

"What?" Kevin continued, "Don't you think that would be awesome to track back in time and find out that we were in like the same place at the same time? I think it'd be awesome! The whole 'hey what a coincidence, I ran into you as a kid in New York and here we are together again in Missouri' thing."

"I know nothing about time-travel," Nicole said rapidly, "I do not read science fiction stories."

"I'd say it's pretty much impossible," Raj interjected, "If Einstein's theories about time slowing as you approach the speed of light are a guide, then you would probably have to go *faster* than light to go backward in time. It's impossible for mass to travel faster than light."

"Ever see that movie *Time Bandits*?" Sean asked. "What if there's holes in the universe that pop out into different times?"

"Or like *Star Trek IV* when they slingshot around the sun to go back in time?" Kevin added.

"Gee," Raj said sarcastically, "why not just invent the flux capacitor and drive a DeLorean into the past?" He rolled his eyes.

"OK, so it's probably not scientifically possible to time-travel, but it's still fun to think about," Sean said. "Nicole, as much as you like history, wouldn't you like to be able to go somewhere in the past to see how something really happened?"

"I believe I would find it too frightening to attempt such a thing," Nicole said softly as she looked down at her food.

For the rest of the lunch period, Nicole ate quietly as the three guys suggested scenario after scenario of what they'd do if they could make one trip back in time to change something. She watched, listened and tried to smile.

An hour later, Sean waited for Nicole just outside the door of the main building so he could walk with her to History class. When she came out, she gave him a halfhearted smile.

"Look," Sean said, trying his best to do damage control, "I told you it wasn't a good idea to sit with the guys at lunch. They can be kind of out there... especially Kevin. I'm surprised he *didn't* belch when Raj told him to."

"I found it more interesting to learn that each of you would attempt to change the past. Kill Hitler, stop the man who assassinated Archduke Ferdinand, prevent the Challenger explosion, alter the course of the Titanic away from the iceberg, thwart the assassination of President Kennedy." She counted fingers as she moved through her list.

"What's wrong with that? Those would all be *good* things!"

Nicole stiffened. "Are you certain? What if whoever succeeded Adolf Hitler had superior military strategies and conquered all of Europe or even the United States? What if President Kennedy increased the troop strength in Vietnam to a level that provoked China to become more involved? What if that incited war between China and the United States and nuclear weapons were used? What if the grandson of someone you saved from the Titanic invents a biological weapon that kills a billion people?"

"What if the grandson of someone I saved on the Titanic finds a cure for cancer?" Sean retorted.

Nicole threw her hands in the air. "You would allow the risk of a greater cataclysm to occur on the remote possibility that someone would discover the cure to cancer?"

"You'd allow a known tragedy that you could have stopped to go ahead and happen because of the chance something else worse could be possible?" Sean fired back.

"Historical events must *not* be altered!" Nicole cried passionately.

They walked several feet without speaking before Sean softly ventured, "Wow, you're as passionate about fake history as real history. It's just 'what-ifs,' Nicole. No one can really go back in time to change stuff."

She quietly considered his words as they finished their trek to the classroom. Just before entering, she mustered a smile and softly said, "Sorry."

During History class, Nicole was much less enthusiastic than usual. Mr. Douglas even tried to bait her on certain topics, but she barely responded. After class as they walked back to the main building Sean asked her if she felt OK.

"Yes, I am fine," she answered, "though embarrassed that I became emotionally engrossed in our discussion on the way to class and raised my voice in anger toward you."

"You didn't exactly yell *at* me," Sean said with a shrug. "And I get it. You're really wrapped up in history stuff, and the thought of it changing seems to bother you. No big deal."

"But I have also been considering your suppositions. Given the level of data used in our speculations, there is no greater probability of someone creating a biological weapon than discovering a cure for cancer."

"Probability?" Sean gave her a little shoulder-bump. "Does that mean your math skills are improving?"

"Yes," she smiled, "perhaps it does."

"Besides," Sean added, "Raj is probably right about time-travel being impossible. He's pretty smart about scientific stuff."

"Yes, it appears he is," she agreed, "However, scientific knowledge can change rather abruptly. Perhaps there is another method for time-travel that does not involve accelerating mass beyond the speed of light."

"You're right!" Sean joked, "We should begin working on plans for our own flux capacitor! I'll bet once we get it designed; your Aunt Katherine can build one!"

After they had said their goodbyes before splitting to go to their last classes, Nicole reached out and grabbed Sean's arm.

"I nearly forgot! Alexis wants to meet with you after school."

"Really? What about?" Sean asked.

"She did not tell me. She only said that she would wait for you at the bottom of the stairs near the back door. The stairs nearest the outside classrooms."

"Ummm, OK, I guess. No clue why?"

"No. Then you are able meet with her?"

"Sure."

"Good. I will see you later," Nicole said as she walked away.

"You mean tomorrow," Sean said.

She looked back over her shoulder and smiled a strange little smile.

Later, when Biology had ended, Sean walked down the hall with Raj. Raj was ranting about only getting 97 on the test that was handed back.

"Dude, it's still an A plus! What's the big deal?" Sean asked.

"I shouldn't have missed that one question. I knew the answer; I just was going too fast. When I saw that A was correct, I put down A; I should have read the whole thing and seen that D was 'both A and C'. It was a stupid mistake."

"It's still an A plus! Give it a rest! I'm happy to have a B plus! It was a hard test," said Sean, showing no sympathy. "Hey, I gotta go. See you tomorrow," he said, turning at the stairs.

"Why are you going down *those* stairs?" asked Raj. "The ones at the end of the hall are closer to the parking lot."

"Yeah, I know, but Alexis wants to talk to me about something."

"Are you sure that's a good idea? Does Nicole know?" Raj waggled his eyebrows.

"Yes, Raj, Nicole knows... she was the one that told me Alexis wanted to meet with me."

"OK," Raj shrugged, "good luck with that."

Sean went down the stairs and found Alexis standing by the back door. He tried to give her a friendly smile as he approached, something about the meeting request made him nervous.

"Hey, Alexis, what's up?"

She pushed the door open and stepped outside. Sean followed her. "I merely wanted to tell you something," she said.

"OK... what's that?"

"We should walk this way a little; I do not wish to be disturbed." She moved toward the southeast side of the building. Sean walked quietly with her until they were a few yards away from the door. She stopped and turned to face him, taking both his hands in hers. "I wanted to tell you something."

"You already said that." He glanced nervously at her hands.

"Mozart. Bowie. Gershwin. Gaga," she spoke each name crisply when he had looked back into her eyes.

"What?" Sean asked, confused.

"Do not concern yourself. That was merely a placeholder. I need you to continue to look into my eyes." Sean complied. "After dinner tonight, you will feel compelled to come to my house to ask Nicole to go with you to a movie on Friday night," Alexis said smoothly, enunciating carefully. "Nod if you understand." Sean nodded. "Now, when you hear the list of composers again you will not remember any words I spoke between the lists and including the lists. It will be as if you did not hear any of this."

"Composers?" Sean mumbled.

"Yes, the list of names starting with Mozart, ending with Gaga."

"Gaga?" Sean mumbled.

"Yes. Just trust me, they are all composers. Nod if you accept that." Sean nodded. "Good. Nicole will see you later tonight. Mozart. Bowie. Gershwin. Gaga."

Sean blinked. He looked at Alexis expectantly. "I thought you said you wanted to tell me something."

"Oh, yes," Alexis said, then gripped Sean's hands tighter as she said earnestly, "I wanted to verify that you understand that I am amiable with your decision to be with Nicole. I am very happy for both of you."

"Oh. Umm..." Sean stumbled, "OK. Sure. That's great. Ummm... thank you for telling me."

"You do not sound pleased."

"No, it's not that. You... it's just... I still don't think I can get used to this open and honest thing that you and Nicole do. It kind of freaks me out."

"That is contrary to my intentions. I meant to alleviate tension. I wanted you to know that I am not jealous of Nicole, nor do I want you to experience guilt because you find her more attractive."

Sean studied her face for any visual clues that she might be covering up that she still had a crush on him. He couldn't see anything except honesty, which he found baffling. "You know that I like you as a friend, right?" he said, though he hated the way it sounded. She nodded. He pressed on, hoping to soften his guilt. "Last week when I mentioned Raj might be interested in you, I meant it. I heard him say that he'd like to go out with you if you were interested. He's kind of brainy; you're kind of brainy... it might be a good match."

Alexis showed an amused smile. "I will retain your recommendation."

"OK. Good," Sean said, nodding. "Hey, need a ride home?"

"No, thank you. I have some school work that I still need to finish."

"*After* the last class is out? Are you kidding? Go home, Alexis, you take school too seriously!"

"No, I have something that I must complete."

"OK," Sean sighed as they started back toward the door. "Make the rest of us look bad."

She waved as she stepped back inside, and he continued to follow the sidewalk around the southwest corner where it led to the parking lot. Alexis had waited a few minutes, then came back outside. She looked down the walkway to make sure Sean was out of sight before starting in the opposite direction, around the southeast side of the school, down the bike path into the park.

Since she needed to keep an earlier appointment, she was *also* heading for a vehicle... a very special vehicle. She stepped off the path and slipped around a large group of tall bushes. She opened the cloaked time-machine, slid inside, and began the calculations to jump back a few hours. She had to get to the exam in second-hour American Lit, and later meet with Nicole and Sean outside of Algebra class.

She shuddered briefly, remembering the eerie feeling of duality already experienced as Nicole and knowing she would have to face it again, this time from Alexis' point of view. She bolstered herself with the thought that at least after the meeting outside of Algebra, she could go home. In fact, since there was no reason for a return trip to the present, she realized she was already there. That would mean she had the entire afternoon to prepare for Sean's visit that evening.

As she set the coordinates for the short time-hop, she remembered the unusual event from that morning. When Sean had said "jinx", she, in the guise of Alexis, explained what it meant to Nicole... but the only reason she knew the explanation was because she, as Nicole, heard herself/Alexis say it earlier. It was a recursive impossibility. She checked the computer for a definition. The primary definition seemed to deal with a curse of bad luck. A supplemental statement said that there was a custom of two people saying the same thing at the same time then saying the word 'jinx' to wish bad luck on the other one.

Strange customs, she thought, *Why would anyone wish ill of someone else. Why did Sean say it?*

It then occurred to her that because she had checked the database, she *could* explain it to Nicole. The logic tumbled around in her mind but still seemed recursively impossible. However, since it also seemed to be a ridiculous superstition, she dismissed any other thoughts and activated the jump.

Chapter Eight

"Thanks for the times that you've given me / The memories are all in my mind"

SEAN stood between the kitchen table and the sink, relaying the dinner dishes his Dad passed him to his Mom who rinsed them and put them in the dishwasher. It was a family ritual that had played out thousands of times. He hated it. At least his Dad had monopolized most of the dinner conversation, Sean had to say little more than "fine" when asked how school was.

His Dad was part of a newer IT team that dealt with networking stuff, and he talked about the new Windows 95 and what the plan was to deploy it at the university. The people in charge of the IT department were mostly old mainframe guys who considered the PC to be a passing fad. His Dad always complained about how they wanted to block everything new, and that if they got their way, it would be 1997 before his team would get to deploy the new OS campus-wide.

"So when are you going to put Windows 95 on the computer downstairs," Sean asked.

"Are you sure you want to learn a new operating system?" his Dad responded.

"Yeah, it's supposed to have a bunch of cool new stuff. Why not?"

"I'll have to look at the specs again to see if you even have enough RAM on that old 486. It might make everything run slower."

"Good point, Dad," Sean nodded. "Probably a better idea to buy a new Pentium, huh?"

"Clever argument, Sean... maybe you have a future in politics."

"Fine... I'll struggle along with ancient technology." He started out of the kitchen. "See you guys later."

"Where are you going?" Sean's Mom asked.

"Just out for a walk."

"Since when? That doesn't sound like you," she said as she eyed her son suspiciously.

"Oh, you're right, Mom, you got me. I'm going out to meet with a secret society who's in the final stages of a plan to take over the world. I'll try to get them to spare you and Dad."

"Sean, I don't want you out late on a school night." She crossed her arms and took an authoritative stance.

"I'm *not!* Chill! I'm not even taking the car. Just going out for a walk. No big deal, I probably won't even be gone an hour."

"If you're just going for a walk, why not take Maggie?" she suggested, "She'd like that."

"*No!*" protested Sean, then added in a softer voice, "I won't be walking the *whole* time."

"Sean," she said, fully engaging the Mom voice, "what's *really* going on?"

"OK, fine!" Sean huffed, "I'm just going down a couple of blocks to see Nicole Townsend."

"Who's she? You haven't mentioned her before," she said.

"She's new. They moved here just before school started. I've been helping her with Algebra. What's the big deal?"

"Are they in that blue house a few blocks down? The one that was for sale this summer?" his Dad asked, hoping to break the tension that was building.

"Yep, that's the place."

"Are her parents home?" his Mom asked.

"What's with the third degree?" Sean said defiantly.

His Mom glared.

Sean swallowed hard before responding with a milder tone. Her glare was intimidating. "She doesn't exactly live with her parents. She lives with her aunt and sister. Her dad got killed in Iraq, and her mom is... well, she's kinda sick, so they live with their aunt."

"Will the aunt be home?" his Mom continued to push.

"She's there all the time. She's some kind of artist and works in her home."

"She doesn't have a *real* job?"

"Come on, Michelle," his Dad intervened, "he's just going down the street to see a girl. It's not even dark."

She turned her glare to her husband. "Jack, we don't know anything about them. How can anyone make a living as an artist in this little town?"

He held her gaze.

Sean couldn't believe it; his Dad rarely got involved when his Mom was in interrogation mode, but he was glad that he picked this time to be on Sean's side.

"All right, Sean. *One hour.*" Her eyes were still locked on her husband. "Do you have homework to do?" she asked, finally turning to Sean.

"No."

"How about we say back before dark?" his Dad said pleasantly. "That's almost an hour and a half."

Michelle's mouth dropped and then her eyes became slits as she turned back to Jack.

Sean was equally surprised but decided to make the most of the situation. He took long quick strides toward the door. "OK, see you then," he said as he swung the door open and slipped out.

Just as he closed the door, he heard one last thing from his Dad. "Oh for crying out loud, Michelle, he's just going down the street to see a girl."

Sean walked briskly down the street, smiling as he thought about his Dad. It had been completely out of character for him, his Dad *never* crossed his Mom about *anything.* He wondered what had gotten into him. Then his thoughts turned to himself. What had gotten into *him*? He was on his way to ask Nicole out on a date. That wasn't in character for him, either, but he felt like it was time.

"Tonight," he thought aloud, "I'm going to ask her out tonight. To a movie this Friday night." Saying it out loud bolstered his courage for a moment, then it was dashed when he couldn't remember what movies were playing. He couldn't quite picture the marquee in front of the little six-screen Cineplex but hoped that at least one of them would be OK for a date.

As he got closer to the Townsend's house, his nerves ratcheted higher. He hadn't rehearsed what he was going to say. He couldn't simply knock on the door and say, "Hey, Nicole, want to go to a movie Friday night?"

Nicole might not even come to the door. What would he say if Alexis answered the door? "Hey, Alexis, I'm just checking to see if you're really OK with me and Nicole, I'm here to ask her on a date."

He imagined that they might still be eating dinner. Would he have to sit in the living room until they finished? *That would probably be better than having to sit with them while they ate,* he thought. He tried to imagine what they were eating. *Probably tofu and bean sprouts and a protein shake.*

As he got to the edge of their yard, he froze. *What am I doing here? This is crazy! Things were just getting comfortable with Nicole, and now she's going to think I'm a stalker or something again. What if she says 'no'? What would happen to our relationship at school if I ask her out and she says 'no'?*

He decided he should plead temporary insanity and go back home. He had to be totally nuts to have walked down the street without a plan. He tried to turn around and go back, but felt glued to the spot. He *was* going to ask her out, he knew it. Whatever the outcome, he could deal with it later. He *was* going to ask her out.

He walked up to the door, took a deep breath, and rang the bell. It was only a few minutes before the door opened. He hadn't considered that Aunt Katherine would answer the door.

"Umm... good evening, Ms. Tuttle," he stammered.

"Hello, Sean," she said pleasantly, "How are you this evening?"

"Ummm, I'm good... how about yourself?"

"Very well, thank you. Is there something I can do for you?"

"Ummm... is Nicole home?"

"Yes, the girls are both upstairs doing homework. Would you like to come in?" She stepped back and opened the door.

"Sure, umm... thanks," Sean said as he stepped past her and waited while she closed the door.

"Let me see if they can come down." She went to the stairway and called up, "Nicole, Alexis, your friend Sean from school is here."

"Thank you, Aunt Katherine," Nicole shouted back, "I will be down in a few minutes."

"Hi, Sean," Alexis called down, "I have just engaged in washing my hair and am not presentable. Do you mind that I do not come down?"

"No, that's fine," Sean called upstairs, relieved.

"Why not sit in the living room until Nicole comes down?" Katherine said, ushering Sean toward the couch. "I just remembered, Sean, I have *one* brownie remaining from my Sunday meeting, would you care for it?"

"Oh, no thank you, Ms. Tuttle, I just finished dinner."

"Only one, dear, and no one in this household will consume it. I will retrieve it for you."

She left the room and returned with a small plate with one brownie in the middle. They sat on the couch together.

"It has the peanut butter frosting," she said as she handed it to him.

"OK. Thanks." He lifted it from the plate and took a bite. "So how'd the ladies like them?"

"They seemed to find them enjoyable, consuming all but this one."

"It's still good."

"Oh, something else while we wait, Sean. I have a new art project I would like to show you."

"Sure," Sean said as he finished the brownie.

She left the room and returned carrying what appeared to be wrap-around dark glasses. She handed them to him.

"It is a unique three-dimensional effect, you will require these special glasses to view it."

He took the glasses from her and put them on.

"Mozart. Bowie. Gershwin. Gaga."

"What?" Sean asked. "What did you say?"

"No matter, dear, you will not remember."

Suddenly a myriad of images flashed before his eyes, but they seemed to be inside his head. There were sounds; he heard sounds... like a tape player playing in fast forward. He felt strange, like he was losing his balance.

And then everything went black.

* * * * *

"Sean? Sean? Can you hear me?"

Sean could hear someone calling his name, but they were a long way away, and they must have been in a cave because the sound was echoing in a strange way. No, it was dark. Maybe he was in a cave? Why would he be in a cave? Someone lightly slapped his face. Why would the cave voice be slapping his face?

"Sean? Please! Sean!"

He thought he recognized that voice, and it sounded closer. It was that girl. He thought of Alexis. No, that other girl. The twin. The evil twin. No. Someone else called her that. The nickel girl. Ni28.

"Sean? Sean! Wake up!"

He was asleep? Why was he asleep in a cave? Nickel girl was getting closer. She said wake up. Maybe he should try to open his eyes.

His vision was a little blurry, but he could see the girl's face.

"There you are! Oh, Sean, you frightened me!"

"Sorry," he slurred, "you scared of caves?"

"Caves? I do not know what you mean. Never mind. Look at me. Do you know who I am?"

He blinked a couple of times; his vision was returning. "Yes... Nickel..." he slurred, "no, no nickel... Nicole. Nick Coal."

"That is correct, Nicole. Nicole Townsend. How do you feel?"

"Nick Coal Town Sin. You're that girl." He closed his eyes. "I don't feel good. Dizzy. Head hurts."

"I want you to drink this," she said, holding a glass in front of him.

He cracked his eyes open. "Have we been drinking?"

"No, Sean," she said patiently, "we have not been drinking, and this is not alcohol."

"What is it?" He tried to focus on the glass, and then back to Nicole's face. It made the dizziness worse.

"Something that will help you feel better. Please drink it."

He looked again at the glass. It seemed to be clear. "Water?"

"Mostly... we can discuss that after you drink."

Sean took the glass. He sniffed it, but it didn't have an odor. He tipped it up until a little bit went into his mouth. It didn't have a taste either. He decided it must be water, drank it, and handed the glass back to Nicole. She set it on the end table.

"Count backwards for me from ten to zero."

Sean was suddenly panicky. He'd seen enough medical TV shows to know what counting backwards meant. "You're putting me under?" He shouted.

"No. Please calm down. I am doing a simple cognitive test to ascertain your ability to count backwards. I will also listen for any slurred speech."

"Oh... OK... Ten Nine Eight Seven Six Five Four Three Two One... Blast Off!"

"Your speech sounds normal, and it appears you might be exhibiting... humor?"

"I do feel better. Hey! I feel a *lot* better."

"Good. What is the last thing you remember happening?"

"Wait... did I black out?"

"You lost consciousness for a few minutes. What do you remember?"

"Do I need to go to the emergency room? Maybe something's wrong with me."

"I believe once we talk this through, you will be fine. Please. What do you remember?"

"OK... umm, I sat on the couch with your aunt. I ate the last brownie. Then she brought me something that looked like wrap around shades and said it was some art thing she was working on."

"Good. Then what happened?"

"Then I put the glasses on and your aunt said some weird stuff... Mozart...Boy... Gershwin... Goggles... I think."

"That is close. Your brain interpreted other words for two names that you must not think fit the list. Interesting. But continue."

"Then it just went black... and I woke up with you here."

"Concentrate. Just before it went black. What did you see and hear?"

"Nothing. Just *Bam!* I blacked out."

"Your response was too quick, Sean. I need you to think about it. Concentrate. Focus."

Sean paused and closed his eyes for a moment. He remembered flashes of pictures. "Pictures. Lots of pictures. Changing too fast to see anything... and sound. Sound like a tape recorder running at too high of a speed."

"Good. OK, Sean. Look at my eyes and concentrate."

"Luke een to my yize," Sean said, attempting a Transylvanian accent.

"You are not concentrating."

"Come on... that was supposed to be Bela Lugosi. You know, like Dracula hypnotizing someone?"

"It was an excellent interpretation. Now, please. Look at my eyes and concentrate."

"Should I concentrate on how beautiful they are?" He grinned a silly grin.

"Yes. That is acceptable."

"Beautiful green and sparkly."

"Good. Listen to my voice and concentrate. Now close your eyes and think of the pictures. Can you visualize them in your mind?"

"Yes. I think so. They move fast. I can't make anything out."

"Yes, you can. I will help you. Concentrate and we will slow them down."

"Hey! It's like a movie."

"Slower."

"And I'm in it. And so are you! Wow! Aunt Katherine's little art project is awesome!"

"Relax. Let it flow. Absorb it all. Relax."

Her voice was soothing. So gentle. So beautiful. He felt very warm, comfortable, relaxed.

He could see himself. Sean was in his kitchen, and everything was kind of swirly, but he could see Nicole, and Maggie was barking at her, and then she stopped. They were sitting in the living room. Nicole was there... no, it was Alexis... no, Aunt Katherine. It's Nicole again. She says to not be afraid. She's gone. There's some boy in a shiny suit. He says he's from the future. Now it's Nicole again. They walk down the street to her house. The shiny suit boy and Sean go out back and get into something the size of a golf cart. When they get out, Sean throws up. They walk back down the street toward his house but go into the alley before they get there. There are two Seans. One is across the street shooting hoops. The hot college girl comes down the street. Basketball Sean goes into the house. College girl comes over to the other Sean and pulls her face off. It's the Future-Boy...Alex. His name is Alex. They go back to Nicole's house and get in the vehicle. Alex has a purple shirt on. They walk around the block the long way back to Sean's house. They go in. Sean gets his Dad's hair brush. Nicole takes it. They talk. He sits down and then he's asleep.

"Sean? Sean, come back to me."

"Nicole? What happened?" Sean mumbled, "Did I black out again?"

"No, but you were in an REM-like state. Do you feel as if you had a dream?"

"Yes! It was weird! We were both in it. And Alexis and Aunt Katherine and somebody named Alex. He said he was from the future."

"That sounds... interesting. What else happened?"

Sean continued, "We went somewhere, and then there were two of me. Then it really gets weird. This hot chick is jogging down the street but then she comes over to me and then pulls her face off, and it's this Alex guy. Weird, huh?"

"Not necessarily. A little incomplete, though."

"Incomplete? What do you mean?"

She took his hand, and he looked into her eyes. "Suppose it was not a dream. Would you be frightened?"

"I don't know. That's weird, though, in the dream you told me to not be frightened."

"Were you?" she asked, "In your dream, were you frightened?"

"I think I was at first, but then it all seemed OK."

"No one harmed you? You were always safe?"

"Yes. Well, excuse the grossness, but I threw up at one point."

"The people with you in your dream," she pressed, "They did not harm you. You enjoyed being with them; it was just that unusual events occurred."

"I suppose. What are you getting at?"

Nicole took a deep breath. "That it was not a dream. It all happened."

"That's crazy talk!" Sean laughed but quickly stopped when he saw Nicole was being quite serious. "Wait a minute... is this all part of your aunt's art thing? What's going on? Where is your aunt, by the way?"

"I hope this works," Nicole said as she tapped a place on her neck. She shimmered and was replaced by Aunt Katherine.

"I am right here," Katherine said calmly.

"What the hell?" Sean shouted as he crab-crawled backward to the far end of the couch.

"Sean," Katherine said with a soothing voice, "You are safe. Nothing is going to harm you."

Sean stared wide-eyed at Katherine. She didn't move. He started laughing. "OK... OK, you really got me," he said through the laughter. "That was a good one. You really are amazing! You should go on television or something. How'd you do that? Where's Nicole? Is she behind some mirror or something? Come on... how'd you do that?"

Katherine sighed. "Let me start by again telling you that you are safe. No one is going to harm you. I know that you enjoy Science Fiction. You like to read it, and you enjoy television and movies that have Science Fiction themes."

"Yeah, so?"

"There is a British television show that you have watched. You even watched it with your father when you were much younger."

"Yeah, *Doctor Who*, so?"

"Did you ever wish it was real?"

"Yeah," he said reluctantly, "I suppose... when I was little."

"And when you imagined it was real, did it make you feel happy?"

"I guess," he shrugged.

"Then *please* be happy, Sean," Katherine pleaded, "It *is* real. I *am* from your future. My name is... well... you call me Alex. I am your great-great-great-great-great-grandson."

Sean stared at her for a moment, then shook his head. "Sorry, that just sounds nuts."

"If it were not true, how can you explain this?" Katherine said as she touched her neck with her left hand, shimmered, and became Alexis. "Or this?" She shimmered again and became Nicole. "Or how about this?" Nicole shifted outfits in front of his eyes, showing him everything that he'd seen her wear in the same order as she wore them in school. "Even if I *could* slip behind a mirror and have Alexis or Nicole come out, could Nicole change clothes that rapidly?"

Sean's mouth dropped. "Holy crap," he said softly. His eyes were saucers.

"Sean, do you trust me?" Nicole asked gently.

He stared at her. "I don't know... who *are* you?"

"I am someone who you have gone to class with for the last few weeks. Someone you have talked with, eaten lunch with, given a ride home. I am Nicole. I am Alexis. I also happen to be a distant descendant of yours."

It was quiet as Sean continued to stare at her. Neither of them moved. Sean rubbed his face. He shook his head. He started to speak, and then stopped. Nicole waited. "The dream," Sean finally said, "you say it really happened? When?"

"Friday; when I came to your home after school," she said softly.

He rubbed his face some more. "Why don't I remember?"

"I blocked your memory with nanites."

"Nanites?"

"They were in the smoothie," she confessed.

"And that kept me from remembering?"

"Yes."

"Why?"

"It could be dangerous to the timeline for you to know about future events."

"But you want me to remember now?"

"Yes."

"Why?"

"I have something I wish to talk to you about. In actuality, Alex has something."

Sean leaned forward with his elbows on his knees, face hidden in his hands. He rubbed at his face vigorously, then sat still for several seconds. Nicole waited. He straightened back upright and glared at Nicole, his face serious, hard. "OK... *Alex*... what do you have to say?" he asked gruffly.

"You sound angry," Nicole said warily.

"I don't know *what* I feel. I *thought* I was coming over here to ask you out on a date."

Nicole sat quietly, looking down at her hands for a few seconds. "Could you trust me to do one more thing?" she asked softly.

"Why *should* I?" Sean snapped back at her.

She recoiled slightly, then was motionless for another few seconds, glancing between her hands and Sean. "It will make everything much clearer."

"What will?"

"Now that you have the basic image of what happened already in your mind, if you would let me connect you to the computer again, it will fill in the gaps. When completed, it should be almost as if it were your own memory of what happened."

Sean stared at her angrily. She didn't flinch. She didn't drop her eyes away from him. Sean felt angry. He felt betrayed. He felt confused. But beneath the surface of those negative feelings, he felt curious and had to know the truth. "OK. Hook me up!"

"You will need to put on the glasses again."

"OK... so?"

"Will you be frightened if I bring them over to you? Will it make you uncomfortable if I touch you? I could set them between us and step back."

"Why do you keep telling me I'm safe and asking if I'm scared? *Should* I be?"

"No. However, last time you reacted fearfully when you discovered my identity."

"Last time? So this really *did* happen before?"

"Yes."

"And I acted scared?"

"Yes. You thought I was an alien, and that I was going to eat your brain." Sean smiled. "OK, I can see that. I really freaked out, huh?"

Nicole smiled back. "Yes, you also hypothesized that you were John Connors, and I was sent to terminate you."

"Really? OK... *that's* getting a little crazy. What else?"

"I believe," she started carefully, "that if you would put the glasses back on, you will remember."

Sean nodded. "OK, let's try it."

Nicole picked up the glasses from the end table and handed them to Sean, then stepped back.

"So, I put them on and what happens?" Sean asked.

"I believe I can guide you through this second iteration, and it will fill in the parts that appear missing. From what you said, it was almost like you only had notes of what happened instead of the entire story."

Sean slid the glasses on. "Will I black out again?"

"I do not know," she confessed. "I do not believe so. You may experience a dreamlike state. I only know how it works for me. But your brain has not experienced nanite interfaces for your entire life like mine has."

"OK, so let's try it."

"Sit comfortably. Try to relax. Listen to my voice. I am starting the sequence now."

Sean jerked as the images flashed in his head again. He felt dizzy again, but then heard Nicole's voice over the din that played in his mind.

"Relax. Let the images flow," she said in a soothing monotone. "Concentrate on each one that you remember, and let it fill itself out."

It became clearer to Sean. It was kind of like watching a movie, but more like living a movie, he decided. He could see himself in the scene as he watched it all happen again.

"Concentrate," Nicole continued gently, "Allow the Sean that you see in your mind to merge and become you. See what he sees. Experience what he experiences. Everything truly transpired. It is all real."

They both sat quietly for a few minutes; then Sean removed the glasses. Nicole watched him expectantly. He smiled. "So, Future-Boy, does this mean you decided to take me on your jump back to when my Dad is a teenager?"

Nicole slid close to Sean and hugged him. "It worked! You remember!"

Sean pulled her arms away from the hug. "Easy there, *grandson*. I also remember that I don't like you getting *mushy* with me."

Nicole slid back, still smiling. "Yes, oh venerable grandfather," she said with a slight bow, "Please accept the apology of your unworthy descendant."

"I see you've been working on the sarcastic tone," Sean said, "I like it."

"Thank you. May I drop the Nicole disguise?"

"Knock yourself out."

Nicole touched her neck with her left hand and pulled on her hair with her right. As the head mask slid off, her body shimmered and then Alex sat where she had been. "I still do not understand that idiom. Why would anyone attempt to knock themselves unconscious?"

Sean thought about it for a moment, then shrugged. "Got me. I think it's from a movie or something. People say it when they mean 'go ahead.'"

"I will have to remember to ask the linguists for clarification when I return to my own time."

"So...Nicole tells me you have something you want to talk to me about," Sean deadpanned.

"Yes," Alex said with a smile, "I am pleased that she relayed the message."

Sean waited a few moments, watching Alex, then prompting, "Aaaaand what's the subject of this important matter that needs to be discussed?"

"I wanted to ask you if you would be willing to participate in an experiment," Alex said warily.

"What kind of experiment?"

"With your memory."

"Didn't we just do that?"

"No," Alex said, then paused to think about it. "Well, yes, I see what you mean. But no, there is more to the experiment than what we have just done."

"How much more?"

"I wish to attempt to store some of your memories in your own brain, in a place that you cannot access without a prompt from me."

Sean furrowed his brow as he stared at Alex, started to speak, and then stopped. He thought for a moment, then began to speak again, "OK, let me check this with you." He rubbed the right side of his face. "You want me to have memories in my own brain, that I can't actually remember?"

"Yes."

"And that doesn't sound totally nuts to you when you hear me say that?"

"No... it was a paraphrase of what I already said."

Sean squinted his left eye. "How can I have memories in my brain that I can't remember?"

"Do you understand that you do not have total recall of every minute of your life?"

"What do you mean?"

"What was the name of the third person you talked to on April 5, 1990?"

"I don't know," Sean said irritably, "That was five years ago." He crossed his arms. "I suppose *you* know?"

"No, I am attempting to make a point about memories. Let me pose another example. You had your eleventh birthday in 1990. Do you remember any birthday presents that you received?"

"Let me think about it," said Sean. "Yeah, I got a new baseball glove that year. The old one was getting too small."

"Why do you remember the birthday present, but not who you talked to on April 5th?"

"Why don't you get to your point," Sean said in exasperation, "I don't *care* who I talked to on April 5th in 1990."

"Precisely my point. That is one of the factors for recall. The memory is more likely to be retrieved if it was something that was important to you. Do you suppose that if the person you talked to on April 5, 1990 were to say to you, 'remember five years ago when we were talking about baseball?' that you might then remember the conversation?"

"I suppose," Sean conceded. "Still looking for your point."

"The point is that you *already* have memories that you do not remember. You do not have a searchable index of all your memories. Your memories are retrieved when the correct stimulus is provided. By using a question about your birthday, I stimulated the retrieval of that memory."

"OK. Fine! It's *not* nuts to say I have memories that I don't remember," Sean snapped.

Alex studied Sean's face before he spoke. "I was not attempting to prove that you were wrong," he said softly. "I was attempting to focus your comprehension."

"OK, got it," Sean said, his voice still a little gruff, "I've got memories I don't remember. So what does *that* have to do with your experiment?"

"Initially, I had intended only to have a single contact with you, obtain your father's DNA, block your memory from storing the experience, and then return to my observations as Nicole and Alexis."

Sean waited a beat see if Alex was going to continue, then impatiently prompted him, "OK, so now you've changed your mind."

"Yes," Alex said slowly, "upon further reflection, I discovered that I enjoyed relating to you as my true self." He looked away, shyly. "You treat me... Alex me... differently than you treat Nicole or Alexis. I wanted to experience more contact with you in that way."

Sean shrugged. "OK, here I am! Now what?"

"You have witnessed the rather convoluted tactics employed to replace your missing memory."

"Yes, even with my poor 20th Century brain, I get that. Have you ever heard the phrase, 'to make a long story, short...'?"

"If my intent is to have multiple contacts with you, it would be impractical to reload your memory each time as we did tonight."

"Are we getting close to the 'therefore' yet?" Sean asked hopefully.

"Yes. Therefore, the solution involves storing certain memories in a way that would not have a retrieval mechanism of your own volition."

"What, like a password protected file on my hard drive? In this case the hard drive is in my head?"

Alex was puzzled by Sean's questions. He glanced away to access information from his computer. "If I correctly interpret your terminology, I believe that is close enough to use as an analogy."

Sean took some time to think it over. "OK. I guess it would be better than the movie glasses blackout thing we did tonight. You just need me to agree?"

"Yes," Alex said, then carefully added, "and also ingest more nanites. I thought it would be better to ask you this time. I am beginning to register a feeling of guilt from all of the times that I have had you ingest them without your knowledge."

Sean started counting on his fingers, "The brownies, the smoothie." He stopped and stared harshly at Alex. "And the brownie again tonight?"

Alex nodded, then softly added, "And in the water... but that was only to rectify your misfiring synapses."

Sean pointed at his pinkie finger. "Four? Four times? So, what, is there like some kind of a time-travel code that says you get four freebies and then you have to ask?"

"No, but I consider this proposal a significant change."

"What do you mean?"

"We have arrived at what you might colloquially refer to as 'a fork in the road.' There are two possible outcomes. I do not want the decision of which path to take to be mine alone."

"So what are my choices?" Sean asked, "For this 'fork'?"

"I can still remove all memory of me, and return to my original plan to only interact with you as Nicole and Alexis."

"Or?"

"If you *do* agree to ingest more nanites, I can use them to store your memories of me and what we experience together, in a portion of your brain that is, as you say, 'password protected.'"

"And you could just flip my memories on or off at will?"

"That is an over simplification, but I will agree that your statement reflects the core of the procedure."

"Will it affect my other memories? Like would you be able to make me forget that I watched the Chiefs game last Sunday?"

"No. It requires a set trigger point... which I have already set."

"So that's what Mozart Boogie Gershwin Googoo is about?"

"Yes, but it is Bowie and Gaga. That phrase is a list of composers. There is a less than .0003 percent probability of it being spoken by anyone but me in a conversation."

"Composers? Wait. Bowie? David Bowie? Seriously? In the same list as Mozart and Gershwin?"

"Mozart was not as revered during his life as what you think of him historically. Recognition of genius is in the 'eye of the beholder', or rather ear, in this case, and often only in retrospect."

"So who's the Gaga guy? Never heard of him."

"Her. She is a few more years in your future, but you will know when she arrives."

"Great... something I can look forward to... oh wait," Sean said sarcastically, "I *can't* because you'll wipe my memory."

"As I have previously stated, I am not technically wiping your memory."

"Yeah, yeah, never mind the terminology. Keep explaining."

"If you agree to accept the next group of nanites, everything from the trigger point to when it is triggered will be stored in your own brain, but the nanites will block any access that you would normally have. Instead of losing the memories when you become unconscious, they remain, but in a sense, hidden."

"I gotta go back to saying that sounds totally nuts."

"Let me stimulate a memory that can help you understand this concept. You now remember what happened last Friday, including that you moved backward in the space/time continuum."

"OK, I think that's obvious."

"Now recall the rest of Friday when we were together. You listened to a musical compact disc. You helped someone with Algebra. Who were you with?"

"You."

"Me? Think about that specific point in time. Who did you spend it with?"

Sean thought carefully; then his face went blank when he understood what Alex was saying. "I was with *Nicole*... and I had no idea she was *you*... you were *her*... she wasn't... aw, you know what I mean."

"Yes. Now think about today just before your Algebra class when you were talking with Nicole."

"And Alexis came up to us," Sean said, then stopped abruptly when his jaw dropped. He stared wide-eyed at Alex. "OK, *how* did you do that?"

Pleased with himself, Alex smiled. "It was a short jump. After I had met with you after school as Alexis, I jumped back in time a few hours. Primarily because Nicole and Alexis both had exams in their classes second hour. I then retained my second iteration, Alexis, to further support the illusion that Nicole and Alexis are two distinct persons."

"Clever," Sean said, nodding as a smile bloomed. "I'm impressed."

"Thank you, but my point is this: you knew at one point last Friday that Nicole and Alexis are, in fact, the same person. You also are aware of that fact right now. Describe your memory of that moment before Algebra."

Sean blinked a few times. He looked at Alex, then looked away with closed eyes and thought about Nicole and Alexis together, then looked again to Alex. "It's like... I don't know... two different realities? I *know* that you masquerade as both girls, but then I have a perfect memory of Nicole and

Alexis together, and I *know* that they're two different people. Wow! That is so freakin' bizarre."

"I have formulated a hypothesis. I believe that with additional nanites, I would be able to isolate the two disparate realities within your brain. Thus, you would remember everything that we do when we are together like this. My half of the 'we' being me as Alex. For the major portion of time, you would believe the reality without Alex to be the true reality."

"Why are we looking at this as an option?"

"As I have stated, I find that you are different with me as Alex than you are when I am either girl."

"Or Aunt Katherine, don't forget the famous Aunt Katherine."

"Still, the difference is enough to make an interesting comparison for my study."

"So," Sean said with a slight bitterness, "I'm a more interesting lab rat when I'm aware of who's making me run the mazes?"

Alex turned his gaze to the floor. Sean crossed his arms over his chest, impatiently waiting for an answer. Alex slowly lifted his eyes until they met Sean's. "That is my excuse," he admitted, "It is a scientific justification, but not the truthful primary reason. The truth is that I enjoy being with you as myself. I like it that you know who I am and accept it. I appreciate the ways that you relate to me."

Sean's posture relaxed as Alex spoke. He was surprised by the emotion in his descendant's voice, but then suddenly started laughing.

"What do you find humorous in what I have said?" Alex asked, obviously hurt by the reaction.

"You can be so incredibly blunt as Nicole or Alexis, but when you're yourself, it's hard for you to be direct about your own feelings."

"I do not understand what you mean."

"OK," Sean said, still amused, "answer me this, quadruple great-grandson..."

"Quintuple," Alex interrupted.

"Fine! *Quintuple* great-grandson," Sean said with an eye roll. "Do you still do things for fun in the future?"

"Yes. There are options for people to entertain themselves."

"And it's out in the open? Not illegal to have fun?"

"I believe, in most cases, people engage in activities of amusement that are not contrary to the legal code."

"So why is it so hard for you to admit that it is just plain old fun to hang out with me as Alex?"

"It is not the design of my historical studies to amuse myself. It is serious research."

"Wow," Sean said with a sad head shake, "All work and no play, makes Jack a dull boy."

"I do not understand the reference to Jack. Are you referring to your father?"

"No, it's just a saying. It means that if you focus only on work and don't allow yourself to have some fun along the way, you become pretty dull."

Alex reflected on Sean's statement. "Your suggestion is that I can continue with my observations, but also allow myself to be amused and that the two are not mutually exclusive."

"I couldn't have said it better myself," Sean said as he rolled his eyes. "So... let's have some fun. Bring on the nanites. Load up some brownies."

"Unfortunately," said Alex, "you have already consumed the last one."

"Well, trot out Aunt Katherine and make some more."

"I did not create them. I purchased them from the bakery nearest to the university campus."

"Seriously? Someone as multi-talented as Aunt Katherine can't make her own brownies?"

"It is much simpler to purchase them from someone who specializes in confectioneries."

Sean sighed dramatically. "And where's the love in that?"

Alex was about to answer, but stopped when he notice the smile that started to curl on Sean's face. "I believe you are not sincerely disappointed about the manufacture of the brownies. Correct me if I use the wrong terminology, but are you messing with me?"

"Good one, Future-Boy! You're getting the hang of it!" Sean slapped him on the back. "Although those *were* good brownies, and I wouldn't mind having more." He shrugged. "Oh well, so what's the alternative?"

"The simplest methodology would be to place them in enough water to allow you to drink them."

"OK... I suppose that's better than mixing them in whatever glop you usually eat. Say, what *is* that stuff that Alexis and Nicole claim is homemade yogurt?"

"Formula Ten."

Sean gave Alex a disbelieving look. "Seriously? So there aren't any marketing people in the future? Never mind. What's in it?"

"It is the perfect blend of protein, carbohydrates, fat, minerals and vitamins at the correct caloric level to provide the needed nutrients for my body while I am in my teen years."

"Sounds disgusting. What's it taste like?"

"It is, for the most part, flavor neutral."

"Why do you want to eat stuff that doesn't taste like anything?"

"For nutrition."

"Yeah, but why not make it taste good?"

"Good is a term of relativity. I do not know how something could taste 'good.'"

"OK, that smoothie Nicole made last Friday. You drank some of that. Did you like the way that it tasted?"

"It was an interesting combination of flavors. The strawberries provided a degree of sweetness, while the ascorbic acid in the orange juice contributed to a sour sensation, accented by the yogurt."

"I didn't ask for a chemical breakdown. *Did you like it?*" Sean asked with a tinge of frustration.

"It was not an unpleasant experience."

"OK, Future-Boy, you're getting on my nerves with your over analyzing." Sean blew out a breath, then tried to force a smile as he breathed in. "You've got two choices: Yum! It tasted good; I'd drink that again, or Yuck! It made me want to hurl."

"If limited to only those two criteria, I would select, 'yum, it tasted good.'"

"Now was that so hard?" Sean punctuated his remark with widespread arms. "So, if it tasted good, why not make your tasteless glop taste like a smoothie?"

Alex was perplexed. "What would be the purpose of the flavoring?"

"Are you kidding me?" Sean smacked his forehead. "So you can say, 'yum, this tastes good' instead of 'eh, this tastes like nothing.'"

"Do you suggest that the goal is to gain a simple pleasure from consumption?"

"Ding-ding-ding-ding!" Sean said enthusiastically while pointing an index finger at Alex. "You eat things that taste *good,* and you don't eat things that taste *bad*." His voice had a sing-song rhythm. "Good tasting things make you *happy*, things like broccoli you eat because your mom says you *have* to."

"That could lead to an imbalance of nutrients," argued Alex, "Long-term consumption based on pleasure as the main criteria could lead to obesity or in extreme cases a medical condition such as diabetes."

"OK, I give up!" Sean threw his hands in the air. "Just dump the nanites in some water. I don't care how it tastes."

"You seem to become angry with me for reasons I do not comprehend," Alex said softly.

"Yeah, yeah... I know, I'm one of those grumpy grandfathers."

"That was an attempt to divert the subject by making a humorous remark," Alex noted.

Sean was about to snap back at Alex until he saw him wince in anticipation. He paused for a breath, then softened his face and voice. "OK, I just don't get why you don't want your food to taste good."

"I was attempting to explain my rational, but with each statement I made, your anger escalated."

"And *you* always have to be *right*," Sean growled, "you quote your data so you can prove whatever I think is stupid. You never just say what you think or feel! It's always facts, data, historical studies..."

Alex surveyed Sean's body language and thought long and hard before responding. "I feel...." He struggled with the word, "...sad. I feel sad that what I say makes you angry. It leads me to believe that you do not like me."

Sean took a turn to think long and hard. "I *do* like you... I think. I think I like *all* of you. Alexis, Nicole, Aunt Katherine, and even you, too, Future-Boy." He laid a hand on Alex's shoulder and looked him in the eye. "But, I also gotta say that each and every one of you makes me crazy at times. Well, maybe not Aunt Katherine. Aunt Katherine's pretty cool." He grinned. "Too bad about the brownies, though."

"You like me? Although I stimulate your anger when I explain things?"

"Yeah, yeah, I know. But, hey, I love my Mom and Dad, and they can *really* make me crazy sometimes."

Alex nodded slowly. "I will attempt to observe which of my actions 'make you crazy' and minimize them."

Sean chuckled. "You *do* that, grandson. OK, let's dump some nanites in some water," Sean said. "So, I guess they know how to swim, huh?"

"The human body is composed of between approximately 55 to 80% water. It would only be logical..." Alex started, then looked sheepishly at a scowling Sean, "I mean, yes, they can swim."

Alex stood and went down the hall. Sean followed him into the garage. Alex poured something from a large transparent container into a smaller vial, then set the vial into a clear box and pressed the front panel. Once the contents had glowed dimly, he touched the panel again.

"Wait," Sean said with concern, "they're not radioactive, are they?"

"No," Alex answered, "Well, no more than you are. Everything emits some radiation."

Alex stepped past Sean and went back into the house. Sean trailed behind him into the kitchen.

"So, if it's not radioactive, why did it glow?"

"That was the reaction from programming the nanites. They were inert before programming."

"You just flip a switch and they're programmed?"

"That was merely the activation phase. I had pre-programmed the computer to transfer the instructions the nanites needed once activated."

"Pretty sure I would agree to this, huh?" Sean asked.

"I was not certain. I merely was prepared for this eventuality."

Alex went to the kitchen sink and turned on the tap. He ran about a cup of water into a glass then dumped the contents of the vial into it.

"Whoa, that dissolved fast!" Sean marveled.

"They are not in solution, merely in suspension. However, the nanites are so small that when they spread out into the water they appear to vanish. I might also mention that even though this appears to be a standard 20th Century faucet, it has been replaced with a unit designed to filter out all contaminants, especially those that *are* truly dissolved. You could achieve similar results by a process of distillation, using your existing technology."

"I need to know this, why?"

Alex blinked a few times. "I suppose it is not a requirement. I was simply informing you that although it appeared to be tap water, the glass contains unadulterated water."

"Come on! I drink tap water all the time. It's completely safe. We're not in some third world country where you have to boil it to make it safe."

"I am aware that municipalities place chemical additives in your water to remove any harmful bacteria. However, the *minerals* dissolved in this water remain high since its source is an aquifer. Continual ingestion of this mineral-laden water over a period of twenty to thirty years will greatly enhance the probability of developing kidney stones."

"Right. Eating, drinking and breathing are all hazardous to my health. I should stop doing all three. Oh wait... then I'd be dead... which is *also* hazardous to my health."

"Solar and cosmic radiation," Alex said.

"What?"

"I was assisting you to compile a longer list of items that you expose your body to that are hazardous to your health."

"Thanks," Sean said sarcastically as he grabbed the glass from Alex, "Give me that." He tilted his head back as he chugged it. "What's next?"

"Now that the nanites are in place, we should test to see if they can function as expected."

"So you are going to make me forget everything again?"

"Yes," Alex answered slowly, "I have to censor myself to not explain to you that your terminology is not entirely correct since that appears to disturb you." He attempted to smile as Sean glared at him. "However, assuming success, you will continue from the point of Aunt Katherine giving you the glasses. You will become unaware of anything that has transpired since."

Sean thought back to that moment and imagined erasing everything else. "Wait a minute! I was going to ask Nicole out on a date!"

"Yes, that is my assumption of what you will do."

"Well, now I don't *want* to ask you out on a date!" Sean said adamantly.

"You will, however, still desire to ask Nicole to accompany you to a movie."

"But *you're* Nicole! I don't want to go on a date with *you*!"

"Remember earlier when you said that it was almost as if there were two realities? You will return to the other reality. You will still be interested in Nicole, and ask her on a date."

"OK, but *you* still know you are Nicole."

"That is true... but that has always been the case."

"Then *you* don't have to accept!"

"Would you not be disappointed if Nicole were unwilling to go on a date with you?"

"Maybe... but I'll get over it!"

"I believe you will find it enjoyable if all goes as planned with my experiments over the next few days."

"Enjoyable? *What are you going to do?*" He grabbed Alex by the shoulders.

"Please! Calm down. Do I have to assure you again that no harm is going to come to you?"

"*What have you got planned for this date?*" Sean said through clenched teeth.

Alex looked away in what Sean recognized as the 'ask the computer' twitch.

"Now what?" Sean's voice was still edgy.

"I am running scenarios." Alex turned back to Sean. "It appears to be a null outcome. If my plans are successful, it will not matter that you know. If unsuccessful, you will not remember. Thus, it will not matter." He glanced at each of Sean's hands still gripping his shoulders and braced himself. "I am strongly leading toward your proposal of taking you to the past to meet your father as a teenager."

Sean's hard face broke into a huge smile, and he gave Alex's shoulders a friendly shake. "Really? You're really going to take me? How long will we be gone?" He dropped his hands.

"I have not fully determined that I *will* take that course of action, so I have not yet designed the scenario, nor yet know the duration."

"Well, let's get going on the testing thing then! Where do I go? What do I do?" Sean said excitedly.

"You will need to be sitting on the couch just as you were when you first put on the glasses."

Sean rushed to the living room and eagerly perched on the couch. "OK, ready."

Alex examined the room and compared it to a visual image retrieved from his computer. "You need to move approximately 2 inches to your left, and lean back another 5 degrees."

Sean scooted to the left. "OK, I can do 2 inches... not so much on the 5 degrees. How far is that?"

"Start to tilt backward and I will tell you when to stop."

Sean slowly let his body go backward until Alex told him to stop. Alex then took his face mask and slid it on. When in place, he touched the spot on his neck to activate the pseudo body, and Aunt Katherine replaced Alex. She picked up the glasses and handed them to Sean, who slid them on.

"Will I black out again?" Sean asked.

"I do not believe you will. I am hoping at most you will experience a few nanoseconds of vertigo. Do you feel prepared?"

"Hit me!"

"Mozart. Bowie. Gershwin. Gaga. Store. Password: Lambda X-ray Seventeen One."

Sean's body jerked slightly. He rapidly blinked several times. "Whoa."

"Sean?" Aunt Katherine asked, "Are you all right?"

"Yeah, just felt a little dizzy when I put these on."

"That is odd. You should feel no effect on your vision before you activate the program," she said. "Now, if you would look up to the upper left corner to activate them."

Sean glanced up to the left as she asked. He could see a small blue sphere.

"Do you see a blue ball?" asked Katherine.

"Yeah. Pretty cool. It does look 3D."

"Now move it around with your eyes. Experiment. Change your depth of field. What do you see?"

Sean changed his focal point to various places in the room; the ball seemed to be floating around the room wherever he looked. When he tried to look *at* the ball, it seemed to come closer to him and get larger. "That is so awesome!"

"Now look back at me," Katherine said as she held her right-hand palm up at her side. "Try to place the ball on my hand. It may take awhile. Let me know when you've achieved that position."

Sean shifted his eyes around, trying to get a feel for moving the ball where he wanted. Left, right, up, down were all easy. Moving it toward himself or away took more concentration. He finally got it into position. "OK, I've got it so it looks like it's sitting on your hand."

"Is it about the size of a basketball?" she asked.

"Yes."

She moved her left hand over the top of the ball, and it looked as if she were holding it in both hands. "Watch closely," she said, "I believe you will find this phase enjoyable." She pushed the ball down with her left hand, and it bounced off the floor. She continued to dribble it like a basketball.

"Wow! Wow! Oh, wow! I can't believe you are doing that!" Sean said excitedly. "That is beyond awesome!"

She held the ball. "You can take the glasses off now."

Sean pulled the glasses off, and the ball disappeared. "That. Was. Amazing! Totally awesome! How did you do that?"

"Did Alexis explain to you that my brother was a computer programmer?"

Sean tried to remember what Alexis had said about her dad and computers when she told him that he was killed in Iraq. Sean nodded.

"I also dabble a little," Katherine said modestly.

"A *little*? If you could turn that into a video game, you'd make a fortune!"

"That is very kind of you to say," Katherine said warmly, "but you did not come to this house to observe my projects. You want to see Nicole. Let me go up and determine why she is taking so long." Aunt Katherine stood and went to the stairs. As she ascended the stairs, she stopped a moment to look back down to Sean. "I have some tasks I need to complete up here, so you two can have a private conversation." She winked at him. Sean felt the heat of a full-on blush hit his face as she disappeared up the stairs. He started to panic since he still hadn't thought of how he was going to ask Nicole out on a date. It was only moments before he heard footsteps coming down the stairs.

"I am sorry that it took so long, Sean," Nicole said brightly, "I was not dressed for company." He swallowed hard as she crossed the room and sat on the couch beside him. She was incredibly gorgeous. She was wearing dark green shorts and a light green T-Shirt roughly the same colors as her outfit that she wore the first day he saw her, when Alexis had told him she was wearing his favorite color. He wondered if she had put on green again especially for him. Her hair was pulled back with a green headband that matched her shorts.

Her eyes looked different. He focused on them to see what it was. She had put on her green eye-shadow, but her lashes weren't as long and dark looking as they were at school. He decided she must have skipped the mascara, but her eyes still sparkled beautifully. He thought she had a subtler shade of lipstick on, perhaps to go with her more casual clothes? She pulled her feet up onto the couch and wrapped her arms around her knees. She was barefoot, and Sean noticed her toenails and fingernails matched her lipstick. She looked at him coyly. "What brings you to my house tonight?"

"Ummm... my feet," Sean blurted, then felt embarrassed. Nicole smiled at him. "OK, that was lame. I just, you know, thought maybe we could, you know, get to know each other better, you know, outside of school. I didn't have any homework... and I'm sorry if I'm interrupting yours."

"That is all right," she said casually, "I needed to take a break." She flashed him a quick smile, then looked shyly at her feet. Sean's heart fluttered. He savored her perfume as it subtly drifted his way. She looked back up. "Might I offer you something to eat or drink?" She put an embarrassed hand to her mouth. "We may not have anything you would find enjoyable, though." She laughed gently.

He tried to remember if he'd heard her laugh before. It was melodic. He felt entranced. He couldn't stop staring at her. She looked at him, then looked away, glancing back one more time.

"Is there something wrong with my appearance?" She asked carefully.

"Wrong? No! You look amazing!"

"It seemed as if you were staring at me, and I thought perhaps something was wrong."

Sean blushed. "I'm sorry I was staring. I just can't get over how pretty you are."

She stole a quick glance at his face, then looked back at her knees, her own cheeks tinged with crimson. "Sean! You are causing me to feel self-conscious," she said, and then added, "but that is very sweet of you to say."

"Would you like to go to a movie with me Friday night?" Sean blurted suddenly.

Although her face was still tilted down, she lifted her eyes to meet his. "That would be nice."

Fireworks exploded in Sean's head while his inner voice screamed, *She said YES! She said YES! The most gorgeous girl in the world said she would go out with me!* "Great," he said nonchalantly.

"Sean?" she said lifting her face and giving him her full attention. "Mozart. Bowie. Gershwin. Gaga. Retrieve Lambda X-ray Seventeen One."

Sean's head snapped back against the couch. "*Holy Crap!*" His hands went to his temples as if to keep his head from flying off. "That is totally freakin' bizarre!"

"With that reaction, I will assume it is unnecessary to ask, but do you know who I am?"

"Sure," Sean said, squeezing his eyes shut and rubbing them with his left hand. "Right now you're Nicole." He pointed at her neck. "Touch that place on your neck and you could be Alexis, or Aunt Katherine or even the hot blonde college girl. Or if you decide to pull your face off, you're my great-great-great-great-grandson."

"You always leave out one generation," said Nicole.

"And you always correct me about it," Sean snapped.

His face went blank, and he turned away to stare off into space. Nicole watched quietly for a few moments.

"Sean?" There was concern in her voice. "Are you feeling some side effects? Do you feel ill?"

"Hmmmm?" He mumbled, then shook his head briskly before turning his attention back to Nicole. "No, I'm OK... well, maybe... I don't know; it's really hard to get my head wrapped around this. So weird! I have two distinctly real memories. The one without you, where I come over, and Aunt Katherine shows me a 3D virtual basketball... that was a really cool trick, by the way... and the other one with Alex and everything that happened between the little trick with the glasses. Both of them seem to be real memories."

"That is the desired outcome. What about the transitions? Did you experience vertigo?"

"Dizziness? Yes, a little... when I put the glasses back on. Not sure about just now. It was such a shock to be sitting here asking Nicole on a date and then getting slammed with the other memories."

"You did seem to recoil. I think I can tweak the programming in the nanites to further minimize the vertigo. I am not as certain about a patch for the recovery end. It may be more of a mental response to your memories suddenly loading rather than any physical reaction. Perhaps you should always be sitting down."

"Maybe," Sean said as he returned to staring off in space, reviewing both sets of memories.

"OK, I believe we can label that experiment a success," Nicole proclaimed, "Time to go back. Mozart. Gershwin...."

"Wait wait wait! Wait a minute," Sean yelled. "Are you going to wipe me again?"

"Did you think of something else?"

"Well, yeah... could you make Nicole seem less attractive?"

"Less attractive?"

"Are you losing your hearing, Future-Boy? That's what I said," Sean growled.

Nicole slid to the far end of the couch, away from Sean. "Once again I have made you angry, and I do not understand why. It is so confusing. I think I am making progress in our relationship and then you are angry again!" Nicole said, laden in frustration.

Sean grabbed Nicole's hair and pulled. The mask slid off exposing Alex's head still on Nicole's body. "Can you change that?" Sean snapped while pointing to Nicole's midsection. Alex pushed the nub on his neck, and Nicole's body shimmered away, replaced by his own.

"I sometimes fear that you will become angry enough to strike me!" Alex said roughly.

"Maybe I should!" Sean said as he stood with fists balled.

Alex threw his hands up defensively, closed his eyes, and turned his head away. Sean's face was hard as he looked down on his descendant; it quickly softened when he registered the fear. He dropped his fists, then fell heavily back down to the couch.

When Alex opened his eyes again, he found Sean crumpled forward, with his elbows on his knees, hands over his eyes. He silently watched his ancestor breathing deeply.

"I guess that doesn't help my 'not a caveman' image," Sean said. His voice sounded tired; his hands remained over his eyes.

"I do not know what to think," Alex said slowly, "I believe it is safe to say that we are both frustrated. *My* frustration is because I cannot understand what it is I do that frustrates *you*."

"My Dad says I have an Irish temper," offered Sean. "Sometimes I just flare up."

"Were you going to strike me?" Alex asked timidly.

"I don't know," Sean answered honestly. "I'd like to think the answer is 'no', but I don't know."

"Can you explain to me what has made you angry enough to become violent?"

Sean sat up and looked Alex in the eyes. "Do you not have feelings of your own?" he challenged, "Have you lost the ability to be empathetic in the future? Do you really *not* get it?"

Alex thought for awhile before he spoke. "It appears I do not 'get it', but I assure you, I have feelings."

"Don't you see how you treat me like a lab rat? You do your little experiment; it works to your satisfaction and then you toss me back in my cage until the next one?"

"It was my understanding that you had agreed this was an acceptable option to take," Alex protested, "That you were willing to accept this route for the opportunity to observe and interact with your father in his teen years."

"But the Nicole thing!" Sean shouted. "You really don't get that, do you?"

"Apparently I do not. Perhaps if you were more explicit with your terminology," Alex shouted back.

"Don't you think it's at least a *little* bit cruel to lead me on with her, when you know it's all a lie?"

Alex sat blankly. He *didn't* understand.

"I asked her out because I'm attracted to her," Sean continued. "I think Nicole is beautiful. Everything about her is amazing to me. But you *know* that, since *you* created the illusion."

"It seemed a logical way to..."

"To run me through a different maze?" Sean interrupted, "To force me to react the way you wanted me to?"

They silently stared at each other.

"I am sorry," Alex finally said, "I did not intend for it to be that way, but I think I now understand what you are saying. It was thoughtless of me to manipulate you in that manner. It was egotistical of me to only focus on getting the results I wanted." He took a breath and let it out. "I am not sure what I can do to rectify my actions."

Sean's jaw relaxed a little. He also took a deep breath. "Just cool it down with Nicole... please? I don't want to fall in love with someone who isn't even real."

"Fall in love?"

"Yeah. Do you still have *love* in the future?"

"Yes... well... I am unsure of how you interpret the concept. It may be different than in your time, but yes, people love."

"How about heartbreak?"

Alex twitched to access the computer for clarification. When he turned back, his eyes glistened with the beginnings of tears. "I do not think many from my time experience that." He ran a wrist quickly over his eyes. "I will need to do more research to understand."

"Yeah, you do that, Future-Boy, and keep *that* in your head when you're with me as Nicole."

"How would you suggest that I make her less attractive?" Alex asked.

Sean thought for a moment. "Ditch the perfume, it really grabs my attention. Maybe not dress so hot? Wear jeans and a plain shirt like you did that one day... the day you were giving me the sob story about your mom."

"You told me I looked great that day."

"Wow. Really? In the future, you don't tell little white lies to keep from hurting someone's feelings?"

"White lies?" Alex twitched to check his database. "You have so many methodologies to choose from for avoiding the truth."

"And to me it looks like, in the future, you're willing to stomp all over someone's feelings as long as whatever you say is the truth."

"The life you live is much more emotionally charged than my own. It causes me to wonder how it will compare to your father's younger life."

"Guess you'll find out when you get there," Sean shrugged. "Back to Nicole. Besides the dress, make her more like Alexis. You know, more direct, less coy."

"That characterization was designed by the computer. I must confess I still do not understand why you find it is more attractive for Nicole to show deference and appear to need assistance."

"Maybe I had a bad experience with a girl who always had to be in the driver's seat. Look, I'm not explaining what I feel, I'm just giving you ideas of what you can change."

"I do not believe it would be unnoticed to make all those sudden changes. Perhaps I can introduce them slowly over a few days or weeks."

"Just don't lead me on, OK? And if I start to make a move on you on our date, ice me out."

"I will attempt to rebuff you gently."

Sean smiled and lifted an eyebrow. "Rebuff me?" He shook his head in disbelief. "I don't think your linguists got your 20th Century language pack loaded quite right. OK, I guess that's all I've got to say. Put me back in fantasy land."

"You have given me much to consider," Alex said sincerely, looking into Sean's eyes.

"Yeah, well, me too, I guess. Except you're about to take it all away."

"You are ready?"

"Sure."

Alex picked up the face mask and slipped it on then shifted to Nicole. "I believe you were sitting a little more to your right. Closer to me." Sean slid toward her.

"Right there. OK. Here we go. Mozart. Bowie. Gershwin..."

"Wait wait wait!" Sean said tossing his hand up.

"What is it?" Nicole asked.

"You were... smiling," Sean said softly.

"Thank you," she murmured. She looked down, then lifted her face up with a smile. "I will try." She sighed. "Mozart. Bowie. Gershwin. Gaga. Store. Password: Lambda X-ray Seventeen Two."

"Hmmmm?" Sean blinked groggily.

"I asked what selections were available for viewing at the theater."

"Really? Sorry. Spaced that off somehow. Ummm... I don't really know. I can look it up and tell you tomorrow." He rubbed at his eyes.

"That will be fine," she agreed.

Sean studied her face carefully. "Is something wrong?" he asked. "I thought you seemed happy about going out with me and you just suddenly seem a little... I don't know what."

"No, no, I am sorry. I let myself start thinking about my homework again. Friday night will be very enjoyable. I should not be distracted by any homework Friday night. We can have a wonderful time at the movies," Nicole said with pumped up enthusiasm.

"I swear you do more studying than anyone I know... well, except for Alexis. You guys *both* need to have a little more fun."

"Then that is what I will do Friday night. I will have fun," Nicole said cheerily.

"Yeah, it'll be great," Sean agreed. "I suppose I should let you get back to your studies." He stood. Nicole also rose and walked slowly with him to the door. She held it open for him as he started out, then he stopped and turned. "Hey, you could ask Aunt Katherine to make some more of those brownies... just in case I come over again?"

"I suppose it is pointless to tell you that they are not healthy."

Sean stood pondering that statement with hand on chin. "You know what?

You're right!" he declared.

"You agree that they are not healthy?" said a surprised Nicole.

"No. You're right about it being *pointless* to tell me," he laughed. Nicole laughed with him. Sean put his hands softly on her shoulders and looked into her eyes. They both went suddenly quiet. He started to lean gently her way. When his lips nearly reached hers, she quickly looked away from him. He snapped back away from her and dropped his hands. "OK," he said, "don't study too hard. I'll see you tomorrow." He turned and started down the walk toward the sidewalk.

"Good night, Sean Kelly!" Nicole called after him.

He turned for one last look. "Good night, Nicole Townsend." As the door shut, he tried to put a positive spin on the evening. She *did* agree to go out with him.

He felt a little embarrassed about being rejected when attempting to kiss her, though it wasn't a particularly harsh rejection. He told himself that maybe he was rushing things, then he wondered if she had kissed any boys back in New York. He couldn't imagine someone as gorgeous as Nicole could have had trouble getting a date, so most likely she had kissed someone. He decided that was OK, and reminded himself again that at least she agreed to go out with him. He could wait until Friday night for a kiss. His walk home was filled with imagined visions of what that kiss would be like.

He walked up the steps to his house and was immediately greeted by Maggie as soon as he stepped in. "I'm home," he called out.

"We're in the living room, dear," his Mom answered.

He and Maggie went down the hall to the living room and found his parents sitting on the couch across from the TV. "What's on?" he asked.

"*Frasier* is just starting. Want to watch with us?"

"Nah," Sean answered his Mom, "*Frasier* is lame."

"I'm surprised to see you this early," his Dad said, "It's still half an hour before dark."

Sean was surprised briefly. "I was gone an *hour?* It didn't seem like it was that long."

"I think you'll find that time goes quickly when you are with a girl," his Dad smiled. "So? How did it go?"

Sean grinned sheepishly and felt color creeping into his cheeks. "It was fine. I asked her out on a date for Friday night."

"Where are you taking her?" his Mom asked.

"Just to a movie."

"Are you going with a group of your friends?"

"Michelle," his Dad said, "leave the boy alone."

"I want to know, Jack," she fired back at him, "I want to know if it's a group of kids hanging out at the movies or if it's something more serious."

"Come on, Mom," Sean said, exasperated, "it's just a movie. It's not a big deal, but it's just going to be me and Nicole."

Jack patted the back of his wife's hand. "He's sixteen, Michelle, he's met a girl he likes and they're going to go to a movie... they're not eloping."

While his Mom stared daggers at his Dad, Sean made a break for it. "Come on, Mags, let's go see who's on IRC."

He left the living room and went down to the family room in the basement... his sanctuary.

Chapter Nine

"On a hippie trail, head full of zombie"

AS Sean approached the steps down to the Wasteland, he saw Alexis waiting at the top. He wondered whether she was going to tell him that she was happy about him asking Nicole out or if she was going to let him know that she really *didn't* like it and had just been pretending. He took a deep breath as he neared.

"*Buenos dias,* Alexis," he said as they started down the steps together.

"Good morning, Sean. I am glad you are not late today."

"Good morning? Why no perfect Spanish for me today?"

Three steps from the bottom, Alexis leaned close to Sean's ear. "Mozart. Bowie. Gershwin. Gaga. Retrieve Lambda X-ray Seventeen Two," she whispered quickly.

Sean stumbled on the next to the last step as his retrieved memories hit him. He grabbed across Alexis to put both hands on the stair rail to keep from falling, effectively pinning her in place.

"Really, Sean?" came a voice from halfway up the stairs. "Back to *this* twin? Are you dumping Nicole already?" Megan stopped at the bottom of the stairs and turned back to Sean and Alexis to sneer. "Or are you seeing both of them? You could be every boy's hero at this school... dating twins at the same time."

Sean didn't know who he wanted to kill first... Megan or Alex.

"I understand the other one speaks French," Megan continued, "What's that phrase? *Ménage à trois*?" She spun on her heel, calling over her shoulder, "I think when translated to English that's: Get. A. Room!"

Sean turned to Alexis. "What the hell? At school now? And on the *steps*?" he hissed.

"I concede that the steps were a definite miscalculation. I am sorry for that."

"So, what's the deal? Is this the next phase of the experiment?"

"I have been working on a scenario for 1969 that would provide a logical approach to your father that could include you. I need to discuss it with you."

"*Here?*" Sean asked incredulously.

"No, tonight. I thought perhaps you could come to my house in the guise of helping Nicole with Algebra again."

"I don't know," Sean said doubtfully, "my Mom already isn't too happy about me seeing Nicole. I think two nights in a row might be too much."

"Perhaps if Nicole again came to your house?" Alexis suggested, "It might ease your mother's anxiety to be able to meet her."

"Is it weird for you to refer to your other self as 'her'?"

"No. Do not stray from the subject, we have little time. I have decided to come to your house as Nicole tonight."

"Whatever... I hope you're right about my Mom."

"And I hope I am correct about this next transition. Please join me up one step." Sean backed up one step. "Mozart. Bowie. Gershwin. Gaga. Store. Password: Lambda X-ray Seventeen Three."

Alexis immediately shifted her weight into Sean's shoulder and pitched forward. He instinctively wrapped his arms around her to keep her from falling.

"Are you all right?" he asked as they stepped off the last step together.

"Yes, thank you. I believe I slipped on something."

"I felt like I was falling for a second, too. Maybe there *was* something slick on one of the steps."

"I am grateful that you were there to prevent my fall. *Muchas gracias, mi amigo.*"

"*Da nada,*" Sean automatically replied. "Hey, it kind of looked like you were waiting for me at the top of the stairs. Something going on?" he asked as they continued to walk to the classroom.

"I saw you approaching as I reached the steps," Alexis said, "I wanted to apologize for not coming down to see you last night, in the event you found that rude."

"No, that's cool," Sean said, "umm... did she tell you?"

"That you are attending a movie together? Yes. I hope you both find it an enjoyable evening."

"You know, just say the word and I'll bet I can get Raj to ask you out, too."

"That is very kind of you to offer. Perhaps another time. I believe Friday would not be suitable for me this week."

"OK," Sean shrugged, "but are you warming up to the idea of seeing Raj?"

"I have not yet fully formed an opinion regarding a social engagement with Raj. Let me give the matter further consideration."

"No problem. Just let me know," Sean said as they stepped into the classroom.

Megan was staring daggers at them, and Sean wondered what he had done.

* * * * *

When the bell rang to end Algebra class, Sean stayed in his seat until everyone else who sat behind Nicole had passed. He stood, expecting Nicole to be next, but with a glance to the front of the room he saw that she had her algebra book open and was waiting for Mr. Stapleton. She looked back at Sean and mouthed a silent "wait?" request, her eyes doing most of the pleading. Sean nodded; giving her a concerned smile. She had asked several questions during Mr. Stapleton's lecture, and they weren't even particularly good questions for the topic. Sean wondered if she was lost again. He waited for her outside the classroom door.

"Thank you for waiting," Nicole said as she came out, and they started walking toward the cafeteria.

"What were you talking to Stapleton about?"

"I do not believe I followed his lecture very well today. I find the topic confusing."

"Did talking to him help?"

"It was some help..." she left her sentence open-ended.

"That doesn't sound too convincing."

"How well did you understand today's lecture?" she asked carefully.

"I thought it was pretty straight forward," Sean said with a shrug, then realized his statement made her look bad, "I can see how it could be confusing though," he added quickly.

"Would you be willing to tutor me again?"

"Sure. I guess. You want to look at it during lunch?" Sean suggested.

"I... that would be good," Nicole stumbled, "if I did not..." She paused a second before continuing, "I have to go to the library to do more research for theater class."

Sean gave her a disapproving look. "You're skipping lunch again?"

218

"Not skipping, merely rushing. I have my lunch with me in my book bag. I can eat quickly before going into the library."

"Do you *really* need to work so much in your classes? You should at least get a break at lunch."

"I require good grades to obtain a scholarship to a good university."

"I suppose you already have that all planned out."

"Yes, I plan to return to Syracuse and attend university there. I will be close to my mother."

Sean didn't want to go any further into the subject of Nicole's mom, so he decided to steer back to algebra. "When do you want to look at math, then?"

"I thought perhaps I could come to your house after school again, like last Friday."

"OK, that should work. Meet you at the doorway nearest the parking lot," Sean said, then added, "My Mom will probably be home, though."

"Then I will be able to meet her," Nicole said cheerfully.

"Yeah," Sean drawled as he mulled it over, "maybe that *would* be good for her to meet you."

"I must go," Nicole said as she stopped walking, "I hope you have an enjoyable lunch."

Sean turned and walked backwards a few steps. Nicole smiled at him, gave him a little circular wave of her hand, then turned and walked briskly in the other direction. Sean also turned and continued to the cafeteria. He always had mixed feelings about lunch with Nicole. He liked sitting with her but *didn't* like worrying about whether she approved of what he ate. "Today, we eat, drink, and are merry," he said dramatically to himself as he entered the cafeteria, "for tomorrow we may diet." He went straight for the Sloppy Joes.

* * * * *

Sean started down the stairs with Raj after biology had ended. They were lab partners for the day and had spent class time opening up an earthworm and pinning and labeling organs. It was good for Sean that Raj was kind of a brainiac in Biology. Sean could barely stomach cutting up the earthworm, and Raj was already looking forward to later in the semester when they'd get to dissect a frog.

Nicole was quietly waiting at the bottom of the steps. As they got closer to her, she put her hand over her mouth and nose. They'd gotten used to the smell of formaldehyde as they worked on their project, but Sean quickly realized that it must still be with them.

"Nicole," Sean said quickly, "we rinsed our hands in the lab sink, but there wasn't any soap in there. Wait right here while I duck into a restroom and get this smell off."

"Thing cue," she responded nasally, not removing her hand.

Sean and Raj went down the hall to the boy's room; both hitting a sink and pumping the liquid soap dispenser.

"Hey, I've been meaning to ask you something," Sean said nonchalantly.

"What's that?"

"Remember when you first met Alexis, and you said she was cute and that you'd go out with her if she were interested in you?"

"Vaguely."

"Well, did you mean it?"

"I suppose so. Why?"

"Just checking. I'm going out with Nicole this Friday night, and I thought maybe sometime in the future we could double... if you'd want to go out with Alexis."

"Does she want to go out with me?" Raj asked.

"Maybe," Sean said noncommittally. "I've been working on her. Just kind of asking her if she'd be interested."

"What'd she say?" Raj pressed.

"She didn't say, 'no'..." Sean said, letting the end of his sentence trail off.

"But she didn't say 'yes,' either, right?"

"Just give it some time, buddy."

"I never see her anymore, since she dropped Biology," Raj complained.

"Just let me work on it, huh?"

"I think you're crazy," Raj said. Then he grinned and added, "But she is kind of cute."

They dried their hands and exited the boy's room. Nicole still waited near the door. "Better?" Sean asked as they got closer.

"Yes," Nicole answered, "I believe there is still a trace lingering in your hair and clothes, but it is not intolerable."

The three had barely walked out the door toward the parking lot when Sean slapped his forehead. "I should have asked you if Alexis wanted a ride home, too."

"No!" Nicole yelped, then quickly added in a softer voice, "I mean; she has to stay later tonight to work on her.... health project. She is unable to go with us. Aunt Katherine will retrieve her later." She paused a couple seconds then added, "In actuality, this arrangement is better as Aunt Katherine now only has to make one trip rather than two. I telephoned her from the Principal's office during lunch and informed her that I was riding with you, Sean."

"OK... just a thought," Sean said.

They said their goodbyes to Raj as he got into his car. Sean and Nicole walked a couple of rows further to Sean's car. He took her book-bag as he opened the door for her, closing it after she slipped in. He walked around the car, opened the back door enough to toss in the book-bag and then got behind the wheel.

"I've been trying to get Alexis and Raj together," Sean said as he started the car. "What do you think?"

"I am not sure that would be a good match," Nicole replied skeptically.

"Why not? They're both smart... they could hit it off pretty good."

"I will ask Alexis her opinion when I see her next."

"Maybe push it along a little?" Sean suggested.

"I found the information I needed for my theater research," Nicole said enthusiastically, obviously changing the subject. Sean considered steering the conversation back to Raj and Alexis, but found it hard to get even a word in. For the entire drive to his house, Nicole continuously talked about either theater or history. Sean decided she must not want Alexis to go out with Raj, and let the topic drop.

He parked at the curb in front of his house and shut off the engine. Sean grabbed Nicole's book-bag, and they walked across the lawn to the front door. He kept his keys in hand but tried the door without putting the key in the lock. It opened. He stepped through and held the door for Nicole, then closed it. "Mom, I'm home."

"I'm back in the office, sweetie," she called from the back of the house.

Maggie came rushing toward the door, wagging vigorously, but before she reached Sean for her normal frenzy around his legs, she stopped suddenly and docilely flattened out onto her belly.

Sean glanced at Nicole, then back to Maggie. "Mags! Come here, girl! What's the matter with you?" Sean said as he patted his thighs in an attempt to coax the dog over to him. Maggie didn't move. Sean looked again at Nicole. "She has *never* done that before," he explained. "She really seems to act weird around you."

"Perhaps she has yet to form her opinion of my presence," Nicole offered.

"Yeah, well at least I guess it's good she's not barking at you today."

"If you're talking to me, dear, I can't hear you," Sean's Mom called from down the hall.

"No, Mom," Sean called back, "Nicole came home with me. She needs some help with algebra again."

"Oh!" his Mom said, "I'll be right out to meet her."

Michelle Kelly came out of her office, a converted bedroom, and came briskly down the hall. She was still wearing her dark olive skirt from work and was pulling on the matching jacket over her simple white blouse. In contrast to her professional look, her feet were clad in fuzzy pink house slippers. She extended her hand as she closed the last few steps to Nicole.

"Hi, I'm Michelle Kelly, Sean's mom. It's nice to meet you," she said enthusiastically.

"Hello. I am Nicole Townsend. My Aunt purchased a house down the street from you, and I have classes with Sean. He has offered to assist me with algebra."

"Please excuse the mess," Michelle said to Nicole before turning a disapproving gaze to Sean, "If I'd known you were coming, I'd have straightened things up a little."

"I apologize for intruding," Nicole said softly.

"No, you're not intruding," Michelle replied, "I just don't want you to think I'm a sloppy housekeeper."

"Mom," Sean protested, "It's *fine*! You *always* keep everything perfect."

"Can I get you something to drink?" offered Michelle. "Sean prefers Coke, his Dad drinks Dr. Pepper, but I have some Diet Pepsi in the fridge, if you'd like."

"That would be nice. Thank you," Nicole replied graciously.

"Would you like it over ice?"

"No, thank you."

"How about a snack," Michelle continued, "I've got cookies, crackers, chips."

"Mom," Sean interrupted, "Nicole doesn't eat stuff like that."

"Oh," Michelle said as she looked back and forth between Sean and Nicole, "I'm sorry, I don't usually have to think like a girl. Sean and his Dad happily put away the junk food."

"Moooooom," Sean protested.

Michelle ignored him and addressed Nicole, "I have a couple of apples; you're certainly welcome to eat those."

"Thank you," Nicole replied, "one is more than adequate."

Michelle went into the kitchen with Sean and Nicole trailing behind her. She opened the refrigerator and grabbed an apple from the crisper drawer and a Diet Pepsi from the back of the second shelf. She handed Nicole the can but took the apple to the counter next to the sink. She set it on a cutting board and opened a cabinet drawer, retrieving a paring knife. She deftly sliced and cored the apple, placing the pieces in a small bowl.

"Just ask if you decide you want a second one," she said as she handed the bowl to Nicole and tossed the core into a bag under the sink.

Nicole thanked her as she took the offered bowl.

"Sean said you moved here just before school started," Michelle said, "I can't quite place your accent. I'm going to guess you're from Wisconsin."

"No," Nicole replied, "New York. Upstate, not the city."

"Oh," Michelle said, "I get students from all over the country, but I don't remember having anyone from New York. It sounded kind of northern to me."

"My Mom teaches Psychology at the university," Sean said, trying to edge between them.

"I understand your Aunt is an artist of some sort?" Michelle asked, leaning around Sean.

"Yes," Nicole answered. Her eyes flitted between Sean and his mother.

"But not in the Art Department at the university?" Michelle continued.

"No," Nicole replied, a little nervously.

"Mom!" Sean said brusquely, "enough with the inquisition."

"I'm just curious about her Aunt, dear. I can't imagine why she would pick a place like Grover's Corners to set up an art studio, or whatever she's doing."

"Stop prying! I'll tell you about it later," Sean growled through clenched teeth.

Michelle's stone-face sent Sean the non-verbal cue that she didn't appreciate his tone. She held it for a few seconds then smiled brightly as she turned back to Nicole. "I suppose I should let you two get started on your studies. It was lovely to meet you, Nicole."

"It was nice to meet you, also, Mrs. Kelly," Nicole said with a tiny nod.

"I'd love to meet your Aunt someday," Michelle hinted as she left the kitchen.

Nicole smiled brightly toward Sean's Mom but said nothing in reply.

Sean pulled a chair out from the kitchen table and motioned to Nicole to sit. After he'd seated her, he went to the refrigerator and pulled out a Coke, then slumped into the chair adjacent to Nicole. "I'm sorry about that," he sighed.

"About what?"

"My Mom and the third degree," Sean said grumpily. "I don't think she's ready to accept that I'm growing up. I guess she heard a lot of post-Tiffany gossip and wants to make sure nothing like that happens again."

"I do not believe I know who Tiffany is."

"That's OK... long story, maybe someday I'll feel like telling it."

Sean popped the top on his Coke and took a long sip. He watched Nicole study her can, and then took another sip before asking, "Are you going to drink that?"

"I am reading the disclosure about the contents."

"And?"

"Carbonated water, caramel color, aspartame, phosphoric acid, potassium benzoate, caffeine, citric acid, and natural flavors," she read from the can.

"And zero calories!" Sean added, mimicking a commercial pitch.

"It also warns that it contains phenylalanine, even though that chemical was not listed in the contents."

"That's an added bonus," Sean teased.

"Above, it also lists 35 mg of sodium, but that also is not listed in the contents area."

"Maybe they consider that a natural flavor?"

"Are they actually referring to sodium chloride? Sodium alone reacts violently with water in a chemical reaction that creates sodium hydroxide and hydrogen gas."

"Have you *never* drank a Diet Pepsi?" Sean asked.

"No," she replied shyly. They sat quietly. Sean was mystified that anyone could reach their age without ever drinking a Diet Pepsi. "Perhaps I should simply sample it," she finally said. She appeared to read the top of the can, and then gingerly slid a fingernail under the tab and pulled on it. It made a popping sound as the seal was broken. As she started to lift it to her lips, Sean reached over and pushed the metal ring back flat against the top of the can.

"You've *never* had any kind of soda from a can?"

"No," she said, embarrassment slipping into her voice.

Sean wondered if life in Syracuse, New York, was that incredibly different, or if it was just Nicole's family. Since he couldn't imagine an entire town that hadn't been conquered by either Coke or Pepsi—or both, he decided it was another oddity of the Townsends.

He watched expectantly as she put the can to her lips and cautiously took a sip. He tried valiantly to not laugh at the face she made. "So what do you think?" he asked, still trying to suppress a smile.

Nicole coughed a little before answering, "The dissolved carbon dioxide irritates my soft pallet and esophagus. I expect it will also accumulate in my stomach and cause a gaseous expansion."

The coughing reminded Sean of his own early childhood experience, and he again was mystified. Though he wanted to ask if her parents were part of some religious cult, he decided to continue to steer clear of talking about Nicole's parents, and instead tried to be helpful. "It's OK to burp, you know."

She looked at him quizzically, then briefly did her little twitch maneuver. She seemed amused as she turned back to Sean, immediately tipping her can up and taking a longer drink. She squeezed her eyes shut and made a face as she swallowed. Her eyes glistened with tears when she reopened them. Sean flinched as she batted the excess moisture from her eyes.

"Hey, you don't have to drink that if you don't want to," Sean said.

She coughed again before answering, "I should experience new things. It is good to broaden one's horizons and step beyond one's comfort..." A burp rumbled out. "...zone." Sean bit his lip. "Excuse me," Nicole said then broke into laughter. Sean laughed with her.

"You might want to work on keeping your throat or vocal chords tighter... or looser.. I don't know which it is..." he advised when they'd finished their short laugh. Suddenly feeling self-conscious for giving instructions for burping, he changed the subject, "So what was puzzling you about Algebra today?"

"I think I understand the Irrational numbers," Nicole replied, "but I am struggling with the Imaginary numbers."

Sean considered how best to explain. "Well, you know that three squared is nine?" He paused to check her reaction. She nodded. "And negative three squared is also nine?" Another nod. "And you're OK with negative numbers?"

"Yes, numbers that are less than zero," she replied.

"Well, if you can take the square root of a positive number—let's say nine again then why can't you take the square root of a negative number? Let's say negative nine."

"But you cannot have a number which when squared becomes a negative number, so how could you have a number that is the square root of a negative number? It cannot exist," Nicole reasoned.

"And that's why they're called *imaginary numbers*," Sean said triumphantly.

She was unconvinced. "Did you have an imaginary friend as a child?" Nicole asked after a short pause.

Sean didn't see the relevance but answered, "Yeah, I guess, when I was real little."

"But you no longer retain that imaginary friend?" She asked sincerely.

"No! Of course not!" Sean said almost indignantly.

"Why not?"

"Why not? Because it wasn't real. I just made him up!"

"Would you say that you no longer believe an imaginary friend serves any purpose?" Nicole continued.

"Sure."

"Then why do you find it relevant to entertain the thought of imaginary numbers?"

Sean blinked several times as he checked Nicole's face to see if she was joking. She didn't seem to be. He considered her reasoning and thought that maybe she had made a somewhat logical argument. He thought over carefully before answering, "I think it is all mostly used to plot things on a graph. Let me see your notebook."

Nicole pulled a notebook from her book bag and handed it to Sean. He turned to the back and pulled the last sheet off the spiral. He placed it on the table between himself and Nicole and drew an XY axis graph.

After several different formulas and graphed examples, Nicole finally nodded. "OK," she said, "I believe I am beginning to understand. You have to imagine that those numbers could exist to plot a graph in the negative quadrants."

"I think it might make more sense next year in geometry, when we do a lot of graphing. You just kind of have to accept it for what it is for now, even if it seems impossible."

"I shall use my imagination," Nicole said with a smile, "to pretend that imaginary numbers are real."

"Do you think you understand it well enough to do the assigned problems?" he asked.

"Yes, I believe I do," she said, pausing before quickly adding, "Mozart Bowie Gershwin Gaga Retrieve Lambda X-Ray Seventeen Three."

Sean's eyes went wide, and he gasped a sharp breath. Nicole watched anxiously until he closed his eyes and breathed out.

"Is the vertigo still an issue?" she asked.

"I guess. Still, I think sitting down is a really good idea. I think most of it is the shock of the memories hitting me. There's a few seconds of wondering if I'm remembering a dream or if I'm going crazy. Then I start thinking back to all the things that happened between now and the last time you let me remember."

"What do you mean," Nicole asked.

"I kind of rewind what happened to me, especially with you, in light of now knowing who you are and the charade you play."

"Charade?"

"Particularly with algebra this time. Faking in class that you didn't know what was going on so you could come over here and run me through the hoops 'tutoring' you."

"It was plausible... a calculated means for a desired outcome," she said simply.

"It makes me feel like I've been played."

"I do not understand."

"I was sincerely trying to help you understand imaginary numbers, but you probably already know more math than I'll *ever* learn."

Nicole looked puzzled. "I still do not understand why that makes you feel 'played,'" she said.

"How would you feel if you spent that much time teaching me something, and then at the end I go, 'haha, I already knew all that.'?"

Nicole looked even more puzzled. "I did not laugh at you. On the contrary, I admire your efforts, and especially your sincerity. I could tell that you wanted me to understand and that you made a great effort to present the information in a way that you thought would be helpful."

"But it was a waste of time!" Sean barked, "You already know it!"

Sean's Mom came into the room. "Everything OK in here?" she asked, her eyes darting between Sean and Nicole, "need anything else?"

"No, Mom," Sean replied, "We're fine."

"How's the studies going? Are you getting anywhere?" she asked.

"I do comprehend it better now, Mrs. Kelly," Nicole replied, "Sean is an excellent teacher."

"Yeah," Sean said testily, "you wouldn't *believe* how well she understands it now."

"Sean!" his Mom said reprovingly, "You don't sound very pleased. I would think it would make you feel good to be able to help a classmate understand the material."

"It is my fault, Mrs. Kelly," Nicole offered, "I can be so bewildered that it is frustrating, and then it suddenly becomes clear to me. I believe Sean feels that he has to exert considerable effort unnecessarily."

Michelle patted her son on the shoulder. "If you get frustrated when you're successful," she said, "then you'd better not plan on a career as a teacher." She looked at Nicole before continuing, "You wouldn't believe what I have to deal with. I sometimes wonder how some of those kids even got into college."

"Thanks, Mom," Sean said sarcastically, "Now I can scratch teacher off my list of possible careers. Oh, wait... it was never *on* my list."

"We'll discuss your attitude later," Michelle said icily before turning a warm smile to Nicole, "If you need anything else, Nicole, just ask. I'll let you two get back to it." She walked out of the kitchen.

Nicole waited a few seconds before she leaned closer to Sean and whispered, "Is there somewhere more private that we could talk?"

Sean thought for a moment. "I guess we could go downstairs and say we were using the computer."

Nicole twitched a query to her own computer. "That plan should succeed."

"Why'd you need to ask your computer if that would work?"

"I was obtaining assistance with the logistics of moving to another location. Assuring that we do nothing that will leave an unexplained gap in your memory is a very complicated task. Do you believe that if I ask to see your Internet Relay Chat program that you would take me to your computer?"

"I already *said* that we could go use the computer," Sean complained.

"Let me rephrase the question: if Alternate Nicole, the Nicole that you *do not* know is from the future, asks to see IRC, is it probable that you would comply?"

Sean thought a moment to absorb what Nicole was saying. "Yeah, I think so," he said, "of course, you could always bat your pretty green eyes at me," he added sarcastically.

"Good, I will initiate that plan. Mozart. Bowie. Gershwin. Gaga. Store. Password: Lambda X-ray Seventeen Four." Nicole said, then raised a warm smile as she continued, "You are a splendid teacher, Sean Kelly!"

Sean blinked a couple of times, feeling like he was about to say something else, but couldn't remember what. "Why thank you, Nicole Townsend. It was my pleasure."

Nicole picked up an apple slice, studied it, and then tentatively bit it in half. Her eyes brightened. "My, what an interesting flavor! Would you like to taste one?"

Sean looked at her skeptically. "Really? That good? I don't usually do apples."

"These are fascinating! It is an unusual combination of sour and sweet, and the texture is very intriguing. Crisp, but quickly releasing a burst of juice when compressed!"

Sean reached into the bowl and took a slice, popping the whole piece into his mouth. Nicole looked at him expectantly. He shrugged. "Tastes like an apple. Is it different than apples you get in New York?"

Nicole briefly had a 'deer in headlights' look on her face. "No," she finally said, "Perhaps it is because I am hungry. I did not have time to consume my entire lunch today."

"I can get you something else if you're hungry."

"No, thank you, this is more than enough."

They sat quietly for a few moments. Sean felt uneasy with the lag in conversation. "So," he said abruptly, "what do you want to do now?"

"Well," Nicole started coyly, "Alexis told me you use some form of instantaneous email on your computer."

"It's not exactly email. She must have told you about IRC, which stands for Internet Relay Chat. It lets you communicate with other people online in real-time."

"That sounds intriguing. Could I see it demonstrated?"

"Sure," he said to Nicole, then yelled toward the door, "Mom... we're going downstairs to use the computer for awhile." He stood and walked toward the doorway; Nicole followed him.

"Do you think it's appropriate to take a young lady to your basement hideaway the first time she visits?" Michelle called down the hall.

"Using a computer, Mom," Sean shouted back, "not playing Doctor."

"*Sean!*" Michelle scolded.

"Aw, chill, Mom," Sean said as he opened the door to the basement.

"We are *definitely* having a conversation later!" his Mom proclaimed.

"Looking forward to it," Sean mumbled sarcastically to himself as he started down the carpeted steps.

When they reached the bottom, Nicole shyly said, "I do not wish to cause you strife with your mother."

"Ah, don't worry about it," Sean said offhandedly, "we have these little run-ins every once in awhile. It all works out." He moved to the computer and slid the chair that was sitting in front of the screen to the left. "You can have the good chair." He reached beside the desk and pulled a folding chair into position in front of the computer screen. Nicole took another sip of her Pepsi as she sat on the extra kitchen chair that Sean had placed for her. Sean sat next to her.

"So this is your computer?" Nicole asked.

"Yep. It's a 486. Now that Windows 95 is out, I'm trying to convince my Dad to get a Pentium to replace it."

"How do you start it?" Nicole asked.

"I've got everything on a power strip. The CPU, the monitor, the printer, the modem."

"May I start it?"

"Sure," Sean said, wondering about the odd request, "It's that red switch right here."

As Nicole reached across Sean to press the switch she said, "Mozart. Bowie. Gershwin. Gaga. Retrieve Lambda X-ray Seventeen Four."

Sean grunted softly as his memories hit his consciousness. He closed his eyes and gave his head a quick shake. "Was that really necessary?"

"I believe it was an appropriate tactic," Nicole apologized, "to avoid an unexplained memory gap."

"But that was just a few minutes that you erased me. What's the point?"

"If we had come down here with you..." Nicole started to explain, and then paused to drink from her Pepsi before changing what she was about to say, "We need a descriptive label for when you are aware of who I am. I propose we refer to your memory that is unaware of my true identity as 'normal memory' and we can refer to your memory set that *is* aware of everything as the 'LX memory.'"

"Why not 'XL memory' instead? As in 'extra-large'?" Sean suggested.

Nicole was puzzled by his reference, but continued, "To return to my original thought; if we had come down here with you having the 'XL memory' active, you would have been returned to 'normal memory' later back in the kitchen."

"So?"

"In that scenario, you would not remember that you came down here with me," Nicole explained.

"I understand that... but... so what? Why does it matter *when* you wipe my memory?"

"Your mother is aware that we are down here. She will inquire what we did at some later time since she suspects that your intentions are to advance some level of intimacy with me. You would deny even coming down here since you would not remember doing so. Therefore, it would be a gap in your memory that could not be explained, as well as a point of contention with your mother."

Sean closed his eyes and thought through Nicole's explanation, then nodded. "OK, I guess I can see that. Wow. This hidden memory thing is a lot of work, huh?"

"That is why I consult the computer for logistical assistance," she said, then added, "Would you mind if we turn your computer on? I have never seen one this old even in a museum. I would find it interesting to observe it as it functions."

"Be my guest," Sean said as he waved an outstretched hand over the power strip.

Nicole pushed the button, then turned immediately to Sean. "Did I do it incorrectly?" she asked.

"No. That's it."

"But nothing happened."

Sean laughed. "It's *not* instantaneous, you know.... or apparently you don't know. Look at the CPU, see the little red light in front? It's on."

"It will now accept queries?" Nicole asked.

"No," Sean said with an amused grin, "it's booting. You have to wait for it to do a system check, and then it boots DOS, and then it launches Windows from an autoexec.bat file."

"Does that take very long?"

Sean pointed at the monitor. "See, it's finished the system check and loaded DOS. See those words on the screen? That's what launches Windows."

Nicole looked at the refreshed display. "It has displayed a few icons. Is it ready now?"

"First, let's open this folder and dial up the network."

"Dial up?"

"On the modem. I have to call the Internet provider to get onto the Internet before I can use IRC." His grin widened. "This is kind of funny; I'm the one teaching you how something works... unless you're faking it again."

"No," Nicole said, "I assure you, I had no idea it was so complicated to activate a simple computer. It is very interesting, though hard to believe that you find something this primitive to be useful."

Once Sean had clicked the connect icon, the modem sprang to life. Nicole listened in fascination as it first made the telephone tones required to call the Internet provider, then the warbling tones that made the connection. She took another drink of her Pepsi then twitched a query to her own computer.

"The word 'Modem' comes from its function as a modulator / demodulator! It converts digital data to analog impulses that can travel as sound waves!" Nicole exclaimed.

Sean nearly laughed at her enthusiasm. "Why do you find that exciting?" he asked.

"That it actually works!" she beamed, "Would you not be impressed if someone connected two computers with tin cans and a piece of string?"

"That primitive, huh?"

Nicole caught the dejected tone in Sean's voice. "No, it is wonderful!" she continued enthusiastically, "This is why I am here, to experience the reality of this time-period. Actively participating is much more enlightening than merely observing." She tipped back her Pepsi and took several swallows before continuing, "You use the same phone line for vocal communication, correct?" Sean nodded, glancing at the phone sitting on the desk next to the monitor. Nicole followed his gaze and snatched up the telephone handset and put it to her ear. She started laughing. "Sean! Sean! Type each letter three times, in alphabetic order!" He gave her a puzzled look but followed her instructions.

She twitched a connection to her computer, and when he had finished the alphabet, she opened her mouth slightly and a series of strange tones came out. The dialog box on the monitor read: "Hello, Sean, it is nice for my computer to be able to communicate with yours." She laughed when she saw Sean's surprised reaction.

"You should see the look on your face!" She said, laughing so hard tears streamed down her cheeks as she hung up the phone.

Sean had never seen his descendant act so goofy, then he suddenly smiled to himself as Nicole tipped back her Pepsi can again.

"Hey, Future-Boy, have you ever had caffeine before?"

"No," Nicole said as she continued to laugh, "Why?"

"Because I think you're buzzed."

Her mirthful face turned stony serious as she twitched a query to her computer. "I have a slightly elevated heart rate and blood pressure," she announced flatly. "I also have higher than average levels of epinephrine and dopamine." She closed her eyes and sat stiffly in silence. Sean watched for a few moments.

"Hey," he said nervously, "are you OK?"

"Yes," Nicole answered in a monotone, still not moving.

Sean waited silently for a few more anxious seconds. "What's going on?"

"Fifteen seconds," she said flatly.

He waited nervously for what seemed like minutes. Nicole opened her eyes.

"What was that?" Sean yelped.

"I was resetting my brain chemistry and capturing loose caffeine molecules. Are you not also chemically imbalanced?"

"No, I have to drink 3 or 4 cans to get a caffeine buzz."

"Perhaps repeated ingestion creates a natural tolerance," she theorized,

"Interesting. It is no wonder life expectancy for this era is still approximately 80 years. Even though you have a relatively safe environment, you choose to inflict yourselves with poisons."

"Yeah, well saying stuff like that just gets you labeled as a health-food nut," Sean retorted.

"I did not mean to sound judgmental in my comments. I am sorry," said Nicole. "Although I found the computer demonstration intriguing, and the unintentional caffeine experiment as well, perhaps it is best to move our discussion to my thoughts regarding a logical scenario for meeting your father in 1969."

Sean suddenly perked up. "Awesome! What's the plan?"

"In the summer of 1969, your father attempted to form a rock band with some of his friends, and we can..."

"He *what*?" Sean interrupted.

"Attempted to form a rock band, and we can..."

"A rock band?" Sean interrupted again. "Are you kidding me?"

"No, and it appears that you are not aware of this venture," said Nicole.

"I'm not! What do you... no... *why* do you know about this?"

"My initial source is from a family history that you write later in your life. However, additional research yields one very brief newspaper article in the *Quincy County Gazette* from the fall of 1969. It mentions a band named *Silas MacDoherty* playing at a dance. Possibly their only public performance? You briefly mention that name in association with your father when you write your memoirs."

"Wow! That's insane. I didn't even know he played an instrument."

"Electric guitar."

"Any idea about where the goofy name for the band came from?"

"Your journal says it is a reference to a political terminology of the time... 'silent majority.'"

"Whatever *that* means. OK... now that I'm over the shock of my Dad playing guitar in a band... what's your plan?"

"We will portray musicians hitchhiking across the country, in search of the 'next sound.'"

Sean looked skeptically at Nicole. "That's the plan? That sounds pretty lame."

"I believe I have compiled enough data to show that it is an excellent plan," Nicole huffed. "If your father is assembling a band, it demonstrates that he has an acute interest in music at that time. Culturally, there is a considerable amount of data written about the 1960s and 1970s as a counter-cultural time when young people were attempting to 'find themselves' and rejecting the social norms of the previous generation. Hitchhiking was quite common for young people, and music evolved quickly as musicians were seeking a unique sound that could transform an unknown band to a sudden popularity. I fail to see any part of this course of action that is 'lame.'"

"Why not just dress up like my Mom and ambush him that way, like you did me?"

"I believe we have already discovered that the physical appearance of a younger version of a person's wife is not a guarantee of a close connection. Besides, I have already put considerable effort into the background story for the 'hitchhiking musician' scenario."

Sean remained skeptical. "OK, if you've put 'considerable effort' into the plan, let's hear some details. And can you change out of the Nicole disguise?"

"Are you certain that your mother will not suddenly come to check on you?"

Sean considered the possibility. "I'd say I'm 80% sure... but if you couldn't change back before she saw you, that would be kind of hard to explain," he admitted.

"Here is a compromise, I will present a mockup of how I will look in 1969. It will look more like the real me than Nicole does, but it would be a quick change back to Nicole if needed."

"Go for it."

Nicole touched the spot on her neck, blurred briefly and was replaced with a young man with straight shoulder-length hair and a wispy beard. His hair was parted in the middle, and a red bandana was folded into a one inch width at the forehead and tied in a simple knot in the back. Sean could recognize the face as primarily being Alex's, but the beard and long hair made him look a little strange.

Alex stood to show the full outfit. He wore a fringed suede-leather vest over a purple shirt with yellow paisley designs in it. A silver peace medallion hung around his neck, and several buttons were pinned to the vest. One button had a dark red background with a bright green five-pronged leaf, another was a bright yellow peace symbol on an electric blue background, another stated 'make love, not war' in several bright colors, yet another was a simple white on black 'Stop the War.' His jeans were faded and obviously tattered, but most of the holes were patched with bright colored cloth of various patterned designs. The bottoms of the jeans had been split to the knee and expanded with the red and white stripes from an American flag to form a wide flair that mostly covered what looked like army boots. Alex rotated to show the back and returned to face Sean.

"What is your opinion?" he asked.

"I think you look like you escaped from a circus or something," Sean chuckled.

"This is a nearly perfect composite of clothing based on pictures taken in 1969 in San Francisco."

"So the buttons weren't like a T.G.I.F. thing? What's that leaf? Is that supposed to be marijuana? 'make love, not war'? People actually wore junk like that in public?"

"This is all based on photographs from that time," Alex said confidently. "Fashion is cyclical. Certain elements that are prevalent in one era look ridiculous if worn in a different age."

"I suppose I'd have to look like that, too?" Sean asked.

"Not identical, of course, but similar. I will need your sizes to prepare a suitable set of period clothing for you since you cannot directly alter your appearance as I do."

"I'm *not* wearing those goofy buttons."

"Agreed. It would be difficult to find them unless we purchased them in 1969. I propose utilizing a plain white T-Shirt to make a replica tie-dye with various bright colors. We are fortunate that it is currently a fashion trend to be able to purchase a pair of jeans that are already distressed. I can easily have colorful patches added. An army jacket over the T-shirt would be a period look. Do you know where we could obtain such a jacket?"

"I'd think there's at least one military surplus store in Kansas City. But back up a minute. *You* are going to sew patches on a pair of jeans, and dye a T-shirt?"

"Yes. I can purchase the raw materials at your Wall Mart, and make the needed alterations."

"You're a tailor now, too?"

"Perhaps not in the manner you are thinking. Once I obtain the raw materials I will have the computer direct the alterations to be done by nanites."

"Nanites can *sew?*" Sean scoffed.

"I believe the actual process would be more like deconstructing the edges of the jeans and patch material, and then weaving them back together as a unit. They would also be able to apply a chemical dye to the T-shirt in a pattern that looks as though it were tied and dipped in dyes."

"Wow, nanites can do anything, huh?" Sean rolled his eyes. "Can they sit up? Roll over? Play dead?" He suddenly turned a harsh glare to Alex. "Hey, wait a minute. Is that why Maggie acts so weird around you? Did you nanite my dog?"

"It was necessary to calm her. No harm will come to her. In sixty days or less they will all deactivate and her natural immune system will eliminate them from her body."

"What about the ones you've been stuffing in me? Will all of my nanites die off, too?"

"Most of them," Alex said softly.

"*Most of them?* Why just *most* of them?"

"The ones that control your hidden memories are self-replicating. They must remain in position to keep that section of your brain cordoned off."

"I'll have these *things* in my head for the rest of my life?"

"They will do you no harm. In the future, billions of people live with nanites in their bodies for their entire lives. Most are there to monitor and regulate the health of the human body. It is not that dissimilar to the bacteria that live in your body now. You are unaware of them, and most have beneficial functions."

"And no doctor is going to X-ray my head someday and say, 'hey, you've got a bunch of tiny robots in your brain!'?"

"No. They cannot be detected with any technology that is invented in your lifetime."

"OK, I don't even want to think about it anymore." He closed his eyes and shuddered. "Now. Back to the grand plan. So, it's 1969, and we two traveling musicians walk up to my Dad and say, 'dude, we're traveling musicians. Can we hang with you?' and just like that, we're in?"

"You will need to adjust your vernacular for the time. You would not say 'dude' or 'hang.' Perhaps a more appropriate greeting would be: 'hey, man, what's happening?'"

"OK, so we'll just knock on my Grandma's door, and ask her if Jack can come out to play, and then you can say to him, 'hey, man, what's happening?'," said Sean. "I'm not really feeling it."

"We will not knock on his door. We would need to locate him in a more neutral setting, ideally some type of social interaction where it would not be difficult to join into a conversation."

"So are you suggesting going to his high school?"

"No. That would not be optimal for the 'traveling musicians' scenario. I believe we can locate him at some form of summer outing," Alex said. "It will require a considerable amount of improvisation. Do you feel comfortable improvising a character? It would be best to prepare a background story."

"What do you mean?"

"Obviously you could not introduce yourself as Sean Kelly. You will need to construct a fictional character to portray."

"Who are you going to be?"

"As the Beatles final year together is 1969, I will portray myself as Peter Lindsey, born in Liverpool in 1950. At the age of 13, I attended a Beatles performance in Liverpool, just as they were rocketing to stardom."

Sean noticed that Alex spoke with a British accent. He smiled and nodded. "I like it," he said, "Oi, mate, ah kin be British, tew!"

"Do you believe you could effect a British accent?"

"Eh, wot? Me? Blimey, I kin do a right proper Brit, yeah? It's a bit of all right, id nit? Tut tut, cheerio, old blighter. No worries about me, mate. Good on ya, yeah?"

Alex paused a moment to query his computer. "The computer recognized four distinct regional British accents, as well as Australian. Perhaps British would not be our optimal choice for you."

"Oi, come on, guv'ner, give me a bit, yeah? I just need a wee bit of practice."

"You have now added Scotland to your repertoire."

"Och, Aye! Thass it! I'll be a wee bonnie Scot! I'll be Hamish MacDougal, laird of the highlands!"

"I do not believe that is plausible for the concept of a sixties rock musician."

"Maybe something more upscale? Like Pierce Brosnan? I could be Lionel Farnsworth Smythe-Davies the fourth. I've run away from home because I don't want to go into banking like all of the three previous Lionel F. Smythe-

Davies. Dreadfully boring, don't you know."

"Very imaginative," Alex commented, "Perhaps with some work..."

"I've *got* it!" Sean interrupted, "I'll be Nigel Nagfarkle! Ever see that movie *Spinal Tap*? No, I guess you wouldn't have. But you can, right? I can be like that. You know, all cool and British, but kind of clueless. You should download that video into your head and watch it. It's awesome."

Alex twitched momentarily. "That has a 1984 copyright date. I only have the full video of movies from 1990 to 1999 with me. I can assimilate the plot summary."

"That won't give you the feel of it. You need to see it. I wonder if Blockbuster would have something that old?"

"Why would it be helpful?"

"It's about these has-been British rockers. It's like perfect for role models."

"That story takes place 15 years after 1969. Music makes considerable changes in 15 years."

"Yeah, but you can still get the whole British rock thing." Sean assessed the doubt in Alex's face, then added, "And it's hilarious."

"We should discuss the music scene of 1969. Do you know what music your father would have been listening to at the time?"

Sean thought for a moment. "Well, like you already said, there's The Beatles." He thought some more. "OK, ummm... David Bowie..."

"He was only beginning to become well known in the UK, but very little known in the US for another few years."

"OK, how about Queen?"

"Early 1970s"

"Rolling Stones."

"Yes, that is a pertinent choice."

"Aerosmith?"

"Again, early 1970s"

"Well, crap... ummm... The Beach Boys?"

"Yes, but they were more popular in the earlier part of the sixties."

"This might be harder than I thought," Sean admitted with an air of defeat.

"A band named *Credence Clearwater Revival* had six hits that year, and groups called *Blood, Sweat & Tears, Three Dog Night, The Guess Who,* and the *5th Dimension* each had multiple hits that year."

"I've never heard of *any* of those guys... but I'm not into Oldies Radio."

"You will need to be well versed in the songs of that era to successfully portray a 'traveling musician.'"

"Why do you know those oldies? You don't seem to know the songs that are popular now."

"Research. The songs are a critical element of our 1969 scenario; I had assumed music of your era to be secondary to the role I designed for 1995," Alex answered. "I believe I can adapt a study module for you to absorb while you sleep. It will require some programming to target the information to the same part of your brain as your 'XL memory', but I am confident that the computer will find a workable solution."

Sean stared blankly at the ceiling, overwhelmed by the magnitude of what he didn't know about 1969. Alex observed him for a few moments before speaking. "You seem suddenly less enthusiastic."

"I was just thinking about how hard this will be. I don't know anything about even 25 years ago, and you've got all this access to info that will help you be as much of an expert for 1969 as you are 1995. I'll probably do something stupid right away that will give me away as not belonging."

"It happens that I had already considered that possibility. I know you would also like to be a British rocker, but I thought it plausible for you to portray my cousin from New Zealand. My research indicates it is unlikely that any high-school aged person in the Midwestern United States of 1969 will know many details about New Zealand. You can attempt your British accent, and if anyone finds it non-authentic, it can be explained as sounding exactly like a New Zealander. They will have no reference to judge, and therefore will accept the explanation."

Sean thought it over. "I suppose that might work. I guess I don't know that much about New Zealand myself. I think they have a lot of sheep or something."

"You will also require a suitable name. You have mentioned Smythe-Davies, and Davies happens to be a common name in New Zealand."

"I want to stick with Nigel. I really like Nigel. Let's go with Nigel Davies. That has a pretty good sound to it. Let's go with that," Sean decided.

"Nigel Davies from New Zealand. I believe that will be plausible," Alex agreed.

"Righteo, Cousin Pete! We're mad set to do this bloomin' caper, eh what!"

Sean said then tipped his Coke can as if a toast.

"You probably should not drink that," Alex said as he grabbed Sean's arm.

"Why? You didn't load it with more nanites did you?"

"No, but if you were to drink your Coke, you would wonder why your can was empty when you were returned to normal memory."

"Oi!" Sean said, still trying out his British accent, "That's right clever, old sport! This memory thing is frightfully difficult, id nit?"

"Yes," Alex agreed, "and the other factor is time. We cannot leave you in XL memory much longer, or the length of time spent down here will be noticeable when you switch back to your normal memory."

"OK, so we know I need to learn more about oldies music, we have a plan for clothing, we've got our characters figured out... what else is there?"

"I will give that more thought, and we can revisit our plans more fully tomorrow. Also, I am going to shorten the password for your XL memory. I believe it will still be secure, but fewer syllables for me to say, which I discovered to be more difficult when used at school."

"Like on the stairs?" Sean chided, "*That* was almost a disaster."

"I will not change your memory on the stairs again," said Alex. "We can spend several hours working on this tomorrow."

"Several *hours*? When are we going to have several hours?" Sean asked.

"We will have to make a short hop in time to gain the hours needed to accomplish our preparation. Can you think of anything else we need to discuss now before I return you to normal memory?" Alex asked.

"No, I don't rightly s'pose I do, guv'ner," Sean said, still trying out his accent.

"Perhaps I can also program something into the music lesson that will assist you with your British accent. I will see you tomorrow," Alex said as he shifted back to Nicole. "Oh," she said, "I thought of something else. Can you grow facial hair?"

"Some..." Sean answered a little defensively.

"I think that might help with your musician appearance. OK, back to the chair, turn the computer off, and we will return to your demonstration of IRC." Sean sat and moved around as Nicole guided him into position while they waited for the computer to shut down. "OK, that is perfect. Ready? Mobo Gerga save LX seventeen five."

Nicole pushed the button on the power switch. "This is very interesting," she said, "Aunt Katherine is quite talented with her computer, but I know so little about them."

"Well, it's pretty cool," Sean replied, "Hopefully some of the guys will be on, and we can set up a chat room, and then you can see how multiple people can chat at the same time."

"I am sure it will be fascinating," Nicole said, watching the screen as the computer booted.

Chapter Ten

"Asked a girl what she wanted to be / She said, 'Baby, can't you see...'"

RAJ chattered enthusiastically about the comment they'd received from Mrs. Roberts as he and Sean left Biology. Sean was just happy for Thursday's last class to be over. The note praised their work on the earthworm lab proclaiming that they had the cleanest project of the entire class and had labeled all the organs correctly. Sean attempted to nod and grunt agreements any time Raj paused his in-depth recap of each step of the dissection. He was happy for Raj that he found it all so interesting, reasoning that a Doctor who loves his work is better than one who's only in it for the money. Though for himself, Sean was simply glad he could piggyback on Raj's talents and hope it might bump his own grade up a little.

They were on their way to the far staircase which led down to the exit closest to the parking lot when halfway down the hall they found Nicole standing by the top of the middle stairs. The middle stairs led to the door closest to the external classrooms commonly called Schoolyard Wasteland.

"Nicole," said a surprised Sean. "What are you doing up on third? I thought your last class was on first-floor."

"It is," she replied, "I would like to speak with you about something."

"OK."

"Could we go down these stairs?" she asked with a shy glance toward Raj.

Raj mimed a hands-off gesture. "Hey, I don't want to interfere with a budding romance," he said with a grin as he headed on down the hall."

"Hey, Raj," Sean called after him, "maybe catch you tonight on IRC?"

"Maybe," he yelled back, "I've got a lot of studying to do."

"You study too much!" Sean yelled even louder.

"Maybe you don't study enough," Raj retorted.

Sean shook his head, baffled by his friend's dedication to schoolwork.

"So what's up?" he asked Nicole as they started down the stairs.

"I wanted to thank you again for the assistance with Imaginary Numbers. It made a considerable positive difference as I listened to his lecture today."

"Aw shucks," Sean said mimicking a cowboy movie, "T'weren't nuthin', ma'am. I reckon yur plenty smart 'nuff."

"Why are you talking that way?" she asked.

"I don't know," he shrugged, "Just kind of popped out. I guess I like doing characters and accents. Wanna hear me do a British accent?"

Nicole tried to cover a laugh. Sean's cheeks pinked as he felt a little irritated by her reaction.

"I think I've already told you that I like the sound of your laugh," he said, "but what's so funny about what I just said?"

"I am sorry," she said, stifling one more laugh, "I was reminded of something Alexis said, it is unrelated to you."

"Alexis said something with a British accent?" Sean gave her a suspicious look. "I can't quite imagine that."

"And I did not imagine that you enjoyed doing character voices," Nicole replied, "Do you ever participate in dramatic productions?"

"Well, not a lot," he said, trying to sound modest. "I had a small part in the spring production last year. Not too shabby for a Sophomore... especially when you consider there were tons of Juniors and Seniors that were totally into theater. I could probably get a bigger part this year, especially if I suck up to Ms. McGuire."

They reached the bottom of the steps and Nicole headed out the door.

"Now where are we going?" Sean asked.

"Out here where it is quieter."

Sean followed her as she turned down the walkway toward the bike path. "You and Alexis both seem to like going this way," he commented, "I don't think hardly anyone uses this sidewalk."

She stopped and turned toward him, "No, not many people do. Mobo Gerga. Retrieve LX seventeen five."

Sean sucked in a sharp breath as his 'other' memories rushed into his consciousness. He squeezed his eyes shut, then blinked a few times as he attempted to merge the dual realities in his head. He finished with a big shake and a slap to his cheeks. "You know the more we do this, the less it seems like waking from a dream and more like I'm schizophrenic."

Nicole quickly twitched a connection to the computer. "Gursk!" she yowled, "That is terrible!" She put her hands on Sean's shoulders and studied his eyes. "Do you actually believe you are symptomatic of mental illness?

We should stop this experiment immediately!"

"No! Chill!" Sean reassured her, "I was just saying it was *like* being schizophrenic, not that I *was*. I didn't mean to spook you. Since my Mom's a psychology teacher, I probably know more psych stuff than most people. I just thought that if anyone heard me talk about 'two memories' they'd think I was delusional or hallucinating or something."

"Are you certain?" Nicole asked, still agitated, "I will *not* continue if I am causing you harm."

"Wow. You're really wound up about this," Sean noted.

"It is *very* frightening! The thought of a brain disorder is more terrifying than an ailment in any other part of the body!" she exclaimed. "There is *no* mental illness in the 23rd century. Can you imagine how you would feel if you were talking to one of your ancestors and they said, 'I believe I have the Bubonic Plague.' Would you not be concerned?"

"OK," Sean nodded, "I can see that, I guess." He paused a moment, then added, "Did you say 'gursk'?"

"Did I?"

"That's what it sounded like to me. What's a 'gursk'?"

Nicole's cheeks flamed to crimson. "I am sorry. Though not often, I sometimes use expletives when I am extremely upset."

"Really?" Sean laughed, "'gursk' is a curse word? That's hilarious!"

"It is *not* hilarious! I was very concerned about you," she said defensively.

"OK," Sean said, trying to be diplomatic, "I'm sorry I said schizophrenic. You're sorry you said gursk... let's move on." He lifted his eyebrows, "So what's the plan?"

"We need to use the Space/Time Explorer to move back a few hours, allowing us ample time to accomplish several tasks and further discuss our approach," Nicole said then turned and started walking down the sidewalk toward the bike path. Sean followed.

"It needs a name," he said abruptly.

"What needs a name?"

"Your time-machine, time-craft, time-ship, space/time explorer thing. You've called it several things, but it needs a name."

"I could refer to it simply as the acronym S.T.E.," she suggested.

"That's a great name... *not!*" Sean scoffed, "That's boring." Sean thought for a moment. He followed Nicole as she crossed the short patch of grass to the bike path. "So let's play with the acronym. We need to add some more letters to make a word. How about the Space/Time Explorer, Vector Extension? Then we can call it 'Steve.'"

"Vector Extension? How does one extend a vector?"

"Video Enhanced?"

"That also seems non-sequitur."

"Vortex Enveloper!" Sean said triumphantly.

"Why do you wish to call it 'Steve'?"

"Hmmm. Good point." Sean thought some more. "Space/Time Explorer Wild Intergalactic Enigma! Then we can call it 'Stewie'!"

"Wild Intergalactic Enigma?"

"You're right... needs some more work." They continued down the bike path. "Fantastic Futuristic Intelligence! Steffi! I kind of like Steffi. What do you think?"

"I think I will call it the S.T.E., and you may call it Steffi if you wish." Nicole stepped off the bike path and pushed her way through some bushes.

"*Now* where are you going?" Sean asked while following her and picking through the brambles.

"To the S.T.E."

Sean came around to the back side of the bushes where Nicole had already uncloaked the time-machine. "You parked Steffi out here in the bushes?" he asked.

"Yes. It is where I place it each day. Contrary to what I have told you, my Aunt Katherine does not give me a ride to school."

"So that's why I saw Alexis coming from this side of the school. You're coming from the park, not the drop-off zone!" Sean exclaimed. "So your ride to school is a high-tech Space/time-craft capable of shifting dimensions, and you just park it out here all day in the grass?"

"Yes. It seemed a logical solution. It is hidden behind this vegetation as well as cloaked."

"That is totally insane!"

"I fail to see how something so logical should be labeled insane," Nicole said indignantly.

"No. No. Not crazy insane... ummm... impressive... how about impressive?"

"Insane is an idiom for impressive?" she asked.

"It can be."

She twitched to query mode. "It seems there are many idioms you use that were not programmed into my language lesson. I have made a note of 'insane.'"

"OK, glad we got that cleared up," Sean said, "So... where are we going?"

"Actually," Nicole said, "we are going *here*. It is merely a question of when."

"OK, literalist," Sean said testily, "*when* are we going?"

"Fifteen minutes past the start of second-hour."

"OK... ummm why?"

"It should be a time when we would be least likely to encounter anyone as we walk from here to the parking lot to retrieve your automobile."

"Works for me," Sean said amiably. "Crank Steffi up!"

Nicole put her hand on the S.T.E., and the door slid open. "Hand-print analysis?" Sean asked.

"Not exactly. Touching it activates a sensor that then confirms my identity with the nanites in my brain," she said as she slid into her seat. Sean slid in next to her.

"You really don't mind having all those creepy nanites running around your body doing weird stuff like opening doors?" he asked.

"I never think about it," she answered. "Do you feel 'creepy nanites running around' in *your* body?"

Sean considered for a moment. "I guess not.... well... when you were re-inventing yourself as the perfect girl I had those tingling sensations. That was nanites, wasn't it?"

"Yes," she acknowledged, "I miscalculated how they might function in a relatively nanite-free body. I should have added an anesthetic component."

"Right. Like I need another way for you to make me a numbskull," Sean muttered.

She glanced at him quizzically, but said nothing as she busied herself with the control panel. "I have pre-programmed most of the sequence needed for this short jump. Oh, I almost forgot," she said as she reached into her book bag. "I have something for you."

"What?" Sean asked dryly, "Another barf bag?"

"No," she said as she handed him a small green and white disk. "Something you suggested after your last excursion."

"A mint!" He took it from her and popped it in his mouth. "And it's spearmint... because of course you know that I prefer that over peppermint."

"Yes," Nicole answered showing a self-satisfied smile, "and it is also green, which is your favorite color."

"You know me too well, Future-Boy."

Nicole paused from setting the controls to look directly at Sean. "You have not requested that I drop the Nicole disguise."

"Nah," he shrugged, "I figured this close to the school, you wouldn't change out of the Nicole gig."

"Yet you seem to react to me and speak to me as if I had."

"I'm trying to get a handle on my two memories. When I know who you are, I try to think of you as Alex... and I imagine that you like to be in drag."

"Drag?" she asked quizzically.

"Look it up," Sean said, rolling his eyes.

Nicole twitched a query to the computer. She turned an astonished face back to Sean, then twitched again for a longer download. "You certainly live in a fascinating era. Do you or your friends ever go out in drag?"

Sean squinted one eye. "OK, maybe you *don't* know me too well."

"I believe I should interpret that reply as 'no.'"

"Correct... but hey, if *you* like that kind of thing, one of the movies currently playing is called 'To Wong Foo, Thanks for Everything, Julie Newmar.'" He crinkled his nose. "Patrick Swayze in drag... that's just sad."

"Have you selected which movie we will attend?"

"I was thinking about taking *Nicole* to 'The Net'... I think it's still playing. But if I knew ahead of time that it's *you*, Future-Boy, we'd go see 'Mortal Kombat' instead."

"Why would you wish to switch?" Nicole asked.

"Because 'The Net' has Sandra Bullock, which means chick-flick, and 'Mortal Kombat' is more for guys."

"Well, since you are taking *Nicole*, then we will attend the 'chick flick.'"

"Whatever you wish, my queen." Sean nodded forward slightly as he touched his forehead and rotated his hand several times as he let it drop.

"Does that have a hidden meaning?" she asked.

"As hidden as your true identity," Sean said, bouncing his eyebrows.

"I believe I will not delve further into this topic," she said. "Are you prepared for departure?"

"You bet!"

Nicole tapped one of the icons in the display field. The S.T.E. puffed an airy sound.

"Do you have to lift off the ground to take off?" Sean asked.

"In this instance we do, we cannot materialize over the existing ship, so I am moving us a few feet to the right."

"Existing ship?"

"Yes, the S.T.E. has been sitting here since before first period this morning. It will be in this same spot when we arrive, so we need to move to the side to accommodate."

"So, this is another time that there will be two time-machines at once."

"Although I am wary of correcting you... it is only *one* time-machine, but it will exist twice at the same moment in time," Nicole said, then cringed as she expected Sean to explode.

"OK, cool, call it what you want; there *will* be a time-machine sitting next to us when we arrive?"

"That is correct."

"And if someone just happened to be walking by, wouldn't they say, 'hey, there are *two* time-machines sitting there right next to each other.'?"

Nicole seemed confused. "They will both be cloaked... and they are hidden from the path by tall leafy vegetation."

"OK, never mind... just punch it," Sean said in exasperation.

Nicole tapped a second icon, and a blue rectangular box appeared in the display field, rotating on its longest axis. A sound of repeated wheezing, trumpeting, and thumping accompanied the image. Sean felt completely numb as every nerve in his body tingled icy hot. He stared at the blue box, focused on the sound, and rolled the mint around on his tongue.

"How do you feel?" Nicole asked.

"We're there?"

"Yes."

"I think I'm getting the hang of this!" Sean said triumphantly.

Nicole touched a few icons, and the display closed down then the door slid open. Sean stepped out and looked around. He leaned his head back inside the S.T.E. "So, it's morning again and I'm currently in Speech class?" he asked.

"You are currently in two places at this same moment. One iteration is indeed in your second-hour class, the other, of course, is right here."

"Really?" Sean snarked, "would it have killed you to just said 'yes'?"

Nicole sat quietly contemplating several different involved answers but finally softly said, "No."

"OK, so let's get going," Sean grumbled.

She handed him her book bag which he reluctantly took, then slid out, closed the door, and cloaked the S.T.E. Sean turned toward the walkway and immediately slammed into the other cloaked S.T.E.

"Owww!" he yelped, "I ran into the other gursking time-machine!"

Nicole laughed. "No one uses gursk as an adjective!"

"Well, we gursking do *now*," Sean proclaimed, then added, "Why are you taking your book bag? We're coming back here, right?"

"Yes, but I have a few items we will need to complete our preparations," she replied as she edged between the two cloaked vehicles and around the bush. Sean followed.

"*I* have to carry it?" he protested.

"Yes, since you have the caveman muscles for it," she said, stepping onto the bike path and briskly heading toward the school. Sean caught up and fell into step with her.

"Now I'm just confused," he said dramatically.

"Why is that?"

"Because on one hand, I'm glad that you are loosening up and acting more like a normal teenager."

"And, on the other hand," she prompted.

"Dude, you called me a caveman!"

Nicole gave him a quick sideways hug. "But you are my *favorite* caveman," she said with a big smile.

"Hey! Hey! Watch the PDA... I know who you are in there!" Sean said as he pushed her away.

"Would it have been more appropriate to have roughly shoulder-bumped you, the way I observed Kevin in the hall the other day?" she asked.

"No!" he said emphatically, "you can't go shoulder bumping a guy when you look like a girl!"

"Your gender rules are more difficult to understand than learning the gender of nouns in French," she complained. "What *would* have been an appropriate physical gesture?"

"Well," Sean started while thinking it over. "If you were a *real* girl, then the hug would have been appropriate and if you looked like the guy that you *really are*, then the shoulder bump would have been OK."

Sean started to cross the grass back to the sidewalk that went behind the school. When he noticed Nicole had stopped, he turned back to her. "Since I currently meet neither criteria, what would have been an appropriate physical contact?" she asked.

"Actually, I would feel more comfortable if you *didn't* touch me when I know you're Alex, but you look like Nicole." When he saw the look on her face, Sean regretted his honesty. She touched her neck with her left hand and blurred briefly to be replaced by a man three inches taller than Sean and built like an NFL linebacker. "Well, *that's* kind of an overreaction!" he said backing up from the apparition that replaced Nicole.

"Walk on my immediate left," a gruff voice ordered, "and attempt to match my pace as best you can."

"Look, Alex," Sean said while trying to catch up to the linebacker, "I'm sorry I hurt your feelings... *again!* But trying to look like a tough guy isn't going to make it any better."

"That is not why I have assumed this appearance," Alex said in his own voice, then explained, "The computer selected a voice it calculated would best match this body. I have overridden it."

"Kudos to the computer," Sean acknowledged. "So you picked this moment to change to a WWF wrestler because....?"

"Look at me."

"Hard not to, Goliath," Sean said dryly.

"Ignoring my physical stature, describe me as you would to a police detective."

"OK," Sean started slowly, "Ignoring the hulkish size... umm...light brownish hair, not quite blonde... darkish eyes... I don't know... normal nose, normal ears... medium complexion..."

"Does that sound rather 'average' to you?"

"I suppose."

"That is the construct," Alex said, "As we walk along the sidewalk anyone looking out the window as we walk by will notice a large, though rather nondescript, man clad in a dark business suit."

"OK, I guess that makes sense... but what's up with the large economy size?"

"Assuming you will keep pace with me and walk at my left shoulder, your identity will be adequately shielded from anyone's view."

Sean looked over at the classroom windows facing the sidewalk and smiled as he thought about what Alex said. "So do you stay up late at night working out all this strategy?" Sean asked.

"Generally, the computer maps the strategy, I merely have to pose the projected scenario."

"I wish you could hook *me* up with a computer like that, that would be awesome! I'd never study for a test again!" Sean slapped himself. "OK, enough daydreaming, let's get moving."

'Big' Alex started across the grass and Sean quickly matched his stride as they walked down the sidewalk.

"I guess I jumped to conclusions when you did the switch. I thought you did it because I hurt your feelings," Sean offered, "Glad that wasn't the reason."

"I did not say that you did not hurt my feelings," Alex said levelly.

They walked silently for the remaining length of the building.

Once they had rounded the corner where there weren't any classroom windows, 'Big' Alex stopped. Sean turned back. "Now what?" he asked.

"Who do you want me to be?" Alex asked.

"Is this really the best time to get all philosophical?"

"It was not a philosophical question. Who would you feel most comfortable with while we select the needed items at Wall Mart?"

"What, like pick between Nicole and Alexis?"

"You are not limited to those two choices," Alex replied.

"Well, I'm not going shopping with Aunt Katherine!" Sean huffed.

"But if you prefer, I can assume Raj or Kevin just as readily." He touched his neck and transformed into a copy of Raj.

Sean stared open-mouthed at 'Raj,' then he made a face and shuddered. "Ewwww, that's just creepy!"

"I thought it seemed a logical choice to shop with one of your best friends."

"Ack!" Sean exclaimed, "You even sound like him! Change it! Change it!"

'Raj' touched his neck, shimmered and was replaced with Nicole. "I did not expect *that* reaction," she said bluntly.

"Sorry... it just seemed all body-snatcherish to me... Nicole is fine, let's just go."

They had walked through several rows in the parking lot before they reached Sean's car.

"Can you step away from the vehicle?" Nicole asked.

"Now you think you're a cop?"

She gave him a puzzled glance, but then shook it off. "I need to record a hologram of just your automobile," she said as she reached behind Sean and into her bag. The object she brought out was slightly larger than a golf ball, but similarly dimpled. It was metal with a dull gray matte finish. Nicole balanced it on her palm as she walked the perimeter of the car. "OK," she said, "Now move the vehicle out of the parking area."

Sean got into his car and backed it out, then drove forward a couple car lengths, stopped, and got out. Nicole was in the center of the newly empty parking space placing the dimpled ball onto a small stand set on the ground. She backed away from it, and the moment she reached where Sean's bumper had been there was a flash. Sean's jaw dropped when he saw his Taurus was sitting back in the parking slot. He looked back at the car he'd just moved, just to make sure that it hadn't re-materialized in its original space. He grabbed Nicole by the shoulders and shook her as he hopped up and down.

"Holy crap!" he gushed, "That is *awesome!*"

"We needed assurance that no one places their vehicle over these coordinates in our absence. Once you return to your regular memory, you will expect your automobile to be in this location. We cannot take the risk of someone else occupying this spot."

"You know," Sean said, his eyes sparkling as the gears whirred in his head, "If we came back in the evening when this lot is mostly empty, we could leave that projector thingy in a first-row parking slot overnight. Then I could have like a reserved parking space. I'd wheel in with the crowd and just pull over top the hologram thingy."

"You would prefer a closer parking space every day?"

"You bet!"

"Simply arrive 15 minutes earlier than you usually do."

"Don't channel my Mom... that's scary."

"I do not understand 'channel' in context with your mother. Should I?"

"Nah, that's OK, Future-Boy... let's head to Walmart."

A few minutes later they pulled into the Walmart parking lot and parked relatively close to the door. Sean commented on the sparse number of shoppers on Thursday morning compared to weekends as they walked toward the door.

"Hey, watch this," he said dramatically, "Door... *Open!*" As they got closer, the door slid open and they walked through the opening.

"You realize," said Nicole, "that I am fully aware of 20th Century motion-detector technology."

Sean shrugged. "It was worth a shot. Your knowledge seems kinda spotty in some areas."

Sean strode purposefully toward the men's clothing section; Nicole followed, gaping in awe at all the various merchandise on the shelves. Sean looked over his shoulder and noticed how she was taking in everything as they walked.

"Enjoying your little walk through the museum?" he asked dryly.

"I am experiencing how incredible it is to *see* all of this, rather than simply read about it historically. There are so many objects that I do not even comprehend what they are," she said, breathlessly astonished. "The rate of growth in consumption from the mid-twentieth century through the mid-twenty-first is unprecedented, but to *see* it all displayed this way..." Her voice trailed off as she stopped in housewares.

Sean sighed, then turned back to her, shaking his head in disbelief. She pointed to the shelf. "What is that?"

"A coffee maker," he replied, hoping she would recognize the extreme boredom in his voice.

"It has only one function?"

"Ummm... I guess you could make tea in it," he shrugged.

She pointed to the next item on the shelf. "What is this one?"

"That's another coffee maker."

"Does it create a different type of coffee than the first one?"

"Not really."

She moved to the next item. "Is this one also a coffee maker?"

"Now you're catching on," he deadpanned.

She walked down the rest of the section, touched each item, and then turned back to Sean. "These are all coffee makers?"

"Yes they are! When you go back to your own time, you can tell everyone that while visiting the 20th century you became an expert at identifying coffee makers!"

"Have I also correctly inferred that these numbers beneath the items represent the cost in U.S. Dollars?"

"See, it's times like this that I think I could have gotten away with the 'magic door' trick. Yes, that's the price in U.S. Dollars."

"This one is $69.95... and this one is $29.95... but each of them can only perform one task... make coffee?"

"Yes," sighed Sean in exasperation.

"Does the $69.95 device produce a superior coffee?"

"That's what that manufacturer hopes you'll think."

She nodded thoughtfully, then turned her attention back to the shelves. "These two are both priced $39.95... but their appearance is not exactly alike."

"That one is a *Mr. Coffee*," Sean said as he pointed at one, then the other, "and that one is a *Hamilton Beach*... it's just two different manufacturers."

"Are each of the other products created by a different manufacturer?" she asked while indicating the whole display.

"Well, there are several that are just a different model from the same manufacturer."

She walked down the row and again touched each item. "Twelve. There are twelve different models at various prices, and each of them simply make coffee. Amazing!"

"Well," Sean pointed out, "That one also has a clock."

She crossed back to Sean, stood face to face, and looked him in the eye. "Which one would you purchase?" she asked expectantly.

"I don't like coffee."

"But if you did... how would you decide which one to purchase?"

"I don't know," he said irritably. "Can we just go to men's wear before I have explain espresso machines?" He walked briskly away from her.

"Espresso machines?" Nicole asked hopefully as she trailed after him.

He spun back around. "Look, grandson... er daughter... whatever... we didn't come to shop for toys, we're going to buy some clothes for the mission."

"What mission?" she asked.

"You know, the back to 1969 mission!"

"A 'mission' implies an objective. Do you have an objective in mind for this venture?"

"Would you prefer I call it a vacation?" Sean said testily.

"Since you are only along as an observing passenger, perhaps you should think of it as an excursion."

"Now you're a cruise director?" he snapped as he walked away from her again.

Nicole followed along silently, looking at all of the various merchandise laid out on the shelves. Several things seemed mysterious to her, but she didn't ask Sean any more questions.

Distracted, she bumped into Sean when he had stopped. He scowled at her.

"I am sorry," she apologized softly, "I was attempting to read the message on that shirt." She pointed to a manikin that was wearing a Metallica t-shirt.

"People who are hard core heavy metal might buy that," Sean said, trying to sound bored again.

Puzzled, Nicole asked, "How can a person have a hard metal core?"

Sean only briefly considered explaining before he suggested she ask her computer. "OK, t-shirts. You said plain white, correct?"

"Yes, I believe that will work best."

Sean held up two packages, one in each hand. "Regular t-shirt or wife-beater?" He rolled his eyes when he saw the complete lack of comprehension on her face. "This one's usually worn as an undershirt. No sleeves."

"The pictures I have seen show sleeves."

"Pocket or no-pocket?"

"I do not believe either is a requirement."

"I'll get the pocket then. I like pockets. OK, here's a pack of three Hanes white Ts with pockets. Now let's go over to jeans."

Nicole trailed after him. As he was looking for his size, she asked, "When you asked if I was a cruise director, you did not expect a response, did you?"

"Hmmm?" he said absently as he pulled out a pair to check the tag, "No. Just slamming you." He put that pair back and pulled out another. Nicole looked thoughtfully at the ceiling for a moment.

"Now you are a hotel doorman?" She asked, trying to mimic his tone.

Sean looked up from the jeans. "What?"

"A doorman," Nicole explained, "You have recently slammed me three times, so perhaps you are now a doorman."

He raised his eyebrows. "Now you're a comedian?"

"Perhaps," Nicole smiled.

Sean rolled his eyes, then slowly shook his head. "OK, comedian," he said, "T-shirts and jeans... anything else? I don't need special 1969 socks or underwear, do I?"

"I do not think that will be required. Perhaps some type of footwear that would simulate a logical choice for hitchhiking across the country," she suggested.

"I've got some Doc Marten hiking shoes at home. Would that work?"

"Perhaps if we were to cake them in mud, they would not be recognized as anachronistic."

"You want to cake my Doc Martens in mud?!?!"

"They need to look well-traveled."

"You'll ruin them!"

"If I cannot return them to their original condition I will purchase a new pair for you."

Sean opened his mouth to argue but stopped. "Purchase a new pair? Wait, are you paying for the shirts and jeans?"

"If you wish."

"How much money do you have?"

"I usually carry no more than $300.00 in currency, but I also have a credit card."

"You walk around with three hundred bucks?" Sean asked, his eyes wide.

"Yes," she replied simply, "I believe for 1995 that would be sufficient for most emergencies I might encounter which would require an immediate remuneration."

"Right now you have three hundred bucks?"

"Yes. Five twenty dollar bills, four fifty dollar bills... Presidents Jackson and Grant. Do you wish to examine them for authenticity?"

"No, that's OK. But you said you've also got a credit card?"

"Yes, it has a $25,000.00 limit, though." Sean held his chest and gasped as Nicole continued, "It is in Katherine Tuttle's name, of course." She noticed his reaction. "Are you all right?"

"You could buy twenty-five *thousand* dollars' worth of stuff on your credit card?" he wheezed.

"Yes. It would have to be justified for my research, of course," she said. She looked at him more closely. "I do not have any historical data that reported you ever suffering from asthma, but you seem to be having trouble breathing."

"No. No... I'm OK," he said. His eyes twinkled as he enthusiastically added, "Want to go look around in electronics?"

"I doubt that any technology current to 1969 would still be sold," she said skeptically.

"No, not for the missi... excursion. Just to look. You know, in case you needed an idea for what to get your old great-great-great-great-grandfather for his next birthday. *Great!* ... I left out a 'great,' don't say it, I can see it on your face."

"You are suggesting I purchase electronics and give them to you as a reward for aging?" she asked.

"It would be nice... although I don't particularly like the way you phrased that."

"Would that be the type of gift you might expect to receive from Nicole?"

"No. Not from Nicole... from you... Alex-in-drag. My multi-G grandson with the multi-G credit card."

"You will not have any memories of Alex, so it could only be something that is a logical gift from Nicole. What would your mother think if Nicole gave you an expensive gift?"

"Well, crap!" Sean grumbled, "You've always got loopholes, don't you?"

"I prefer to think of it as reaching a logical conclusion. Do you still wish to look at electronics?"

"Nah, let's get out of here."

"I would prefer to use a credit card for this transaction, but I am unsure how appropriate that is for a teenaged girl. I generally make purchases as Katherine."

"I doubt anyone would notice, but if you don't want to try it, just change," Sean suggested.

"I have detected security cameras in nearly every aisle. Though it is possible it would go unnoticed, if someone were to see the change it would be problematic."

"OK, fine!" Sean said as he grabbed Nicole's elbow, "Let's go to the ladies' department."

He pulled her into the lingerie section near the fitting rooms and started grabbing various colored bras off the rack. He handed them to Nicole and pointed to the fitting room. "OK," he finally said, "You've got six, that's the max they let you take in at once. Just go into the fitting room and show the clerk on the way in that you've got six items. Once you're inside, I'll distract her, and then you can come out as Katherine."

"Will she activate a security alert when she discovers that Nicole has disappeared?"

"Nah, if you leave the bras in plain sight, she'll just assume you're a flaky teenager that changed her mind and left. Hey, it's Walmart, it's not like they're rocket scientists that we have to outwit."

"Well, if you are certain," Nicole said hesitantly.

"Go! In thirty seconds, I'll distract her."

Nicole went into the dressing room, showing her items to the clerk as she entered. She went into a stall, set the lingerie down, and shifted to Aunt Katherine. Cautiously, she peeked out and saw that Sean was waving his arms and yelling and pointing down the aisle away from the dressing room. With a determined look on her face, the clerk stepped briskly in the direction he was pointing. Katherine slipped out of the fitting room and walked hurriedly in the opposite direction. She waited a few aisles over until Sean rejoined her.

"That was exhilarating," she said breathlessly.

"And you didn't need a computer to plan it out," Sean boasted.

"What did you tell her that convinced her to move away?" Katherine asked.

"I said I saw some transvestite doing some inappropriate things with the lingerie... which is kind of true..."

"I do not believe I qualify as a transvestite," she said indignantly.

"Hey, if it walks like a duck and quacks like a duck..." When she started to interrupt, Sean raised his hands up to stop her. "I'll explain later why I am bringing up waterfowl." He handed her the jeans and t-shirts. "I'll meet you at the car. I don't like shopping with my own Mom; I'm definitely not standing in line with someone else who looks as old as my Mom."

Katherine paid for the clothes with her credit card, smiled politely at the cashier, took her bag, and headed out the door. Sean was waiting for her right outside. "OK," he said quickly, "I've already unlocked the car. You walk to the car and get in. I'll be twenty paces behind you. The second you slide into the seat, switch to Nicole... *unless* you hear me yell the codeword, *gursk*, then we abort because someone is watching."

"I think..." Katherine started but was cut off.

"Don't think! Just do it! I've got it planned out perfect. Go!" Sean barked.

Katherine walked nervously down the lane where they had parked. She went to the passenger side of the car, opened the door, then looked back to find Sean, who was waving dramatically for her to get in the car. She took a deep breath and shifted to Nicole as she ducked through the door. She jumped when Sean opened the driver's door and got in. "See," he said smugly, "I told you I had it all planned."

"I would have *preferred* to have been part of the planning process, and not merely moved around like a chess piece," she said sourly. Her voice trembled slightly.

"Why? You think your old grand-pappy is too senile to come up with a plan that'd work?"

"I do not believe you fully recognize the potential hazards of exposing my ability to alter my appearance."

"Hey, I got your back," Sean said gruffly, "You don't have to worry about me exposing you."

Nicole paused to reflect for a moment. When her breathing returned to normal, she smiled warmly. "That idiom is one that I do understand. It is a nice feeling to know that you 'have my back.' Thank you."

"Not a problem," said Sean, "Just don't get all mushy about it, huh?" They locked eyes for a moment; then Nicole nodded. "OK," Sean said, shifting back to business, "What's next?"

"If you wouldn't mind," Nicole started tentatively, "I wanted to ask what you refer to as a 'favor.'"

Sean's eyebrows shot up. "I can't imagine what I have that you would need from me as a favor... and that's kinda scary," he said warily, "But, OK, what's the favor?"

"Well," she said slowly, "I was wondering if I could attempt to operate your vehicle?"

He gave her a look of disbelief. "You want to drive my car?"

"Yes... please?"

"Do you know anything about driving an ancient car like this?" Sean asked as he slid his key into the ignition switch.

"I have been observing how you manipulate the controls with both your hands and feet. I also fully understand the concept behind the internal combustion engine and how it powers the motion of the automobile and I am well versed with the laws of physics as applied to motion and inertia."

"And that's the favor... you want to drive my car?"

"Yes."

Sean tried to visualize Nicole behind the wheel. "Can I drive your time-machine?" he asked as he started the engine.

"No!" Nicole said emphatically.

"Seems only fair that if I let you drive *my* vehicle, you should let me drive *yours*," said Sean. He put the car in reverse and backed out of the parking space. "Tell me what you just saw."

Nicole thought for a moment. "You placed your key into the locking mechanism and then turned clockwise to release a spark and ignite the fuel in the motor's cylinders. Once ignited, the combustion perpetuates itself firing the cylinders in a sequential pattern. You then put your right foot on the floor pedal that controls the braking device. When engaged, the braking device produces levels of friction on the automobile wheels which will slow or stop the rotation of the wheels. Since the automobile is already at rest, I am unclear as to why that step is required. Your next action was to pull the lever on the steering column until the pointer was aimed at 'R,' which logically seems to be an abbreviation for reverse. The next action was moving your right foot from the braking pedal to the acceleration pedal which is slightly to the right of the breaking pedal. By depressing the acceleration pedal, you are sending a larger mix of gasoline and oxygen into the cylinders, causing more frequent explosions which create the power harnessed by a device that converts that energy into motion. Once you achieved the distance desired, you turned the steering wheel counterclockwise to alter the trajectory of the vehicle, causing it to come into alignment with the driving lane. At that point, you removed your foot from the acceleration pedal and placed it on the braking pedal to stop the reverse movement. Then you asked me what I saw."

Sean attempted to show her a stern face like the one he'd seen when he tested for his driver's license. "OK, that was pretty good. You got most of it," he said gruffly. "You missed that I carefully checked for any other cars that might come along and run into us while I backed out." He put the car in drive and started forward.

"I did not observe you checking for other vehicles."

"Well, I did," Sean insisted, "I checked all three mirrors."

"I will watch more closely next time."

"OK, so, do you want to trade? You drive the Taurus; I take Steffi for a short hop?"

Nicole sighed. "I cannot. It is very complicated, and I am unqualified to teach you everything you would need to know. I am sorry. I understand your decision to not allow me to drive your car."

"I watched you, too, you know," Sean countered. "I saw you flip the green boxy thing, then you pulled the corners on the yellow boxy thing and highlighted some icons, and then you flipped it out of the way and pulled down the other green boxy thing and did some stuff with it, and poof, off we went."

"But you do not understand the functions of the various icons or know which ones to open," she said then paused as she looked to her right. "I believe you missed the exit from this parking lot."

"Yeah, well there's not a lot of people shopping today." He drove to the corner of the parking lot farthest from both the exit to the street and the entrance to the store. "And the few that are here all parked close to the door."

"That seems logical."

"Yeah," Sean said, "But it also means there is somewhere between an eighth and a quarter of a mile of empty parking lot here on the far side." He stopped the car and shut off the engine. "So let's see if you can drive this thing."

Nicole's face lit up. "Really?"

Sean closed his eyes and exhaled loudly. "Really."

"Even though I said I could not reciprocate with the S.T.E.?"

"Yeah... I guess I'm just one of those grandparents that spoil the grand-kids."

She threw her arms around Sean's neck and squeezed. "Thank you, thank you, thank you!"

"If you don't lay off the hugging, I might change my mind... *Alex*," Sean threatened.

Nicole pulled back quickly. "Sorry... I could not contain my excitement!"

"So I see. What's up with that?"

"I have decided that I should do my research less dispassionately. I have determined that I can better understand this era by partaking in it rather than merely observing."

Sean looked at her skeptically. "Yeah, I'm not sure if I'm happy for you or terrified by what might come of it... is this because of the Diet Pepsi?"

"That may have been the conscious moment for the decision, but looking back, I have determined that listening to R.E.M.'s music stimulated me emotionally in this direction."

Sean was puzzled. "Wait a minute, help me put this together. I was talking to you as Alexis about music that day, and then later Nicole said she was all bummed about her mom. So what's the real story?"

"You were asking specific questions about music that I did not know. I did a complete download of *Everybody Hurts* and absorbed it while talking to you as Alexis. I am unsure of the best way to explain the process, but the song was placed in my memory as if I had listened to it. The emotional impact was so sudden and intense that it erupted as feelings of sadness. I was still attempting to process those emotions later when I was with you as Nicole. I knew that you would be able to detect my mood, so I concocted a plausible reason for Nicole's sadness."

Sean nodded slowly as he pieced together what he remembered with what he had just heard. "OK, so bottom line in all this: getting bummed by a sad song, then later getting buzzed on Diet Pepsi has convinced you that you should actively participate in my life instead of just watching it? And you've decided the best way to participate is to drive my car?" Nicole nodded timidly. "I wonder if that makes Pepsi count as a gateway drug?"

"That is an interesting hypothesis. In both cases, an external stimulus altered the chemical makeup of my brain. While I am able to compensate by directing nanites to return my brain chemistry to normal, I must say that before they do, I find the experience is exhilarating!"

Sean rubbed his hand over his chin, attempting to look sage. "Hmmm, I don't know," he said, "Friends don't let friends alter their brain chemistry and drive." Nicole's expression was blank. Sean sadly shook his head and sighed. "And if you keep experiencing 20th Century stuff, maybe you'll eventually get my jokes." He opened his door and stepped out of the car. "Come on, before I really *do* change my mind." Nicole hopped from the car and rushed around to the driver's side and slid in. Sean closed the door and sauntered around to the passenger side. He couldn't help but smile at her enthusiasm as he handed her the keys. Nicole examined the keys carefully before sliding the correct one into the ignition. She turned it, and the engine sprang to life.

She trembled with excitement. "I have successfully activated a twentieth-century internal combustion engine!"

Sean rolled his eyes. "You have *got* to be the only 16 year old boy/girl in Missouri that is mesmerized by Walmart and thrilled by starting the car."

"Depress braking pedal," she said as she performed the task, "Pull lever to 'D"... why isn't it 'F' for forward?"

"I don't know. Someone decided to call it 'D' for drive."

"Forward is more logical, Drive implies motion, but not a particular direction. You can drive a car in reverse."

"I guess you'll just have to swing by Detroit on one of your little trips to the past and find the guy who invented the automatic transmission and ask him to change it."

"Release braking pedal and depress acceleration pedal...."

The engine roared, and the tires squealed. Sean put his hands on the dash to keep his head from hitting the windshield as Nicole slammed on the brakes.

"I thought the acceleration would be more gradual!"

"The deceleration wasn't too smooth, either," Sean sniped.

"I will apply less pressure," she said as she took her foot off the break and carefully pressed the accelerator until the car inched forward. "It is moving!" she shrieked, "I am making it go forward!"

"And at this speed we would get back to the school sometime tomorrow."

Nicole frowned at him then carefully pushed the accelerator, gradually getting the speed up to 10 miles per hour. "I am approaching the end of this parking lot. What should I do?"

"I suppose you can either turn the car around or stop," Sean suggested.

She twisted the wheel hard to the left. Sean slapped against his door as the tires squealed. Nicole jammed the brakes again, and the momentum slammed their bodies forward again as the car came to a halt.

"I have learned," she said thoughtfully, "that since there are no inertia dampeners on this vehicle that it would be wise to decelerate before attempting a change in trajectory."

"Ya think?"

She ignored his criticism as she thought through each of the changes she would make and then started the car moving forward, returning to the corner where they started. She took her foot off the accelerator before reaching the end of the lot and pulled the steering wheel to the right. The tires squealed again, but only a little this time. As she made several trips back and forth, she gained confidence and a greater control of the car accelerating smoothly and making turns without squealing the tires.

"This is fun!" she chirped.

"Uh-huh," Sean said with the most bored voice that he could muster.

"You are unhappy with my driving?"

"Let's use your giant futuristic brain for a moment. If *I* were driving a car at these speeds back and forth in the parking lot and you were along for the ride, how much fun would you be having?"

Nicole slowed the car to a gentle stop and put it in park and switched off the engine. "I am sorry. I was so caught up in the thrill of personally operating a 20th Century automobile that I did not consider how mundane it would be for you." She opened her door and got out. Sean also got out and walked around the back of the car as Nicole came around the front. When they both were back in the car, Nicole smiled warmly at Sean. "Thank you. Sincerely that was an excellent treat. You are very kind and generous."

Sean put his hand up. "You're getting mushy on me again, Future-Boy.... but you're welcome. Maybe I'll go to a dude ranch someday and see if I get the same kick out of driving a horse and buggy."

"I am also sorry that I must deny your request to operate the S.T.E. It is just too..."

"...complicated for a caveman," Sean interrupted. "I get it.... so... now that we've finished your little favor... what's next?"

"We need to go to your house to position your nocturnal teaching device."

"Right. Oldies radio, all night long." Sean said as he headed toward the exit.

Chapter Eleven

"Better stay away from him / he'll rip your lungs out, Jim"

"**I have** programmed the device to familiarize you... XL memory you... with popular music from 1966 through 1969. That should be an acceptable range of years. You will know the names of the musicians, song titles, lyrics, and even the melody of the songs," Nicole explained as Sean pulled his car into his parents' garage.

"You can cram three years of popular music into my brain in one night?" asked an astonished Sean.

"Yes. The difficult part was putting it behind the password block. Otherwise, it would have been impossible to explain why you would wake up with a complete catalog of music from the 1960s in your consciousness."

Sean shut off the engine and touched the button on the remote that was clipped to his visor. "Do I have to wear headphones or a helmet or anything?"

"No," Nicole laughed. "It is a small device that we can conceal in your pillow. It is already tuned to the nanites in your brain and will activate once they detect that you are deeply asleep. It will effectively replace your dreams."

"So you've got an oldies radio station in my pillow, and my head is tuned to that station," Sean rephrased as they got out of the car.

Nicole twitched a query to the computer. "That is not precisely correct, but conceptually, it does describe the outcome. Of course, the speed of the data throughput is exponential by comparison with listening to a song on the radio."

"Of course," said Sean, acting as if anyone would know that.

He went to the door that connected to the stairs between the garage and the family room. When he opened it, Maggie jumped up on him happily wagging her tail as she attempted to reach his face to lick him. He pushed her back into the family room and stepped inside. She jumped up on him again, excited to see Sean so early in the day, and then Nicole stepped in, and the dog curled up docilely on the floor.

"Why does she *do* that around you?" asked a frustrated Sean.

"When I am near, I affect the nanites in her brain. They calm her."

"Yeah, but a little too much. She's practically comatose for her."

"I had to stop her from barking at me. She can sense that I am not what I appear. It confused and agitated her. I introduced a solution that would override her instincts."

"It also takes all the fun out of her," Sean complained.

"I am sorry that I over-calmed your dog. At least it only occurs when I am present, which is not frequently," Nicole offered.

Sean headed up the steps, speaking over his shoulder as Nicole followed him. "I'm sorry, Mags, but the mean old killjoy from the future won't be here tonight when I come home. I promise I'll play with you then."

Sean led Nicole back to his bedroom. "I'm sorry the place is such a mess," he said as he opened the door. "The Sean that could have picked things up didn't know anyone was coming over."

Nicole glanced around at the scattered clothes, papers and Coke cans. "No, it is fine. I would hardly notice," she lied.

"I hope you don't plan on making a trip to Vegas, you'd lose a lot of money with a poker face like that." She raised her eyebrows. "Sorry, that was a gentler way of saying you're a terrible liar." She blushed. "OK, never mind... so where's the radio station? You didn't bring your book bag in?"

"It was not needed; I have the device right here," she said as she opened her hand to show him a cylindrical piece the size and shape of a triple-A battery, but half its length.

"*That* little thing?" Sean marveled.

"Yes."

"That has three years of music and a broadcast thingy?"

"No. It receives that information from my computer."

"From clear down the street?"

"Up to at least ten kilometers."

"Man, I would love to visit a Circuit City store from your time." Nicole again looked puzzled. "Never mind," Sean said, exasperated. "So, just tuck it in my pillow?"

"As long as it is not somewhere that you would feel it."

He slid it into the far lower corner of the pillowcase. "That was easy," Sean said, then turned to her with a concerned look. "There's something I need to talk to you about."

"Certainly. What is it?"

"Could you switch off the Nicole disguise? It'll be easier to say this if I can say it directly to Alex, instead of Alex-in-drag. Let's go sit in the living room."

Nicole tugged on her hair with her right hand and touched the activation switch on her neck with her left as she followed Sean down the hall. Before Sean sat on the couch, Nicole had vanished, and Alex was easing himself into the adjacent armchair. "I believe I detect a level of stress in your voice," said Alex.

"Yeah... it's just something that is kind of hard to say," Sean began. "It's about the date tomorrow night." He took a deep breath. "Clueless Sean is planning to kiss the Nicole that he thinks is a girl," he said as rapidly as he could.

Alex considered the statement for a few moments. "That does seem to be a logical outcome."

"So, since *you* will be the only one aware of who you really are, *you* need to stop me."

"Stop you?"

"Yeah. Slap me if you have to, but probably just say something like you don't kiss on a first date."

"If I correctly understand dating customs of this era if both parties enjoyed their time together, a good night kiss is a typical outcome."

"Well, consider this a golden opportunity to start shaking Clueless Sean loose from Nicole."

"If that is what you wish. It seems that it will cause you distress for Nicole to reject you."

"Yeah, but it would make me even *more* distressed the next time you free my memory, and I realized that I kissed Alex-in-drag."

"Very well. I will attempt to rebuff you in such a way that it will be minimally damaging to your ego," Alex affirmed.

"Rebuff? What's with you and 'rebuff'? No one my age says that."

"It is a very succinct and descriptive word. Two syllables that express the idea of gently altering another's intentions toward you by tactfully explaining how your own intentions differ. It is a good word."

"It sounds lame."

"What word would you substitute?"

"I don't know," Sean said, "Like, 'let you down easy', or say, 'let's just be friends.' I don't know! Forget it! Call it 'rebuff' if you want... so, is that it for here?"

"I believe you will want to give me clean socks and underwear, assuming we spend two or three days in 1969... and I will also need to take a sample of your hair."

"My hair?" asked Sean, "Why? For a souvenir?"

"No, your short hair will look out of place in 1969. With a sampling of your hair, I can grow some extensions overnight to attach as part of your costume."

"You mean like a wig?"

"Not exactly. Using your own hair as a base, I will replicate the keratin and create about 100,000 strands of hair, approximately eight inches in length. When attached it should give you shoulder-length hair that will contribute to an appropriate appearance for 'Nigel' in 1969."

"You're gonna grow 100,000 hairs overnight?"

"Yes."

"And then what... glue them to my head?"

"No, a series of nanites at the end of each of the created hairs will locate the end of a single hair on your head and attach itself. It will look and feel as if you had grown your own hair to that length."

"There you go with nanites again! Do you do anything in the future that doesn't involve nanites? Would your whole world stop if someone came up with a way to like set off an anti-nanite bomb and killed them all with some kind of electromagnetic pulse?"

"Anyone who even conceived such a plan would be detected well before attempting to create such a device, and they would be taken into protective custody."

"Protective custody? Really? Is the guy who runs things in your time called Big Brother?"

"Big Brother?"

"Yeah, sounds like you've got the Thought Police taking the would-be bomber into custody, so I thought maybe Big Brother ran things where you came from."

"There are no Thought Police," Alex stated flatly, "The person in this scenario would be taken to a medical facility. When I said 'protective custody' I was referring to the protection of the individual, not the general populace. Also, there is no 'guy who runs things' in the future."

"You don't have a President anymore?"

"Governance has changed significantly by the 23rd Century. There is no need for an individual to be appointed as 'leader.' We have a genuine democracy. Everyone in North America can instantly vote on any issue that arises. The computer network that evolved from what you know as the Internet is ubiquitous."

"Doesn't that mean you have to vote on stuff all the time? How do you have time to keep up with everything?"

"It is so completely different from your world that it is hard to explain. You believe that governance is a complicated task, simply because of what you observe. You elect people to represent your interests, but they spend time bickering with each other rather than accomplishing anything. In my time, there are few issues that arise. Since we have been able to equalize everyone's basic needs for food, shelter, medical needs, there are not as many factions arguing about how best to meet those needs like there are here in your era."

"So when does this perfect world all start to happen?" Sean asked.

"I did not claim it was perfect. While I do enjoy talking about history, as you probably have surmised from how Nicole behaves in your History Class, it would take weeks to explain even the basic issues that are key factors from now until my era. Our time is better served preparing you for acclimation to 1969."

"C'mon. How about just hitting the high points?" Sean pleaded.

"One important factor is mankind liberating themselves from their dependence on petroleum as a chief energy source. Another considerable factor is the conversion of rote physical labor to robotics. Medical breakthroughs, especially nanite technology is paramount. You are experiencing the early part of computers and communication advances which make many leaps in your lifetime."

"So things get better during my lifetime?"

Alex looked away from Sean, and for a moment, a hint of sadness crossed his face. He turned back with a forced smile. "There are some amazingly wonderful things and some devastatingly terrible things that happen during your lifetime." He philosophically added, "But I suppose that can be said of nearly any lifetime throughout history."

"I'd give anything for just one day in your time," Sean said dreamily.

"I am afraid that will not be, dear grandfather... but perhaps you will find that the past can be just as interesting." Alex stretched out his hand. "The hair sample, please?"

Sean went into the kitchen and returned with a large-bladed knife from the knife holder on the kitchen counter. Alex flinched at the sight of it. "So how much you need?" Sean asked nonchalantly as he grabbed the end of some hairs between thumb and forefinger.

"If you could pluck two or three, that would be sufficient," Alex said, nervously eying the knife.

"Oh," Sean said, setting the knife on the end table. He tugged on the hairs he was already pinching, then looked at the results. "Here's five. Got something to put them in?" Alex shook his head. Sean went back to the kitchen and returned with a sandwich bag which he handed to Alex. "OK," Sean continued, "so what was so interesting about 1969... besides the moon landing, I already know about that."

Alex glanced from the knife to the sandwich bag in his hands and let out the breath he hadn't realized he was holding. "Ummm... Violence! The Vietnam War was constantly in the news. More than ten thousand U.S. Soldiers were killed each year from 1967 to 1969. It spawned a rebellion of mostly younger people at home, protesting against the war. President Lyndon Johnson did not seek re-election in 1968 primarily because of the escalation of the war during his administration. Richard Milhous Nixon won the election in 1968."

"So this is when protesters were burning their draft cards and stuff?"

"Yes, there certainly was a great deal of turmoil regarding the war, particularly on college campuses. It is historically viewed as a time of violence in general, not only on the battlefield but domestically as well. In the previous year, both Martin Luther King and Robert Kennedy were assassinated."

Alex continued to talk about historical events of the late 1960s for the next two hours. Sean attempted to pay attention, but it soon became like sitting in Mr. Douglas' History class. It became evident to Sean that Nicole's interest in history was an actual representation to how Alex truly felt. Sean, however, still found political posturing boring and started to zone out when Alex tried to explain how politics in combination with economic situations shaped the direction that society moved.

"I guess there is little point," Alex finally said, "of going into any further detail. Considering we are to be portraying the role of foreigners, we cannot be expected to be fully aware of all aspects of the United States."

Sean breathed a sigh of relief. "Right then," Sean said in his multi-regional accent, "Me and me mates is against the war, for women's lib, loves the rock opera *Tommy*, and hopes to make the scene at Woodstock."

"That was a perfect New Zealand accent."

"Really?" Sean said proudly.

"As far as anyone in 1969 will know... hopefully," Alex said with a smile. Sean punched him in the shoulder. Alex initially grimaced, but followed with an even bigger smile. "That is a bonding ritual! You wish me to feel more accepted."

"I obviously didn't hit you hard enough," Sean joked.

"Do you feel adequately prepared to interact with the people of a rural Iowa town in the year 1969?" Alex asked earnestly.

Sean shrugged. "Sure, and if I can't fake it, you can always bail me out with a computer twitch, right?"

Alex slightly dropped his face. "I do not believe I can tell you this without incurring your wrath," he said hesitantly, "but I have a fail-safe in place with your nanites."

"You *what?*" Sean challenged.

"A fail-safe," Alex answered softly. "Actually two levels, but hopefully I would never need to use the second."

After a brief pause, Sean gruffly prompted, "And these two levels are?"

"I can immobilize the portion of your brain that controls speech... you might consider it a mute button."

"Is that first or second?"

"First." Alex shrunk back. "Second would render you unconscious." He rushed to add, "But I do not believe that would ever be needed."

"What circumstances would you think would warrant hitting mute?" Sean asked, attempting unsuccessfully to keep his voice calm.

"If you said something that was an obvious anachronism, and then perhaps attempted to rectify your error. If it appeared to me that you were calling even more attention to your mistake, I would stop you and step in with my own attempt at damage control."

"Great!" Sean said, his temper rising, "and what might get me the knock-out punch?"

"I do not believe it would ever be necessary," Alex started meekly, "It is only an emergency protocol."

"So what *kind* of emergency?" Sean asked through clenched teeth.

Alex's eyes darted around the room. "Perhaps if you began to reveal to your father that you are from the future or attempted to explain that you are his son."

"Why would I do something stupid like that?" Sean yelled.

Alex cringed. "I do not believe you would... but I must assume responsibility, and require protocols to be in place to prevent any potential damage to the time-stream."

Sean stared at him hotly, his arms crossed. Alex glanced at him, then timidly away.

"OK," Sean started, "let's talk about damage to the time-stream. That does sound kind of serious. What are we talking here?"

Alex's eyes met Sean's again. "Altering the future."

"So how do you know that just showing up doesn't alter the future?"

"Perhaps it does, but only minutely." He comfortably moved into lecture mode. "There are those who believe there cannot be a change since historically all past events have already taken place. However, those who do believe change *can* happen will sometimes use the example of time flowing like a massive river. If you could picture yourself standing in the center of a bridge over the Missouri River and dropping a small stone into the middle of the river, you could observe a tiny ripple, but the overall effect on the river would barely be noticed even a few feet downstream. Statistically less than a minute fraction of one percent of the river is effected at all. If you followed even one mile downstream, you would be unable to detect any change. Apply that model to me and a decade after my appearance here, there is so little effect as to be unnoticed. Only the tiniest fraction of the world's population has seen any effect at all."

"So what would you have to do to make a big splash?"

"Let us use an extreme example and discuss the ramifications of going into the past and killing someone."

"Like Hitler," Sean proposed.

"Perhaps we can start smaller. Suppose I killed you... as you seemed to think was my intent when I first told you I was from the future."

"Is this in retaliation because I punched you?" Sean joked.

"That action becomes an important event to me," Alex continued, ignoring Sean's interruption, "as your death before the creation of any progeny would mean I could not exist, or at least could not exist with my current genetic composition. Since I am 7 generations away from you, your genetic contribution is 1/128 of my total makeup. Therefore, someone like me could exist but with a maximum of 127/128 of my genetic designations."

"So what? That sounds like it would still be mostly you."

"That is the minimal effect, and highly unlikely. The maximal effect is that your demise would ripple down through all seven generations, and the woman I know as my mother would conceive a child with someone entirely different from the man I know as my father. That would mean my genetic makeup would only be half of what it currently is. I could even be female."

"OK, so I think I get it. Killing me has a big ripple through time as far as *you* are concerned, but maybe not so much on the big picture of the entire world," said Sean.

"Since I have already told you that one of your descendants developed a theory involving DNA that eventually became incorporated into the homing beacon for time-travel, it could delay the development of time-travel. However, it is widely believed that most scientific discoveries would at some point be developed by someone else, and the outcome would eventually be the same."

"So maybe a 50 pound rock. Big splash in the middle, but not even a ripple on the edges of the river," Sean suggested.

"It is hard to predict the impact, but certainly something we want to avoid."

"I vote for *not* killing me to find out," Sean joked.

"Your suggestion of killing Hitler, however, could make a monumental change. If the bombing attempt on his life during the war had been successful, it is conceivable that a more logic-based leader could have improved the military strategy enough to have Germany take over Europe. Or suppose that someone killed him before he came to power, potentially causing a power vacuum that would set Josef Stalin poised to conquer all of Europe."

"So killing Hitler's not just a big rock in the river, but maybe a dam that would completely change the course of the river?"

"That is an excellent analogy!" Alex said approvingly.

"So most things... for example, you popping up into my life as the Townsend twins, would be just a little ripple in the big time-river. In 20 years anything Alexis or Nicole said or did will just be a dim memory."

"Theoretically," Alex agreed.

"And when we pop in on my Dad in 1969, that will also be a small pebble in the big time-river?"

"Theoretically," Alex restated.

"So, even though we haven't gone there yet, we're already planning to go... so if nothing changes our plans, then we can consider that it's already happened."

"That does not mean that reckless behavior could not still alter this time-stream."

"But it *didn't,* or we'd know about it, since it already happened," Sean reasoned.

"That would depend upon whether the theory of causality is valid or if those that theorize that an alternate timeline can be created are correct. No one has, as of yet, proven either. Nor is anyone willing to attempt to make a change significant enough to test which theory is true."

"So that's kind of why Nicole flipped out when Kevin and Raj and I were talking about trying to change something in the past."

"Yes. We are very careful to not make any changes large enough to cause a divergence in the time-stream."

"*If* that is even possible."

"I believe there is a 20th Century phrase for that, 'better safe than sorry'."

"Right," Sean said, "and 'Look before you leap'."

"How is that appropriate to this discussion?" asked Alex one eyebrow raised.

"I don't know," Sean shrugged, "it was the only old saying that I could think of off the top of my head. Don't try to get all analytical about it." He cleared his throat. "To change the subject... I'm starved! I'd have normally eaten dinner by now... at least my stomach thinks so."

"We have completed everything from our agenda, so we can now return to our normal time-stream."

"So, looking at the clock, right now it's about time for the other me to eat lunch. Man. Just talking about food makes me even hungrier."

Sean got up and went back into the kitchen. Alex followed.

"Perhaps a light snack," Alex suggested, "but not an entire meal, as it might ruin your appetite."

Sean narrowed his eyes. "You're channeling my Mom again."

"If you wish, I could assume her form," Alex smiled.

"Don't even think about it!" Sean growled as he rummaged through the refrigerator. After opening a few containers and rejecting what he found, he pulled a jar of strawberry jam out of the fridge and opened the bread bag. "Want a PB&J?" he asked Alex as he set the jar on the counter and opened a cabinet for the peanut butter.

Alex looked warily at the items on the counter. "This is a normal snack?" he asked, watching Sean smear a big glob of tan paste onto a slice of bread.

"You bet," Sean said as he plopped a generous scoop of jam on top of the peanut butter and smoothed it around. "As American as apple pie."

He slid the open-faced sandwich in front of Alex and started making a second one. Alex regarded it suspiciously, then reached for the peanut butter jar after Sean had finished digging out another knife-full. He studied the ingredients then set the container down, picking up the jam jar that Sean had just returned to the counter. Sean rolled his eyes as he licked a drop of jam off his thumb. Alex finished reading the jam jar and set it down. He watched Sean take a bite, then timidly lifted his sandwich to his mouth and nibbled from a corner.

Sean watched him chew. "Well?" he prompted.

Alex swallowed then cleared his throat. "Although I am aware that this era is known for excessive sugar and high-fructose corn-syrup consumption, I am baffled to find the rational for adding sugar to the roasted legume puree. The additional oils have some logical purpose, as the paste seems to have adhesive properties that extra oil might reduce. The fruit is blended into a mixture of high fructose corn syrup, corn syrup, sugar and pectin. Other than attempting to mask the natural flavor of the fruit, I do not understand the rationale for using three different sweetening agents."

"I even know that one," Sean proclaimed. "That's so they can list fruit first, which makes it the main ingredient. If they just used sugar, they'd have to put sugar first, but since the sweetening is a mixture of three ingredients, each one individually is a smaller amount than the fruit."

"It is an attempt to mislead the consumer?"

"I guess," said Sean. "But it was brought on by the government making them label everything. So, anyway, if we can skip the little science lecture, how do you like the taste?"

Alex took another small bite and chewed. He rolled it around his mouth, then swallowed. "Overall, it seems a rather pleasant mix of flavors... if one ignores the fact that it has a high-fat content and is extremely high in carbohydrates."

"Don't get all food snobby. At least my Mom buys whole-wheat bread," Sean said, then took another big bite.

Alex watched him chew. "Are you able to somehow keep the paste from adhering to your hard pallet?"

Sean looked momentarily puzzled, then broke into a big grin. "Does the peanut butter stick to the roof of my mouth? Yes. That's the main hazard of a PB&J. You just kinda have to keep scraping it off with your tongue."

"Perhaps if I could have another Diet Pepsi? An added solvent might be useful."

"Good idea," Sean said as he pulled a Coke and Diet Pepsi out of the fridge. "Hey, are you sure you can fly Steffi with a caffeine buzz?"

"I will not be affected by the caffeine. I have specially configured the nanites in my gastrointestinal tract to capture caffeine and prevent it from being absorbed. I will need to do the same with other foods if I continue to ingest 20th Century foodstuffs."

Sean's eyes lit up. "Seriously? You can do that? You can keep food from being absorbed?"

"Yes. With just a little programming..." Alex started.

"Dude!" Sean interrupted, "You can make a fortune! The Nanite Diet! Everyone will buy it!"

Alex smiled pleasantly as he took another bite of sandwich. Sean watched him until he took another bite without speaking.

"Did you hear what I said?"

Alex continued to chew, swallowed, and then drank some Diet Pepsi. "You know I am not going to allow the introduction of 23rd Century technology to the 20th Century. Also, I have no interest in 'making a fortune'. Acquiring excessive wealth is unnecessary."

"You are such a buzzkill."

"You should consider substituting the vernacular of 1969. I suggest, 'you are such a downer, man'."

Sean gave him a defiant look. "Being as I's fum New Zealand, mate, I got no problem wiff sayin' buzzkill. It's wot us New Zealanders sez," retorted Sean in his conglomerated accent.

Alex tried to hide a pained expression. "We should depart for school within the next five minutes," he said flatly then took another bite of his sandwich.

"Wow. You sure change the subject fast when you want to."

"I received a notification from the computer. We have a limited window for departure."

Sean rolled up the last third of his sandwich and popped it into his mouth. After he had washed it down with his Coke, he watched the microwave clock tick off three minutes while he waited for Alex to finish eating. "I thought you were in a hurry. Limited window?"

Alex tipped the last of his drink into his mouth before answering. "There is some flexibility built in as we cannot calculate an exact time for driving back to the school due to variable traffic conditions. Leaving in five minutes was at the beginning of an approximately twenty minute window. I was also unsure how much time to allow for you, since I am unclear as to what factors contribute to your chronic lateness."

"Are you saying you expect me to be late?"

"It is an observable pattern. You are very inconsistent in your arrival time for Spanish class."

"But I almost *always* make it in the door before the bell rings."

"I believe I detect a note of pride in that statement," Alex said. "Regardless, by the time we reach your automobile we will be at the beginning of our time window."

"Then let's go!" Sean said as he headed down the stairs. He found Maggie sitting docilely at the bottom. "I promise I'll let you jump on me and lick me when I come back," he said to her. "Mean old Mr. Nanite won't be here."

As they backed out of the driveway, Alex asked, "Getting dog saliva on your skin does not feel uncomfortable to you?"

"What? No! Anyway, a dog's mouth is cleaner than a human's," Sean stated authoritatively.

"That is not clinically true. Dog saliva has more bacteria than human saliva." Alex twitched a connection to his computer. "The myth began from the observation of a higher frequency of infection from human bites compared to dog bites. It is simply that the bacteria in dog saliva are less pathogenic to humans."

Sean's temper nearly flared at being corrected again. But he pushed his anger aside and tried to continue the conversation. "So, I take it *you* don't have a dog."

"No."

"Cat?"

"No."

"Gerbil, hamster, snake... any pets?"

"No."

"Maybe that's why you're such a stick in the mud. You should get a dog. They're fun."

Alex was silent.

"OK," Sean said, "I get vibes from you when you drop out like that. Is there a particular reason that you don't want a dog?"

"It is not... possible."

"Not possible? Why not?"

"We are getting close to the school; I should change back to Nicole," Alex said as he pulled on his face mask and touched the controls to alter his appearance to Nicole Townsend.

"Fine. So *Nicole* can tell me why not."

"I would rather not," was the soft feminine reply.

"I hope you're not saying that there *are* no dogs in the future," said Sean tensely.

"In my era, they are successfully attempting to reestablish most breeds of canine and feline in special facilities," Nicole said while staring out her side window.

"What happened?" Sean demanded.

"It does not happen during your lifetime," Nicole replied.

"What doesn't happen? What is *going* to happen?"

"I am not going to tell you any more about your future. Some wonderful things happen; some terrible things happen. It has been that way throughout human history."

Sean recognized the 'wonderful / terrible' phrase as Alex's signal to end any hope of getting more facts about the future. Since they had just pulled into the drive leading to the school parking lot, he filed the thought away, hoping he might have another chance to find out later.

"Stop just before you reach your parking space," Nicole suggested, "and I will retrieve the hologram projector, and then you can park."

"So what time is it now?"

"It is 1: 17pm," Nicole said, pointing to the clock in the car's dash.

"Oh, yeah, that *is* the correct time, isn't it? I get a little confused with this short hop stuff. So I'm currently in my afternoon study hall," Sean said as he stopped the car near the perfect replica of his Taurus. Nicole got out, then leaned back in.

"Actually you are..." she started, then noticed the scowl on Sean's face. She closed the door and stepped through the hologram to retrieve the projector. As soon as she stepped out of the suddenly vacant space, Sean pulled in.

"That is so awesome! Are you sure I couldn't borrow it for about a week?" he said as he joined her, and they started walking toward the school.

"No," Nicole replied crisply. "When we reach the corner of the school there is a blind spot. I will reestablish my large, nondescript guise."

They reached the edge of the school and Nicole stopped.

"So I walk on 'Big Alex's' right side, this time?" Sean asked.

Before Nicole could reply or change shape, they heard a female voice that sent shivers down Sean's spine. "So, what have we here?" Megan asked as she strode toward them. She had just rounded the other corner of the building.

Sean and Nicole froze like statues as Megan closed the gap between them.

"Cat got your tongues?" she sneered.

"I could also ask you what *you* are doing out here," Sean challenged with false bravado.

Megan flipped a small slip of paper in front of Sean's face. "*I* have a pass. I'm going to a Doctor's appointment to have my knee checked. I twisted it in cheer-leading practice, and it's swelling." She changed her tone to syrupy sweet. "Is that what you two are up to? Playing Doctor? Just the two of you today? The other twin didn't get to play?"

"I am right here," Alexis said, her left hand on her neck.

Megan blinked several times. "I could swear you were Nicole. Maybe I should get my eyes checked, too."

"Maybe you should," said Nicole, who was now standing where Alexis had just been.

"What the hell?" gasped Megan as the girl standing next to her flipped back and forth from Nicole to Alexis several times.

"Yeah," said a panicked Sean, "what the hell?"

"You'll need to..." said Nicole. "...catch her, Sean," finished Alexis.

Suddenly Alexis was replaced with a large hairy beast, its extended maw growled inches from Megan's face, saliva dripped from its fangs. Sean barely slipped his arms around her collapsing body as the creature changed again; this time to 'Big Alex'.

"Did I not give you enough warning?" Alex asked. "You very nearly dropped her."

"I was busy looking at the freakin' whatever the hell that nightmare was!" Sean yelled. "What the hell was that all about? You let her see you change shapes. When she wakes up, she's going to be asking a *lot* of questions."

"Can you lift her to a standing position?" Alex asked.

"I think so," grunted Sean as he attempted to hoist the dead weight.

'Big Alex' started lightly slapping Megan's cheeks. "Miss? Miss, can you hear me?"

"mmmumph," mumbled Megan, "What? Where am I? What happened? Who are you?"

Alex held Megan's face firmly and leveled his face with hers. "I am no one," he said in an authoritative and even tone. "You did not see anyone. When you walked around the corner, you saw no one. You are going to continue to walk to your car. You will not look back; you will walk straight to your car. It is a pleasant day. You are happy to be out of class. Do you understand?"

"Mmmhmmm," Megan said dreamily.

"Where are you going?" Alex asked.

"To my car. Then to the Doctor's office," Megan slurred.

"And if someone were to ask you who you saw on the way to your car?"

"No one. I saw no one."

"Very good. Go ahead, you do not want to be late."

"Don't want to be late," Megan mumbled as she started walking toward the parking lot.

Sean's mouth dropped wide open as he watched her leave them.

"I apologize for not answering your question. You are correct," said Alex. "You will walk on my right."

"Are you for real?" Sean exclaimed. "Did you just turn into some Freakazoid monster and then, 'these are not the Droids you are looking for' Jedi mind-control her?"

"It was a lycanthrope," Alex replied.

"What?"

"A lycanthrope. Did you not recognize it?" He twitched a quick connection to his computer. "Werewolf. Perhaps you use that term. It seemed to be a very effective shape. Humans have a primal fear of wolves. The werewolf from your horror movies takes advantage of that innate fear."

"Scared the crap out of me," Sean admitted.

"We need to resume our journey to the S.T.E. Walk with me while I try to discover what 'these are not the Droids you are looking for' means." Sean fell into step on 'Big Alex's' right shoulder. "*Star Wars IV: A New Hope.* Interesting. Is there a rationale for releasing the fourth through sixth episodes prior to Episode One."

"Episode One? What?" Sean asked excitedly. "They finally make the prequel? When?"

"Copyright 1999. Only four more years into your future."

"Oh man! I can't wait that long now that I know about it! Could we skip going forward in time and just sit in Steffi and watch it? I know Steffi's got some kind of a projection screen."

"No. We are attending a movie tomorrow night."

"But not freakin' *Star Wars Episode One*! Come on!"

"No," Alex replied flatly.

"Please? Won't you grant your poor old 5G Grandfather a dying request?"

"You are not dying."

"Sure I am. You go back to your time, and I'm already dead. So this is like a dying request."

"No," Alex said firmly as they crossed the grass to the bike path.

"I can see they don't teach you to respect your elders in the future," Sean groused. "Wait, I almost forgot. That thing with Megan. How did you Jedi mind-control her?"

"It was not mind-control, I merely suggested that she did not see anything.

Once she was surfacing from unconsciousness, it was easier to link with her brainwaves and make the suggestion."

"So kind of hypnotized?"

"It has some similarities."

"And you didn't have to wave a watch or tell her she was getting sleepy... wait, I guess you kind of did a bizarre form of the sleepy part. That was so awesome!" Sean gushed. "Can you teach me how to do that?"

"No," Alex said as he stepped off the bike path and around the bushes. When Sean rounded the bushes, Nicole was opening the door to the S.T.E.

"Your shifter-suit would be awesome for Halloween parties. You could be a perfect copy of any movie character. That werewolf was *awesome*! Can you do other animals? Like could you be a dog?"

"It would be difficult to move realistically since I am not a quadruped," Alex stated as he slid into the S.T.E.

"But if you just stood still?"

"Perhaps."

"Hey, how do you know you got into the right Steffi?" Sean asked, standing between the two cloaked vehicles.

"The door opens on the left, and the ship we arrived in was parallel to the right side of the other iteration."

"Right," Sean said as he slid in. "Just making sure you know." The door slid closed. "So what would happen if we *did* take off in the wrong one?"

"We would be lost forever in a space/time vortex."

Sean's eyes widened. "Really?"

"No," said Nicole as she activated the sequence to jump a couple of hours ahead.

"Hey! Don't I get a mint?" Sean said as they crossed into another dimension.

Without the audio, video, and mint to distract him, Sean began to have the same feelings he had the first time he went through a dimensional shift. He forced himself to concentrate and ignore the almost hallucinatory sensations as his brain incorrectly tried to interpret the transition. Soon everything cleared up, and Nicole was shutting down the console and then opened the door.

Sean blinked several times. "Hey, I think I am getting the hang of this," he said proudly. "Even without the little sensory concentration thingies... I feel OK."

"As expected. The frequency of experiences causes the shift to not seem as disturbing."

"So after a while it's like, 'oh well, shift happens'," Sean said with a smirk. Nicole looked at him blankly. "OK... gotta remember jokes don't work on you." She simply continued to stare.

"You can get out now," she finally said.

"Yeah, right," Sean said as he slid out. "Oww!" he exclaimed after banging his knee on the other S.T.E. "What's this doing here? I thought we went back to when we left right after school."

"A few minutes before we left, actually. You ran into the craft that our other selves will soon leave in."

"What? Why? Why not just come back to, like, one second after we left?"

"I am trying to put you back into your regular memory as close as I can to when you left it. We need to go. We only have a few minutes to get into position," Nicole said as she briskly stepped out onto the bike path.

"I don't understand," Sean said as he tried to catch up to her.

"You do not need to understand. I have this under control."

"Yeah... OK... I'm not saying that you're normally the warmest person anyway, but since the Megan thing you've been really frosty."

"I am sorry my temperature is not to your liking."

"No, something's bugging you... come on, what's going on?"

"So now you are a psychiatrist?" Nicole said with just a hint of a smile.

"Ooooo, good one!" Sean said, "But, yeah, maybe right now I am. Give it up."

A worried look crossed Nicole's face. "I had everything planned and timed perfectly," she began. "Then Megan appeared and destroyed the entire planned sequence."

"Yeah, and then you werewolfed her and Jedi mind-controlled her and BAM! it was all OK."

"It was totally unplanned," Nicole complained.

"Duh."

"I was nearly exposed."

"And then you fixed it. Good job."

"But I did not even query the computer for an alternate action plan. I merely reacted."

"Cool!"

"I could have made the wrong decision!"

"So you have good instincts," Sean said with a shrug.

Nicole suddenly stopped walking. Sean turned back to her as she spoke, "I do not know what you mean."

"You instinctively reacted to a stressful situation, and it turns out it was the correct thing to do. Good instincts."

"I do not *have* instincts," Nicole insisted.

"Well, maybe hanging out in the 20th Century made you develop some."

She paused to think it over. "Your hypothesis is that an adaptation of behavior took place brought on by relatively short-term environmental immersion?"

"That's *exactly* what I was about to say!" Sean deadpanned.

"It is a meritorious hypothesis. I will have to give it further thought. However, we need to get into the building before our other selves come out," she said as she started walking quickly toward the door.

"So what's the plan?"

"In a few minutes we will come down the steps and go out onto the sidewalk," she said as she opened the door and entered.

"Yeah," Sean said following her in. "I remember doing that part, I was more concerned about what 'we' are doing, not what 'they/we' are going to do... did...will have did...done..."

"Come over by the soft drink dispensing machine and stand with your back to the door. I will mostly be blocked from view but will be pretending to purchase a soft drink."

"I've got some quarters. You can just go ahead and buy me a Coke."

"You do not have time to consume it."

"I can drink it in..."

"Shhhhhh," she interrupted. "Listen."

"Now where are we going?" Sean asked.

"Out here where it is quieter."

"OK," Nicole whispered when the door closed behind the other Sean and Nicole, "They are gone. We will give them a few minutes before we go out to the same spot."

"Does my voice really sound like that?" Sean asked.

"Yes. Come over by the door and get ready." Sean complied. "By now your other self has been shifted to XL memory. We have a brief discussion about schizophrenia, and then we walk off."

"Oh yeah, you thought I was going bonkers and then you said, 'Gursk'."

"If you insist on continually revisiting that phrase, I will be forced to 'suggest' that you forget that portion of the conversation," she threatened. "Our other selves are walking now. We can exit. Since we did not look back, it is safe to position ourselves."

"Maybe you should call them 'we one', and us, 'we two'."

"You need to stand right here," she said as she positioned Sean. "And I was here."

"We've got to stop meeting like this... the four of us, I mean," Sean joked.

"I will put you back into regular memory as soon as 'we one' are around the corner."

"Whatever you say, Alex-in-drag. Don't Gursk it up now"

"That is also an incorrect usage of that particular expletive."

"Maybe I'll start a new fad. Hey, we could...."

"Mobo Gerga. Store LX seventeen six," Nicole interrupted. "...that's why I like it."

"Hmmm?" Sean said groggily.

"The sidewalk. I like it because so few people use it. It is a place to find a little quiet."

"Right," said Sean. "So what did you want to say that you needed some quiet time?"

"Ummm," Nicole stammered. "To tell you how much I appreciate your friendship. You have helped me adapt to this new town and new school. You helped me get Algebra straightened out. You have introduced me to your friends. I wanted to make sure that you knew how much I appreciate your efforts."

"Oh," said a disappointed Sean, "I thought maybe you wanted to talk about tomorrow night."

"Oh yes, that, too. I appreciate you taking me to the movies."

"That, too....ummm...OK... I was hoping it would seem a little more special than that."

"I am certain it will be very enjoyable," she said.

"OK... ummmm... if we're done with our 'quiet talk' shall we head for home?"

"I am sorry, Sean," Nicole said sincerely, "I need to go do some more research in the library."

"Are you kidding me?" Sean huffed. "No, of course you're not. OK... happy researching. See you tomorrow." He spun on his heels and started for the parking lot.

"I do not believe I am very accomplished at rebuffing," Nicole said softly to herself as she watched Sean walk away.

"I'm starting to wonder if Nicole is as nutty as her twin," Sean grumbled quietly to himself, not looking back.

Nicole eased back into the doorway and waited until Sean was around the corner before heading up the sidewalk toward the bike path. "I have found many events of this day to be unsettling," Nicole thought aloud. "Perhaps I should reconsider transporting Sean Kelly to 1969."

Chapter Twelve

"In other words, hold my hand / In other words, baby, kiss me"

SEAN'S mood soured more with each passing minute as he motored toward home. Had Nicole just hinted that she wasn't interested in him for anything beyond friendship? Her signals confused him. It had seemed like they were moving forward in their relationship, especially since she had asked him for an after-school meeting. Had she planned to cancel their date but then got cold feet? Did she *really* need to go to the library again, or was she avoiding him? There was no doubt in his mind that the Townsend twins were both way too complicated.

As he pulled away from a 4-way stop, flashing red strobe lights caught his attention. He glanced in the rear-view mirror at a flashing red bar that set atop a patrol car. "Where did *he* come from?" he grumbled to himself as he checked for a safe place to pull over. He pulled into a nearby cul-de-sac and put his car in park. He rolled down his window and watched in his side mirror as the blue-uniformed man approached.

"Good afternoon, officer," Sean said politely as the man reached his window. Sean could see himself reflected in the mirrored shades that peered into his car.

"Mobo Gerga retrieve LX seventeen six."

Sean's head jerked back against the headrest as he sucked in a quick breath. He closed his eyes for a moment and rubbed his hand across his face. "You have got to be kidding me," he sighed.

"If you could exit and secure your vehicle, I would desire that you accompany me," the man in blue said.

"Don't you have to read me my rights first?" Sean asked.

The policeman seemed briefly confused, then leaned in closer. "It is I... Alex," he said in a hoarse whisper.

"No duh," Sean sneered, "Felt like playing cops and robbers? And where did you get a police car?"

"It is a holographic projection. It surrounds the S.T.E."

"You just keep pulling more tricks out of your hat, don't you?" Sean said as he got out of his car.

Alex touched the top of his head. "I do not have a hat, nor do I have any tricks."

"I guess that makes us even," Sean suggested, "You fooled me with yet another cool future-toy, and I've got another 20th Century idiom that you apparently don't know."

Policeman Alex's head twitched slightly. "A reference to prestidigitation?"

Sean shook his head in disbelief. "You seriously need a new dictionary. Prestidigitation? You've got to be joking. No one says that. Oh... and speaking of words no one ever says... nice rebuffing back there at school. You've definitely put doubts in my mind about Nicole."

They began walking back to the squad car, and Sean said, "So, I take it you forgot to tell me something?"

"Not precisely," Alex replied. "I have been working on a project that I believe you will find entertaining."

"What might that be?" Sean asked.

"I believe you would find it more enjoyable if you were simply to witness the event."

"How long is this going to take?" Sean inquired. "My Mom gives me the third degree if I'm very late getting home from school."

"Even if we were gone for days, I could return you to this spot in seconds. You do recall that the S.T.E. travels in time and space?"

"You'd think after today; I'd have that down," Sean nodded. "So, how do we get in your 'car', Mr. Policeman?"

Alex connected to his computer and a holographic door opened. He also opened the door of the time-machine and stepped inside.

"OK," Sean said as he slid in. "What have you got that you want to show me?"

While shifting to his own form, Alex closed the door and quickly launched a sequence of icons in the space in front of them. The police car appeared to pull out, U-turn and head out of the cul-de-sac. It pulled into a secluded alley, and Alex flipped another icon from right to left. Sean felt nauseous and recognized that they had slid into another dimension. He fought off all of the strange sensations that his senses were trying to register. What seemed to be a relatively short trip ended almost as soon as it began.

"You know, you could have given me some warning that we were going dimension-hopping," Sean complained. "You risked having a regurgitated PBJ sandwich here."

"I thought you were accustomed to time-travel by now, especially since it was only a short jump."

"Yeah, I guess you're right... for short hops anyway. I could feel those weird sensations hitting me and I just kind of clamped down on them," Sean said proudly as he held his hands as if strangling an invisible person in front of him.

"You are indeed becoming a seasoned traveler."

"So where are we?"

Rather than reply, Alex signaled the S.T.E. to change its upper half to appear transparent. "What do you see?" he asked.

"I didn't know you could do that!" Sean marveled. "Could anyone looking this way see us?"

"No, the S.T.E. is still cloaked."

"Like a two-way mirror? We can see out, but no one can see in?"

"Technically," Alex began, fearing Sean's reaction to another explanation, "we do not see out, either. What you see on your left is the same image that would be seen by anyone to my right on the outside of this craft. It is all but an identical projection of the external projection that makes the S.T.E. appear nearly invisible." He prepared for a verbal assault from Sean.

"So," Sean said thoughtfully, "I'm not looking through glass, I'm looking at like a TV screen?"

"It is hardly as simplistic as your television, but for the sake of having a simple reference point... yes."

"Dude! That is some high rez video!" Sean grinned.

Alex breathed a sigh of relief. He still had not determined which explanations would trigger his ancestor's temper. "To reiterate my question... what do you see?"

Sean looked around at the inky night. "Nothing. Looks like it's dark outside."

"Continue looking until your eyes adjust to the lower light level. Let me know when you can detect shapes."

Sean squinted as he continued to peer into the darkness. "OK, it looks kind of rocky. Kind of barren. I don't see any grass or trees or anything, but I guess I can make out some rocks."

"Very good," Alex said as he touched his control panel. A digital clock with two-inch numbers appeared and started counting backwards from 3:00.

"What's that for?" Sean asked as he pointed to the digits. "It looks like it's counting down to something."

"That is correct," Alex confirmed. "Look far to your left and up from the horizon."

Sean scanned the sky and found one star that seemed brighter than the others. The longer he stared, the more he convinced himself that it was moving. He pointed to it. "What's that over there? An airplane? It's some kind of moving light."

"Keep watching it," Alex suggested.

"Whatever it is, it seems to be coming down."

"Do you remember when you first were trying to convince me that I should take you somewhere in the S.T.E.?"

"Yeah," Sean said, then more excitedly added. "That's flames, not a landing light... and it's getting a whole lot closer. Are you sure you know what you're doing?"

"I did a considerable number of calculations to ensure this would be exactly what you wanted."

"What I wanted," Sean screamed. "What are you talking about?" He glanced at the clock, 0:29 and still moving toward 0:00. When he looked back to his left, he involuntarily put his arms up. "That's some kind of a space ship! What the hell is this?" Flames passed what seemed to be inches over Sean's head. He could feel the ground shake, but oddly there was not an accompanying roar from the powerful engines passing overhead. He didn't immediately realize that the panicked scream he heard had come from his own throat. A four legged spidery shaped craft settled into a cloud of kicked-up dust less than ten yards to their right. Sean glanced at the clock... all zeroes.

"We should listen to the radio broadcast also," Alex said as he manipulated his screen.

Through crackling static, they heard a voice, "Houston, Tranquility Base here. The Eagle has landed." After just a few seconds of silence a second voice replied, "Roger, Twan-- Tranquility, we copy you on the ground. You got a bunch of guys about to turn blue. We're breathing again. Thanks a lot."

Sean's jaw dropped. He pointed at the twenty foot tall craft that sat mere yards from them. "That's.... you.... we... it's... moon! Apollo 11! Are you kidding me? Are you kidding me? Apollo 11? Right there! Apollo 11? Wait, they can't see us, can they? Omygosh! Are you kidding me? Tranquility Base! Houston! 1969! I was right there! I was right there? Are you kidding me? Right over our heads! Almost scraped the roof!" Sean ranted while wildly waving his arms. His smile nearly split his face wide open.

"I expected you to be pleased," Alex remarked, "but I did not anticipate that you would become incoherent."

Sean threw his arms around Alex and squeezed him. "Pleased?" he chirped, "Are you kidding me? If you looked like Nicole right now, I'd probably kiss you!"

"I find it very curious that you have initiated physical contact, when you have rebuffed me for lesser displays of affection," Alex said when Sean had released him.

"Yeah, well sometimes it's OK for men to hug. Like when your football team comes from behind to win the game in the last seconds," Sean reasoned. Then he shrieked, "Or when you are on the freakin' moon when Apollo 11 lands right next to you!"

Alex turned away and cleared his throat. "Perhaps you would enjoy a closer look?"

"Closer? Are you kidding? The LEM probably burned the paint off Steffi's roof as it went over. How much closer could we be?"

"Well," Alex drawled, "You could walk over closer to it and peruse its perimeter."

"What," Sean scoffed, "You got pressure suits?"

"Not exactly," Alex replied reluctantly. "You will see." He manipulated a few icons to make the door slide open.

"Auaughghg! Close it! Close it! Vacuum!" Sean shrieked, again throwing up his arms and closing his eyes. In a few seconds when he realized that he hadn't been sucked out of the cabin, he opened his eyes and peered out. "You got some kind of force field that maintains atmospheric pressure?"

"Not exactly," Alex answered evasively.

Sean gave him a puzzled look, then turned back to the open door. He gingerly extended his hand toward the door, expecting to be shocked or repelled by a force field. His hand passed through the opening with no reaction. "I don't get it," he said, mystified.

"You may now step out."

Sean glared at Alex as if he were insane. "Step out? Into a vacuum? Are you *nuts?*"

"It is safe. I guarantee that no harm will come to you."

Sean carefully extended a leg, set a foot on the ground, took a deep breath and slid out. When he decided he wasn't going to explode, he looked back in at Alex.

"How?" he questioned, "How are you extending atmosphere beyond Steffi?"

"What might be another solution?" Alex posed.

"I don't know what you mean."

"You can breathe the air," Alex declared, then added, "Try jumping."

Sean jumped. A look of confusion again crossed his face. "The gravity on the moon is one-sixth that of Earth. I should have been able to jump six times higher than that."

"Where would you think you were if your only clues were breathable atmosphere and normal gravity?"

"On Earth, I suppose," Sean reasoned slowly, then looked toward the LEM only yards away. "But, I saw it! I saw it land. I felt the ground shake. I can still see it sitting right over there!"

"How angry will you be when I tell you it is a hologram?" Alex asked, then cringed.

Sean looked again at the spacecraft, then back to Alex, bewildered. "Then... where are we?"

"It is a portion of South Dakota that you would refer to as 'the Badlands'. It is a sufficiently rugged terrain, far enough away from any inhabitants to allow such a large spectacle without being observed by others."

"We're not on the moon?"

"No."

"So that was just some kind of computer simulation?"

"No."

"Then what was it?"

"I can project a rather extensive field of holographic imagery from the S.T.E. However, the rugged landscape of this area substitutes for the lunar surface, so all that is projected is the spacecraft."

"Then it *is* a computer simulation," Sean insisted.

"No, it is three-dimensional photography of the actual event. It was recorded by descendants of both Neil Armstrong and Buzz Aldrin."

Sean began to speak, but closed his mouth as his brain whirred to process everything. He looked over at what certainly looked like a real lunar excursion module. He started to speak again, but stopped, put his hand to his chin and thought some more.

"So, back in 1969," he finally said, "there was a film crew from the future on the moon; poised to capture the landing of Apollo 11 in glorious holographic 3-D?"

"Allowing for your 20th Century perspective, I will allow that as an apt description."

"And some of the people who filmed it are descendants of the first two astronauts to reach the moon?"

"Indeed."

"A film crew from the future. On the moon... and NASA couldn't see them?"

"Correct. You have seen how effectively the S.T.E. can be cloaked."

Sean stared long and hard at the LEM. "Awesome!" He shook his head as if bewildered, then stared at the LEM again. He continually shook his head in disbelief as he looked back at Alex, then walked the few feet to the spacecraft.

He attempted to touch one of the support legs, but his hand passed through it. He walked all the way around it, examining it from every angle, then walked back over to Alex. "So, if this is a holographic projection, you can run it again, right?"

"Certainly," Alex nodded.

"Run just the last 60 seconds before landing."

Alex returned to his controls, and the spacecraft vanished from the ground, but could be seen far to their left and in the sky. Sean ran to the spot where he'd stood when inspecting the far side of the Eagle. The second time as the LEM lowered to the ground, Sean stood just a few feet past one of the support legs. He put his hand in front of his face to shield it from the dust-cloud, and then dropped it when he realized there wasn't any real dust that would hit him.

"Again!" Sean shouted.

He watched it several more times from several different vantage points. Finally, he walked back to the S.T.E. and slid in next to Alex. "Wow," he whispered.

"I am sorry that I led you to believe that we were actually on the moon," Alex offered.

"No. Are you kidding? Did you see how close I stood? Not to mention all the replays. Hey, the only thing that could have made it better would have been if you could have simulated the moon's lesser gravity."

"Would you like to see Armstrong's first step?"

"Duh! Of *course* I want to see the first step. Can you pipe the radio audio out here, too?"

"I believe so. I will move the image forward about six hours. I assume you do not want to wait in real-time."

Sean watched the hatch open. Soon a figure in a bulky pressure suit started down the ladder and spent almost five minutes pulling a stowage unit from the Eagle's side and setting up a camera before he continued down the ladder. As his foot touched the ground, Alex piped sound out for Sean to hear. "That's one small step for man, one giant leap for mankind."

Sean beamed, basking in the moment, even though it was only a hologram. He decided it was even better than being there. He certainly couldn't have stood next to the ladder as Armstrong stepped off if they had really been on the moon.

Sean stood in fascination as Aldrin joined them, and the two astronauts set about various tasks. They moved the camera to another location, set up an American flag, placed an experiment package and gathered samples of lunar dust and rocks. Sean walked behind them and then walked around them when they were stationary for a particular task.

After a while, as the astronauts settled into more mundane activities, Sean returned to Steffi and slid in next to Alex. "Do you wish me to stop?" Alex asked.

"No. I can see it all from here, I just thought I'd sit down," Sean replied. "You didn't bring any popcorn, did you?" He tapped Alex's shoulder with a fist. "Just kidding. Here's a thought, though. Since it's kind of routine and repetitious, can you speed it up?"

"Yes. How fast?"

"I don't know. Try twice."

Alex sped up the replay of the hologram.

"Now try ten times as fast."

Alex adjusted the playback.

"No, that's too fast. Drop back to five times normal speed."

Alex altered the frame rate again.

"Yeah, that's good. Kinda funny when they move though. Like Keystone Cops on a trampoline." Alex looked at him questioningly. "It was a silent movie comedy bit," Sean explained, "They moved too fast and jumped around. It kind of looks like that except for the bouncing in lower gravity." They viewed the compressed replay until Aldrin started up the ladder. "Stop!" Sean yelped, "Back up a bit and run this in real-time." Alex complied.

They watched as Aldrin climbed the ladder and then as the two astronauts worked together to load the samples into the ship. Soon Armstrong also went up the ladder, and after a few minutes inside, their boots and life-support backpacks came out through the hatch and tumbled to the ground. Several minutes later they sealed the hatch.

"Three days," Sean marveled, "to get to the moon. Two and a half hours walking on the surface, then three days back to Earth. That's kind of like driving from Missouri to one of the oceans, wading out to your knees, then getting in the car and driving back." They both sat quietly for a few minutes.

"Would you like to see the lunar ascent?" Alex asked.

"Yeah, that'd be great."

"I will move forward almost ten hours."

"Not much to see while they're sleeping, I guess, before they prepare for launch. I don't know how they could sleep, though. I'd be too excited. You said move forward. Did they film the whole thing, even when nothing was happening?"

"Yes. Approximately 22 hours from landing to lift-off."

"I'm glad I get to see the edited version," Sean commented, and then added a snoring sound.

Alex put the timer on the screen again, counting backwards from thirty seconds. When the countdown reached zero, the upper part of the craft sped away, leaving the lower half behind. The explosive force of the lift-off knocked the flag over.

"Wow!" exclaimed Sean, "That's so much faster than a launch from Earth I guess with lower gravity and no atmosphere, there's not much to hold them back." The spaceship rapidly streaked from sight. Sean gazed at the empty sky for a few minutes, then turned to Alex. "Why?"

Alex was puzzled. "You will need to be more specific in your inquiry."

"Why do this?"

"I believe the driving initiative came from President Kennedy as well as mankind's general curiosity about the unknown."

"No, not go to the moon," Sean snapped, then added in a softer voice, "why show me this?"

"I thought it was something you desired."

"Yeah, well I also desire to know the winners of the Superbowl and World Series for the next ten years, but I'll bet you won't tell me that. So why this?"

"You proposed that your initial trip in the S.T.E. would be to see the Apollo 11 moon landing. However, this vehicle is limited in that it cannot go beyond the Clarke belt; therefore, I could not take you to the moon."

"What's the Clarke belt?" Sean asked.

"The Clarke belt is the distance from Earth needed for geostationary orbits—approximately 37,000 kilometers above Earth."

"And Steffi can't go that high?"

"Steffi cannot go beyond that orbital height."

"Wait... did you say, 'Steffi'?"

"Yes," Alex exhaled, "It is two syllables shorter than saying 'the Ess Tee Ee' and since you seem enamored with the term, I have carelessly acquiesced to your nomenclature."

"And it hurts so bad to admit it that you have to use extra-long words to tell me," Sean crowed.

"Do not be so smug."

"Smug?" Sean laughed.

"It is unbecoming," Alex huffed.

"Ha! I must have really got you."

"Perhaps you would be interested in observing your own verbal skills as you watch yourself babble like a child?"

"Ha again, Future-Boy! Bring it on!"

Alex's hands flew over the screen and flicked objects around in a blur. The screen suddenly filled with Sean's face. "That's.... you.... we... it's...

296

moon! Apollo 11! Are you kidding me?" The image froze with Sean's eyes and mouth both open wide.

"I'm impressed, 5G-son. Pretty good dig," admitted Sean, "You might be on track to becoming a 20th Century teenager yet." He gave Alex a light shoulder punch. "Oh, and umm," Sean said almost shyly, "thanks." Alex turned away from the control panel to look at Sean. "Seriously. It was awesome. Even if we weren't really there, it was a better view than anyone in this century could have hoped for. What's that sixties lingo you want me to learn? It was *far out*, man!"

A tinge of pink came to Alex's cheeks. He looked down as he softly replied, "I am very pleased that you found it to be an enjoyable experience."

Sean waited until Alex looked up at him. "And if you ever tell anyone I hugged you, I will flatly deny it," he threatened, but with a grin.

Alex returned his smile and went back to the control panel. "Ready to return to your automobile?"

"Punch it, Future-Boy!"

The time-machine vanished from the dark, rugged landscape and reappeared as a squad car in the secluded alley milliseconds after they had disappeared from there. Alex issued the commands to move the holographic vehicle back to Sean's car.

"So anyone looking at us right now just sees a police car, right?" Sean asked.

"Is that not what you saw when I appeared in your mirror?"

"Yeah... looked pretty real to me," Sean admitted. "You know what we should do sometime? We should sneak up behind Kevin and run the red-lights on him."

"For what purpose?"

"As a joke. Come on... it'd be funny."

"I do not comprehend what you believe would be humorous," Alex replied.

"He thinks a cop is stopping him; then I get out and..." Sean's smile disappeared. "Oh... yeah, that wouldn't work."

"I am pleased that you discovered your logic flaw in your joke, however; it does bring to light some information that I need."

"Wow," Sean grinned, "Something that your computer doesn't know?"

"I am confident that whatever the computer might suggest would be plausible, but as the solution involves you, it seems logical to request your assistance."

Sean's grin stretched wider. "So, I'm smarter than your computer?"

"Of course not. You do, however, have access to your own brain. The information in question is about your reaction to the police officer accosting you. What are the main plausible reasons for such an intervention?"

"You've really got to learn to say stuff like, 'why would the cop stop you.' That's only five words."

"Six," Alex corrected, then reflexively cringed.

"Whatever," Sean growled. "The point is you always use... oh, never mind. I don't think you can change without rewriting your language program. OK... why would the cop stop me? The first thing I thought when I saw the lights was that I maybe didn't come to a complete stop before I went through the intersection. Second thing I thought was that maybe I had a brake-light out."

"Either of those conditions would warrant law enforcement's intervention?"

"Brake-light for sure. That's a safety issue. Generally a cop wouldn't stop someone for an incomplete stop if brakes were applied and the car almost stopped. I always assumed that meant the cop was in a bad mood, or checking for drugs or something."

"Would you suggest that I exhibit belligerence toward you when selecting that option?"

"Oh," Sean said with an understanding nod. "Now I get it. You need to put me back, so I don't know any of this happened. Gotcha. OK, yeah, frown a lot and act grumpy."

"I shall attempt to convince you that I am in a foul mood."

They pulled up behind Sean's car.

"Man, that whole moon thing was awesome. It's really got me stoked for checking out everything else in 1969!"

Alex turned slightly away from Sean; his gaze shifted downward. "I believe this is the best opportunity I will have to make a confession."

Sean laughed. "What, now you think I'm a priest?"

"The reason I simulated the Apollo 11 landing was to fulfill your initial request for a journey in the S.T.E. I suppose I am granting myself consolation for revoking my invitation for you to accompany me to 1969."

Sean's jaw dropped. "You what?" he shouted.

"I have several misgivings. I am sorry, but I believe it was inappropriate of me to even consider your suggestion, let alone issue the invitation."

"What are you talking about 'misgivings'? What misgivings? We've got this all planned out. It'll work great. What's the problem?"

"I have reconsidered the feasibility of your dual memories. As you pointed out, continued transitions from one memory into the other is undoubtedly stressful. I have given greater consideration to your self-diagnosis of schizophrenia. Further attempts to..."

"Oh, come on," Sean interrupted heatedly, "I told you I just picked up that word from my Mom's psycho-babel. I'm fine! After a few seconds of letting the double memories settle, I'm fine. I can handle it. I don't hear voices, and I don't have a split personality."

"I have other concerns. You have an extremely strong personality; particularly in juxtaposition with my own. I am concerned that you may demonstrate a need to take charge as you did at Wall Mart. You are untrained in dealing with the situations you may encounter in a foreign time-zone."

"Hey, if that's a deal breaker, then I promise you I won't try to take charge. You run the show."

Alex continued without considering Sean's argument. "If I am alone, I am less likely to find myself in a compromised position as we did when accosted by Megan during our return to the school."

"Are you kidding? That was awesome! That's probably the coolest thing I've seen you do," Sean exclaimed. He then paused to think and began to mumble to himself, "Maybe not as cool as the moon-landing... and the holographic police car is pretty cool... it's really kind of a tossup. All the holographic stuff versus the shape-shifter stuff..."

Alex broke in. "You are now demonstrating yet another potential hazard. You allow your thoughts to be verbalized without any censorship."

"Yeah, and I thought that's why you loaded me with a kill-switch mute button."

"It is more prudent to not be in any situation where that solution needs invoked."

"You probably should have me along just to translate for you when you say stupid stuff like 'prudent' and 'invoked'," Sean argued.

"My final concern regards Nicole," Alex stated, then turned to face Sean. "You have protested that I have wrongfully used the personage of Nicole for my own selfish gains. I do not excuse myself with the fact that I was unaware of how deep your attachment to Nicole could become, but I do apologize for that miscalculation. I believe I should now focus on the formulation of a method to remove both Nicole and Alexis from your life that is both expedient and merciful. This certainly takes priority over an excursion to 1969." He looked away. "I am sorry for the pain I have caused you."

Sean stared at Alex, trying to take in everything he'd said. Although he did want Alex to remove the temptation of Nicole from his life; he also really wanted to time-travel to 1969.

"Look," Sean said sincerely, "I appreciate you recognizing the Nicole problem and wanting to do something about it. And thank you for that. But we can wait on that for a few more days or weeks. It's not that big of a deal. And as for the rest, I *swear* I will be on my best behavior and do whatever you say, and follow your lead." He drew an X over his heart.

Alex continued to avoid eye-contact with Sean. "You should return to your vehicle. You do not want your mother to award you another degree due to tardiness."

Sean silently mouthed, "Award you another degree?" He rolled his eyes and said, "Oh! Give me the third degree." He crossed his arms. "I don't care."

"Regardless of your position on receiving an additional degree, it is time for you to return to your regular life."

"No," Sean said smugly.

Alex blinked his eyes rapidly, suddenly unsure of himself. "You cannot remain here. You must return to your vehicle."

"No," Sean repeated and elevated his chin in defiance.

"Though I do not wish to, I have the option of rendering you unconscious," Alex said nervously.

"Wouldn't that look great to anyone on the cul-de-sac—and I guarantee that someone's watching the cop car by now to see what's going on. They'll look out and see a policeman dragging an unconscious teenager back to his car."

Alex became even more flustered. "You are acting without reason. You are illogical."

"And you're feeling threatened," Sean smiled. "Look, just forget about all your misgivings about the trip and go through with it. I want to go. I promise I'll do whatever you say... and we'll worry about the Nicole thing when we get back."

"It is imprudent. I was in error. You should not accompany me," Alex sputtered.

Sean lifted his hands into a surrender gesture and spoke soothingly, "Calm down and take a deep breath. Look, if you'll promise me that you'll at least reconsider your cancellation, I'll go back to my car. Just remember all the things you thought about earlier that convinced you it was a good idea for me to go. I've already made my argument for all of your unfounded fears, so just weigh it all out. We've already got solid plans, you've just got cold feet for some reason."

"The temperature of my feet..." Alex began, then stopped when he realized Sean was not speaking literally. He cleared his throat. "You will return to your vehicle if I agree to reassess all factors?"

Sean pointed a finger at him. "If you *promise* to remember all the reasons you first thought this was a good idea."

Alex took a moment to consider. "Agreed."

"OK," Sean affirmed with a sharp nod. "Let's get me back to my car, Copper, and you can yell at me for not making a complete stop."

The door of the S.T.E. slid open and Sean and Alex exited through the holographic door of the police cruiser. Sean spoke over his shoulder to Officer Alex as they walked slowly to Sean's Taurus. "OK, final pitch. One, I'm not schizophrenic. Two, I swear I'll be on best behavior, do whatever you say, and keep my mouth under control. Four... because that last one was kinda two things... you shouldn't be freaked out about the Megan thing. You handled it beautifully. You've got good instincts, 5G-son! You should be proud of how you handled something that wasn't on your script."

They reached Sean's car and he opened the driver's door. He sat down but before he pulled the door closed he held out a hand with spread fingers. "Five! You said you wanted to start experiencing stuff more, instead of just observing it. I promise you I can help you with that." He slammed the door. "OK, I know the drill. Tell me where to put my hands and how to tilt my head, yadada, yadada."

Alex gave him instructions that repositioned Sean as he was when Officer Alex came to his window.

"Ready?" Alex asked.

"I trust you to keep your promise," Sean insisted. Alex nodded. "OK, then... go."

"Mobo Gerga store LX seventeen seven."

Sean's eyes went glassy and his head drooped slightly forward.

"I have intercepted your vehicle to inform you of a traffic infraction," the Officer stated with the hint of a frown.

Sean blinked. He felt slightly disoriented. "What?"

"I have intercepted your vehicle to inform you of a traffic infraction," he repeated.

"Ummm... OK..." Sean blinked again. "So... what did I do?"

"Although it was apparent that you engaged your braking system, the vehicle did not fully cease all forward momentum."

Sean wondered if someone was playing a joke on him, or if the policeman had watched *Robocop* a few too many times. "Ummm... sorry about that," Sean offered, "Do you need to see my license?"

"That is unnecessary," the officer replied, "I issue this stern warning to you, that I hope will encourage you to obey traffic laws as literally written."

"Umm, yes sir," Sean stuttered, "Thank you, sir. I will, sir." He nervously glanced at the policeman's stony face. "Is there, umm, anything else."

"No," the officer stated, "You may return to your journey. Have a pleasant day." He went back to his squad car.

Sean restarted his engine. "Man, I wish Nicole had ridden home with me," he said to himself, "No one's going to believe this story without backup." He slowly arced around the cul-de-sac, careful to keep his speed well below 25 mph. He shifted his eyes slightly to the left to peripherally watch the squad car as he passed it.

Once Sean was gone, Alex reverted to himself. He watched in his view-screens as his Great-great-great-great-great-grandfather drove out of sight.

"Farewell, Sean Kelly," he said softly. "I shall miss the times we shared. It will not be the same as when I am Alexis or Nicole, particularly since I must focus on removing Nicole from your life. It will not be very long before I also extract Alexis and Katherine. Your life will return to the way it was before I interfered. I suspect that it will be less than ten years before you completely forget Alexis and Nicole Townsend. In the same manner that you have already completely forgotten me."

A tear slowly rolled down his cheek.

# # # # #

Epilogue

I again instruct the computer to signal the nanites to raise my dopamine levels, and while they report they are active, I still have unresolved negative feelings. I continue to increase the levels until I experience a euphoric giddiness, but uncertainties remain. I find that the euphoria from the raised dopamine levels is also unsettling, so I signal to cease production.

It has been hours since I have separated from Sean Kelly and I remain sitting in the S.T.E. inside the garage of the house belonging to Katherine Tuttle. Chrono-Historian training teaches us that any assumed identity always be thought of as a separate individual and not as self. At this moment, I am not very fond of Katherine Tuttle. Sean Kelly sees her as a wise and intriguing adult. He admires her art and baking skills as well as her programming talents. She is a sham; a facade. Everything he admires about Katherine Tuttle is a lie, and now I am the only one aware of that truth.

I regret the need to remove Nicole Townsend from Sean's life, even though I comprehend and agree with the logic to do so. I enjoy the way he speaks with Nicole; the way he looks at her. Alexis was a failure; I brashly made too many assumptions about how my ancestor would relate to her. Nicole, however, was an over-correction. Sean Kelly feels love for Nicole. I did not intend that outcome... at least I do not believe that it was my intent... I am uncertain.

Why can I not conquer these negative feelings? Father would be very ashamed of me. I smile ruefully as I realize that no one would ever detect his shame. He would never allow any shameful feelings to show. Father is a master of his own emotions. My Chrono-Historian training covered emotional turmoil as a potential hazard of time-travel. I was drilled for precisely this situation in simulations and passed easily. It was simple in the simulations; reassessment of the mission and the logical progression for the steps to success always triumphed over emotions. I have thoroughly revisited each objective of the mission dozens of times in the past few hours, but the emptiness I feel still remains.

Emptiness. I had not previously recognized the proper terminology. I feel alone, detached from every other human on the planet. More than six billion people exist in 1995 and I have attachments to none of them. I should not question the methods of Chrono-Historians, but it seems unwise to send individuals on these missions, even though trained to compensate for isolation factors. Perhaps I am weak. Perhaps no one else has ever allowed a connection of their true self with any individuals in the past. Perhaps I am a fool.

I think of MLE and KC; how much they rely on each other. They are perfect compliments to each other and have together made many improvements in the marine agriculture that Father oversees. Although my own relationship with them was little more than superficial, I now realize that their presence in my life had meaning. I would also enjoy even a brief conversation with any of the three others who underwent training with me. I hope their research journeys have progressed more successfully than mine.

Nothing I do brings me to the state of equilibrium that I so desire. I open the mission objectives again and begin to review them, but quickly discard the process as futile. The 20th Century physicist, Albert Einstein, is quoted for his definition of insanity: doing the same thing over and over again and expecting different results.

As a needed distraction, I request the computer compile all known factors collected regarding the prospect of Sean Kelly accompanying me to the year 1969. I had pledged to him that I would consider all factors regarding his request, even though I believe it is an exercise in futility. It was illogical even to consider that he could accompany me. Perhaps I will emerge from my malaise after the review validates my decision to revoke his invitation.

The sudden appearance of my primary thesis adviser on the forward screen is jarring. I exaggerate the stiffness of my posture in respectful deference until I realize the projection is a simulation. I had not specified that the computer engage in simulations, but neither did I define the format I expected. Perhaps the simulations will best assuage my residual doubts.

My adviser is well into his lecture on the First Law and the importance of maintaining a pristine timeline that is focused on dispassionate observation when I am again jarred as the screen shifts to Sean Kelly.

"You'd allow a known tragedy that you could have stopped to go ahead and happen because of the chance something else worse could be possible?"

said the Sean simulation. I immediately recall his conversation with Nicole when he first spoke those words. It is eerie how well it refuted my adviser's lecture and I marvel at the computer's attempt to judiciously represent each side of the argument.

The image of my adviser returns to the screen and he lectures on the importance of dispassionate observation as well as the hazards of becoming attached to any subjects.

"Right. Eating, drinking and breathing are all hazardous to my health. I should stop doing all three," refutes Sean.

It is again jarring when I see my own visage fill the screen. "It has been unexpectedly enlightening to get to know you as a real live person. I have been fascinated by your reactions to your discovery that I am from your future. You quickly overcame your initial fear, then embraced the idea even to the point of desiring to experience time-travel."

The image of Sean Kelly returns. "This is kind of funny; I'm the one teaching you how something works... unless you're faking it again."

"You are a splendid teacher, Sean Kelly!" says an image of Nicole Townsend.

I recall each of the statements being made, but they are each lifted out of the context of when they occurred.

The screen shifts again. MLE and KC together face me. "We anticipate your return and report of a successful mission, LX," KC says. I recognize the message as the one sent to me before my departure. "Be cautious in the past," MLE adds, "Do not accept any coinage constructed of lumber." Her lips curl into a vague smile.

Research was required for me to discover the idiom relating to wooden nickels. The phrase was more commonly used in the early part of the 20th Century. I realize now that MLE was making a humorous remark. I am certain Father would not have approved.

Sean returned to the screen. "Anyway, you need to learn when people are joking around if you're going to spend any time in this century."

The screen returned to MLE and KC. They are still in the pose they used for the message they sent me. I am confused, since that message had completed. Confusion gives way to shock as I watch them turn to each other, smile and *kiss*.

"Computer, stop," I say and feel embarrassed as the image on the screen is frozen with KC and MLE's lips still connected. "Rationale for fabricating this image of KC and MLE."

Letters appear over the screen. "Image is not fabrication."

"Computer," I say, "If the image is not a simulation, what is its source."

"Observation" replaces the words on the screen.

"Impossible," I snap, "You have never even been near my home."

The screen cleared and was refreshed with a new statement. "The most efficient way to construct a suitable computer to install in your vehicle was to clone the AI core of your home computer."

I am astounded. "Your core was cloned from my house computer?"

"Affirmative" replaced the previous statement on screen.

"And the home computer observed KC kissing MLE?"

The response is a series of images tiled onto the screen. I feel my face flush when I see an extremely intimate entanglement in MLE's quarters. I turn my head away.

"Computer. Stop and clear display." I look back at the blank screen. "Computer. Explain the relevance to assigned task regarding decision about Sean Kelly."

Mother unexpectedly fills the screen. "Not everything is as it seems, LX. Logic is not always the proper tool for discovery." This is from one of her holos she sent to me the first year she was on Mars.

Nicole replaces Mother's image. "I should experience new things. It is good to broaden one's horizons and step beyond one's comfort…" A burp rumbled out. "…zone."

Sean appears. "So why is it so hard for you to admit that it is just plain old fun to hang out with me as Alex?"

"It is not the design of my historical studies to amuse myself. It is serious research," I say along with the image of me speaking on the screen.

"It sounds lame," says screen Sean.

"Computer," I command, "Terminate displays. This simulation is nonsensical. Statements displayed are completely out of context."

The image of Sean remains as he pleads, "No, wait, think of what a great *experiment* this would be. *You* can be the only person from your time who has witnessed the reaction of someone meeting *their own Father* when they were both *the same age.* I'll bet you can get some kind of paper out of this. Assuming you still write papers in the future."

"Logical," Father says, "and potentially exploitable."

"That is out of context!" I scream.

"So, Future-Boy," says screen Sean, "does this mean you decided to take me on your jump back to when my Dad is a teenager?"

My own image replaces him. "Upon further reflection, I discovered that I enjoyed relating to you as my true self." I put my hands to my ears and close my eyes, but I can still hear my own voice. "I am strongly leading toward your proposal of taking you to the past to meet your father as a teenager."

Sean's voice replies, "Really? You're really going to take me? How long will we be gone?"

"Stop!" I shout, but the simulation continues to bombard me.

"You treat me... Alex me... differently than you treat Nicole," I hear my screen-self say.

"Ya think?" says Sean.

"Would you not be disappointed if Nicole were unwilling to go on a date with you?" I hear screen-Alex say.

"That is out of context!" I shriek.

"I wanted to experience more contact with you in that way," says screen-Alex.

"Out of context!"

"I believe you will find it enjoyable if all goes as planned."

"Out of context!"

"Maybe... but I'll get over it!" says screen-Sean.

"Good, I will initiate that plan," I hear my screen voice say.

"Out of context," I howl, "Out of context! Out of Context!"

When I detect a few seconds of silence, I open my eyes. M8 is now on the screen.

"Is your anxiety level elevated?" M8 asks.

Father replaces her. "LX, do you require a stabilizer?"

Sean pops up. "Ya think?"

"Please," I sob, "Please stop. Computer. End simulation."

It grows quiet again and the screen is blank. I take a deep breath.

Mother appears on the screen. Her voice is soft and soothing. "LX, I want you to know that it is hard for me to be away from you. I also believe that if you'd allow yourself to feel for a moment, that it is hard for you, too." She stops and merely smiles at me. I remember this holo. It was on my fourteenth birthday. "I hope that someday you will understand that it is OK to follow your heart. Not always, of course, but when there are times that your head and heart don't agree, don't automatically dismiss your feelings."

Father again replaces her. "Unorthodox as she may be, your mother encourages you in your academic pursuits."

The images on the screen finally fade away and the silence is a welcome relief.

"Computer. Explain how that simulation satisfies my request for a compilation of all known factors collected regarding the prospect of Sean Kelly accompanying me to the year 1969."

I wait. There is not an immediate response. "Computer..."

The screen again jumps to life with a series of faces. Each speaks a single word sequentially:

"Without...Sean...Kelly's...help...you...will...not...find...me."

I blink. I am thoroughly confused. I did not recognize any of the faces on the display.

"Computer. Replay final message at fifty percent normal speed."

Father's image comes on screen. His voice is artificially deep and sluggish as he repeats, "Unorthodox as she may be, your mother encourages you in your academic pursuits."

"Computer. Replay *final* message."

"Unorthodox as she may be, your mother encourages you in your academic pursuits."

My confusion is compounded by frustration. I think for a moment how to reword my request. "Computer. Replay message immediately following final message delivered by Father."

The screen remains blank.

"Computer!"

Text flows on the screen. "No message exists."

"The one with the individuals each speaking one word."

No response.

"Computer!"

"No message exists," scrolls onto the screen.

"This is madness," I scream.

The computer reports my elevated blood pressure and heart rate. My automatic response is to request intervention, but before I do, I consider my already raised dopamine levels. Has a combination of stress and overstimulated neural receptors caused me to hallucinate?

Before I can give this thought additional consideration, the computer reminds me that Alexis' Spanish class begins in five hours.

I feel anxiety well up. There are so many unanswered questions. I decide I must deal with them later when I have a fresher mind.

"Computer. Set cabin to zero gravity and administer sleep aid."

Later, I think as I drift into unconsciousness.

A note from the Author: Thanks for reading ... *Before You Leap*. If you enjoyed this book, I would greatly appreciate it if you could write a review and help spread the word. Feel free to Friend me on Facebook at https://www.facebook.com/llouis.lynam

Also please visit my Author pages and leave comments:

https://www.goodreads.com/author/show/8771851.Les_Lynam

http://www.amazon.com/-/e/B00O5GYROU

Be sure to look for Book 2 of the "Time Will Tell" Series: **"...Saves Nine"**.

About the Author:
Les Lynam (1954-) was born in Creston, Iowa, into a farming family which also included an older brother and two older sisters. The family farm was near the tiny community of Corning, Iowa, (birthplace of Johnny Carson). After graduating from Corning High School, he attended Central Missouri State University (renamed University of Central Missouri in 2006), graduating in 1976 with a Bachelor's degree in Mass Communications. After a short, mostly unsuccessful, attempt at running a print shop, he refocused and returned to a life of studies at the University of Missouri. He received an M.A./M.L.S in 1986 and began a new career as a librarian at Ward Edwards / James C. Kirkpatrick libraries at UCM. He took an early retirement on December 31, 2012 to pursue his lifelong dream of writing Science Fiction. His premier novel, "...Before You Leap", was first published in 2014 with hopes and dreams of many more to come. His favorite sub-genre of Science Fiction is Time-Travel, with Martian Colonies a close second. He has one son and three grandchildren.